Praise for the works of I

Winter's Moons

Lise MacTague's writing is wonderfully descriptive, and the story is beautifully built up, allowing the reader to become immersed in the wolven world she has created.

-The Lesbian Review

MacTague has delivered another gripping and gritty urban fantasy. ...The author immerses the readers in the dark in-between world of werewolves, distrusting alphas, other non-humans, possible conspiracies, growing despair and a glimmer of hope. I really liked the many unexpected twists and turns.

-Henrietta B., *NetGalley*

Breaking Out

This was a lovely, feel-good romance with minimal angst and lots of sweet moments of sapphic love and family... With an enemies to defence partners to friends to lovers evolution of the main characters' relationship, it was fun to see how Adrienne and KJ's relationship grew without the overly angsty moments that sapphic romance novels can be filled with.

I strongly recommend it to those who love hockey, and those who know nothing about it.

-Gillian F., *NetGalley*

Demon in the Machine

...is an exquisite steampunk and paranormal mashup permeated with action, mystery and romance! This book had my heart thundering in my chest on so many levels! One of the many things I love about MacTague's writing is her ability to create strong, complex and "real" characters and the wonderful dynamic she develops between them. This book is no exception! All great steampunk features wonderful gadgets and contraptions and this novel is rife with such inventions as multifunctional goggles, powerful jump suits enabling the scaling of tall buildings and, of course, the new horseless carriage. ...So, if you enjoy layered, well realized and imperfect but enticing characters, then this book is definitely for you!

MacTague is really suited to steampunk! She excels at writing stories with strong women and Briar and Isabella are no exception. *Demon in the Machine* is a wonderful mélange of mystery, steampunk, paranormal and romance that is appealing on so many levels!

-The Lesbian Review

Five Moons Rising

MacTague completely knocks it out of the park with this one, one of the best lesbian paranormals I've read. This book blew me away. Not just for the imagination MacTague demonstrated around the different creatures that haunt the darkness and the work Malice and her colleagues have to undertake to defeat the rogue ones, but also because of the underlying themes and threads that hit on so many subjects. Family, commitment, what it means to belong, what it means to trust—MacTague covers them all and in writing that's so powerful it took my breath away at times.

It's another winner from MacTague, who is rapidly becoming one of my all-time favorite lesfic authors.

-Rainbow Book Reviews

This book is absolutely brilliant. It is filled with memorable characters and a plot that will keep you coming back to it even when you know you should be working or sleeping or doing something else. MacTague really got into her head and gave us a beautiful account of what it would be like to be a werewolf. It was so wonderfully done that I now have a massive book crush.

-The Lesbian Review

Vortex of Crimson

MacTague does it again... A fantastic end to the saga that has seen Jak and Torrin fight all sorts of battles, both physical and emotional. I love how MacTague mixes in the action scenes and conspiracy theories alongside the touching and sometimes angsty romance between Jak and Torrin. Neither the action nor the romance ever takes over completely, the balance is always spot on.

-Rainbow Book Reviews

Heights of Green

What a rip-roaring sequel this is to *Depths of Blue!* There are layers within layers in this book, and the subtle ways they are revealed is brilliant in its execution. It's clear something is going on, but MacTague teases this out, strand by strand, and brings it all to a stunning ending. There's politics, intrigue, action, and lots of emotion. Both Jak and Torrin's actions and reactions are explored in just the right amount of detail alongside the story itself, and it's a fantastic blend. The book finishes on a great cliffhanger, ready for book three, and I can't wait to get started on that.

-Rainbow Book Reviews

The ending had me standing on my feet. Reading it had me pumped and the teaser at the end did nothing to slow my heart rate down. The way Jak's and Torrin's journeys split apart and then come back together had me turning pages so fast I got a digital paper cut and those SOBs hurt! But it was worth it.

-The Lesbian Review

Depths of Blue

I thoroughly enjoyed the story and the characters that Lise MacTague has drawn in *Depths of Blue*. The world building is top-notch and the backstories of the characters are told in such a way as to move the story along and not in a pedantic, expository way. I would recommend anyone who likes a good sci-fi book give this a try.

-Lesbian Reading Room

This is a proper sci-fi/action/adventure story with two very strong female leads and I absolutely loved it! Both Torrin and Jak are kickass women, and that was such a refreshing change—there's no tough butch here rescuing a weak femme damsel in distress. They can both look after themselves and they therefore have a lovely tension between them from the start. This is part one of a trilogy and I cannot wait to get into book two—I love MacTague's story-telling, her narrative and descriptive skills, and the universe she's created. Excellent lesbian sci-fi, of which there isn't enough, so this is a brilliant addition to that genre.

-Rainbow Book Reviews

MOONBREAK

LISE MACTAGUE

Other Bella Books by Lise MacTague

Breaking Out
Demon in the Machine

Five Moons Rising Series
Five Moons Rising
Hunter's Descent
Winter's Moons

On Deception's Edge Trilogy
Depths of Blue
Heights of Green
Vortex of Crimson

About the Author

Lise writes speculative and romantic lesbian fiction (often in the same book) in all sorts of different flavors. She has written a contemporary hockey romance, a space opera trilogy, one steampunk novel (but she'd love to write more), and a mess of paranormal urban fantasy. She grew up in Canada, but left Winnipeg for warmer climes. After flitting around the US, she settled in North Carolina where the winters suit her quite well, thank you very much. These days, there isn't nearly enough hockey in her life. She makes up for that dearth by cramming writing in around her wife and kids, work, and building video game props in the garage, with the occasional break for podcasting. Find some free short stories and more about what she's up to at lisemactague.com.

MOONBREAK

LISE MACTAGUE

BELLA BOOKS
2024

Bella Books, Inc.
P.O. Box 10543
Tallahassee, FL 32302

Printed in the United States of America on acid-free paper.

First Edition - 2024

Editor: Kayla Mancuso
Cover Designer: Medora MacDougall

ISBN: 978-1-64247-496-1

PUBLISHER'S NOTE

Aknowledgments

I need to start by thanking my beta readers: Lynn, and Amy. I appreciate you reviewing my writing while it's less than sparkling. These stories would be much poorer without your assistance. Thank you especially to KD Williamson, Stephanie Goldman, and Ashly Rodriguez for your excellent feedback as sensitivity readers. Any and all errors of characterization are my own.

As always, a huge thanks has to go to my editor, Medora MacDougall. I look forward to working with you every time. Those little errors keep sneaking in, and I'm glad to have you on my side when it comes to squashing them.

Thank you to everyone on the Bella crew. No book comes out in a vacuum, and I appreciate all your efforts on behalf of my stories. I especially need to thank Kayla Mancuso for being patient with my requests in relation to the book cover. What you've come up with is fantastic, and I'm truly proud to have your artwork on my book. This time around, I also need to thank the Bella staff for your support as it relates to my cancer treatment. I'm thrilled we didn't have to shelve this book, and that we only had to postpone it a little bit.

To my readers: thank you so much! I'm always excited to hear that one of my stories has made an impression. I'm going to keep writing, but it's your reactions and feedback that keep me from sticking my stories in a drawer and forgetting about them.

To the staff and doctors at UNC-Rex who have worked tirelessly on my behalf on the cancer detour I was forced into making this summer: thank you. Since my diagnosis in June, I've felt taken care of. Cancer treatment isn't easy to go through, but with the team I have working with me, I feel like my bases are covered. At least as much as they can be.

And finally, but never lastly, to my wife and kids (Lynn, Whit, and Ce), thank you for everything. Your bemusement at the strange things that come out of my brain is endlessly entertaining to me, but you continue to put up with them.

Lynn, thank you for being my love, my best friend, my project partner, my sounding board, and so much more. I wish I didn't have to add caregiver to the list, but I do. Having you on my side means everything to me. I honestly don't know if I could have done this without you. I love you so very much, and I can't imagine my life without you.

Dedication

To my editor, Medora MacDougall. You make my stories better.

CHAPTER ONE

"You?" Cassidy stared at the ghost who grinned at her from the plushest office chair the world had ever seen. "You're dead. Mary said you were dead."

The last time she'd seen Stiletto, the Hunter had been less than thrilled to discover her existence. She'd been frightening then, in her form-fitting black combat garb, her short black hair slicked back from her face. She was even more imposing now, despite being in an exquisitely tailored pantsuit of deepest crimson that served to emphasize the androgynous lines of her frame. The sienna of her skin was only a few shades darker than her clothing, and her hair floated about her head in short strands now allowed their freedom. All of her considerable menace had been honed, distilled, then remade into this creature who was barely the right side of terrifying. It was a good thing Cassidy wasn't human anymore either.

Stiletto's smile widened until Cassidy was certain it would split her face, her obsidian eyes glinting with malice. "She should know." Sharp teeth gleamed shockingly white against her dark lips.

Cassidy blinked as she tried to sort out what that answer could possibly mean. "She was there."

"That she was." Stiletto stood, pushing the chair back in a smooth motion. She made her way around the desk slowly, almost languidly as she trailed one hand along the sharp edge. "So what do you need from me, Alpha? What can the Lord of Chicago do for you?"

"So you're a vampire now." Cassidy stepped back, trying to keep out of Stiletto's reach, but she kept coming. Cassidy clenched her fist around the black canvas jacket she still carried.

"Hm."

"And you're the one who took over from Carla."

"You catch on quickly."

The statement was faintly mocking, and Cassidy flushed. "Then you know what happened to my pack."

Stiletto kept advancing, and Cassidy kept backing away.

"I know things have gotten a little hot for you, recently," the vampire said.

Anger sparked inside Cassidy's brain, and her wolf snarled in response. She stopped in her tracks and held out one hand, stiff-arming Stiletto back even as she tried to close the gap. Cassidy hefted the jacket and slammed it down on the desk.

"You don't know anything," she growled around lengthening teeth. Her claws scored through the blotter on the desk's top, gouging out little curls from the hard wood beneath. "My pack is gone. Taken."

Stiletto stilled. She cocked her head and waited, as unmoving as a statue carved from petrified wood and carnelian.

"What kind of a 'Lord of Chicago' doesn't even know about the goddamn military pulling shit in her territory?" Cassidy sneered, displaying teeth that rivaled Stiletto's in length and surpassed them in number. "Carla would have known."

"Military?" Stiletto's gaze drifted down to the jacket on the table. She snatched it up so quickly that Cassidy almost didn't see it. The vampire spun away, her form blurring until she stood next to the lamp on the top of the desk. "The design is consistent with the BDU the military uses for night maneuvers."

"Why does the military want our wolves?"

Stiletto settled into her chair, her brow furrowed. "There's been a contingent of black ops troops in the area. They're available to support the local Hunter, and they take on their own missions against supras who get"—her face took on a pained smile—"out of control. They don't have the firepower to take on a werewolf pack."

"Wolven." Cassidy's correction was quiet, but no less intense for its lack of volume. "And it was four packs. Maybe five."

Stiletto's carefully shaped eyebrows climbed her forehead, and Cassidy found herself leaning forward, trying to catch a whiff of the vampire's scent. Was she lying? It was impossible to tell. She might as well have been sniffing a stone.

The vampire tossed the fabric down while shaking her head. "None of this is conclusive. Just because it's consistent with what my former employer's foot soldiers might wear, it doesn't mean it was them."

"Former employer?"

"I couldn't very well keep being a Hunter with all this going on, could I?" Stiletto gestured down the length of her body. "They don't take kindly to the undead joining their ranks. Something about conflict of interest, I'd guess."

"There's a policy that covers this—" Cassidy shook her head. "No. It doesn't matter. None of this matters. The only thing I care about is where the kidnapped wolven have gone and who took them. Not necessarily in that order. If you can't help me, then you're of no use at all."

"I don't have any current information, but that doesn't mean I will never have something for you." Stiletto leaned forward, steepling her fingers in a way that was so stereotypically villainous that Cassidy might have laughed if the situation hadn't been so dire. It felt like someone had removed everything from inside her ribcage and replaced it with an ache somehow both dull and vicious that showed no sign of subsiding.

She closed her eyes and took a deep breath. "I'll leave my number. If something comes up, you can call me."

"I can do better than that." Stiletto looked her straight in the eyes and reached into the desk. "These…events concern all of us. If someone was strong and organized enough to pull off the kidnapping of dozens of werewolves, then they could come after us. I will reach out to you if I find anything." She pulled a necklace out of a drawer and pushed it over to Cassidy. "If you need anything, show this at any entrance to the building at any time of day. Someone will bring you directly to me."

The blood-red jewel on the silver-disked pendant winked up at Cassidy. She licked her lips, wondering how much of her soul she would be selling if she took it. An intact soul wouldn't bring her wolven back. She reached over to pick it up, then froze when Stiletto's hand closed over hers.

The vampire's skin was colder than its warm brown suggested. Cassidy wasn't being held tightly. She pulled back, and Stiletto's grip firmed.

"I would ask a favor," she said, a quirk of a smile forming at the corner of her mouth.

"And there it is." Cassidy let go of the necklace.

"Nothing you won't willingly offer, I'm sure." Stiletto turned Cassidy's hand over and pressed the pendant into her palm, then let go. "If you run across my predecessor again, let me know where she is."

"Again?"

"She went straight to your home after things got…messy here. I know you took her in."

"I owed her a favor." Cassidy shoved her ticket into the club deep in the pocket of her pants and hoped she never had to cash it in. "You know my den burned. It's probably still burning. Chances are good she never got out."

"Carla is too cunning to be caught by a group of mere humans, no matter how well armed they might have been."

"Unlike my wolven," Cassidy said flatly. She refused to leave the subtext hanging between them. If Stiletto was indeed the new Vampire Lord of Chicago, then she needed to know that Cassidy wouldn't be pushed around or manipulated. Better to make that clear now than to have Stiletto try to keep stringing her along.

Stiletto inclined her head. It could have meant anything, but Cassidy chose to believe that the vampire was acknowledging her overstep.

"Whatever the reason, I won't believe she's dead until I have proof or the word of someone I trust."

"I can't promise anything, but if I hear, I'll let you know."

"And I have your word on that?"

Cassidy bit her lip. It felt like she was about to step off a pier into shark-infested waters. Still, Stiletto had phrased the request as if there was a favor in play. Maybe Stiletto was too new to nonhuman politics to understand what that meant, but Cassidy did and would hold her to it. "You do. I will do you the favor of letting you know where Carla is, if I ever find out. I promise."

Stiletto nodded. "I'll hold you to that. And if you see your sister…"

"Yes?" Cassidy asked when the silence had gone on too long.

"Tell her 'thanks.'"

"Sure, I guess."

"I'm sure we'll see each other again." Stiletto leaned back in her chair.

"Yeah." Turning on her heel, even though it made the hairs on the back of her neck prickle to have Stiletto behind her, Cassidy left the room. The vampire greeting party had dispersed and the hallway beyond the door to Carla's—no, Stiletto's—study was empty. A bass line thudded dully, the sound matching the rhythmic press of her brain against her skull.

She'd gotten little from Stiletto but had somehow given up much. How was that even possible? The vampire might be new, but she'd pushed out the decades-old previous lord, and already Cassidy was dancing to her tune.

She strode through empty halls. Those in the nightclub were nearly as desolate as when she'd reached them. Even those most committed to late-night revelry were dispersing, some in the arms of vampires, others alone or in pairs. She smelled as much disappointment as anticipation among them as she wove her way around the various groups. Why someone would be crushed not to be a vampire's late-night snack was not something she could understand. She was already drained, and Stiletto hadn't even hinted at putting her teeth to Cassidy's flesh.

After the oppressiveness of the club, the cool night air was a welcome balm. Cassidy paused at the top of the steps at Faint, wondering what to do next. Snow had the Kenosha Alpha and Beta in her van and was going to drop them off somewhere. The remaining Alphas who had made it out of the ambush in the woods had dispersed to their dens to see what awaited them.

Her gaze shifted, focusing north toward her own home. She had nothing else to do until noon. That was when she would meet back up with the surviving Alphas. Technically, Marrow and Bone were Alpha and Beta, or maybe it was the other way around. She hadn't had enough time to figure out how to differentiate them before soldiers overwhelmed their meeting. It was something to dwell on, rather than allowing her mind to delve back into the dark memories of that brutal skirmish in the snow. Her recollection was already fragmenting into stark shots of muzzle flashes in the dark, blood splattered on white, the glare of the helicopter's light piercing the night, then the brutal end of the same copter in fire and heat. It was a miracle they'd made it out with as many as they had.

Cassidy blinked, trying to make sense of her surroundings. She was wandering, her feet taking her back to the hotel, where more fire awaited her.

She chewed on her lower lip, disregarding her wolf, who tried to tell her that obsessing over the previous night's events wasn't helpful. If there was a better argument for how ill-fit she was for leadership, Cassidy couldn't see it. Wherever her wolves were, they were there without her. It might have been better if she'd been taken with them.

Her head exploded in sharp pain as her wolf scored the inside of her brain with sharp claws of fierce disapproval. As long as they took breath, they would search out those who had been taken from them. Retrieving their own was much easier from a position of freedom than it would have been from captivity.

Cassidy shook her head, trying to clear it both of the pain and her own concerns. She'd gone to try to clear up the reason for the disappearance of a few of her wolves and had ended up losing them all.

The wolf nipped at her, more gently this time, herding her thoughts away from the abyss that threatened to pull her in. The adrenaline of the previous night had allowed her to coast, but now that she was alone…Now that Snow wasn't there…

It was a lot easier to be optimistic with the lone wolf around. To think that Snow had only been in her life a couple of weeks, and now Cassidy was lost without her. Oh, she'd fallen hard, far harder than she'd intended. She'd been told lone wolves were dangerous and never to be trusted. With no pack loyalty, their motives when they showed up in pack territory was questionable. What they wanted was to worm their way into a pack, any pack, but there had to be a good reason they weren't already in one. The members of the North Side Pack certainly clung to that belief, but they could be forgiven their suspicion. After all, a lone wolf had killed their previous Alpha, then had taken over the pack, treating those wolven who hadn't been able to escape with cruelty and neglect.

She shook her head. She hadn't met MacTavish, which was just as well. Her wolf snarled inside her head. They would have taken him down if they'd ever crossed paths. Dean was another matter. The true former Alpha had been beloved by all his wolves, who still felt his loss with a keenness that Cassidy wished she could blunt, Snow most of all. As Dean's sister, she had the most reason to be angry at Cassidy for her bungling of the situation. Cassidy had truly proven what a fantastic successor she was to Dean. Her tongue curled at the bitterness of her sarcasm. Still, it wasn't a misplaced emotion. She'd managed to lose them all.

Somehow, she still had Snow. That was something she could cling to. She wasn't part of the pack, but she'd put her neck out just as far as any of Cassidy's packmates. If she ever wanted a place in the pack, Cassidy would offer it to her. For now, she was going to have to settle for putting aside a place for Snow in her heart. The lone wolf might be amenable to that. She wasn't going to be into mating—Snow had no desire for physical intimacy—but she wasn't averse to cuddling.

They'd gotten pretty cozy, and Cassidy could only hope that she wouldn't change her mind.

Her feet took her across city streets lined with slumping piles of rotting snow. Every step took her closer to the remains of her den. The least she could do was witness the end of the place she'd called home since October. After that, she would meet up with the others and work on moving forward. She would allow herself to wallow until then.

CHAPTER TWO

The pale yellows and oranges of the rising sun were a marked contrast with the blackened bones of the building that had been her pack's den. The roof where she'd posted up did little to block her from the wind that whipped in off the lake. The night had been cold, and the day promised to be nearly as bad. It was fitting.

Cassidy's fingers were warm with her own blood. The claws on their tips pierced her palms as she watched the firefighters roll up their hoses. Others toppled what remained of standing walls toward the center of the burned-out hulk. They would be dangerous if allowed to stand, their stability stolen by the fire that had gutted them. Just as Cassidy had been gutted by the government forces who had robbed her of her pack.

She smiled, lips stretching enough to crack dry skin. The thoughts were grim. They were melodramatic. She'd expected her wolf to reprimand her, to radiate silent displeasure or rake her claws along the underside of her skin, but the wolf was in complete agreement. She was all for wallowing now, though for how long she'd continue to permit it, Cassidy wasn't sure.

Together they watched as the hotel was soaked and leveled until nothing remained but smoldering ashes among the rubble. She checked the web of lights that represented the wolves she'd gathered to her: those in the pack and those she didn't want to lose track of. Her own wolven were still accounted for, if far enough away that she couldn't determine in which direction they'd been taken.

Ruri's star was still gone. What the absence implied was worse than she wanted to contemplate. Ruri was her sister's girlfriend. She and Mary Alice had gone on some trek to the North Woods of Wisconsin at the behest of Mary's bosses. The same bosses who'd probably set the soldiers on them at the Alphas' meeting and who'd taken advantage of that same meeting to burn down her den and kidnap her wolves.

Had the trip been a ruse to get Mary out of town? While Cassidy had still had contact with Ruri's star, she could be assured that Mary was also alive. Now that it was gone…Had the government attacked them too? Or was some other force involved? The whole situation was a wretched tangle.

Her wolf whined. Couldn't they go back to wallowing in the misery of their own plight?

Heat prickled the backs of her eyes. Cassidy squeezed her eyelids shut, but tears overflowed anyway. Hot tracks painted twin paths down her cheeks. They'd left things in such a bad place. Mary wasn't the one who had turned her, but her job had put Cassidy in the crosshairs when the rogue Alpha known as MacTavish decided to use Cassidy to get back at her. Not only had Cassidy been turned into one of the wolven, but she'd also learned that Mary had been lying to her family about her life for the past five or more years. Mary was a Hunter, a genetically engineered supersoldier who took down rogue nonhumans. Cassidy didn't know who she was anymore, only that Mary wasn't the person she'd thought. She'd lied and lied, living a double life for so long. Had she laughed about it, thinking how stupid her family was to fall for the deception?

Family. There was no sign of her mom either. For all Cassidy knew, the charred rubble was Sophia Nolan's grave. She could only hope her mom had gotten out. But if she'd survived, why hadn't she reached out to Cassidy? Her phone hadn't so much as twitched.

Nearly everyone she cared about had been stripped away from her in the space of a few terrible hours. Cassidy should have turned her mom. That way, she would be on Cassidy's internal starscape. Then she might have known if Sophia was even alive.

A gust of wind from behind her brought with it a thread of silver at the same time as Snow's star snapped into bright focus in her mind. Half the tension left her body in a rush. Her wolf leaped up inside her, tail wagging frantically as the aroma of the lone wolf encompassed her.

* * *

Snow shook her head in equal parts relief and concern. "I thought I might find you here. Isn't this dangerous?"

Cassidy sneaked a look back at her. The gold of the sun's rays illuminated the pale skin of her face in stark relief, darkening the shadows under her eyes and washing away the faint spray of freckles across her nose. Her unbound hair barely brushed the tops of her shoulders. The sun picked out lines of gold among the mousy blond, turning the strands into a light curtain that obscured some of the pain in her gaze.

She turned and held an arm out in a mute invitation to join her. Snow picked her way across the roof, avoiding treacherous patches of ice that would have been difficult to navigate even with the pads and claws of furform. She relaxed into the embrace and allowed Cassidy to pull her in against her body.

The Alpha closed her arms a little too tight. She buried her nose in the exuberant curls of Snow's hair and inhaled deeply. Snow luxuriated in the contact and the way their scents mixed in a way that felt right. Her wolf settled within her, offering the comfort Cassidy craved.

"They can try me," Cassidy finally said.

Snow blinked up at her, eyes tired. "Sorry, what?"

"That this is dangerous."

"Ah." Snow closed her eyes and laid her head on Cassidy's shoulder. "It is. If I was trying to flush someone out, I'd be keeping an eye on the area. It's not a trap if no one's checking the snare."

"Is it wrong to wish they'd find me? I'd take so many of them down." Cassidy's scent was raw and erratic. It skittered between murderous rage and deep despair. Neither emotion was unwarranted, but she couldn't allow them to run her, not now.

"Only in that I'd miss you if you got killed. And it wouldn't help your pack come home." Snow took a deep breath, then let it out in one long exhale. "Your mom and sister wouldn't be thrilled either."

"If they're even still alive."

"Hey." Snow lifted her head, and reached for Cassidy's face. She gently took the Alpha's jaw and turned her head around until their eyes met. "It's hard to lose family. Don't make it harder by assuming it's happened when you don't know for sure. Where there's doubt, there's hope."

"Hope?" Cassidy blinked as tears poured down her cheeks but made no further attempt to stop them.

"It's better than the alternative." Snow leaned forward and gently kissed first one cheek, then the other. "And you're not alone."

"I'm not." Cassidy squeezed Snow against her.

"You've got more powerful arrows in your quiver than me."

"Maybe." Her grin was cheeky, even through her tears. "Hammer's not nearly as cute, and I'm not sure anyone could come between Marrow and Bone."

"You're hilarious." Snow couldn't help but smile, even if the statement was ridiculous. Cassidy trying to make jokes was a much better proposition than Cassidy looking to pick a fight.

"True." Cassidy scrubbed at her wet cheeks, then turned back toward the burned-out ruins of her home. Thin trails of smoke and steam had replaced the dense clouds of the earlier conflagration. A few firefighters carefully walked the ashes putting out the remaining hot spots, but most of the fire engines had left the area, leaving mainly police cars.

"Let's find somewhere more comfortable to spend the time until we meet up with the Alphas," Snow suggested.

"I don't think there's anything else to do here," Cassidy said. "Except maybe getting picked up by the cops for loitering." She stood and stretched.

Snow mourned the departure of the warm spot at her side, but got up as well. Her own muscles had grown tight. Oddly, she'd been sitting too much. Yes, there had been the mess in the woods. She'd scrambled to avoid the soldiers and had been forced into taking the lead to get the remaining Alphas back to her car and safety. After that, she'd had her ass parked in the driver's seat, when she should have had Cassidy's back with the vampires. The North Side Alpha didn't look like she was sporting tooth marks, but they probably would have healed already.

No, her contribution to the cause that night had been to drive the Kenosha Alpha and Beta to an emergency vet in Wisconsin. Some hero she was. She didn't even know if Jane would live. The Kenosha Beta hadn't fared well after being at ground zero when the helicopter exploded. Dale thought she might survive, but Snow had watched wolven with injuries that bad slip away.

"How about a nap?"

Snow eagerly took Cassidy's offered hand. "I could use a few hours." She shook her head. "Or days."

"We can do days when we have everyone back," Cassidy said. "Hell, you can have weeks then."

"Some quiet weeks with you?" Surprised at the cozy warmth that flooded her chest at the suggestion, Snow looked over to be sure Cassidy was serious. At her nod, Snow grinned. "I'd like that."

"Me too." Cassidy sighed.

"The van's that way." Snow pointed in the direction she'd parked. They would have a bit of a walk. Parking too close, especially with a vehicle as recognizable as her van, had seemed like a risky proposition. "Come on." She hopped over the edge of the building, landing on her feet a good fifteen feet below.

Cassidy followed but stumbled on the landing as taxed muscles protested their treatment. Snow reached out to steady her and got a grateful smile in thanks.

She returned the smile with a grin of her own. "There are advantages to avoiding fights." The Alpha had to be running on fumes. Snow was fatigued enough and she had experienced a fraction of the exertion that Cassidy had. Never mind the multiple shifts in and out of her three forms, Cassidy had also been in the thick of the fight after soldiers had ambushed the Alpha meeting.

"Clearly." Cassidy linked her arm through Snow's, who pretended not to feel the weight the Alpha was putting on her.

They crossed the street and into the neighborhood. The smell of blood lingered in the air, thickening as they approached the van until Snow could taste it.

Cassidy wrinkled her nose.

"It was way worse an hour ago," Snow said.

"I bet." Cassidy's eyes flashed bright red and blue for a moment before settling back to their usual hazel and brown.

Snow unlocked the driver's side and slid in, then leaned across the front bench seat to let the Alpha in. Cassidy clambered into the front seat. She hesitated before turning to take in the mess in the back. Snow knew what she was seeing. The sun shed golden light onto a multitude of blood pools. By far the worst was the bench seat where Dale's Beta had been tended to. The cushions were drenched in blood that had dripped down to soak into the carpet. Where Hammer had been sitting there was a smaller crimson stain. The sheets on the bed all the way at the back were rumpled and dotted with blood from Bone and Marrow.

"I'm sorry," Cassidy said, her voice quiet. "I didn't think…"

"No one did." Snow flipped a dismissive hand at the disaster that was her living area. "I'm just happy we were able to get everyone out."

"Not everyone." Cassidy squeezed her eyes and shut the stench of despair rising from her until it choked out the blood that painted the back half of Snow's van.

No, they hadn't all gotten out. Hammer had to have lost his Beta; there was no way he would have left the area if Briella had still been alive. The Aurora Alpha, Crag, and his Beta had been among the first to go down. And then there was Hazel's troubling absence. The Joliet Alpha was senior to the area's Alphas and a steadying hand. There was no way they would have missed the gathering unless something catastrophic had happened. The implications of their absence were especially troubling.

Snow fumbled getting the car in gear and had to wiggle the gearshift back into place. She was quick to recover, but there was still a slight lurch as she pulled away from her parking spot.

"What do you think?" Snow asked. "Should I find somewhere busy or secluded to park?"

"Busy." Cassidy's response was immediate. "Whoever's after us has taken a lot of trouble to fly under the radar. Let's find somewhere they'd have to expose themselves if they want to come after us."

"Fair enough." Snow chewed on the inside of her lip as she reviewed their options. "I have an idea," she said finally. "See if you can catch a bit of sleep."

"'Kay." Cassidy slouched down in the seat and closed her eyelids for a moment before sitting straight back up again. "Nope." A sudden return of anxiety suffused her scent.

"Problem?" Snow asked with a sympathetic half-smile. "It won't be long. We'll try again when we get there."

They headed south across city streets. Cassidy peered out the windows, her eyes on the sky above them. Snow appreciated the lookout. She couldn't watch for both cars and helicopters.

True to her estimation, it took maybe fifteen minutes to get to the parking garage of Northwestern Memorial Hospital. Snow stopped for a ticket at the entrance, then pulled into the garage. It would be a good place to lay low before their meeting. The number of civilians in the area should give pause to anyone with designs on kidnapping the two of them like they had Cassidy's pack.

Snow pulled away from the ticket station with a sardonic wave at the driver behind her who was already leaning on the horn. The constant stream of traffic coming and going from the massive parking garage was perfect.

The interior was tight, but Snow still backed them into an open spot surrounded by other vehicles. She'd deliberately picked the level with a pedestrian overpass into the hospital complex.

"Let's get some Z's," Snow said, putting the van into park. She peered out the windshield one last time, then crawled over the seats to the back.

"I don't know if I'm going to be able to sleep," Cassidy admitted as she followed suit. "I keep seeing the moment where everything broke bad."

"I figured. But just try." Snow popped open two of the back windows, then stripped the blood-stained sheets off the narrow bed. She tossed them into the corner, then opened the hatch with her clean linens. There was no point in making the bed, but some blankets would help. "It's going to be chilly."

"We can cuddle." Cassidy didn't move until Snow slid onto the bed, then crawled up onto the narrow mattress. There was enough room for both of them if they got cozy. It was a good thing wolven liked sleeping in piles of their packmates.

Snow turned over onto her side and snugged Cassidy against her. She didn't mind being the big spoon, and someone needed to support the Alpha. She couldn't do it all on her own. If someone was going to come after Cassidy, they'd have to get through her first.

Cassidy relaxed back into the embrace and heaved a sigh at the same time as Snow. They shared a quick grin.

Snow slid her hand down between them, rubbing the small of the Alpha's back in circles she hoped would be soothing. She watched as Cassidy's eyes drifted shut, then pressed a kiss to the back of her neck. She allowed herself to stay awake for a while, watching for any sign that they'd been found, but when there was nothing except the passage of the occasional human on the way to or from the hospital, Snow found herself drifting. She let go, permitting herself to settle lightly into slumber, trusting instincts honed over more than a century to wake her at the least sign of trouble.

CHAPTER THREE

They circled the massive building one final time, but nothing seemed untoward. It took up a city block in downtown Chicago, not far from where they'd bunked down to catch a few hours of sleep. Snow's instincts had woken her a couple of times when humans got too close to the vehicle, but Cassidy had slumbered deeply. That in itself was a testament to her exhaustion. The North Side Alpha still held herself stiffly and her face was creased by lines of fatigue and stress, and yet she still looked so much better than she had before the nap.

They'd found parking not far from the library, but it had taken what remained of Snow's stash of cash to convince the valet to let her park it herself on the outer edge of the lot. There was no way a human could have been permitted to enter the van, not when the back was as spattered with blood as it was. She'd had to give up her keys, but she'd held onto the extra set. Despite no sign of a tail to the library or when they parked, Snow knew they had to keep acting as if someone was coming after them. Living her life assuming others had negative designs on her continued existence had kept her alive and relatively safe so far.

Snow nodded at Cassidy as they crossed through the front entrance. Cassidy was as on edge as she was. There was hope for her yet.

"We didn't set a meeting place in the building," Snow said quietly. Her voice still carried further than she would have liked it to. The main foyer was filled with marble and stone, with nothing to soften even the quietest whisper. A balcony ran the perimeter of the room, and she eyed the railings carefully. No one on the second level seemed out of place or paid them any special mind.

"We're a little early." Cassidy lifted her head and inhaled deeply, then let the breath out through her mouth. She grimaced. "But we're not the first to arrive."

"Ah." Snow took her own deep breath, tasting the air in the entryway. Hammer's distinctive aroma floated among the building's other smells. It had had some time to dissipate, but not so much that they couldn't follow his trail. It would take quite a long time for an Alpha's scent trace to completely evaporate, but enough time would make it difficult to track it directly to the wolven.

He hadn't bothered with the elevator. It seemed he'd been certain of his destination. His trail led directly to the stairs heading up.

"Have you been here before?" Cassidy asked in the hushed tones characteristic of those talking in a library.

"A number of times. I was one of many who took a tour when it was first opened to the public. You?"

"I stopped by once, just to check it out. The library on campus had what I needed for classes." Cassidy shrugged. She paused on a landing to sniff again, then pointed upward.

"That makes sense." Snow hesitated. Cassidy's scent had taken on deep sadness when she'd mentioned school. "Do you miss it?"

Cassidy barked a humorless laugh as she mounted the next set of stairs. "You're going to have to be more specific than that."

"School, I guess. Do you miss taking classes?"

"Classes, sure. I suppose." She paused for a moment. "I think what I miss most is the idea that everything was wide open in front of me. I could have been anything. Anyone. And now..."

"Is it feeling like you've been pinned down?"

"Maybe." Cassidy's lips twisted. "Of course, I'm suddenly at loose ends."

"Yeah." Snow sighed.

"Why do you ask?"

"Mostly making conversation. Well, that and I was going to assure you that you could still take classes. I do all the time."

"Maybe when this is over." They stopped on another landing, and Cassidy took a moment to cast about for Hammer's scent. "He's that way."

"The history and genealogy section."

"Let's hope he's not looking into his ancestry. I can think of better times to work on a family tree." The words might have been meant as a joke, but there was venom behind them.

"Genealogy is difficult for us," Snow said quietly.

"Wolven don't keep records?" Cassidy stalked toward the far side of the section where Hammer's scent grew steadily stronger.

"Not so much."

The South Shore Alpha was seated at a table in the corner. The Black man's large frame dwarfed what would otherwise have been an average-sized table. The dreadlocks that were normally pulled back into a neat bundle now hung free. He gripped his dense black beard with one hand, the other he used to scribble on a legal pad with a tiny golf pencil. Snow had known him long enough to see him in all sorts of moods, but today he radiated ill temper.

He looked up as they approached, more to acknowledge them than because he had any need to see who it was. After deliberate eye contact with Cassidy, he bent his head back down to his book. He had a stack of volumes around him and seemed to be methodically flipping through them, stopping only to jot down more notes.

Cassidy slid into a chair opposite him, then squeezed in so Snow could get past her. It didn't slip Snow's notice that Cassidy was giving her the chair by the wall. If someone attacked, she would be protected on two sides. Three if she counted Hammer across the table.

"What did you find?" Cassidy asked. She glanced around to see who was nearby. Hammer had chosen his spot wisely. The stacks ended not far from them in one direction. There was another table across the way, but no one was at it. With the anger that Hammer exuded, both in the scent that roiled around him and the tension in his frame, Snow would have been surprised if any humans could have stood to be in his immediate vicinity.

"The house is standing, but it's empty." He might have been discussing the weather except that the pencil in his hand snapped. He gently placed the pieces on a small pile of writing utensil shards by his left elbow.

"Shit."

"Those who weren't home were taken. Probably right after they left work." He flipped a yellowed page and perused it quickly before flipping the next.

"I called everyone in for the evening," Cassidy said. She leaned her forehead on her interlaced hands. "Maybe some of them would have stayed free if I hadn't."

"Not based on what I found when I got back to my den. Once we left…" He didn't blame her out loud, but his scent made it clear he was furious. It wasn't difficult to guess the target of his anger.

"Once we left." Cassidy's voice was muffled by her hands.

"This isn't anyone's fault," Snow hissed. "At least no one at this table."

"Who's talking about fault?" Dale's voice came from behind them as the Kenosha Alpha emerged from the stacks.

"No one," Cassidy said.

"Not yet." Snow glared at Hammer's chin. She didn't quite dare lift her eyes to meet his. "How's Jane?"

"Recovering with the pack." Dale swung a chair around and plopped into it, straddling the back. She moved like a bird, from one burst of speed to the next, with only enough time in between to look around or take a breath. Her round face was better suited to smiles than the bland facade she was showing the human world. She'd taken the time to brush the blood out of her long black hair and bind it back in a simple bun. It would take more than doing her hair to dispel the exhaustion from her hooded dark eyes.

"Your pack wasn't taken?" Cassidy leaned back in her chair, watching Dale carefully.

The Kenosha Alpha shook her head. "I moved them before the meeting. Someone hit our old den, though." She pursed her lips. "Pretty sure we all know who."

"The same bastards who—"

"—took our wolves."

Marrow and Bone strode up to the table. Snow glanced around to see if anyone had heard them. The Gary Alpha and Beta were making no effort at being quiet. They'd found clothing somewhere, but it fit poorly. On one, the clothes were too baggy, on the other too tight. A too-small shirt displayed wrists crisscrossed with scars, the pale lines a few shades lighter than her skin. Similar scars on the side of Hammer's neck were much darker. They all sported visible signs of old battles, all except Cassidy. She hadn't collected nearly as many, and for the moment, they could still be concealed by her clothing.

"Did they burn out your den too?" Cassidy asked.

"Nothing left but ash and ember." Marrow leaned against the wall near Snow, the scent of woodsmoke wafting from her with each movement. Bone propped herself up on the nearest windowsill. Or at least, Snow thought it was Marrow who was closer to her. They gave off a restless energy, even when they weren't moving. Each always seemed aware of the other, either leaning toward her twin or one sister facing the other.

"We dug through it anyway." Bone spread her hands. Soot caked black under her fingernails, visible from across the table, even against her ochre skin.

"No one was home." Marrow stared off into the distance. The tight curls of her hair had been flattened in places. The shorter sides usually gave the style a playful look, somewhere between mohawk and afro. There was no sign of humor to either of them now. Snow had always thought they'd go to their own deaths with a joke on their lips. Apparently it was possible for the Gary Alphas to take something seriously.

"Did you lose any of them?" Cassidy asked.

The four Alphas looked at her as if she'd sprouted another head. One that was cursing up a storm. In church.

"My pack is safe," Dale said slowly.

"That's not funny, Five Moons," Bone said. "Very poor taste."

"And that's coming from us." Marrow cocked her head at Cassidy. Flecks of gold flared to life in her irises.

Cassidy waved her hand impatiently. "I know they were taken. Did any of them die? I can still feel all of my wolves."

The combined weight of the Alphas' gazes would have been more than Snow could have taken, even as the glares shifted from outrage to curiosity.

"What do you mean you can feel them?" Hammer asked. He put down his latest pencil.

"You mean you can't?" Cassidy looked from one Alpha to the other.

"That's not one of my gifts," Dale said. "Do you mean to say you have the ability to sense the wolves bound to you even when they're not close to you?"

Cassidy nodded.

"So you know what direction they're in," Marrow stated.

"What are we waiting for?" Bone pushed herself away from the window. "We'll take Snow's van and go get them."

"It doesn't work like that," Cassidy said.

"I don't think my van's big enough for everyone," Snow said at the same time.

"I can't get you there even if Snow could get every single lost wolf into her van." Cassidy looked from one Alpha to another in turn. "I know they're alive. I'm not close enough to get a fix on them."

"Kinda useless." Bone sneered, her full lips pulled thin on one side as she leaned back against the window.

"If I can get close enough, I'll be able to tell a direction, but that's it."

"Maybe we can work with that," Hammer said. "We use Five Moons as final confirmation."

"Final confirmation for what?" Snow asked, grateful for the distraction. Anything to cut the tension between Cassidy and the twins.

"There's only so many places they can take our wolves," Hammer said. He indicated the stack of volumes at his elbow. "Think about it. They've picked up dozens of scared and angry wolven. Even if they're drugged, you know our people will metabolize that shit out of their systems in no time. They have to get them somewhere they can be secured. So what fits the bill? Somewhere away from human civilians. Somewhere fortified, both from the inside and outside." He grinned, exposing teeth already grown sharp. "They have to know we're going to come after them."

"So prisons," Dale said thoughtfully.

"But not current ones," Bone said. "Something that's been decommissioned or closed."

"Better include old mental hospitals, then," Snow said.

Hammer nodded and made a note on the legal pad.

"Hospitals with prison wings would also meet the bill." Marrow leaned forward, rubbing her hands together. "What about old army bases?"

"Hospitals are probably too small, but the bases are a good idea." Hammer's pencil was flying across the page now.

"We should give more weight to federal facilities," Cassidy said. "The vamps seem to think the jacket I took came from a military uniform."

"And look outside of Illinois," Bone added. "We're not that far from a bunch of other states, especially by freeway."

"Or helicopter," Marrow said grimly.

It was amazing how a bit of direction shifted the group's mood. The Alphas no longer eyed each other with suspicion. Cassidy reached over and snagged a sheet of paper from Hammer. He pulled a spare golf pencil out of a pocket and slid it over to her.

"I'll see what I can find online," Cassidy said. "You keep looking wherever you're looking."

"These are city directories and lists of state government property," Hammer said with quiet dignity.

"I'm sure your moldy books will be very helpful." Cassidy's grin held the first glimmer of true amusement Snow had seen since the previous day. "Bet the Internet will give me way more hits than you can get with print."

"You're on," Hammer said.

Cassidy stood and headed toward the nearest bank of computers. Snow scooted after her. After a moment, Bone followed along with them.

When Snow quirked an eyebrow at her, the Gary Alpha shrugged. "Marrow will keep an eye on Hammer and Dale. I get to babysit you two."

"Might as well make yourself useful, then," Cassidy said. "How good are you with computers?"

"Do you have a library card?" Snow asked.

Bone shook her head. "I'll copilot."

"Good thing we still have our wallets." Cassidy pulled hers out of her pocket. "And that I signed up for a card the only time I was here."

"I've got mine." Snow glanced at the crowded banks of public computers. "Now to find a couple that are open."

"Allow me." Bone wandered to the end of the closest computer table. She loitered for a few moments without saying anything.

She didn't have to. It wasn't long before the entire row decided they had something, anything, to do anywhere else. She smirked as Cassidy and Snow took the end machines and logged in.

"Let me know what else I can do," she said. She hooked her foot around the leg of a nearby chair and dragged it so she was sitting behind them with an eye on both screens.

Snow fired up Google and began working her way through the search results, keeping an eye out for the kinds of locations they'd talked about as a group. Cassidy searched next to her in bouts of furious typing that was punctuated with clicks of the mouse and scribbles on the scratch paper she'd gotten from Hammer. The Gary Alpha watched both screens and quietly suggested more place names as they worked their way through clickbait articles of haunted buildings and old government facilities.

Their list grew in fits and starts, with more and more suggestions from Bone. Eventually they were investigating ideas and muttering amongst themselves if they seemed like reasonable candidates. They were clicking along at a good rate. Snow felt her chest expand, like she could finally take a deep breath again. It was good to have a plan, rather than panic and blind reaction to events out of their direct control.

"This is looking really good," Cassidy said.

"One more," Bone said. "How about the Historic Iowa State Pen—"

The lights went out around them, plunging the area into semidarkness. All the computers went dark, including the two they were working on.

"What now?" Cassidy asked.

CHAPTER FOUR

As soon as the lights went out, Cassidy's wolf went on the alert. They scanned the immediate area, as Cassidy's jaw ached. She clenched it to keep from changing. They were far enough from the exterior windows that it was fairly dark, but their eyes had no problem piercing the half-gloom of the library's sixth floor. Beside her, Bone's irises held a dark amber glow, and Snow's shone brilliant silver.

"Get the wolf under control," Bone whispered. She blinked twice, and her eyes returned to their normal light brown.

"Right." Snow's eyes dimmed almost immediately.

Cassidy had to clench her eyes shut and force the wolf back down. She didn't want to go, but she finally conceded to relinquishing her grip on their body when Cassidy pointed out that an enemy coming up on them would know them immediately.

"Power's out, people," came a woman's voice from the far end of the floor. "You need to evacuate the building."

There was a collective murmur of irritation around them, then the rustle of humans pulling together their belongings and making their way toward the exit. A moment later, some handful of lights came back on as an emergency generator somewhere came to life.

Bone was already heading back to where they'd left the other Alphas. By the light from the window, Hammer was scribbling frantically as he flipped his way through another directory.

"We need to go," Cassidy hissed. "They're evacuating the place."

"One more second," Hammer murmured. "I just need to…" He kept writing.

"This could just be a random power outage," Marrow said.

"And if you believe that, I have oceanfront property in Arizona to sell you," Bone replied. They shared a strained smile.

"I don't believe in coincidences," Cassidy said. "Not anymore." The outage could be coincidental, but if it wasn't, they were making nice juicy targets of themselves.

"If it's a ploy, there will probably be government forces waiting for us outside." Dale craned her neck at the window, trying to get a good look at the street below.

Marrow grabbed her by the elbow and yanked her down. "If there are government forces, that could mean snipers. Watch the windows."

"So we go out the back." Cassidy scanned the room, looking for other exits than the main stairs they'd used to access the floor. Nothing jumped out at her as a reasonable alternative.

Bone ducked and scooted past the windows, heading toward the outside walls.

"Follow my sister," Marrow said. She shook the table. "Hammer, if you don't have it now, you're not getting it. We have to move."

"Where are we going?" Dale asked. She started after Bone.

"Staff exit," Marrow whispered. "Trust us. We have some experience navigating the back areas of government buildings."

It struck Cassidy as being a very specific set of skills, but Snow didn't seem to have any qualms in following the Gary Alphas. Cassidy came along, as much to watch Snow's back as to see what had ended up on Hammer's list. She was conscious of the folded paper in her back pocket. What she wouldn't give to compare his list to hers.

Bone led them around the perimeter to a staff service point. Sure enough, a green exit sign was illuminated over a door. A large sign with "Employees Only" in stark white on black font took up half the width of the door beneath a small, diamond-shaped window.

"That's only for staff," Cassidy whispered to Snow.

"You're worried about niceties now?" Hammer asked from behind her. His voice rumbled with amusement and Cassidy's face heated. Her wolf snarled quietly, yearning to put him in his place.

"Five Moons," Marrow hissed from behind the South Shore Alpha. "Your eyes."

"Yes, yes." She squeezed them shut, trusting her other senses to keep her with the group. The wolf didn't want to calm down; she wanted action. There was too much talk and not enough attacking those who'd dared confront them. She was willing to subside only when Cassidy promised that if they ran into anyone they could legitimately take out, the wolf would be unleashed.

When she opened her eyes, the group was moving through the door. Hammer had squeezed past her to the front and Dale had dropped back next to Marrow, who still took up the rear. Dale whispered with Marrow, but their voices were too low for Cassidy to make out the words.

The room behind the staff door was disappointing. It wasn't huge, but row upon row of metal filing cabinets dominated the space. Here and there, a large volume or a stack of white folders broke up the monotony of the cabinet tops. It smelled overwhelmingly of old paper. She'd thought the sixth floor had smelled strongly of the stuff, but it was so thick here she could almost see the scent as a beige miasma in the air. The room was dark. No one had thought to install emergency lights back here.

Bone came to a crouching stop in front of the door on the other side of the room. She pressed her ear to the gap where the swinging door almost met the frame. It had been designed to allow someone to push through from either side. As long as no one came barreling through to catch their odd group skulking in the gloom, they would be fine.

Cassidy's palms and feet itched, as much from the wolf holding herself in readiness to ascend, as with the need to keep moving. They had a plan, or nearly a plan. She wanted to be past this part already, to where they tracked down her wolves so she could go find her mom and Mary Alice. There was so much to be done, and lurking in the dark was taking too much time.

For too long, Bone stayed crouched and listening before nodding and pushing on. The other Alphas' eyes were shining brightly, except for Marrow's and Bone's.

The room beyond the file cabinet room was echoingly large and dotted with square pillars. Bookshelves crammed with papers formed the edges of ad hoc office areas. Some desks were clear, while others were buried in documents that reeked of age and dust. Snow muffled a sneeze into her upper arm as they moved through. Bone glanced back long enough to mouth "Bless you," at her.

Hammer grinned, and the Alphas behind Cassidy smelled briefly of amusement. Then Dale sneezed.

Cassidy's nose itched in sympathy. Her wolf's disdain mounted. This place was for the past. They had no time for such things. Ruminating on what had come before was pointless and they had work to do. Cassidy pointed out that the human obsession with the past had given them somewhere to start for in looking for their packs. The thought surprised the wolf, and she subsided into irritated grumblings.

They were halfway across the room when the scent of something inhuman tickled Cassidy's nostrils. The other Alphas smelled it too, and they swiveled almost as one.

A dark-haired white woman whose hair was pulled back in a tight bun sat in the shadows next to a large table strewn with documents. She looked human, but her eyes shone in the dark with an eerie red shimmer that flashed as she met each of their gazes in turn. She nodded gravely, then held a gloved finger to her lips and pointed in the direction they were headed.

"What—" Bone's soft query was cut off when Hammer bumped her with his shoulder. There might be more questions to be had here, but the woman didn't seem inclined to rat them out.

The rest of the room was empty of humans or otherwise, and they were able to cross it quickly. Despite the cluttered appearance of the area's many desks, the walkway was clear.

Again, they paused at the next door. This one was thicker, and Cassidy held her breath as Bone listened at it. She glanced over at Snow, making sure the lone wolf was holding together, then past her to see if the woman whose scent was of thorns and dark pleasures was coming up on them. The way behind them was clear. Whatever interests the woman had weren't with them.

Snow looked fine, and her scent wasn't any more concerned than the situation called for. Of all of them, she'd taken the least amount of damage the previous night. She must have been tired, but the bone-deep exhaustion of the Alphas was absent from her frame. Her brown eyes caught the light more sharply. The brown of her skin was warmer, missing the tinges of gray that fatigue brought to the others. Snow caught Cassidy looking and shot her a fleeting smile. Her aroma brightened as she did so, and Cassidy found herself smiling back. She edged closer to Snow and reached out toward her.

Snow grabbed her hand, lacing their fingers together in a tight grip. Cassidy squeezed back and held on, even as Bone nodded, then opened the door.

Dim light filtered through the doorway. A pair of emergency lights halfway down a featureless hallway were more than enough to illuminate the area. Hammer crossed immediately over to the opposite side of the hall, then waited to see where the Gary Alphas would lead them next. Dale went a short way in the opposite direction, then also paused. For a moment, Cassidy wondered where they were going, then realized that the two Alphas were keeping the group from clumping together.

She wondered if she should move, but that would take her away from Snow. No, it was more important that she and her wolf stay by the lone wolf's side in case they needed to protect her.

Bone scanned both sides of the hall, then pointed to the right. Another green exit sign gleamed over a door.

When it was pushed open to reveal a stairwell, Cassidy couldn't fully throttle a small gasp of relief. Even though the air that came through the opening was stale, she inhaled it deeply. This was their way to freedom. Unlike the wide stairs they'd climbed to get to the sixth floor, these were narrow, the stair treads deeper. The emergency lights revealed bare concrete with no carpet to cushion each step, only a strip of black nonstick materials. The metal handrails along the outside walls were alligatored with years of paint having been applied, chipped away, then reapplied without removing the remnants. As their little group trooped down the steps as quietly as only wolven could, Cassidy caught the smell of stale cigarette smoke.

She paused in her tracks, Snow almost running into her back. Marrow grunted a quiet question.

A quick glance at the nearest door with the big number five painted on the industrial gray surface confirmed that they'd only gone down one story. She'd assumed the smell of cigarettes would be from staff members going out for a smoke, but they were awfully high up to be smelling it.

At the front of their little group, Bone was looking back at her, head cocked. Cassidy lifted her nose in the air and inhaled deeply. There was that whiff of cigarettes, in a tangle of brown so light as to be almost imperceptible. She breathed in the strand of scent, closing her eyes and savoring its component pieces. The cigarette smoke made her want to gag, but she held it in. Beneath the smoke was sweat—human sweat—and another scent that she wasn't as familiar with. Some kind of oil perhaps? She'd smelled it before.

Her eyes popped open. She'd smelled that oil the night before. It had been nearly obliterated by the stench of gunpowder.

Hammer had also closed his eyes. When he opened them again, they glowed brilliant orange. His lips pulled back from his teeth to match the snarl that was stretching across her own face. Her knees wobbled as the wolf raked her claws along the underside of Cassidy's belly. She'd promised, and the wolf was eager to collect.

Her skin prickling with gooseflesh that hailed the return of her fur, Cassidy had enough presence of mind to empty her pockets and shove the contents into Snow's hands. She kept her jaws clenched as the wolf roared into her, shoving their humanity aside in a burst of fluids. Agony ripped through her as her bones snapped and reformed, the muscles not so much writhing as springing into place. It was over in seconds and without a sound from their throat.

The other Alphas waited, but as soon as their own furforms settled, they were moving again. There wasn't a dim eye among the group. Hammer was holding onto betweenform, his dark skin blotted out by charcoal gray fur that looked black in the stairwell's low light. A muzzle jutted from his face, displaying long teeth that glittered in the dim light of the emergency lamps. His legs bent backward like a wolf's, but he stood upright on them. Furred arms ended in long fingers tipped with full wolf claws. Betweenform was typically only used for Alpha challenge fights, but it was helpful for things like opening doors, even if it wasn't ideal for most fights. It was difficult to hold onto, but Hammer didn't seem to be having any trouble. His orange eyes glittered with rage seeking an outlet.

Dale, Marrow, and Bone had held onto skinform, but with claws and teeth prominent. Snow was in full skinform, with nothing to distinguish her from a human except her eyes glowing white so bright that there was no sign of pupil or cornea.

Each step was soundless. The wolf swallowed the warning growl she wanted to release. You didn't warn your enemies of an ambush. You sprang it, obliterated them, then moved on to the next one.

The smell of cigarette smoke was stronger to those in furform, as were the scents that wafted along with it. They sniffed deeply, separating them further. There were at least six humans. Their ears twitched. Whoever advanced up the stairs was trying to be silent, but concrete did little to muffle the scrape of boots on each new step. It was difficult to tell how far below them the interlopers were.

Each step down wound the tension in their belly ever tighter. With each flight of stairs, they crept closer to the front of their little pack. They sent frequent glances back at Snow to make sure she was still with them. Marrow was also keeping a close eye on the lone wolf, and Dale was falling further back through the group toward her as Cassidy and the wolf moved up. There was no surprise that a group of Alphas were closing ranks to protect the most vulnerable among them.

They were out in front of the group when they turned the corner on the landing of the third floor. The scrape of boot on concrete was the only warning they got, but it was enough.

When the soldier came around the corner at the bottom of the flight, they were already launching themself through the air.

The woman's eyes widened on the other side of her iron sights, her finger tightening to squeeze off a round, but the wolf had already bowled her back. The report of her first shots bounced around the hard surfaces that surrounded them. Bullets whined and ricocheted off the walls. A line of fire scored across their ribs, but the wolf paid it no mind.

Their jaws snapped just short of the soldier's face, and their claws shredded the black battle uniform, unable to pierce the Kevlar vest beneath her jacket. Her legs had no such protection. Her struggles slackened suddenly as a jet of blood spurted through the rent in her thigh. They dug down further, glorying in the heat of the blood that painted their abdomen. The femoral artery pumped the soldier's lifeblood onto the cold concrete. Before she'd stopped twitching, they were already flinging themselves forward.

Cassidy was little more than a passenger as the wolf danced and weaved among the squad of soldiers. They wore the same uniform as the group the night before. One of them perished as he tried to shove the blade of a silver knife up under their jaw. The soft metal crumpled between their teeth.

Mere moments had passed, and they'd taken down half the group. The remaining Alphas rushed to dance death among the soldiers. More shots rang out as their would-be assailants belatedly realized they were the ones under attack. The lights dimmed, then went out, leaving the space lit only by the staccato muzzle flashes of their enemies' rifles. Each crack illuminated a scene of carnage. The wolf concentrated on the next throat to rip out, the next gap of flesh to savage. The sparks of light grew less frequent until they stood panting in a suddenly quiet battlefield.

A grunt and snap broke the silence, and a human's last gasp accompanied the final soldier's death.

They stood panting, their ears swiveling, listening for any sign that this wasn't the only group of soldiers, but the only sounds were the quick breaths of the other Alphas, and the drip of blood pooling on concrete. They made a quick count of the eyes that glowed around them. Hammer's citrine was closest, with Bone or Marrow's gold behind him, and echoed at the top of the flight. Dale's bright lavender glowed in front of the other Gary twin. Their heart stuttered in their chest when they realized there was no sign of Snow's white eyes.

They let out a whuff of relief when the lone wolf's face appeared slowly around the edge of the wall at the top of the flight. Her eyes flickered across the scene, taking in the dead humans in all their gore.

"Let's keep moving," Hammer said quietly. The shape of his muzzle garbled the words somewhat, but the suggestion—command, really—was unmistakable.

The wolf agreed. Cassidy half-heartedly reached out to try to wrest back control, but the wolf wasn't giving it up. Cassidy didn't have the energy to muster up a good fight. The wolf was in charge now, for good or for ill. As long as they could keep Snow safe from those who hunted them, she didn't really care who was running things.

CHAPTER FIVE

Snow picked her way through the carnage the Alphas had made. It wasn't that she was too concerned about getting her clothes dirty, but one of them should be free of the evidence of their demolishment of the humans. There was no way of knowing what waited for them at the bottom of the stairwell, but they would have to cross at least one street to get to her van.

She shoved Cassidy's phone and wallet deep into her pockets. A quick pat revealed that her own wallet and car keys were still there. She only needed the ID for driving, really, and replacing it was a pain since she didn't really exist in the eyes of any government.

The van was their first escape plan, but this was Chicago. They had other options if they couldn't get to the car. Her mind was already running through them and prioritizing each one. All would be complicated by a group of blood-covered people and a wolf who was positively drenched in gore, but they'd be able to clear the immediate area.

They kept on moving cautiously down the stairs. Cassidy was still in furform, but she drifted back to Snow's position at the group's rear. Marrow had been taking up the tail, but she'd moved forward during the short but brutal fight. She and Bone now took the lead with Hammer close on their heels.

Destroyed clothing hung from Cassidy's frame. She would occasionally shake a front paw as the remains of a cuff still somehow attached to the remnants of a sleeve restricted her movement.

"Hold on," Snow whispered after they'd negotiated another flight of steps.

Cassidy looked up at her, red and blue eyes gleaming in unspoken question.

Snow reached down and yanked the dangling piece of fabric away from the cuff. She twisted and pulled with her other hand, separating what remained of the collar of Cassidy's shirt. It took only a few seconds to remove the remaining shreds of clothing. She worked quickly, but carefully, taking care not to transfer too much blood to her, at least no more than she could wipe off her hands.

Cassidy stood quietly, letting her work. As soon as Snow was finished, she leaned her heavy brindle head against Snow's hands. Her eyes shut for a fraction of a second, then popped back open. The red eye winked shut, then Cassidy was moving forward again.

The rest of their trip down the stairs was uneventful. Occasionally, the squawk of a radio would echo down from the remains of the human soldiers, but no one else started up toward them.

The Alphas gathered at the landing next to the metal door with the number one painted on it. The stairs continued down further toward a basement level.

There was no window to check what might await them. After a quick look back at the group, Bone pushed the door open a crack. She took a moment to inspect whatever was beyond, then moved through the doorway. The area behind it linked up with another featureless hallway. Double doors at the end leaked daylight and fresh air through small gaps.

Bone pushed one open a fraction of an inch, then eased it back into place.

"We've got humans," she whispered.

"Military?" Hammer asked.

Bone nodded. "Looks like a cordon."

"My car isn't far," Snow murmured. She closed her eyes, allowing her wolf's unerring sense of direction to lock into place around them. She pointed to the left and back. "That direction. We parked in the lot across from the main entrance."

"We'll be completely exposed if we make a run that way." Dale drummed tan fingers with blood-stained tips against the top of her thighs. Her bun was mostly intact, but it had loosened a bit in the tussle. She tucked a stray strand behind her ear.

"Not if we go up," Snow said. "The stairs up to the El are on this street. We break through, then head up there. With luck, we can get over the cordon and down to street level before anyone knows we've broken containment."

"It's risky," Hammer rumbled.

Cassidy bristled next to Snow. She pawed at the door and snarled. She was ready to take on the world, it seemed.

"The other option is to hide out here and hope they don't find us," Snow said.

"Now that we've let the cat out of the bag—" Bone said.

"—I don't think they're going to just walk away," Marrow finished.

Dale lifted her hands. "We did leave a big bloody calling card."

"We did." Hammer grinned, his teeth bloody in the muzzle of his betweenform. "Looks like the only way out is through."

"We're going to have to move quickly." Dale ran a critical eye over the group. The Alphas looked back at her, each as bloody as she was. "We'll stick out. Our only chance is to be fast and decisive."

"I like a solution—"

"—that calls for brute force," Bone finished her twin's statement.

"Maybe you should…" Snow made brief eye contact with Hammer and gestured at her face.

Hammer's scent went spiky with irritation, then subsided. "We're already going to be obvious."

"There's obvious, and then there's panic-inducing."

He sighed and shook himself, fur receding to expose skin. Such was his physical presence that without the fur, his bulk reduced only a little. Fluids sluiced off him, rinsing off a lot of the blood and soaking clothes now ripped at the seams, but still holding together. He kept the claws and teeth, grinning for a second, before clamping his lips shut and folding his fingers into a fist.

Bone and Marrow reached for the doors in unsettling unison, then shoved. Dale and Hammer rocketed through the sudden opening.

The soldiers outside the door had been facing away. Three dropped as the Alphas tore through them.

"Come on," Bone and Marrow shouted in stereo.

Snow started forward, heading for the gap in the thin line of military men and women who were turning their way in slow motion. Cassidy flowed forward at her side, near enough to touch but not so close as to get in Snow's way.

The doors slammed shut as Marrow and Bone followed behind them. Two more soldiers in black fatigues went down, one missing a large chunk of throat, the other bleeding profusely from deep gouges to the eyes.

Dale was halfway up the steps to the El platform before the rest of the group had hit the bottom. She crouched and looked back behind them.

"Here they come," she shouted. "Keep moving."

Vehicles screeched to a halt as more soldiers spilled out onto the street to flank their group. Snow kept running, her knees pumping as she took the steps two at a time. She braced herself for the feel of rounds puncturing her flesh, but the sound of gunfire never came. The terrified faces of human civilians stared down at them from the top of the El platform. However bold the military had gotten to try to scoop them up from the middle of the city, it seemed they weren't brash enough to incur civilian fatalities.

"Try not to kill them," Snow yelled. She'd meant the soldiers behind them, but with the way the loose throng at the top of the stairs scattered, the humans didn't know that. It made for a much easier dash across the platform, so she wasn't going to complain. The screams of terror made her cringe, but she couldn't close her ears to them.

The tracks were free of trains and Dale waited impatiently by them. When the rest of the group ran past, she darted back to glance down the steps.

Shots rang out and she ducked away.

"They're still coming," she called out as she dashed back to the group.

Snow hopped down onto the tracks. It couldn't be long before the next train came along. She kept one eye down. Wolven could take a lot of damage, but she didn't know how they'd fare against the voltage of the electrified rail that gave the trains their power. "Watch your feet," she yelled.

The rails were a quick way out, but they were open, with no civilians to keep soldiers with a line of sight on them from firing. Fortunately for them, she didn't plan on being up there long.

Snow sprinted as quickly as she could while keeping one eye on her feet to avoid becoming barbecue. She kept the other eye on the side. When they'd cleared the platform, she veered off to the edge of the tracks and vaulted the railing, Cassidy right behind her. The gap between the El and the closest building was relatively narrow. The fifteen-foot drop was negligible. She bent her legs to absorb the shock to her knees but was already looking around as she did so.

Pedestrians littered the sidewalk, most looking her way. Between the commotion above and her sudden arrival, there were far more eyes on her than made her comfortable.

More wolven in skinform dropped out of the sky, and Snow was already pushing past the gawkers.

"Move!" she yelled, gesturing at the humans to make way for them. A businessman in suit and tie froze up ahead. He held his attaché case in front of him as if it might be any protection if she decided to unleash her wolf. Cassidy ripped out an angry snarl, high and harsh, and he jerked back.

The North Side Alpha bounded past him, turning her head to make sure Snow was on her tail. She needn't have checked. Snow's legs churned, propelling her forward and away from their pursuers. A quick jump off the edge of the El might gain them some time, but she doubted it would make them give up the chase.

A fresh din arose at their backs. She risked a quick glimpse over her shoulder as they turned the corner of the building. Black-clad bodies were streaming down the stairs of the El. More lined the bridge where they'd just been. They raised rifles and took aim, but Snow and the Alphas were around the corner before anyone could take a shot.

Civilians stared as the wolven in their bloody garb pounded down the sidewalk among them. The more bystanders they got between them and the soldiers, the better the chances they would slip the net with their skins intact.

They were almost at the next corner when figures in black filed in to block the sidewalk in front of them. There was no more barrier of civilians, scant protection though it had been. Triumphant shouts rose from behind as their pursuers thought they were trapped.

With a burst of speed, Cassidy flowed out in front of the group. She tracked a zigzagging route toward those who dared bar their way. She was quick, but when Dale darted forward, she was a blur. Even in skinform, Dale reached the soldiers first, despite Cassidy's head start.

"Keep running," Marrow shouted in Snow's ear.

"We've got you," Bone hollered in the other. They linked arms behind Snow's back and propelled her forward, even as she instinctively tried to slow to avoid the soldiers ahead. The way behind them was a mass of black as their pursuers finally caught up.

Cassidy and Dale were carving a path through the dozen or so humans who thought they could stop a pack of determined wolven. And now that the soldiers were facing each other, it seemed none of them dared to fire their rifles for fear of hitting their comrades.

A series of deep booms filled the air. Snow was propelled forward when the center of her lower back was hit. It felt like she'd been walloped by a sledgehammer wielded by a determined wolven. She was kept from tumbling by the Gary Alphas. Bone shifted so her torso was behind Snow's. She grunted, the curls on her head trembling as another series of reports rang through the air and she took whatever rounds had been meant for Snow.

Ahead, Cassidy and Dale had opened a channel through the soldiers. Human bodies lay on the ground. Most were still moving, and there was a surprising lack of blood.

Marrow hustled them into the opening. She used her free hand to slash at anyone who got too close. Her eyes glowed liquid gold, even in the bright sunlight. As the humans closed in behind, Bone shifted to Snow's other side. When she let go, a pang of anxiety shook Snow. This was not her kind of fight. The brawl swirled around them. It was much too close. There were no shadows in which to hide and leap out from when the time was right. There was only keeping her head down and swinging at anyone who got within arm's reach.

Despite the opening Cassidy and Dale had provided for them, they were slowing down. There were too many humans, and desperation was starting to set in. Marrow hooked her arm around a man's neck and threw him to the ground as he attempted to stab her in the belly. With an extra twist at the end of the throw, the man's head snapped to the left at an unnatural angle. When he hit the sidewalk, he wasn't moving.

The shouts of the soldiers grew in volume even as they deepened in pitch. A force like a freight train hit their knot, snapping Snow's head back with enough momentum to give a nonwolven whiplash. The roar hadn't come from the crowd of brawlers; it had emanated from Hammer's throat as he shoved them free of the mob.

Snow looked back and threw out her hand toward him as he was nearly swallowed by the angry human throng. He grabbed hold, and their collective momentum popped them free.

Cassidy and Dale were heading back their way, causing traffic to screech to a halt while they bounded across the road without any thought to the cars honking at them.

"Dale," Snow yelled. "Get ready!" She reached into her pocket and pulled out her keys, then threw them toward the Kenosha Alpha. The lob was a little off target, but Dale leaped up and snagged them out of the air one-handed.

Cassidy hesitated, clearly torn between making her way back to where half their little pack was struggling free of those who were still trying to stop them, and accompanying Dale. Hammer shoved against the knot of Snow, Bone, and Marrow while making eye contact with Cassidy. Something passed between them, then Cassidy was bounding away. The cars that had just started moving were forced to slam on the brakes again. A cacophony of horns filled the air, accompanied by the angry shouts of drivers.

Hollered curses were replaced by concern as the rest of the wolven started to dash across four lanes of traffic while being chased by armed figures.

Bone staggered as someone opened fire behind them. The smell of wolven blood hit Snow's nostrils. These weren't the same nonlethal rounds that had been employed seconds ago. While the soldiers weren't willing to fire if it might take out one of their own, apparently they were pissed off enough that civilian deaths were no longer a concern.

Despite the injury, Bone kept on. In a move so seamless it was as if they'd practiced it, Hammer slipped into Bone's spot, freeing her up from Snow's weight.

The assistance was no longer necessary, but Snow couldn't shake the Alphas' iron grips. She'd lost sight of Dale and Cassidy, and she cast around desperately for them. Everything was a blur. Too many people were moving too quickly. The din around them didn't help. She wanted to find somewhere quiet and protected to crawl into it until the disturbance passed. There was nowhere to hide, nowhere to go but forward.

A new sound joined the morass of noises. Metal scraping on metal grew louder and louder until the unmistakable shape of her van pulled up in front of them in a squeal of abused tires. The side door was already open.

"Get in," Dale shouted from behind the wheel. The instruction was unnecessary; Snow had already been pitched into her own car. Marrow was pulling Bone in behind her, while Hammer braced himself in the doorway.

He gritted his teeth as his burly frame shook from more impacts. Snow winced at the pain in his eyes and at the sound of slugs burying themselves in the side of her beloved Volkswagen bus.

Marrow grasped Hammer's forearm and pulled him into the van as Dale laid down more rubber on the pavement as they pulled away at ridiculous speed.

The impacts on the side of the van traveled down the side. Each concussion was followed by a rain of shattering glass. A handful more shots rattled against the van, then stopped.

Silence reigned inside the van, so profound it pressed in on Snow's eardrums.

"Are you all right?" Dale's voice sounded like it was coming from far away. Snow wondered if that was from shock or damage to her hearing.

"Been better," Hammer grunted. He rolled onto his front. Multiple bullets had pierced his skin. Blood welled out, crimson on warm umber that was shading into cool ebony as he endured still more agony.

On his other side, Marrow was inspecting Bone's torso. A bright red flower disfigured her shirt and the warm terracotta flesh beneath.

"Hold on tight," Dale said. "I'm going to try and lose 'em."

CHAPTER SIX

Cassidy and the wolf dug their claws into the carpeted back area of Snow's van. They pitched to one side or another after every one of Dale's sharp turns, then sunk their claws in once again. Buildings and cars whizzed past them. Dale apparently drove at the same swift pace she moved, not that the circumstances didn't call for it. If Cassidy had been driving, she would be as heavy on the gas as the Kenosha Alpha.

Dale laid on the horn as she blew through a red light. Honks responded quickly but fell behind them in an instant.

Snow was crouched half over the front seat. One hand anchored her to the back of the bench seat, the other directed Dale through the congested grid that was downtown Chicago. The van's interior darkened as they passed through some sort of tunnel, then Dale jerked on the wheel. A squeal of metal on metal filled the van as she forced her way between two cars that waited at yet another red light.

The cars gave way, then she was on the horn again. After a bare pause to see if the intersection was clear, Dale slammed her foot down on the gas. They juked left, then right. Squealing tires and more angry honking filled their ears.

A moment later, they were heading straight, and the canyon of buildings had opened up. The road smoothed out under the van's tires.

The wind whistled through shot-out windows as Dale was able to pick up speed and finally sustain it. The wolf didn't know what it meant, but Cassidy knew they'd gotten to the freeway. Their panting breath slowed when the wolf realized they'd be able to open some distance between them and their hunters.

The air rushing through the car had the added bonus of dispersing the smell of blood. Now that they weren't moving so erratically, Marrow was able to finish tending to Bone's wound and was turning her attention to Hammer.

"Can you shift?" she said to the South Shore Alpha, her voice raised to be heard over the sounds of the road.

"Not sure I'll be able to shift back anytime soon," Hammer responded, his teeth gritted around the pain.

"You won't be much use to us in your current condition," Marrow said. "Reaching furform will go a long way to jump start the healing process." She looked down at the carpet that was soaked with even more blood.

"You make good points."

Snow looked back at them. "If you're worried about ruining the carpeting, that ship has sailed." A half-grin quirked the corner of her mouth, robbing the words of any possible accusation.

Still, Cassidy couldn't help but feel some responsibility. She knew how much Snow cherished the van. She silently vowed that the lone wolf wouldn't have to spend a cent of her own money to bring the van back up to its previous excellent condition. She owed Snow so much. Each Alpha did.

"Seems like I'm outvoted." With ponderous effort, Hammer pushed himself up to all fours. He bared his teeth and clenched his eyes shut. His transformation was slow. Cassidy wondered if that was on purpose, or if he was as low on energy as she was. As he labored through the change, bullets popped out through their entry holes before the skin was covered with the coarse deep gray pelt of Hammer's massive furform shape.

He moved more easily but seemed unsteady on his feet. Bright orange eyes cut over at Cassidy, then he followed her example by hooking his claws through the carpet and underlayment. He hunkered down, lowering his center of gravity to keep from swaying so badly. His ribcage expanded and deflated in a slow but steady rhythm and his ears drooped. Hammer was the picture of exhaustion. The same deep tiredness threatened to drag Cassidy down as adrenaline drained from her system.

Marrow and Bone leaned their heads against each other, mussed black curls mingling together, eyes shut as they braced against the side of the van. Snow and Dale were deep in conversation, but Cassidy couldn't make out what they said. The wind whipped their words away before they could come to the wolf's ears. That was all right, they trusted Snow, and Dale had nothing to gain by steering them wrong. What she and the wolf needed was some time to recuperate, to regain some of the energy they'd been putting out with no chance to rebuild their stores. A whole deer probably would have gone a long way toward their recovery, but those were going to be hard to come by on a Chicago freeway.

Instead, they crept forward to where Hammer hunkered down. He whipped his head around when they rested their shaggy head on his flank. They froze, eyes on his. Surely he could use the closeness as much as they could. His body was stiff, though, practically vibrating with tension.

Marrow reached out a foot and tapped his front paw with her shoe. "Give it a rest," she said. "Literally. She's not going to try to eat you. Not now."

Bone grinned, her teeth stained with blood, though no longer pointy. "And if she tries, we'll be sure to protect you."

Impossibly, his back stiffened further. An indignant scent rolled off him in a vibrant orange not too far from the shade of his eyes. It was chased by rueful amusement, and he sighed, then flopped his head onto the ground.

The wolf laid their head back onto Hammer's flank. They closed their eyes, blocking out the occasional building or vehicle that flew past with unsettling speed. Hammer wasn't pack, but the proximity of another wolven was a balm that lulled them into a light doze.

They hadn't been snoozing long when a new sound yanked them out of half-sleep. If they'd been in human form, Cassidy would have cursed until the air turned blue around them. There was no mistaking the rhythmic thumping. What was it with helicopters lately?

* * *

Snow crouched and glared out the window at the aircraft that hovered in front of them. It was black, sleek, and dangerous. At least this time the side door wasn't open with a machine gun pointed at them. Other cars on the freeway were taking note of the helicopter but didn't seem to be too concerned.

"How did they find us again?" Snow asked.

Dale's wispy eyebrows met in a ferocious scowl. "It has to be your van."

"What do you mean?"

"You've been LoJacked." Dale cut hard on the wheel, slipping in behind a semi in the lane to their right.

Snow clenched her fists on the back of the bench seat. "What do you mean?" she asked again, even though she already knew the answer.

"They're tracking your car." With another twist of her forearm, Dale slid over again, then accelerated, putting the truck between them and the helicopter. They couldn't see it, but the sound of its rotors were audible, even over the rush of air through the shot-out windows.

At least the windshield is still intact. Snow stared forward, wondering if it was the wind or the pit yawning in her stomach that was making her eyes water. "You don't know that." The denial was quiet, but not quiet enough.

"Can we take that chance?" Dale asked.

"What chance?" Marrow leaned forward until she was next to Snow. "Is this about our new visitor?"

"It is." Dale looked over her shoulder at Snow. Her glance brimmed with empathy, but beneath it was resolve as hard and deep as bedrock. "The car is compromised."

"Of course it is." Marrow closed her eyes for a moment. "They probably all are. Were. Those bastards knew what we were doing, and when it was time to move." She opened her eyes, revealing brightly glowing golden irises shining in the warm sepia tones of her face. "We need to ditch it."

Snow clamped her lips shut. All that came through was a quiet whimper. From the bloom of sympathy she smelled off Marrow and Dale, they'd heard it.

Marrow clapped her on the shoulder, then gently guided Snow to the bench where Bone sat with her eyes closed.

The other Gary Alpha looked up as she sat down. "Welcome to the timeout couch," she said. "What did you do to end up here?"

Marrow was back speaking urgently in Dale's ear, one hand gesturing as she made her case for something. Dale was nodding along, but Snow couldn't make out what was being said.

Bone bumped Snow with her shoulder. "Come on, talk to me."

Cassidy wriggled away from Hammer and crept forward. She laid her patchwork quilt of a head on Snow's lap and considered her soberly.

"Dale thinks we're being tracked through my car." She clenched her hands into fists. "We need to ditch it." The words were so cavalier. "Ditch it." As if she hadn't had the van for longer than she'd known anyone inside it. The Volkswagen bus had come to her brand new off the assembly line. She'd used money squirreled away for years while her previous vehicle, a World War II military surplus Jeep, slowly rusted out from under her. She'd vowed not to let the same thing happen to the bus, and she'd kept that promise. She was the primary mechanic for the vehicle, and she'd learned so much about car maintenance as a result. If she was being honest, the van was her longest relationship, and now she was supposed to simply walk away from it?

She looked around, taking in the interior she'd retrofitted herself, improving it from barely adequate living space to a comfortable refuge from the pressures of pack life and the human world. The recent bloodstains and rents in the carpet couldn't hide the love she'd poured into it.

Cassidy sat up, balancing carefully against the car's swerves as Dale continued to slip from lane to lane. She snuffled at the underside of Snow's chin, then treated her lower jaw to a thorough tongue bath.

"Oh, Cassidy." Snow leaned against the massive wolf, wrapping her up in a tight hug and burying her face in the dense fur. Dried blood flaked off the long guard hairs, but the soft downy fur beneath smelled of Cassidy. It also did an excellent job of sopping up the tears streaming from her eyes, now that she had a place to shed them where the other Alphas couldn't see. There was no way to stop them from smelling her pain, but having them watch as she cried felt too vulnerable.

"Everyone hold on," Dale yelled. She yanked hard on the wheel, jerking them to the right.

The helicopter juked to follow, then pulled up as they raced down an exit and passed under the freeway without bothering to stop at the light.

When they emerged from the underpass, the helicopter was close on their tail. The side door opened and a soldier stepped into view. He had some sort of large weapon on his shoulder, and it was trained on the vehicle. There weren't many other cars on the road here. That had clearly been a tactical error on Dale's part. Without innocent bystanders, their pursuers were once again growing bolder. Before he could fire the weapon, Dale slammed on the brakes and spun the wheel, drifting left across two lanes of traffic and coming to a brief stop pointed in the opposite direction. Tires squealed as she hit the gas, then posted up behind a box truck. It didn't provide the same amount of cover that a semitruck would have, but the soldier didn't fire.

The helicopter hovered, watching them as they headed back through the underpass. Sure enough, as they came out on the other side, it was following them again.

"Which way?" Dale yelled at Marrow.

The Gary Alpha gestured left as she crawled over the front bench seat. Dale yanked them into a turn at the next intersection. In a pell-mell zigzag, they wove their way through Chicago's side streets. The wolven in the back held on grimly as they were jerked about, even as Marrow directed Dale according to directions known only to her. The buildings around them changed from houses to blocky, low industrial buildings. The quality of the street deteriorated, sending them bouncing from one pothole to the next.

Marrow was standing half-crouched, one eye out the window on the helicopter that clung to them with frustrating determination despite their winding path. The rest of her attention was through the windshield. They went under another overpass and Marrow held up her hand.

"Stop!"

Dale slammed on the brakes and they all lurched forward as one.

Marrow turned to the wolven, who were still holding on for dear life. "Everyone out. Leave the car running." Her eyes locked with Bone's. "We're pulling a Wrecking Ball."

Bone's face lit up as if she'd been offered her favorite treat. "Dibs on puncher." She lunged forward and threw open the side door and stepped out.

As soon as her feet touched the pavement, she puffed herself up and pounded on the front passenger door. "Get the hell out here!" She jiggled the handle, but it was locked. "I'm gonna kick your ass so hard you'll be eating shit for days."

Hammer flowed out and paused as he emerged, his massive gray head waving in the air as he tested the smells of this place. He moved on to stand not far from Bone as she continued to act like she was trying to get into the van. If she'd wanted to, she could have pulled the handle right off the door.

"Eating shit for days?" Marrow roared back through the shattered window. "I'll show you eating shit, you jumped up, no good, bulldagger bitch."

"Bo'dagger?" The warm ochre of Bone's skin flushed even redder. "You gon' bo'dagger me?" She reached through the window and snatched Marrow by the collar. With a heave, she dragged her sister from the van, then swiveled and pushed her hard away from the car.

The driver's side door slammed as Dale came out. Snow hesitated in the large passenger door. She wasn't sure what was going on, but Marrow and Bone didn't smell angry at all. Bone punched her sister in the gut, shoving her back when Marrow doubled over her fist. Through it all, she smelled happy, almost gleeful. Marrow's scent was just as jazzed.

Snow stepped down from the van, with Cassidy at her heels. The Gary Alphas were trading blows and insults. The punches weren't at all fake. Blood dripped from the corner of Bone's mouth, and Marrow sported a cut above one eye. The mechanical chop of the helicopter's rotors wasn't enough to drown out the sounds of impacts on flesh and the insults they continued to fling each other's way.

They'd gathered an audience. People were craning their heads to watch the brawl that had spontaneously erupted at the side of the road. Dale had stopped them in the middle of a makeshift homeless encampment. Tents and lean-tos were haphazardly clustered against the back wall of the overpass. It was a fair-sized gathering of people, and it didn't take long for Bone and Marrow to be surrounded by a dozen or more onlookers who muttered and pointed. Marrow wrapped her arm around Bone's midsection, taking her down to the concrete. The Alphas rolled around, trying to wrestle the top spot from each other, but they were so evenly matched that neither could maintain the upper hand for long.

More people joined the onlookers, drawn in by the excitement. Dale pushed her way into the crowd, leaving Snow with the two Alphas in furform by her side. No one was paying the massive wolves much mind. All the attention was on the fight.

There was no way Snow was going to jump into the mob. She was already feeling exposed being around so many humans. Who knew when more would show up? If it hadn't been for the Alphas sticking to her side like burrs in fur, she would have made a break for it.

At the slam of the car door behind her, Snow whipped her head around. She had time to make out a human form in the driver's seat of her van before they were pulling away from the curb. Snow took a couple of steps toward it, but the driver saw her coming. They sped up, the wheels squealing loudly at the sudden acceleration. Seconds later, her van was too far away to even consider giving chase.

Cassidy tried, but the car outpaced even her in furform. The North Side Alpha skidded to a stop twenty feet from Snow. She looked back, clearly torn between chasing after Snow's beloved car and returning to her side. Snow dropped to sit on the curb. Cassidy trotted back, taking up a sentry point in front of her, while Hammer posted up at her back.

The South Shore Alpha let out a deep whuff of satisfaction. The excited noises of the crowd were already abating. It wasn't long before the gathered humans dispersed. Dale muscled her way back through the remaining gawkers.

"So that worked," she said as she made her way up to Snow's little group.

"What worked?" Snow asked dully. "Some asshole stole my car."

"And now that damned copter is their problem."

Snow blinked. She cocked her head and realized that it was a lot quieter under the bridge.

Marrow and Bone staggered up, leaning against each other.

"These two really sold it," Dale said. "Didn't pull any punches."

"I believe it."

Bone's nose was gushing blood, lending her grin a ghoulish cast.

"Might as well have some fun while we're at it," Marrow said. One hazel iris was disappearing under the puffy lid of a rapidly swelling black eye. Even that couldn't diminish the sparkle of excitement in it.

"Had to sell it," Bone said. "For the good of the group."

"The group," Snow said flatly. "Yes, I'm thrilled."

Dale shook her head. "I know it's hard, but it was the best way to get the heat off us."

"We could have slipped them, then found and ditched the tracker."

"Before or after they pasted us with whatever ray gun was pointed at us?" Bone asked. The words were blunt, but her tone was sympathetic enough to start Snow's eyes prickling again.

Cassidy licked the side of her face, warding off her tears before they could fall.

"Well, I can't do anything about it now," Snow said bitterly. "What's the next part of this wonderful plan no one knows about except you two?" She glared at Marrow and Bone, willing them to know exactly how angry she was about the whole situation.

"We need a new car." Marrow gave her sister's stomach a playful slap and straightened up.

"Yep." Bone scrubbed drying blood off the lower half of her face, then wiped her hand off on Marrow's shirt. "One that's at least as roomy as the old one. Something tells me we're going to be sharing it for a while."

CHAPTER SEVEN

The new van was a marked downgrade from Snow's beloved bus. Cassidy's heart ached as she gazed down at the lone wolf. Snow was snuggled in under her arm and was sleeping so hard she might as well have been sedated. Her full lashes spread out across her cheeks. Her cheekbones had always been high, but the stress of the past couple of days had opened hollows up under them. Cassidy vowed to catch her as many plump rabbits as it took to rid her of the faint gauntness she had developed during their escape from Chicago.

They were in the first row of seats, with Marrow and Bone sacked out in the second. The twins had opted for furform. They were as identical wearing fur as they were when in skinform, and it was difficult to tell where one ended and the other began. They could have been one gigantic wolf of silken chestnut fur, except for the plumed tails at either end and the twin heads lying aside each other in the middle.

Hammer sat in the passenger seat, his muscular mass and ebony skin in direct contrast to Dale's lithe, tan form. She was at the wheel again. The Kenosha Alpha drove like the van was an extension of her body. They sped north, slipping between and around cars on the Tri-State. The South Shore Alpha peered at a damp and bedraggled piece of paper. Somewhere in all the chaos and while in furform, he'd eaten his list rather than lose it. After Marrow and Bone had boosted the new van, he'd disgorged the contents of his stomach on the sidewalk and had refused to move, staring at the sodden paper until one of them picked it up. It had been a smart move, but Cassidy was glad she'd still been in furform at that point. Marrow or Bone had snagged it.

They'd left town, stopping in a suburb only long enough to pick up clean clothing for all of them. Now that they were moving again, Cassidy felt like she should have taken advantage of a nap, but even with Snow pressed against her she couldn't relax enough to drop off. She kept watching the skies, waiting for that inevitable moment when the helicopter would swoop in again.

Part of her was daring to hope that getting as close as they had to the Wisconsin state border meant they were in the clear. The other part of her had decided they couldn't afford to be wrong about being ambushed. Again. There had been three in the past two days. At this point, she wasn't taking anything for granted.

Try as she might to keep a focused eye out, her attention kept drifting. Her own list of potential places their kidnapped wolven might be hidden was burning a hole in her pocket, but she couldn't get to it without disturbing Snow. That wasn't going to happen. The lone wolf deserved her sleep.

Cassidy refocused her attention on the scenery. Fields passed by, half-covered with snow that was melting under the sun's rays. Drifts accumulated in shaded areas. It wasn't warm enough to melt anything that wasn't directly exposed to the warmth of the sun. She looked again to the sky, but it was still empty. Her ears caught no sounds except the drone of concrete beneath the van's wheels and the occasional growl of another car's engine as they passed it. Bone and Marrow would occasionally gasp or murmur in their sleep. Snow was so far gone that all Cassidy heard from her was deep and even breathing.

A low buzz in Cassidy's pocket caused the lone wolf to stir, her brows pulling down into a faint scowl for a moment. Cassidy scrambled to pull out the device. Who was calling her? Her heart leaped at the prospect of seeing Mary's face on the lock screen.

An unidentified number greeted her instead. She stared at it for a moment. Hammer had swiveled around to regard her. Dale watched her through the rearview mirror. Snow and the Gary Alphas slumbered on.

Still, there weren't many who had the number. If it was a scam caller, she could always hang up on them. Cassidy stabbed her finger down on the green icon, then held the phone up to her ear, waiting.

"Hello?" The voice that quavered down the line to her was weak, but as known to Cassidy as Mary's.

"Mom?" A terrible tension left Cassidy's body and she melted against Snow. "Thank god you're okay."

"I'm so glad to hear your voice." Sophia Nolan sniffled audibly on the other end of the line. "I was so worried something had happened to you."

"Same." Cassidy held back her own tears, but it was a close thing. "When I saw the hotel on fire..."

"It happened so fast. Carla was able to get me out..." Cassidy's mom paused for a long moment. "The things I saw. Oh, Cassie-bean. Is this what your world is like?"

Cassidy shook her head. "Not until the past couple of days. It's usually pretty low-key. Where are you?"

Snow stirred at her elbow and opened her eyes. She blinked a couple of times, then reached an arm over and wrapped it around Cassidy's waist.

"I'm not sure, not completely. It's somewhere west of Chicago. Carla got us onto a train. Someone smuggled us off about ten hours ago. We were kept in the dark, because—Well, you know."

"I do." Her mom was safe for now, but was she really out of danger? After all, Carla wasn't just any vampire. She was being actively sought by the new vampire leadership of Chicago. The same leadership who'd ousted her less than a week ago.

"She got me a phone so I could call you and let you know we're okay. And so I could see if you answered." Sophia sighed. "This isn't what I wanted for you."

Cassidy laughed. She had to rein it in before the cackle became too deranged. "Turns out the universe doesn't really care what we want for ourselves or others. I'm just trying to get through this fucked—I mean effed—up set of events."

"You can say fuck in front of me," Sophia said dryly. "If ever there was a situation for it..."

"The world really has ended." Cassidy cracked a smile. "Never thought I'd hear you say swearing was fine."

"It's not a blanket approval."

"I'll try to stay out of more trouble, then."

"I'd appreciate it. I don't know how much more of this excitement my poor heart can take."

Cassidy sat straight up in her seat. "Are you having palpitations or something? Does your arm ache? How about your jaw?"

"I'm fine, sweetie. A little hyperbole, that's all."

"Oh." Cassidy slouched back in the chair.

"I'm sorry, Cassie-bean, but Carla is telling me to wrap it up. I'll call when it's safe."

"But, Mom—" The phone beeped in her ear as the connection was severed. Cassidy swiped her thumb across the screen to get a look at the number. The area code was 902. She had no idea where that was. A quick search told her it was off the east coast of Canada. "Where the hell is Nova Scotia?"

She looked up to see all the Alphas in the car watching her. Snow tightened her grip around Cassidy's waist but kept her eyes closed.

"Your mom was in your den?" Hammer asked carefully after the silence had stretched too long.

"With the former Vampire Lord of Chicago." Cassidy lifted her chin and pushed it out pugnaciously toward him. "You have a problem with that?"

He grinned but broke their gaze first, turning to look out the passenger window. "No problem, just getting a handle on how… complicated your life was when someone dropped a bomb in it."

"You think that's complicated—" Cassidy snapped her mouth shut on the rest of the sentence before she could finish it.

"It gets more complex?" Dale's voice was neutral, but her scent balanced on a knife edge of bright blue concern and sharp red anger.

"Either we're all in this or we're not," Hammer said. He watched the passing scenery as if it was the most interesting thing in the world and he wasn't commenting on Cassidy's reticence.

"Ha." Cassidy looked down at Snow, trying to ask her without words. *Do I tell them about Mary?* she tried to convey, as if she and the lone wolf had some sort of telepathic bond.

Bone and Marrow flopped their shaggy lupine heads over the back of the seat, watching everyone with rapt attention as their tongues lolled from their mouths.

"What kind of answer is 'ha'?" Dale asked.

"One where I'm not sure how you're going to take what I have to tell you."

"Now you have to share," Dale said.

"I do." Cassidy swallowed hard. "I don't want to, but I should. Don't freak out, okay?"

"Freak out about what?" The wheel creaked alarmingly under Dale's grip.

Hammer didn't say anything, but his back was ramrod straight. If he'd been in furform, both ears would have been swiveled back to point at her.

"Malice is my sister."

* * *

"Cassidy!" Snow shot up from her half-reclining position against the North Side Alpha's body. Her nose was assaulted by a riot of emotion-laden scents. It was enough to send her into a sneezing fit, even in skinform. Amusement of a pitch that bordered on hysterical emanated from the Gary Alphas. Hammer was a spike of anger and fear. Dale's was the only scent not an assault on the nostrils. Snow didn't have the time or attention to carefully parse it through, but it seemed like a mix of chagrin, sympathy, and concern. Cassidy stank of fear and resignation.

"She's what?" Hammer roared from the front seat. His eyes flashed orange.

Dale reached over to place a hand on his arm, but he shook her off.

The twins were panting so hard the seat was shaking. If they'd been in skinform, Snow was sure they would have collapsed in peals of helpless laughter.

"She's my sister." Cassidy was also sitting up straight. All her attention was on Hammer, which Snow didn't think was wise. Bone and Marrow could attack in the middle of deepest humor. Snow had seen it once and hoped never to again.

"And you didn't think to share that little tidbit until now?" Hammer's voice dropped into an accusatory hiss. He was turned all the way around in the front seat, rage radiating from him. The tension was picked up by Cassidy and fed straight back to his face. Snow recoiled, trying to move out of the range of the terrible anger that was brewing between the two Alphas.

"Are you really going to have a full throwdown in a stolen van in the middle of the freeway?" Dale asked acidly. Her sharp gaze cut to both Alphas. "Hammer, save it for when you have ground under your feet. Five Moons, maybe we don't drop bombshells like that in the middle of our getaway from the same forces your *sister* works for?"

"It's not like that," Cassidy said. After Hammer reluctantly turned away, she sank back into herself.

"And you'll have all the time you need and more to explain it to our satisfaction," Dale said. She turned her eyes back to her driving, but her attention barely wavered from the two wayward Alphas.

Marrow was wheezing as she panted, and Bone had collapsed against her. The only sound in the van was of their lupine mirth.

Cassidy was biting her lip, and Snow hesitantly put a hand on her thigh. The Alpha closed her eyes and took a deep breath. Then another. It was Snow's turn to support her, so she wrapped both arms around Cassidy and pulled her close. The frightened edge to her scent eased a bit, but the anger was still sharp. As far as Snow was concerned, the announcement had gone about as well as could be expected. No blood had been shed, no one had tried to shred Cassidy to pieces while they hurtled down the freeway at eighty miles an hour. There were scarier things than fraught emotional conversations.

CHAPTER EIGHT

The Alphas cloistered together in a shed, a point of tense quiet in the bustle that was going on outside the small structure. Dale's first stop on returning to her den had been to check on Jane's progress. After finding out that her Beta was on the mend, she'd pulled her people together for a quick meeting in which she imparted the unwelcome news that they were moving yet again. Her wolves had been distressed, but they'd jumped into action. It had helped that they hadn't had enough time to unpack. As they'd split up, the larger half had started packing up, while the smaller started dismantling cars to make sure none of the pack's remaining vehicles had trackers on them. Dale had pointed at Cassidy.

"Now," was all she'd said. The Alphas of the disappeared packs had watched her like she was a bug under a magnifying glass.

Marrow and Bone still seemed highly entertained by this latest turn of events. Hammer's eyes still hadn't returned to their normal dark brown. He glowered at her like a broody storm cloud from the furthest corner of the shed. It was a small space and he took up a lot of it, but he'd still done his best to be as far from her as possible.

Dale's black eyes drilled into hers. Her lips were drawn thin, nearly disappearing into her broad face. Cassidy refused to look away. Her wolf was adamant that they couldn't show the slightest weakness, not in front of four Alphas.

Snow hadn't been invited. Hammer had deliberately shut the door before she could join them. Part of Cassidy was glad the lone wolf wasn't there. If things went badly, Snow would be out of danger. Her selfish side wished Snow had been able to come. Cassidy missed her. Beyond that, Snow's presence helped her think more clearly, especially when emotions were high.

"Spill it." Hammer ground out the order through gritted, pointed teeth. The spiky orange-red scent that surrounded him reflected the rage he kept contained, making him seem larger than ever. How did the wolven manage to loom, even when he was more than arm's reach away?

"Malice is my sister," Cassidy said matter-of-factly. She didn't break eye contact with Dale. "I know her as Mary. She's older than me by a few years."

"It's awfully convenient that your sister is in with the people who are after us," Dale said. "And here you are as well."

"We don't talk much these days. Not since I became this. One of you." Cassidy resisted the urge to look down. "I don't even know if she's alive."

"How could you not tell us that you're related to the Hunter?" Hammer asked. "And we're supposed to just take your word that you don't know what's going on with her. Seems like that disappearance is awfully good cover for some serious shit disturbing."

"She's mated to a wolven." Cassidy broke Dale's stare to intercept Hammer's. "She's not the enemy you think she is. She wasn't. She just…"

"Just?" Cassidy didn't know which twin had asked, but her tone was encouraging.

"She just lied to me and my mom about what she was doing and who she was for years. She poked the wrong bear, and I ended up catching her shit." Cassidy shook her head in a harsh chop that sent her hair flying about her face. "So when I say we're not really talking right now, I think I have a good reason. And that's before she disappeared into the wilds of Wisconsin with Ruri."

"Ruri?" The other twin leaned forward, exactly mimicking her sister's interested posture. "Velvet's Ruri?"

"Velvet?" Cassidy cocked her head, then nodded when she remembered Dean's Alpha name. "Yes. Ruri was Velvet's Beta. She and my sister became an item when they were trying to keep me from losing myself in the wolves after I was bitten."

Dale shook her head. "I'm going to need a more coherent explanation."

Cassidy frowned. "Why am I explaining myself to you all anyway? You want me to air my dirty laundry so you can sit in judgment. I don't owe you anything."

Dale made an exasperated noise. "See it from our point of view. You're the one who pulled us all together, which doesn't happen often. You change the agreed-upon timeline, and all hell breaks loose. That can be hung on coincidence, but when you drop this latest revelation on us, it starts to feel less like chance and more like a setup."

"And don't you think I would know that, if I was this big mastermind?" Cassidy gestured expansively with her arms, causing Marrow and Bone to lean away from her. "That's a big hole in your theory. I didn't have to tell you. There's no way you'd know, otherwise. Especially if Mary and Ruri really are dead."

"You keep saying that," Marrow said. "What makes you believe they're gone?"

"I could feel Ruri. She was part of my starscape."

"Your whole deal on how you can feel the wolves in your pack," Bone said.

"That's the one. If I concentrate, I can nearly see them." She mimed reaching out and plucking something out of the air. "If they're close enough, you can pull their star into your orbit. You called them gifts before. Which ones do you have?"

Hammer shook his head. "I don't see what bearing this has on our discussion."

"We can talk to each other telepathically," Bone said.

"It's only fair that you know ours if we know yours," Marrow added.

"She could be a plant." Red spiked Hammer's scent all over again.

Marrow and Bone snorted in unison.

"If she is, she has the worst OPSEC either of us has ever seen," Bone said.

"If she's a mole, then I'm a house cat." Marrow smirked.

"What do either of you know about OPSEC?" Hammer demanded.

The twins' grins mirrored each other, but they didn't elaborate.

Dale sighed, grabbing the bridge of her nose. "Five Moons, would you tell us how you came to be Alpha of the North Side Pack? Let us smell you so we all know you're on the level. Gary might be willing to take your words at face value, but I need some assurance."

"Fine." Cassidy closed her eyes as she prepared to revisit memories still raw and jagged even six months later. "It started when Mary—Malice crossed MacTavish." With as few words as possible, she outlined the events of the previous October. How she'd been in the wrong place at the wrong time and MacTavish had set his wolves on her as a way of punishing Malice and warning her away from the North Side Pack. How Mary had pulled Ruri in on keeping Cassidy alive as she struggled with a dangerous shift from human to wolven made all the more treacherous for the circumstances under which she'd been turned. How Malice and Stiletto had taken MacTavish on while Cassidy had joined the exiled remnants of the North Side Pack to wrest those who had been stolen by MacTavish away from him. It had culminated in her taking over the pack.

"There was no one else," she said quietly, her eyes clenched shut. "And now we're here."

"Did anyone smell anything untoward in all of that?" Marrow asked.

"Because I sure didn't," Bone replied.

Dale shook her head. "She told the truth."

"As she knows it," Hammer said. His scent had lost the heavy overlay of rage and was subsiding into simmering orange suspicion.

"It all tracks," Dale said. "If you're not convinced, we can put this to a vote."

Hammer waved a dismissive hand. "I know how that'll go."

"You don't have to like me," Cassidy said.

"Good." Hammer grinned, flashing sharp teeth at her. "Because I don't."

"We just have to be able to work together." She turned her gaze on the others. "Are we quite done here?"

"With that." Dale massaged the back of her neck with one hand. "What's next?"

"I want to know what this has to do with the Hunter being dead," Marrow said.

"Maybe dead," Bone said. She smacked her twin on the arm. "That's her sister," she hissed.

"I could feel Ruri. I never claimed her, not officially, but I could feel her like she was one of my pack. Or maybe it's that I did claim her, but we don't talk about it."

"Which means…?" Bone asked.

"Nothing really. I'm tired, and I'm losing focus." Cassidy sighed. "I was able to feel Ruri, so I knew she was still alive. That changed last night."

"So your wolven drop off your 'starscape' when they die?" Marrow asked.

Cassidy grimaced. "Maybe? I haven't lost anyone yet, so I don't know for sure. The only others I haven't been able to see are a couple of wolven who asked to be released."

"So she could have joined another pack." Bone tapped her fingertips together. "Or maybe she's so far away you can't feel her."

"And you're concerned about her dropping off your radar because she's with the Hunter," Dale said. "Your sister."

Cassidy nodded.

"That's some high stakes."

"I hadn't noticed." Talking it out with the Alphas was only making each loss more tender.

"And your mom called while we were in the car."

"Yes."

"Damn." Dale shot her a sympathetic look. "That's a lot."

"It is." Cassidy shrugged. "But it doesn't change that my pack is out there, and so are all of yours."

Marrow rubbed her hands together. "Now we can get to next steps. Which are?"

Hammer pulled the rumpled piece of paper from the front pocket of his pants. "We start knocking the locations we found off the list."

Cassidy pulled her own list of locations from her back pocket. It wasn't as soggy as the South Shore Alpha's, but it was creased. She smoothed it out on her thigh. "We found some places too. I figured we could compare and make a master list."

"That could work." Hammer reached out to Cassidy.

She hesitated for a fraction of a second, then handed the paper to him.

* * *

Snow sat in the open door of the van they'd stolen in Chicago. Around her, the Kenosha pack's vehicles were being packed up. A steady stream of wolven moved to and from the old farm's buildings. There wasn't much to pack, but with nearly thirty wolven, including half a dozen cubs, it was taking a while.

"Snow, right?" The voice was unfamiliar, but when Snow turned to regard the woman who'd approached her, she felt a shock of recognition.

Jane was upright. She stood with a bit of a hunch. The last time Snow had seen her, the gash below her ribs had been weeping blood. Her pale skin was nearly white and her eyes were bright with the same pain that threaded through her scent. It wasn't agony, though. She seemed well on her way to recovery.

"That's right." Snow smiled.

"Do you mind if…?" Jane gestured to the space next to her.

"Not at all." She scooted over to allow the Kenosha Beta some room.

"Thanks." Jane sat with a relieved sigh. "Being up and about is a lot right now." She laughed softly. "I've been ordered to take it easy."

"You look…" Snow paused. Jane looked terrible. She'd lost weight, which wasn't surprising. Their heightened metabolism-fueled systems allowed them to heal with unreasonable speed, but it didn't confer invulnerability. She'd watched too many wolven die the previous night. "…alive."

"And I'm glad for it. I hear I have you to thank for that."

Snow lifted one shoulder. "I helped as much as I could."

"I had no idea you were even out there." Jane shook her head. "And I like to think I'm pretty observant."

"I have a lot of practice going unnoticed."

"It shows." Jane allowed her eyes to track over to the storage shed into which the Alphas had shut themselves. "Do you know what they're planning?"

"I don't." Snow lifted her nose to test the breeze. She'd ended up at the van not only because it was out of the way, but because it was downwind. If she got any whiff of blood, she would have to decide what to do next. She was staying still only because she was caught equally between hiding until she knew Cassidy wasn't under threat and getting closer to be there if the Alphas decided to turn on Five Moons. Not that she'd be a whole lot of help if it came to teeth and claws, but she didn't know if she could stand aside while Cassidy was savaged. Her wolf was stuck in the same dilemma, though for once she seemed to be leaning toward the side of violence.

"We got lucky," Jane said. "I thought Suni was being paranoid when she had everyone move dens before we headed to the meet up."

It took Snow a moment to realize Suni was Dale's given name. She hadn't spent enough time among the Chicago-area packs to pick up on the Alphas' real names. Her time in the Midwest had mostly been spent with Dean. "It's a good thing she did."

"It absolutely is. I need to remember that you can't be too vigilant when you're Alpha. It's only that things have been so quiet for so long, you know?"

"Aside from losing pack members."

"Aside from that." Jane stared off into the middle distance. "I was hoping they'd left on their own."

"Yeah…" Snow allowed the conversation to lapse. In the silence, Jane retreated into herself and watched the storage shed with as much interest as Snow.

After a few minutes, Snow stood. She didn't dislike the Beta's presence, but she couldn't quite relax with her so close.

"I'm going to go…" There was no good excuse, so she allowed the phrase to fade off as she wandered away. She took care not to get any closer to the shed, but she also made sure to keep both eyes on it.

Another thirty minutes passed before the door opened and Marrow and Bone strolled out. The sun wasn't quite setting, but it had developed that golden quality that promised the end of the day was coming soon. It highlighted the tight, looping curls in their hair, shading the deep brown to something a few shades lighter. Their skin warmed further, lightening shades of red into orange that presaged the coming sunset. They flowed along as if they hadn't a care in the world. Maybe they didn't. Snow wasn't close enough to smell them.

After them came Cassidy and Dale, their heads bent together as they conferred quietly. Dale's black hair was out of its bun and hung like a sheet much lower than Cassidy's shoulder-length, mouse-brown locks. Dale tucked one side behind her ear, but Cassidy seemed to be taking advantage of the protection her hair offered. Her skin soaked up the golden rays until it nearly glowed. At her side, Dale was deeply tanned. The angle of the sun outlined scars along her forearms. She was small, and many challengers had mistaken her size for weakness, but she was at least as deadly as Hammer, despite being dwarfed by his presence.

The South Shore Alpha took up the rear, a hulking shadow whose bad mood was nearly as dark as his skin. At least his eyes had stopped glowing, but they peered out beneath brows drawn together almost tightly enough to be a scowl. As it was, he just looked extremely peeved. The hood on his jacket was up, confining his dreadlocks and removing what little definition he had for his neck. His shoulders had always been so muscled that his neck wasn't visible unless he stood to his full, considerable height. Right now, he'd pulled his head down in a posture that protected him from attack. Snow couldn't tell if he was expecting another ambush or if he trusted the other Alphas that little.

This was the group that was supposed to pull together and rescue dozens of missing wolven. They were already fractured and disparate. Body language spoke of mistrust and lines being drawn. Hopefully, they'd find the kidnapped wolves quickly. It would help if they'd come up with a plan.

Snow angled herself back toward her van. She grimaced when she was confronted with the bland white monstrosity that wasn't her beloved bus at all. The thought of her van being taken for a joyride and being abandoned made her heart ache. It had been her home, and now the best she could hope was that it would be left by the side of the road somewhere. If she was really unlucky, their tail had caught up to it and shot it up, thinking the wolven were still inside. That wouldn't go well for the human thief.

Cassidy broke off her conversation with the Kenosha Alpha and turned to face Snow as she rejoined the group. Bone gave her a wink and a wave as she settled herself behind the wheel, ignoring Hammer who seemed to have thought he was going to drive. Marrow slithered into the passenger seat as he made his way around the front of the van.

"So what's next?" Snow asked.

Dale nodded toward the sheet of paper Cassidy held. Her untidy scrawl had been added to by a neater and bolder hand. "There's the list," she said.

"We're going on a road trip," Cassidy said. "Join us as we crisscross the beautiful Midwest to check out abandoned hospitals, prisons, and insane asylums."

"That's such an attractive offer." Snow glanced over at Dale. "I take it you're not coming?"

Dale shook her head. "I'm happy to help in whatever way I can that doesn't take me away from my wolves."

Cassidy sighed. "She's going to be our home base. Somewhere we can shower, I guess."

"Would you do any differently?" Dale asked.

"You know I wouldn't." Cassidy tried to quirk a half-smile, but it quickly slid off her face. "I'm just jealous."

Dale smacked the North Side Alpha on the arm. "You've got a hell of a crew. If anyone can do it, this group can."

As long as they can get everyone rowing in the same direction, Snow thought. She looked over to where Hammer was stewing in the van's furthest seat while the Gary Alphas seemed to be trying to find the most offensive station on the radio.

"No pressure," Cassidy said.

"No more than you'd put on yourself anyway," Snow replied. She leaned over and bumped her shoulder against Cassidy's.

"That's probably true."

"You have our next location," Dale said. "Swing by whenever you need, just remember to check for bugs, trackers, or whatever first."

"You got it." Cassidy took a deep breath and held it for a moment as she gathered her confidence. It seemed to help a little bit. By the time she exhaled, some of the anxiety in her scent had been replaced by resolve. "We might as well knock the first one off our list tonight."

CHAPTER NINE

In a scene that had become all too common over the past few weeks, Cassidy glared out the front windshield as they left the sprawling farm in rural Wisconsin. Her hair was still damp from her hasty shower. The wolf hadn't been thrilled. She considered showers to be wastes of time and uncomfortable beyond that. Cassidy didn't care. Skinform had been starting to feel greasy. And besides, she wasn't the only Alpha who'd decided on a quick cleanup in human form.

The wolf shifted. They both knew her poor mood wasn't because Cassidy had dared wash up. They'd been looking for over half a month and were no closer to tracking down their missing wolven. The list had gotten shorter and shorter, and with each location that was crossed off the list, Cassidy's worry that they would never find the wolves grew. And as if all that wasn't enough, Cassidy's heat was coming on. She didn't have time to deal with it and wasn't in the right mindset to try to figure it out. It was one more inconvenience on top of the crap sandwich she'd been eating for too long.

She sneaked a look over at Snow. The lone wolf stared out the windshield, her brown eyes sharp on the road, but the perfect arches of her eyebrows weren't pulled down in concentration. She handled the wheel with a confidence that made Cassidy want to snuggle in against her. Her full lips looked especially kissable, though while she was driving seemed like a bad time to lean over for a smooch. Maybe if Cassidy placed one along the subtle curve of her jaw… The skin of her face was smooth, devoid of the scars the Alphas seemed to collect like trophies at an elementary school field day. The day was overcast and drawing to a close, the light coming from the sky was cool, but that did nothing to dim the warm sepia overtones of Snow's skin. Cassidy longed to bask in the fire of Snow's regard. Yes, her heat was definitely here.

Their relationship was in a weird place. Not bad weird, but it hadn't quite settled, and Cassidy wasn't always certain how to bring up sexual topics with the lone wolf. As inconvenient as her heat was, Cassidy was going to have to deal with it, but how did she broach the topic?

And who did she take care of it with? Snow was out unless she made the first move, though she would have been Cassidy's preference. The wolf didn't care too much about which of the others would make a good match, which left only Cassidy's own preferences to come to a decision. Hammer would normally have been her first choice, since she did prefer the company of men for sex, but they'd been finding it difficult to see eye to eye on just about anything. Plus, she had a dim recollection of Luther telling her that the more dominant her male partners were, the more likely it was that their mating could end in conception. Dominant enough himself that she'd chosen him as her Beta, his advice had been invaluable. Until he was taken. His kidnapping had led to her pushing up the time of the Alpha meeting. Was it her fault the meeting had been attacked?

Her wolf whined softly within her. Fault didn't matter. It had happened and now they had to deal with it. Cassidy laughed softly. Cubs would be a terrible addition to their current situation. They had to deal with their missing packmates, not be making more. That was without considering the complications of custody for cross-pack liaisons. Was there already a policy in place? Or a tradition, whatever the wolven wanted to call it? She shook her head. No, cubs were nothing she could even consider.

On the other hand, Bone and/or Marrow were her other current options. Could they put aside their irreverence for long enough to get it on with someone? And would they both want to mate? They certainly did everything else together. Not that they weren't attractive. Of course, at the moment, everyone in the van was hot enough to make her mouth water.

The wolf's disapproval washed over her, dampening Cassidy's rising ardor somewhat. In the wolf's opinion, Cassidy was overthinking it. Their heat was here. They would mate. They would be sated. Everyone would move on. It wasn't difficult.

Cassidy jumped as a warm hand closed over her forearm.

Snow gave her a sideways look from the driver's seat. "Are you all right?"

Cassidy was glad she'd kept her voice down. Marrow and Bone were closest to the driver's and passenger's seats. Hammer was hunkered down in furform as far back in the van as he could get. The seats were gone. They'd ripped those out almost immediately. The carpet remnants that layered the back weren't pretty to look at, but they were soft enough to lounge and sleep on.

"What's going on?" Snow asked again.

"I'm not...I can't..." How did she explain to the lone wolf who didn't like sex that she really needed to get off, and in such a way that the Gary Alphas weren't falling over themselves at the hilarity of the situation. "Can we talk about this later?"

"Or you could talk about it now," one of the Gary Alphas said. She propped herself up on one elbow. "You stink of libido, and it's working everyone up."

Cassidy ground her teeth together hard enough that they squeaked audibly. "I'm aware of that, and I'm handling it."

"Doesn't smell like it," the other twin piped up. Neither was bothering to keep her voice down.

Down the length of the van, Hammer's ears twitched, and he lifted his head to regard the rest of them.

"We struck out again, and all you can talk about is getting me laid?" Cassidy stared in open irritation at Marrow and Bone.

"It's obviously on your mind," Marrow said. At least Cassidy thought it was Marrow. She was getting better at determining which of them was which, but it was difficult. Not only were the two Alphas indistinguishable visually and olfactorily, but they took glee in never correcting someone who had addressed them incorrectly. Both would answer to either name, except to Snow. They felt a little different in Cassidy's starscape. She was at a bit of a disadvantage because she couldn't pull their stars into her web, but she could view them, even if it was at a bit of a remove.

"And if you didn't stick your nose in where it doesn't belong, that's where it would have stayed."

"And in our noses." Bone wrinkled hers, then eyed Cassidy up and down. "If you want a hand with that, I could help out." She leaned over to look at Snow. "With your permission, of course."

"Let's just get to our overnight spot," Cassidy said. "I'll get it handled when we're not driving. Not that it's your business." She glared down at Marrow. "Or yours."

Hammer sneezed from the darkness in the back of the van.

"And certainly not yours."

"I'm sorry I asked." The sympathetic smile on Snow's lips and the light blue of her scent took the sting out of the words.

"We should talk," Cassidy admitted.

"And we will soon." Snow glanced down at the phone on the dashboard mount. While the lone wolf still resisted getting a phone of her own, she liked the GPS feature on Cassidy's, especially the estimated arrival time. And although Snow had an amazing mental map of the country, they were sticking to out of the way places, some exceedingly so. The coming night would be no exception. They'd noted a dirt road along an isolated stretch of county highway. There had been no houses or barns in the vicinity, so the Alphas had agreed that they would spend the night there.

"Good." Cassidy reached over and gave Snow's hand a squeeze, then went back to staring out the window. About the only good thing she could say about her sex drive being out of control was that it was blunting the edge of her anxiety and frustration over their lack of progress. Really, she was trading one frustration for another, but the sexual one didn't feel as dire.

They drove on through the dark, Snow mostly ignoring the muted turn-by-turn directions on the phone, though she started paying more attention the further they got from the highway. When they bumped their way onto the dirt road, Cassidy reached over and snagged the phone, turning off the screen and stowing it in her pocket. Snow cut the lights and opened the window. There was enough of the half-moon's glow to see by. She drove slowly, looking for a likely place to camp overnight.

"I smell water," Cassidy murmured after a few minutes.

Snow nodded. "That's a good place to stop." She peered out into the gloom, as if she could see through the sparse trees on either side of the van. "That way, I think." She pointed off to the left.

"Sounds good to me." The lone wolf had an amazing sense of direction, one Cassidy had come to rely upon over the past couple of weeks. None of the Alphas questioned her anymore. It was taken as gospel that if Snow said something was in one direction, then it was.

Sure enough, a minute later, they were parked. Moonlight sparkled back at them off the surface of a small stream that was only partially obscured by trees.

Cassidy stepped out of the van and stretched, forcing her arms wide enough that the muscles in her shoulders strained with delicious tension.

A hand trailed along the small of her back, reigniting the fire at her center. "Think about it," Bone said in her ear. The Gary Alpha winked, then followed along behind her sister. Marrow was already pulling her shirt over her head, exposing sepia skin that would soon be covered by silky chestnut fur. Their breaths steamed in the light of the moon. The smell of spring was on the air, but the nights were still chilly.

Hammer hopped out of the van, a dark blot that was swallowed up by the shadows under the trees almost immediately, leaving Cassidy to close the door behind him. It galled her to do so, but she did anyway. It wasn't like he could in furform, but he could have taken on betweenform for a few seconds. Instead, he chose to try to put her in her place by refusing to do the task himself.

She slammed the door with more force than required, then leaned her head against the van's white paneling.

"Should I come back later?" Snow asked quietly from right behind her.

"Don't you dare." Cassidy turned and opened her arms. To her relief, Snow didn't hesitate before stepping into them. She closed the lone wolf in a fierce embrace that gentled after a few seconds. "We don't have time for me to get tied up in knots over something as insignificant as sex," she said into Snow's shoulder. The words were muffled, but she knew the lone wolf's sharp ears would still make out what she was saying.

"Just because I don't like it doesn't mean it has no value to others." Snow slid an arm around Cassidy's waist and wrapped the other around her neck so she was cradling the back of her head. "If it has you so turned around, I could..." Her voice trailed off, but she couldn't hide the pungent aroma of distaste that suffused her scent.

"No." Cassidy shook her head against Snow's shoulder. "I don't want to put you through that." She tried to wrap her brain around the best way to ask to have sex with someone else, without it sounding like she thought what they were building between them was in any way inadequate.

"Hey." Snow grasped Cassidy's chin between her fingers and gently lifted it so they looked each other in the eye. "It's okay. I know your heat is upon you. I know you're probably about to crawl out of your skin needing to scratch that itch. I'm all right if you get it taken care of by somebody else."

"Really?" Cassidy stared deep into Snow's eyes, searching for a hint that she was putting on a brave face. Snow's eyes shone with sincerity, and her scent was as steady as ever.

"Really. I mean, it would be a bit weird if you scratch it with Bone, because we used to see each other, but that's my damage, not yours. And it was twenty years ago." She closed her eyes and tipped her head forward until their foreheads rested together. "I know going without sex will be hard for you. Maybe impossible, but I think you're getting all wound up in human attitudes around it. Even I know that it means as much or as little between two wolven as they want it to. If it'll take the edge off and you'll feel better and be able to focus more on the issues at hand, that's fine. Hell, if you want to fuck some other wolven just because you like it and your heat isn't forcing you too, I'm as fine with that as I am you going for a run and catching yourself a couple of rabbits. It's a physical act." She tapped the side of Cassidy's head. "What I'm interested in is here…" Snow placed her other hand over Cassidy's heart. "…and here. Does that make sense?"

"It does." Cassidy swallowed hard. Tears were unaccountably about to well up in her eyes. "Does this mean we're girlfriends?"

The quiet question surprised a laugh out of Snow. When Cassidy stiffened and tried to pull back, she wrapped her arms around Cassidy's shoulders and pulled her back into a tight embrace. "If that's what you want to call it. Yes, we're dating, going steady. I'm keen for you, Cassidy Anne Nolan."

Now it was Cassidy's turn to chuckle. "I'm super keen for you too, Snow." She lifted her arms around Snow's ribcage and returned her embrace. "We haven't talked about this, at least not in these terms. I know I like spending time with you, and I think you like hanging out with me. It's good to know what the status of our relationship is."

"Relationship." Snow said the word as if she were savoring it.

"That's the word."

"It sounds better than girlfriend."

"Why's that?" Cassidy laid her hand on Snow's shoulder, looking off into the distance. She could hear her girlfriend's heart beating and savored her warmth.

"I don't know. It sounds frivolous, I guess. What I feel for you isn't frivolous." Her scent took on a brittle edge.

"So what's a better alternative?" Cassidy grinned. "How about lady friend?"

"That's awful. I'd settle for main squeeze."

"Really?" Cassidy pulled her head back to see if Snow was serious. When the lone wolf stared back at her, with no trace of humor, Cassidy nodded. "I guess I can do that."

"Of course not," Snow said, her cheekbones flushing red while her eyes danced merrily. "I don't know what to call us, we can experiment with some terms, but I know that I want to be with you. So there."

"So there." Cassidy considered Snow for a moment. "How about my boo?"

"Absolutely not." Snow let go of her and grabbed her by the shoulders and turned her to where the other Alphas had disappeared. "Go get that itch scratched. I'll be here when you're done."

"You got it." Cassidy took a couple of steps away from the lone wolf and shucked her clothes quickly. She dropped to her hands and knees, allowing the wolf to ascend within her.

By the time her hands hit the ground, they were already paws. There was a brief burning irritation to her skin as fur rolled over her in a wave. Fluids sluiced off the ends of each strand as it pushed its way through her skin. Cassidy and the wolf took half a dozen steps away from where Snow was starting her own transformation into furform before giving themself a brisk shake to get rid of the effluvia that still clung to them. The wolf panted, tasting the air to see where the various Alphas had ended up. It was time to relieve the terrible pressure that had built up inside them for the past day.

Tail held high, they trotted off in the direction of Marrow and Bone. One or both of them would be willing to give them what they needed.

CHAPTER TEN

When Cassidy and the wolf opened their eyes, the sky was still dark, though starting to lighten. What they could see of it through the trees was gray and sullen, but that did little to dampen Cassidy's mood. The wolf was in fine fettle as well. The previous night's romp had been exactly what they needed. The pressure of their heat had subsided, and now they could enjoy Snow's company. The lone wolf wasn't stirring yet, and they were content to stay wrapped around her, breathing in her scent. It was so nice to dwell in a present when their only care was staying still enough not to awaken their companion.

The perfection of the moment didn't last, such things never did. Hammer rose from beneath a tree across the small clearing where the wolven had settled. He moved into a deep bow, producing a long whine as he stretched his muscles to their limit. Cassidy and the wolf watched him through slitted eyes while he crossed the open area and disappeared into a thicket of tall grasses. They were dead and dried from the long winter, but the shelter of the tree boughs above had protected them from winter snows and winds. Despite the size of Hammer in furform, he slipped neatly between bundles of dead grass with barely a trace.

Marrow and Bone were in a boneless pile not far from where Snow and Cassidy had curled up. At first glance in the relative gloom, they looked like a two-headed beast. There was no indication that either was awake.

Now that they were up, the wolf's bladder reminded them that it hadn't been emptied in hours. With a sigh, the wolf slithered to her feet. Snow's ear twitched and she cracked open one set of eyelids to glance at them. The wolf leaned in close and whuffed the scruff behind her ear. An aroma of contentment rolled off Snow and she relaxed, dipping back into sleep.

Cassidy and the wolf trotted soundlessly over to the tall grass, following the bright orange banner of Hammer's scent trail. He was headed toward the river. They strayed off the trail before they got to the river and took care of the bladder problem, then picked his trail up once again.

He hadn't gone far, but he had shifted. Hammer stood in skinform, half-submerged in the creek that had attracted their group in the first place. Water ran down cool umber skin. It had to have been freezing, but there was little sign of discomfort on his face or in the way he held his body. They couldn't make out even the smallest patch of gooseflesh on him.

When the wolf emerged, he locked gazes with them for perhaps longer than necessary, then went back to scrubbing handfuls of water over his bare skin.

Cassidy wasn't sure why she decided now was the time. There had been other opportunities before this moment to confront him. Maybe it was that she felt good about where she stood with Snow, or maybe she and the wolf had dispelled some of their tension the previous night. Whatever it was, the wolf stepped back and allowed Cassidy to come to the fore. The fluids from her change chilled instantly in the freezing morning air, but she resolved to put it out of her mind. If Hammer could ignore the cold, then so could she.

Amusement wafted from him, a redder orange than the color Cassidy associated with his scent. "It's actually warmer in the water."

Cassidy didn't answer but stepped into the stream. The cold water, only a degree or two above freezing, was a shock to her system. Goose bumps flashed to life over her skin, and she couldn't stop herself from briskly rubbing her hands over her upper arms.

"Give it a moment," Hammer rumbled. He bent forward to duck his head into the water, before wringing the excess from the long dreads that hung down past his shoulders. The ends were faded almost to orange, then darkened steadily the closer they got to his scalp. He took a minute to work water through his beard.

"If you say so." Cassidy clenched her jaw shut after the words to keep her teeth from chattering audibly.

They washed up in reasonably companionable silence for a few minutes. The muscles in Cassidy's legs and buttocks cramped from the cold, but she was determined not to leave the stream until Hammer did.

Eventually, and with a curious sideways glance, Hammer stepped up onto the bank. His eyes flashed amber and coarse charcoal gray fur flowed up over his legs, up his torso, to the ends of his fingers and the tips of his ears. His muzzle lengthened and his legs reformed with a snap of muscle and tendon that echoed over the water. A moment later, he stood in resplendent betweenform.

Cassidy followed his example. The reemergence of fur felt like sliding into a cozy bed in the middle of winter. Despite the discomfort of the transformation and of maintaining betweenform, she closed her eyes and enjoyed the sensation of being warm, before slicking the remaining fluids from the change down off her arms.

"So why'd you do it?" Cassidy asked casually, as she turned her attention to the effluvia still sticking to her legs.

"Do what?" Hammer asked. He had assumed a half-erect crouch, one that allowed him to relax while keeping watch across the creek and into the trees on the far bank.

"Why did you break with me at the Alpha meeting? I thought we'd agreed to head to my pack's fallback territory." She struggled to keep the question as matter-of-fact as possible, but accusation still bled into her tone. Carla had warned Cassidy about her allies. Had she known Hammer couldn't be trusted?

"First of all, we didn't agree to anything." Hammer might as well have been reading out of the dictionary for all the emotion in his tone. "Second, you didn't know Crag or the other Alphas."

"So you could just do your own thing, while letting me believe you had my back?"

"We're Alphas," Hammer growled. "We do not have each other's back. We have temporary alliances and truces. Respect is permanent but earned. You had none of those things."

Stung, Cassidy drew herself up to her full height. "So your alliance was so temporary it didn't even last three days? If you're trying to earn my respect, then you're going about it the wrong way."

Hammer's eyes flashed an orange so brilliant it was nearly neon. "Earn respect from you? I have no need for your respect. I have that of the other Alphas in this area and beyond. I had a functional pack and, beyond that, a happy one. Something you couldn't manage. And then you lost it. For both of us!"

Each accusation hit Cassidy like a separate slap. She stepped back a couple of paces, staring at him and wondering why the words hurt so much.

"If you'd been able to see beyond the tip of your muzzle, you would have known that I was maneuvering Crag around to where he *might* have seen things your way. But no, you're too prideful, too arrogant, too sure of your own self while knowing nothing of us." Hammer sneered, exposing long teeth and the true depth of his contempt for her.

"As if I could believe that for a second," Cassidy spat. "This sounds like the backpedaling of someone who knows he fucked up. You didn't think to move your wolves before the meeting. Dale did, and she still has a pack."

It was Hammer's turn to rear back as if struck. "Crag was never going to follow you."

"I didn't want him to. I don't want any of you to!"

"Then why do you act like you're the one in charge of our group?"

"Maybe because I'm the only one with a phone who can look up where the next location is on *your* list. The list that's drying up pretty damn fast."

Hammer launched himself at her, allowing himself to slip the rest of the way into furform. As soon as his form began to blur, Cassidy dropped away and the wolf popped up in her place. Before the wolf could dig her nails into the dirt to sidestep, Hammer's bulk slammed into them like a Mack truck. He bowled into them, dropping his shoulder under their neck and popping up to send them tumbling in a tangle of limbs. They let the momentum take them as far from the South Shore Alpha as it could, then smoothly bounced to their feet.

Hammer was on them an instant later, but they were ready. They danced out of the way, their teeth clashing together just shy of his ear. A wolf that large shouldn't have been able to spin so deftly, but Hammer's teeth were already coming for their muzzle. Cassidy tried to jerk their body out of the way, but the wolf had the wheel. She batted aside Cassidy's attempt and ducked, sliding beneath the other Alpha's forelegs.

With a quick snap of her jaws, the wolf shredded the skin and fur behind his right elbow. They missed severing his tendon by a fraction of an inch when he jerked the leg away. Then his weight was dropping down on them. They eeled away, but he sank his teeth into the back of her neck, yanking out a sizable chunk of their hackles. As they got to their feet, blood dripped down the sides of their neck. Cassidy tried to pull them back, but the wolf paid her no attention. Cassidy was limited to doing little more than watching the wolf take on the other Alpha.

And they were losing. Hammer was everywhere, snapping at their paws, harrying their hindquarters, backing them into the root system of a large oak. With nowhere else to retreat to, the wolf exploded in a flurry of aggression. Tooth clashed against tooth, claws ripped at fur and flesh. The two Alphas were locked together on their hind legs, teeth wet with blood and saliva, claws shredding large furrows out of haunch and underbelly. All Cassidy could do was feel every blow, every puncture, and hope that the wolf would wear Hammer down enough to stop him from killing them.

CHAPTER ELEVEN

The faint sound of Cassidy's footsteps were receding when Snow opened her eyes again. She'd hoped to be able to sleep a little longer, but without Cassidy curled up alongside her, she was feeling exposed. Not that she was concerned about the presence of the Gary Alphas, but they were out in the open and down two Alphas. If they were happened upon by a farmer, she had no doubt that Bone and Marrow could handle them. Hell, she could handle a human farmer. However, another visit from their friends in the military was a completely different proposition. As soon as her mind wandered to that scenario, Snow knew she wouldn't be able to sleep again for a while.

She yawned, reveling in the way the muscles of her jaw stretched when she was in furform. A yawn was so much more satisfying as a wolf than it was as a human, especially the emphatic snap of the teeth back together at the end. With a quick hop and a stretch, Snow was up and ready to face the day. She'd eaten the night before. Cassidy had come back from her little romp smelling like she'd mated with one or both of the Gary Alphas, with two rabbits hanging from her jaws. They'd shared a postcoital meal, the smell of fresh kill thankfully blunting the smell of sex that still clung to the North Side Alpha. The interlude seemed to have been exactly what Cassidy needed.

She made a quick pit stop behind a tree to relieve herself on the way back to the van. Once there, it took the normal excruciating length of time to shift from furform to skinform. After the last of the fur dropped from her, Snow wasted no time in briskly rubbing the remaining fluid from her skin before pulling on her clothes. She sat on the edge of the van's doorway to pull on her boots.

She knew the moment the chestnut wolven emerged from the brush next to the van. The Gary Alpha shifted out of furform as she joined Snow.

"Bone?" Snow asked.

The Alpha nodded. She and Marrow never tried their identity tricks with her. Snow had been concerned that the notoriously prankster wolven would try to trick her by passing Marrow off as the one she was seeing. She'd had no desire to be the butt of such a joke and had told Bone straight out that if she wanted them to spend time together, she would be open about her identity. Bone had sat her sister down and forced her to promise not to try to fool Snow. Despite their relationship never quite taking off, Bone and Marrow had held to the promise and still did decades later.

"Pass me a towel?" Bone held out one hand and waited while Snow leaned back to snag it. "Thanks."

"Any ideas what our next stop is?" Snow drew her knees up to her chest and stared out into the trees.

"Not really." Bone popped her head out from under the towel. Her black curls were shorter on the sides than Snow's, but the drying had fluffed the top and back way out. "Five Moons told me one thing and Hammer another."

"In front of each other?"

"Separately."

Snow sighed. "Those two gotta work out their differences. And soon."

Bone's chuckle was dry. "Not all Alphas work together as well as me and Marrow."

"Because they're not twins."

Bone cocked her head. "Maybe. We're used to sharing. Five Moons is young, she can be forgiven. And she shows some capacity to learn. Hammer is…"

"Hammer's been at this a long time. Longer than you and Marrow."

"Definitely longer than your Cassidy." Bone reached for a shirt and pulled it on over her head, muffling her next words. "You two are getting along well."

Heat suffused Snow's cheeks. She covered them with hands that were cold from the chill morning air. "Checking up on me?"

"We didn't end up as mates, but I still care. I want you to be happy. If she makes you happy, then I'm ecstatic for you. If she doesn't..." Bone grinned, displaying sharp teeth. "Well, I think Marrow and I could make short work of her."

"I don't need you to protect me." The rebuke was sharp, far sharper than Snow would have dared use on almost any other Alpha.

"Maybe you don't need me to, but I want to." The teasing mask dropped off Bone's face. "You're important to me. To us." She glanced back to where they'd made camp. Snow had no doubt that she was looking in Marrow's direction. Her scent oozed sincerity, an odor Snow had smelled on her ex only rarely and only when they'd spent time alone together.

"She listens to me," Snow said quietly. "Lets me take the lead."

"Hard for an Alpha."

"Maybe." Snow smiled gently. "But Cassidy is so earnest about making sure I'm comfortable in what we're building together." She shrugged. "If it weren't for the massive mess we're in, I could see myself making a life with her."

Bone smelled faintly surprised. "Is your wolf interested in a mate bond?"

Snow considered the question for a moment. "I don't think so. There's too much of that"—she waved her hand to indicate sex— "bound up in mating and the mate bond. But we like Cassidy a lot. She doesn't make me feel deficient. It's been a long time since I've had that." None of her romantic relationships had ended without making her feel less than. She was beginning to have confidence that the gentle intimacy she was cultivating with the North Side Alpha could flourish without growing in uncomfortable directions.

"Then I'm really happy for you. For both of you. She seems like a good kid."

"She's not a—" Whatever words Snow had for the defense of her girlfriend were cut off when far-off snarls came to her ears. She pushed away from the van, turning her head to zero in on the noise. "Do you hear that?"

"I do." Bone barked a short laugh. "Sounds like Hammer and Five Moons are working out some of those differences."

"I should—"

"Maybe leave them to it."

"I don't know." Snow pushed forward through the light underbrush with Bone on her heels, despite the Alpha's own words to leave the situation alone.

Marrow stood in furform in the middle of the clearing where they'd spent the night. The snarls continued, increasing in pitch and intensity. They stopped suddenly, replaced by the meaty sound of one body hitting the other. The loud yip of pain that followed was unmistakably Cassidy's. Snow froze, torn between an urge to hide and the need to see what was happening to her girlfriend.

A flash of peeking over the edge of a warehouse balcony filled her mind. In the scene her memory served up, her mama's eyes met hers as she was borne to the ground. Teeth flashed in the light from the skylights above as they closed around her throat. Her eyes stared into Snow's soul, even as the light left them, and her neck was obliterated in a gout of blood and ruined muscle.

"Hey."

Snow jumped as hands closed around her elbows. Bone kept her grasp and pulled her into a loose hug. "It's okay. This won't end like your mama did."

"You don't know that," Snow gasped. "Can't know that." She ripped her arms free and pushed her way out of what was meant to be a comforting hold, but instead felt like it was dooming her to inaction. She ran forward, her heart pounding in her ears while she cursed the weakness that prevented her from calling the wolf to her as she ran.

The snarls and growls had been replaced by the sounds of impacts and tearing. Hammer and Cassidy were doing some serious damage to each other. They weren't difficult to find. The racket of their confrontation led Snow and the Gary Alphas right to them.

When they emerged along the edge of the stream, Hammer had Cassidy backed up against a large oak tree. The smell of their blood filled the area, and it splashed liberally across the crazy quilt that was Cassidy's pelt. Hammer's dark gray fur was much more effective at hiding his wounds. He ignored Snow and the others and continued to press his advantage. Cassidy's feints and darts weren't enough to slip around him and get to where she could evade his attacks. Speed and guile were little match for sheer power when cornered.

"Enough!" Snow shouted. The order sounded weak even to her own ears, and already she was quailing at daring to speak to an Alpha in such a way.

Hammer ignored her and moved to intercept Cassidy as she tried to push off the tree's trunk and spring past him. She came away missing a chunk of fur. Blood wept from where Hammer had torn the skin away.

She hesitated, neither able to leave nor to come to Cassidy's rescue. Hammer would demolish her without even thinking about it if she dared to enter the fray in skinform. Did she call the wolf to her? By the time she could assume furform, Cassidy would be down or worse. Maybe she could distract Hammer long enough for Cassidy to get past him.

Snow strode forward, yelling. What she said, she had no idea. She opened her mouth and words came out.

One of Hammer's ears twitched. Two wolven in red-brown fur that bristled with shared aggression dashed past her. Remains of clothing flapped from Bone's frame. She dived between the battling Chicago Alphas. Marrow slid into the gap she opened and stopped nose to nose with Hammer, a deep growl sounding within her chest. Behind her, Cassidy was able to slip around the tree. She seemed intent on circling to get a line on Hammer's flank, but Bone harried her further into the underbrush.

Even as Hammer lifted his lip at Marrow, his hackles started to go down. He looked around for his quarry, but when he didn't see her, he turned away. Marrow kept at his heels, making sure he wasn't trying to get her to move off him so he could go after Cassidy again.

Snow dodged around the tree, following the sound of paws scuffling in dead leaves to where Bone was barring Cassidy's path back to the stream. The North Side Alpha must have been exhausted. There was no other way Snow could explain that she hadn't simply overpowered the Gary Alpha. Cassidy lifted her head, tasting the wind. She turned toward Snow, her eyes shining brilliant blue and red. This time, Bone let her past. Cassidy made her way over to Snow, who dropped to her knees.

Cassidy's weight in furform was the same as in skinform, but it felt like so much more when it leaned into her. Snow braced herself and wrapped her arms around Cassidy's lupine shape. The fur was warm and sticky in places from a mixture of her and Hammer's blood.

"Let me see you," Snow murmured and pushed Cassidy back. She gave the Alpha a thorough onceover, checking that none of her wounds were continuing to bleed. To her relief, they were starting to heal. Despite the seeming viciousness of Hammer's attack, none of the damage was anywhere close to lethal.

Cassidy deployed her tongue to bathe the side of Snow's face.

"Yes, yes." Snow sat back on her heels and locked eyes with the Alpha. "Care to fill me in on what happened?"

CHAPTER TWELVE

Cassidy glared at Hammer from the back of the van. Snow sat beside her, not seeming too put out by the irritation she must have been radiating. Everyone was acting as if nothing had happened, and she didn't know if she should be outraged or relieved. It didn't help that they'd all witnessed her defeat by Hammer. Her wolf grumbled deep inside. They both simmered with rage, but it no longer demanded that they act. Instead, it held a watchful quality. They'd been bested for now, but their time would come. After all, they'd beaten Hammer in their first meeting.

For now, they were dancing to his tune. Marrow and Bone had asked about their next destination, and he'd jumped in. They were headed to Iowa to check out a shuttered maximum security prison that was now a historical site. It wasn't even the next one on their list. Cassidy would know; she'd put it together based on her estimation of which would be the most likely place for their packs to be stashed. The Iowa one was pretty far down. At least it was sort of on the way, so the decision to deviate from the plan didn't burn as much as it could have. No, it was the casual way he'd inserted himself into the position of decision-maker. Who had died and made him king?

"Hey." Snow bumped Cassidy's shoulder with her own.

"What?" The question was snappish, and Cassidy closed her eyes. "Sorry," she said, gentling her tone. Snow wasn't the problem here.

"Do you want to talk about it?"

Cassidy cast a quick glance forward. Hammer was in the front passenger seat while Marrow drove. Bone was slumped down and leaning against her sister's seat. Her eyes were closed, and her head nodded along with the van's movement. As usual, the front windows were open, providing those inside with some fresh air but also enough noise to cover up a quiet conversation in the back of the van. Probably. Hopefully.

"Talk about what?" Yes, that was an excellent way to encourage a dialog about getting her ass handed to her by another wolven.

Snow raised one eyebrow, and Cassidy's cheeks flushed in response to the quiet challenge.

Her wolf perked up inside her, ready to respond to anything that felt remotely like it might be treading on their autonomy. Cassidy took a deep breath, deliberately disassociating herself from the residual anger the wolf insisted on carrying.

"Sorry," Cassidy said again. She licked her lips, trying to buy enough time to understand her own tangled emotions before attempting to explain them to her girlfriend. "The wolf is being...difficult."

"I bet." Snow eyed her for a long moment before continuing, "Have you lost a fight before?"

Cassidy shook her head. The deeper wounds she'd picked up in her brawl with Hammer still ached, though the bleeding had stopped thirty minutes before. Some of them would scar for sure, adding to the collection she was building. There weren't as many on some wolven she'd seen. Luther had a gnarly collection, and Naomi wasn't far behind. All of the other Alphas sported twice as many even as her Betas, while Snow's skin was marred only by a few. Maybe some scars would go toward earning Hammer's good regard.

The wolf shifted. They didn't need his respect. They were his equal whether he wanted to admit it or not.

"Is that a no?" Snow prodded gently.

"Yes." Cassidy grinned a bit at the confusing answer. "It's a no." It was her turn to raise an eyebrow. "Does that make a difference?"

"It can. Even Alphas don't win every fight. It doesn't make you any less Alpha. Unless it was a challenge fight, of course. And this wasn't one of those."

"How do you know?" Cassidy sat a little straighter. She shouldn't have needed someone else's approval to feel like she still mattered, and yet Snow's words held a disproportionate amount of weight.

"For one thing, you're alive." Snow's grin was dry as bones left to bleach in the sun. "Not to mention Hammer didn't follow the forms for that. Not that everyone does."

"They sure don't." Dean's death at the hands of a rogue Alpha was proof enough of that. "If Hammer doesn't want my pack, why did he pick a fight?"

"Is that what happened?" Snow was watching her carefully now. Funnily enough, she almost never avoided Cassidy's gaze anymore.

"Of course it is…" Cassidy's voice trailed off as she reexamined what had gone down between the two of them. "I may have pushed him," she finally admitted. "A little bit."

"Ah."

Stung by the judgment in the single syllable, Cassidy hastened to explain herself. "All I wanted was to know why he let me twist in the wind at the Alpha meeting. I thought we had a plan going in, but then he started to tell Crag that we could split our forces. I thought we'd agreed that everyone would go to my pack's fallback."

"Did he ever come out and say that he would back you in that plan?"

"Well, no. But it was implied."

"Hammer is a canny operator. He's faced down half a dozen challenges to his position and come out on top every time. Most Alphas don't have to contend with even half that many before stepping down or being stripped of their title."

"And their life." Cassidy sighed. "How was I supposed to know that?"

"You aren't." Snow shook her head. "I doubt Marrow and Bone know that. I do because I've been around longer than all of them, and I keep track of this stuff. Why didn't you ask me what my take was?"

"Oh." Cassidy looked down at her hands. The wolf had grown subdued within her, settling into a stillness she only maintained when she was paying very close attention to their surroundings. "I don't know."

Snow patted her on the leg, the motion managing to feel somehow comforting and accusing at the same time. "I'm here for you. Remember that. I may go to great lengths to be overlooked, but I see a lot."

"Why don't you just tell me?"

Snow laughed loudly enough that Bone cracked open one eye for a moment. She gave her ex a little fingertip wave, to which Bone responded by snorting and closing her eyes again. "I haven't lived as long as I have by presuming to tell an Alpha what to do. Any Alpha, even one I'm dating."

"Dating." Cassidy chose to take offense at the term, rather than delving more deeply into the irritation she'd felt at Snow's laughter. It hadn't been malicious, but her first response had been one of anger. "We need a better term than that."

"Well, we can't call it friends with benefits."

"Why not? The benefits don't have to be sexual. I do have access to your encyclopedic knowledge of the wolven, after all."

"That is true."

"See, I listen." Cassidy's grin felt forced, but as she held Snow's gaze, it loosened, becoming more natural. "I'll try to do better."

"One of the things I like so much about you is how you pay attention. I don't think I've seen you make the same mistake twice."

"I'll try to take some comfort in that," Cassidy muttered. "It doesn't change the fact that Hammer handed me my ass."

"You'll get him back the next time." Snow watched Cassidy out of the corner of her eye. "There will be a next time."

It wasn't a question. "I don't think—" Cassidy's protest was cut off by a surge of determination from the wolf. The other Alpha might think himself on top for now, but that would change soon enough.

"Your instincts are going to tell you to take him down. Just don't forget what we're here to do. I don't think any of you are getting your packs back without help from the others."

"I know." Even the wolf knew, though that didn't seem to slow down her thoughts on ways to best Hammer. He was bigger than they were, stronger too when you gauged muscle against muscle. They'd been cornered so they couldn't use their speed and cunning to its fullest extent. They wouldn't allow him to trap them like that again.

"Your eyes are glowing."

"Are they?" Cassidy squeezed them shut.

"We have a task." Snow closed her hand over Cassidy's forearm and squeezed. "Try to remember that. You two can tear into each other once you have your packs with you again, right?"

"Right." Cassidy took a couple of deep breaths to calm her racing heart and to force the wolf back down. They could plot how to put Hammer in his place later. They had a target, and even if it wasn't the one Cassidy would have chosen next, it still needed to be cleared.

She only hoped that they wouldn't run out of list before they could find their wolves.

CHAPTER THIRTEEN

Snow moved her weight slightly to ease some blood back into her arm. Cassidy was a dead weight on it. The Alpha had gone from fuming to asleep, likely before she even realized it. When she woke up, Snow would have to make sure she got some food and drink in her. A hungry Alpha gave new depth and breadth to the meaning of the word hangry.

She knew Cassidy was unhappy with Hammer. For her first loss in a scrap between Alphas, she'd come out pretty well. Her wounds had already healed. Most of them had disappeared, and only a few had left behind light-pink scars a few shades lighter than even her pale skin. Either Hammer had gone easy on her, which Snow doubted, or Cassidy had defended herself reasonably well. All Alphas lost battles, but if they walked away, it was still a partial win. Every fight between Alphas had the potential to end in death. It was rare for Alphas to be killed outside of an official Alpha challenge, but it happened often enough that it wouldn't be remarked upon.

Eventually, Cassidy might even realize that her anger with the other Alpha was a textbook case of transference. Not that Snow would be the one to tell her. Maybe if the relationship lasted a little longer than the handful of weeks they'd known each other. It would be so nice to be close enough to someone else that she could point out when they were being a little ridiculous. That Cassidy was an Alpha, and a new one, probably meant things would take longer to reach that stage, but Snow was trying not to hope that this time it might work out.

When she was in furform, it was so much easier to live in the moment. Skinform might have the advantages of opposable thumbs and speech, but she sure had a tendency to wallow when she was in it.

Cassidy snuggled deeper into the crook of Snow's arm. Snow smiled, even as she could feel the circulation to her hand being cut off once again. She really liked this one. Her body filled with cozy warmth when she contemplated their future together. Yes, there was an undercurrent of concern that things wouldn't work out and she'd be alone once more, but when Cassidy did such adorable things, it was easier to pretend the river of anxiety didn't exist.

"Five Moons?" Hammer turned in his seat to peer back into the gloom.

"She's sleeping," Snow said.

"We're getting close to the location. We're going to need her."

Maybe he had taken it easy on her. Certainly, they all relied on Cassidy's ability to feel her wolven when in close enough proximity.

Snow looked down at the sleeping Alpha cradled against her right side. "How much further? You know she can't feel anything unless she's really close."

"Close enough. Wake her."

Snow couldn't make out much through the side windows of the van. They were lying on the floor and at that angle all she could see was the tops of trees. They whipped past at a rapid pace, so it seemed likely they were still on the highway. She made no move to shake Cassidy awake. Nor did she look up at Hammer.

She was intensely aware of his presence at the front of the van. Alphas always took up a lot of space, but it felt like he was spreading into every unoccupied corner of the vehicle. She bit her lip as he exerted his will, silently demanding she comply.

"Hammer, c'mon." Bone kicked the back of his seat. "You're making my skin itch."

Cassidy was stirring, her wolf rousing to respond to the one who had challenged her.

As soon as he saw her moving, Hammer's presence receded in a tide's slow ebb. Snow let out a long breath, trying not to show that she'd been affected.

"What's going on?" Cassidy's voice was rough with sleep. When she opened her eyes, they glowed dimly.

"Hammer says we're almost there." Snow reached out to a canvas tote. It was in the far corner and she had to stretch to snag it. When Cassidy sat up, she mourned the loss of the Alpha's warmth along her body.

"Good." Cassidy's voice sharpened, taking on the snap that meant she was sliding into Alpha mode.

Snow hesitated, not sure if Five Moons would appreciate having a bag of beef jerky being thrust into her hands, then shrugged. She'd seen mates of Alphas do the same for decades. There was no reason she couldn't, even if they weren't properly mated in the eyes of their pack. Even when they got Cassidy's wolves back, they might never be.

"Here." She shoved the bag over at Cassidy before she could make her way to the front of the van.

Cassidy accepted the offering with a small smile, and the scent of gratitude wafted off her briefly. Snow grabbed a couple of Gatorades, then joined the group at the front.

The Alphas were staring intently out the front windshield. Cassidy had positioned herself behind Marrow's chair, temporarily evicting Bone from her preferred spot as the wolven closest to her sister. Bone let the encroachment into her space go without comment. A faintest whiff of irritation colored her scent, but that was it.

Snow posted up behind Cassidy.

"So where is it?"

Hammer gestured at Cassidy's phone in the dashboard mount. "The device says we're two minutes out."

"Then we're nowhere near close enough that I'll be able to feel anything," Cassidy groused. She grabbed a handful of jerky from the bag and stuffed it into her mouth. "'S way too early."

"Perhaps you could see your way to being ready," Hammer said. His voice was a study in patience, and Cassidy's cheeks reddened at the exaggerated calmness of his face.

"It's fine," Cassidy said. She made no attempt to hide the edge in her tone. "I'm not the one who's wasting time."

Snow placed a hand on the small of Cassidy's back where Hammer wouldn't be able to see it. She didn't move it, only allowed the warmth of her skin to soak through Cassidy's shirt. The Alpha's shoulders eased a little. It wasn't much, but the tension in the van lowered enough that Marrow uttered a small sigh from the driver's seat.

"We're knocking one off the list," Hammer said easily, as if the two of them hadn't been at each other's throats that morning. "That's all that matters."

"Right." Cassidy continued staring out the windshield.

A sign whipped past them, warning that a drop in the speed limit was coming up. Marrow obligingly eased off the gas. The trees gave way to thin strips of dormant farmland. Another sign announced another drop in speed. As they drove past it, houses came into view up ahead, along with a small sign with peeling paint that welcomed them to Burson. The speed limit was less than half what it was on the open highway, but they were through the outskirts of the small town in no time and into its tiny downtown. In contrast to the farmland around the town that was resting in anticipation of spring planting, downtown had gone from dormant to neglected. Boards covered the windows of half the storefronts; those that remained were dark and dusty. Only a handful appeared to have actual tenants in them.

It had the same feel as the area around the North Side Pack's den, only this town didn't have the wolven to thank for the loss of its inhabitants. She wasn't aware of a pack in the immediate area. There was a small one on the Wisconsin side of the border in Prairie du Chien. They were close enough that one or all of the Alphas should have considered stopping by to make their presence known. Aside from that, Snow had stopped by the Cedar Rapids Pack a few times over the decades. The Iowa packs were a little odd in that they eschewed the state's big cities, choosing instead to inhabit towns and villages where their presence should have been more difficult to hide.

Snow had gotten the feeling that the packs were all offshoots of a larger pack that had either completely disbanded or had moved on. Those who were left seemed to enjoy their quiet lives, and she certainly wasn't prepared to cast aspersions on the life choices of other wolven. Long-term loners like her were rare among their kind. Sooner or later, a lone wolf would settle into a new pack. She didn't know of any who'd been on their own as long as she had.

The phone announced an upcoming turn past the city hall, whose brick needed a good cleaning. Marrow guided the van through the left turn, and moments later they were passing back into the woods. The road took them up at a reasonably steep angle. Unlike the highway that had brought them here, this road was showing its age. Potholes and cracks had been mended time and again, but even that couldn't stop the edges from crumbling away, leaving large drop-offs from the concrete onto a gravel verge that was mostly taken over by dead weeds. The road might have been two lanes at one time, but erosion made it closer to one and a half lanes in places. The road climbed some more, then turned, sending them up the side of a steep hill. If Snow hadn't been intimately acquainted with the Rockies out west, she might have termed it a mountain.

They switched back and forth twice before reaching the top where a massive structure dominated the landscape. Trees had been cleared away from it, giving them an unobstructed view of tall cut-stone walls. Tall towers marched the length of those walls, their metal roofs pitted with more rust than paint. The Silent Heights Penitentiary had seen better days. According to Cassidy's information, it had been closed in the late 1990s. But someone was still here.

A large gravel parking lot took up space directly in front of them as the van turned to follow the road. A handful of cars were parked in the row nearest to the prison. There weren't many, but Snow thought perhaps there were more than would be required for a small security force to keep vandals and urban spelunkers from breaking in.

A small flame of hope bloomed in her heart. All eyes were on Cassidy, except Marrow's. She was watching the road, but even she couldn't stop herself from sneaking glances at the North Side Alpha through the rearview mirror.

Cassidy's knuckles were white where she had grabbed onto the sides of the driver's seat. She steadied herself as she stared fixedly at the prison during their slow pass. She didn't breathe until they'd cleared the long outer wall that ran along one side of the prison.

"Anything?" Hammer asked.

Cassidy shook her head.

"Let's find somewhere to park," he said.

Even Cassidy didn't exactly know what her range was. This was a scene that had played out a dozen times already, so why did Snow feel such disappointment? Probably because getting closer had never yielded results. Still, they didn't want to miss out on finding the wolven just because they weren't thorough enough.

No one said anything as Marrow continued down the road that ran along the top of the escarpment. There was a sheer drop down to the Mississippi River below. Now that they'd cleared the penitentiary, the trees had closed back in around them. Marrow pulled off the road onto an overgrown dirt trail. She drove them barely far enough not to be noticed from the road, then put the van in park.

"Let's go take—" she said.

"—a closer look," Bone finished.

CHAPTER FOURTEEN

Cassidy downed the last of the bottle of Gatorade that Snow had discreetly handed her. She shucked her clothing. Snow and Marrow had opted to stay with the van, which left her with Bone and Hammer. At least she was pretty sure it was Bone. She'd finally pinpointed the subtle difference in how they appeared in her web of stars. They twinkled at slightly different rates, or at least that's how Cassidy would have tried to describe it had anyone asked her. Marrow's twinkle was a little faster and a hair more erratic than Bone's. If Cassidy hadn't spent so much time with them, she doubted she would have been able to tell at all.

The fact that she was Snow's ex also made things a little awkward, at least in her own head. Bone had never said anything to her about it. To the best of her knowledge, she hadn't said anything to Snow either.

And of course there was Hammer. Her wolf wanted nothing to do with him, but she also refused to seem like they were avoiding him. The fact that their indecision was likely incredibly obvious in their scent only served to frustrate the wolf further. She'd settled into a hypervigilant mode that Cassidy found uncomfortable. They twitched at every sound, their heart racing at every unfamiliar scent.

The shift from skinform to furform went quickly. The wolf snarled at Hammer's back, then darted into the undergrowth before he'd finished shaking the fluids of the transformation from his fur. They'd started at about the same time, and the wolf took great satisfaction in the fact that they reached full furform first.

Cassidy wondered if Hammer had known he was in a race, but the wolf ignored her pointed rumination. There were more important considerations than how quickly Hammer could shed his skin.

While Cassidy floundered in the utter hypocrisy of the wolf's thoughts, she took them through tangled underbrush at a quick clip. They bounded down game trails, forged their way through bramble patches, and leaped over a couple of rills. Bone and Hammer were on their tail, and it pleased them to be leading the chase.

If only it was a real hunt. There was game to be had up here and more than the rabbits, squirrels, and groundhogs they were used to chasing in the city. The scents of deer drifted by on the wind, tantalizing them to deviate from their more important quarry.

As much as they wanted to follow those aromas, they stayed on the track they knew would take them to the building that probably didn't have their packmates. They'd been here before, even if this was one of the nicer environs in which they'd done this important work. The wolf knew from Cassidy that the possibility of their wolves being here was low. She wanted to get this search over with so they could take a quick break for some fresh game, then to get on with the important hunt. Cassidy couldn't disagree.

It took longer than they would have preferred to reach the edge of the trees. An open field stood between them and the walls. From Cassidy's sketchy recollection of the complex's layout, she knew that the old cell blocks were held at the other end of the enclosed area. The closest walls separated them from an old exercise yard. There might have been some satellite footage of more recent buildings within that yard, but she couldn't say for certain. She'd looked at a lot of images of abandoned prisons and asylums. After a while they all mushed together.

The grass hadn't been mowed recently, but winter had done a number on it. They wouldn't be able to rely on it for great cover, but it was better than nothing. At a full sprint, they could have crossed the field in ten or so seconds.

Bone and Hammer joined them as they hunkered at the field's edge. Hammer raised his nose and tasted the wind. He didn't seem too concerned by whatever he smelled on it. The occasional trace of human came to her nose, but that wasn't unexpected, given the cars in the parking lot.

They moved before Hammer could give the okay and pretended not to see his irritation in the way his limbs stiffened nor to smell the sour green scent that rolled off him. Bone's scent was a mix of light-blue resignation and warm-red amusement. The Alphas followed in their wake, with Hammer next and Bone taking up the rear. They stalked closer in a tight file. If anyone happened on the group's tracks, they would see only one set of prints as each made certain to step in the pawprints of the one in front.

It took far longer than ten seconds to cross the field toward the high stone wall. The wolf kept her eyes open for thicker patches of grass and small shrubs to maximize their cover. They were almost to the base of the wall when they were brought up short by a sharp tug on their tail.

The wolf stiffened, ready to whirl about and confront whoever had dared, but the nip at their left flank stopped them dead in her tracks. After another tug, this one stronger than the first, they looked over their shoulder. Hammer released his grip. He nodded upward to the top of the wall, pointing at the roof of the nearest guard tower.

There was nothing too sinister at first glance, but when they looked again they saw it. A small camera was fixed to the underside of the roof's overhang. It was pointed toward the road. Hopefully, it hadn't caught their advance. Cassidy wondered if the camera swiveled. It would be foolish to assume it didn't. They checked the tower at the opposite corner of the wall but didn't see another camera, which made sense as the only thing back that way was a sheer drop.

Why did this place have cameras? None of the other abandoned installations they'd been to had. Either this was left over from when the prison had been functional, or it had been installed since then. It did look small to have been installed in the midnineties.

A kernel of excitement burbled up inside their chest. This was the first good sign they'd had in two weeks. There was no sign that their wolves were any closer than they had been, but if they were being held in cell blocks on the opposite side of the prison, they might not be close enough.

The front of the prison was obviously out of bounds. They dropped their muzzle once to Hammer in acknowledgment, then turned and faced in the opposite direction. This time they waited for the Alphas to fall in line before starting out. Cassidy and the wolf prowled carefully forward, secure in the knowledge that the two wolven approved of their actions.

They kept an eye out for more cameras as they moved carefully through the grass. While they'd been moving slowly before, now they inched past at barely more than a crawl. The less the grass moved as they passed through it, the less chance that they'd be caught out. Cameras were a problem. Cassidy fervently hoped that whoever was recording was doing so only on the visible spectrum of light. If what was up there had heat-sensing capabilities, they'd already been exposed.

But there were no sirens, no booted feet running their way. They kept their ears sharp for any sign of alarm but heard nothing.

If the tower on the escarpment side had a camera, neither Cassidy nor the wolf could see it. With no signal from Hammer or Bone that they had seen anything untoward, they kept creeping forward, around the corner of the wall. The strip of ground between the wall's base and the sheer cliff that overlooked the Mississippi River was narrow, too narrow, apparently to have gotten a lawn mower back there. All sorts of small shrubs and healthy weeds had been allowed to grow. They might be devoid of leaves, but her pelt would camouflage just fine against the dead greenery that was left behind. They had no doubt that Bone and Hammer would blend in as well.

Cassidy and the wolf took one more long look at the tops of the walls and the guard tower. Razor wire ran around the top of the walls and around the perimeter of each tower. The towers themselves were dark, but it was difficult to tell if they were empty or if the windows were tinted. From their angle, they had no way of knowing for sure. The fur along their hackles prickled and lifted. Not knowing if they were being watched was not a sensation either of them enjoyed.

Still, there were no cameras, and no one had opened a window to lean out and take potshots at them. The wolf dived into the gap between a bush and the wall and they made their way forward once more. It was easier to move without being spotted, so they were able to build up a bit of speed, almost reaching a trot that was only slowed when they had to squeeze under a bush.

They were emerging out from under yet another scraggly shrub, when a point in Cassidy's internal starscape blazed to life. They froze, reaching out toward it. It was Luther. A howl of triumph tried to push its way out of their throat, but they kept their muzzle clamped against the fierce joy within.

They turned their head, trying to get a bead on where Luther was at that moment. He was definitely on the other side of the wall, maybe twenty or thirty feet away. His was the only star to light up.

A bump on the withers and a questioning whine startled them, and they whirled around. Bone tilted her head. Her scent was hopeful, if guarded. Hammer stared straight at her as if he might divine her thoughts through sheer force of will.

Their mouth dropped open in a happy pant. It wasn't everyone, but it was something. At least one of her wolven was inside the walls of this place. They closed their mouth when they realized they would have to leave. The wolf was already agitating that they should take betweenform and scale the walls. The razor wire might be a bit of an inconvenience, but they'd survive it.

Would their other wolven? If they moved now, they risked tipping off whoever was holding Luther. There was no way he would stay without some force to keep him bound. The thought didn't calm the wolf. At the realization that their Beta was in all likelihood being held against his will, she tried to muscle Cassidy aside.

Cassidy let her. The wolf couldn't reach betweenform without her cooperation. It took the wolf long moments before she would admit defeat, but without Cassidy to provide the balancing act between furform and skinform, they might as well have tried to turn into a bird.

While the wolf raged, Cassidy reached out to that glittering point. She pulled it toward her with metaphorical hands and cradled it. Was it her imagination, or did the star pulse more strongly when she did so? Joy and despair combined within her, creating a dizzying vortex of emotions when the wolf's anger swirled among the mix. Cassidy wanted nothing more than to stay and see how many more of her wolven she could reach, but Hammer and Bone were retreating. She couldn't do this without them, whether the wolf would admit it or not.

Cassidy gave Luther's star one last caress, then let it go. It floated slowly away from her but didn't stray far. She closed her eyes, then turned to face her wolf. It was time to leave. Throwing themselves at this problem would lead to their death. If they were lucky, they would be the only ones to die. If they weren't, they would take some or all of their wolven with them.

It was time to get over their pique at Hammer. They needed him, and that wasn't going to change anytime soon.

The wolf snarled in angry agreement. She dug their claws into the cold, hard ground, tearing long furrows into it. But try as she might, she couldn't refute Cassidy's words. Their anger, however justified it might be, was dangerous. There would be time for such things later, and if they were truly fortunate, they could take that rage out on those who had stolen their wolven.

This was the right move. Her mind made up, the wolf squeezed herself back under the bush. Snow would be so excited to hear about the discovery of one of their packmates.

CHAPTER FIFTEEN

Marrow leaned back in the passenger seat, her feet up on the dashboard. "How is your girl taking getting her ass handed to her by Hammer?"

Snow grinned at the acknowledgment of their relationship. "My girl is doing just fine."

"Really?" Marrow raised one eyebrow and lolled her head to one side to get a better look at Snow. She knew Snow didn't like looking other wolven in the eyes as a general rule, but that didn't stop her from trying to snag her gaze.

"Do you remember your first loss as an Alpha?" Snow raised a hand when Marrow took a breath to answer. "That wasn't to your sister?"

"Touché." Marrow furrowed her brow for a moment. "I do. A lone wolf made a play for the Gary Pack not long after Noor and I took over."

Marrow didn't use Bone's real first name often. Never where Cassidy and Hammer could hear it. The twins were cagey about their identities in front of outsiders.

"You must not have lost too badly."

"The little shit tried to ambush me. I was Alpha, Noor was Beta. He waited until I was alone on a nighttime run, then got the drop on me." Marrow grinned. "He was nearly successful, but he hadn't counted on me being able to let my sister know what was going on. She showed up just as he was closing his jaws around my neck." Her grin shouldn't have been able to widen as far as it did. "He didn't know what hit him." She lifted her throat to show a series of raised bumps, each slightly lighter than the terracotta skin around it. "I have my necklace to remember it by."

"And I bet you bounced right back from looking death in the face. Am I right?"

"Huh." Marrow bounced her leg against the dashboard. "Noor helped."

"I'm sure she did." Snow looked out the van's side windows. "Maybe give Cassidy—Five Moons—a chance to get past this before getting shitty about it, all right?"

"No skin off my bones." Marrow shrugged. "Just don't want her to take us along for the ride if she loses it."

"She's not going to lose it."

"If you say so."

If Cassidy did lose it, Snow would have been shocked. The Alpha wasn't exactly in the best of spirits at the moment, but she'd been dealt a blow. Absorbing blows was what Alphas did. Snow had every confidence that Cassidy would step up to this challenge as she'd been doing to all the ones previous to this.

Marrow twisted around to look right at her when Snow didn't rise to the bait again.

"I'm going to check the perimeter," Snow said. She pushed open the side door and stepped out onto packed dirt and leaves before Marrow could say anything. Direct orders from Alphas were difficult to shake off. She made a point of it when it wasn't her Alpha, but that didn't mean there wasn't effort involved. She was tired of the amount of work Bone's sister was. Marrow had been a subtle needle in her side since she and Bone had spent time together a couple of decades back. She wasn't going to let Marrow under her skin again.

There wasn't much to the perimeter—it was only a van after all— but that didn't stop Snow from walking out into the surrounding trees until the van was barely visible through the branches. Its white paint had dulled to grungy gray from being driven through snow-covered streets and down melting gravel roads. The thing was an eyesore, lacking any of the character or refinement her beloved bus had carried. It felt silly to be mourning her van. It was only a hunk of metal, after all. Its loss paled in comparison to the loss of the Alphas' wolven. She knew that, and yet every time she had to view the ugly box of a replacement, she felt a pang in her heart all over again.

It didn't help that she had to share it with the Alphas. There was no space to call her own. Out of the van and in the woods felt a little better than being cooped up with Marrow, but it wasn't the same. Tears pricked at her eyes, and she let them fall without trying to stop them. No one was there to see her weakness.

It wasn't fair. She would never have the chance to see how it felt to have Cassidy stay with her in the bus. They'd had those few hours snuggled together in a Chicago parking deck, and that had been it. It had felt right to have the Alpha in her territory, small though it was.

As if the thought had conjured her, Snow caught a glimpse of brindled brown and gray through the trees. Cassidy was back, with Hammer and Bone close behind. She ghosted her way back up to where Marrow waited.

The three Alphas shed their furform as they moved. Each was in skinform by the time they reached the van itself. Bone skimmed fluid from the change off her skin as she turned to watch Cassidy. Marrow came around the back of the van, pausing to throw the doors open, then move out of the way as the naked Alphas helped themselves to their clothes.

"You found them." Bone's voice was tight with hope she didn't want to reveal, but it still spilled out around the edges.

Cassidy grinned tightly. "One. Luther."

"You didn't feel any of your other packmates?" Hammer asked. "What about ours?"

"I don't know." A curious mix of elation and disappointment layered Cassidy's scent. "I have to be very close to feel wolven who aren't mine."

"How close is very close?" Bone demanded.

"I don't know." Cassidy shook her head in a sharp chop of frustration. "I keep telling you all that I don't know, and it never sinks in."

"What are the chances they'd be holding Luther alone without anyone from the other packs?" Snow asked as she left the cover of the trees. On the face of it, this was the first good news they'd had in weeks. Why was there so much tension?

The question brought the Alphas up short. They exchanged glances ranging from disgruntled to excited. Sometimes Snow felt like she was chaperoning a group of grumpy toddlers. Except this group was used to getting their way. Just like most toddlers.

"That's a good question," Bone replied slowly.

"And if it is just Luther in there, he's still being held by someone, right?" Snow asked patiently.

"I don't see a world where he's hanging out inside a prison of his own volition," Cassidy said.

"So worst-case scenario is it's just him, but there are people there who know more about what's going on than we currently do."

Hammer nodded. "And if it's the best-case scenario, the rest of our wolven are there as well."

"Or it's somewhere in between," Cassidy said slowly. "We really have no choice except to go in after him."

"A plan would be good," Snow said, her voice mild. She stared off into the trees across the track.

"It needs to be a good one," Marrow said, her eyes locked on her twin's. "Even if it's only Luther in there, we can't tip our hand."

Bone nodded. "And if it's more than just Luther…We need a team."

"I thought we were a team," Cassidy said.

Hammer grunted. It could have meant anything. At least Cassidy ignored him. She seemed to have gotten refocused on what was important.

"Of course, we'll be the masterminds," Marrow said.

"Excuse me?" Cassidy sputtered.

"Hammer is in good shape to be our muscle," Bone said as if Cassidy hadn't spoken.

Cassidy frowned. "I can be muscle."

"Snow will do as getaway driver." Marrow turned her gaze toward the lone wolf. "You have a steady hand at the wheel."

"There were cameras along the walls," Bone said. "We're going to need a hacker. We need to get a handle on the prison's layout." She turned her head to watch Snow carefully. "Do you feel up to being the wheels?"

"I drive a lot, but not like that. I try to avoid notice, remember?" Snow was glad Bone had checked in with her. "I'm sure I can be helpful with research and support. I'm not going to be a whole lot of good at pulling this thing off, I'm afraid."

"So we need someone who's good with a fast getaway," Marrow said.

Bone looked back at her.

"Byron," they said at the same time.

"Do we know where he is?" Bone asked.

"We can find out," Marrow replied on the heels of the question. "Who do we know who can hack stuff?"

Cassidy raised her hand. "I can—"

"You?" Marrow's question was full of scorn. "You'll need to be able to do more than call your mom."

"Yeah, I know, Marrow. I'm not some secret hacker. What I was going to say is I can work on finding us one."

"How do you plan to do that?" Hammer asked.

Cassidy hesitated. She was struggling with something. That much was obvious to Snow. If she could see it, so could the others.

"I have an in with Chicago's new Vampire Lord," she finally said. "I bet she's got plenty of hackers lying around." Cassidy shrugged, exuding uncertainty. "I'll just broker that favor for what we need."

"You're bringing the vamps into this again?" Hammer's eyes flashed orange, but his voice stayed soft, dangerously so.

Bone shook her head. "Seems risky."

Marrow pursed her lips and all eyes turned to Cassidy as they waited for her.

"Look, we don't have a lot of options," Cassidy said, before Marrow could weigh in against her. "No one here is good with computers. Half of you can barely turn one on. If we had the time, we could interview half the Midwest and find someone with the skills, but I don't want to wait that long. Do you?" She looked each Alpha in the eye, pinning each in turn with a stare, moving on before it could turn from pointed to aggressive. "I don't want to go to the vamps. If I had any other choice, I'd go with it."

"You're taking on the favor," Marrow said. "They'll want payment, but it comes out of your pocket."

"Yes." Cassidy smelled unhappy but resolved. She closed her hand around something in her pocket.

"If this blows up in our faces, I'm taking yours off," Hammer growled.

"You'll be welcome to try, after I get my own back from the vamps." Cassidy drew herself up as much as she could and met his glare with her chin up. They locked eyes for long moments.

Hammer looked away first, satisfaction bleeding into his scent. "Very well. It sounds like you all have people to reach out to, and I don't. I'll stay behind and keep an eye on the prison. If they try to move Luther or anyone else out, I'll know."

"How will we contact you?" Cassidy asked.

"When you're back in the area, come and get me. If I have to move out, I'll leave a message there." Hammer pointed off to a downed log by the side of the overgrown track.

"I don't anticipate being gone longer than a day or two," Cassidy said.

"I don't know how long we'll be gone," Bone said.

"Probably closer to three days," Marrow finished.

"You'll find directions here." Hammer grinned and rubbed his hands together. "Our quarry doesn't know we've sighted them. The most successful hunts start with stealth."

"That they do." Cassidy stepped up and grasped Hammer's shoulder. "Thank you for staying behind and watching over my Beta."

He nodded somberly. "We may have our differences, but I know you'd do the same for one of mine if the situation called for it."

"I would." The words were quiet, but Snow smelled the of truth of them.

Cassidy turned toward the twins and Snow. Hammer had already shucked his pants and shirt. He dropped to his hands and knees and his pelt of charcoal gray washed over him. Before they'd gotten into the car, he'd disappeared back into the trees.

Snow trudged around to the driver's seat and got in. Marrow was climbing between the front seats into the back. She held up a finger, indicating for Cassidy to wait.

"Take a couple of pictures of the back of the van, would you?" she said.

Cassidy wrinkled her brow. "Why?"

"Oh, and a couple from the inside out the back door," Bone added. "And some of the van from the outside."

"I'm not doing any of that until I know what the point is." Cassidy crossed her arms.

"We need the photos for our contact," Bone said. "It's not a joke."

"Promise," Marrow said, with a wide grin that implied otherwise.

Cassidy looked back and forth between them, then sighed and climbed in the back of the van.

"One out the side doors and one out the back," Marrow piped up.

"Or just one for every side of the van," Bone added.

Snow could hear Cassidy's teeth grinding, but she complied with the twins' strange directions. They kept lobbing suggestions at the other Alpha until they were satisfied.

"Just one in through the side door, then," Bone said.

"Fine. But I'd better not be wasting my time." Cassidy snapped another quick picture. "What am I doing with these? Neither of you has a phone."

"Email the lot of them to Lordy dot B at Gmail.com," Bone said.

"Put 'From the Skeletwins' in the subject line," Marrow said on the heels of her sister's instructions.

"Skeletwins?" Cassidy raised an eyebrow as she fiddled with her phone.

"An old nickname," Bone said.

"If you say so." Cassidy tapped the screen one final time, then stashed the phone in her pocket. She headed toward the passenger seat.

Marrow grabbed her arm. "One last request. After you get back with your hacker, bring the van back here for an hour every day. Between—" She cut off and looked over at her sister.

"Nine to ten should be fine," Bone said. "It'll account for the time zone."

"Time change?" Cassidy yanked her arm back. "Why on Earth would I do that? This sounds like a setup for one of your ridiculous pranks."

"It isn't," Marrow said.

"Promise," Bone chimed in.

"Mm hm. This from the two who stuffed the toes of my boots with dead fish for three mornings straight."

"Hmm." A huge grin creased Marrow's face. "The best part was the fourth day when you practically turned your clothing inside out looking for where we'd stashed that day's offering."

"And there wasn't one." Bone was smiling just as wide as her sister.

"No, that was the day you smeared jam on the inside of the car door handle. Where did you even get jam?"

"We helped ourselves to some from Dale's place."

"So you can see why I'm having problems believing this isn't a setup, right?"

"Five Moons." Marrow placed her hands on Cassidy's shoulders. "I don't joke on the job."

"Is that true?" Cassidy looked over at Snow.

The twins' past was almost as murky to Snow as it was to Cassidy, but she had no problem believing their background was sketchy. Marrow smelled like she was taking things seriously, aside from a thin veneer of amusement which probably stemmed from memories of Cassidy's irritation with their shenanigans.

"It could be," Snow said.

"You're no help." Bone rolled her eyes at Snow. "Look, we're on the level with this one, I promise." Sincerity rolled off her in a wave.

"Ugh. Fine." Cassidy pulled her shoulder out of Marrow's grasp. "Can we get on with this? We're wasting daylight."

Marrow and Bone piled into the back of the van.

"Drop us somewhere with enough cars that we can hotwire one," Bone said.

"You know," Cassidy said as Snow put the van in reverse and began the long, arduous process of driving backward down the narrow track. "It occurs to me that you and your sister have a lot of knowledge of the shadier side of things."

"We watch a lot of movies," Marrow said blandly. Her scent shifted from determined to smug, then back again.

"Is that so?"

"Sure it is," Bone said. She leaned back against a pile of blankets to one side of the van's back area and laced her fingers together behind her head. "Heists mainly."

"I see." Cassidy's tone said she wasn't buying what the twins were selling for a second, but she allowed the matter to drop.

Snow had known for quite some time that Bone and her sister had some unconventional approaches to things, but it hadn't occurred to her they might have an actual criminal background. She didn't say anything as she continued backing, the main road only now coming into view. It wasn't really her business. When you lived beneath society's notice, you had to make money somehow. A lot of packs engaged in enterprises that ranged from questionable to illegal. It wasn't her place to judge, even if it was an area she avoided as much as she could.

Still, it seemed like their talents were about to come in handy.

CHAPTER SIXTEEN

Cassidy had plenty of time for second, third, even fifteenth thoughts as they drove back from Iowa to Chicago. Was trusting Stiletto, and by extension the vampires, the best way to go? No matter how many times she twisted the question around in her head, the answer still came back as a reluctant yes. She had no other options, no favors to call in. Anyone she knew from her life before the wolven wouldn't know what to do about the pickle she'd landed herself in, and everyone she knew from afterward had either been sharing a van with her for the past weeks or had been taken.

Snow hadn't been thrilled at the plan, and away from the Alphas, she hadn't been shy about sharing her reservations.

"Gifts from vamps have a tendency to leave toothmarks," she'd said while tapping her fingers along the top of the steering wheel. "I need to know you've thought this through, considered all the angles. If you have and still want to do this, I'll back you up. I just need you to be sure."

Cassidy was sure, or she had been, but the long ride had given her plenty of opportunity to doubt herself, then talk herself back around to the plan. The Alphas were understandably hesitant, but they hadn't been there when she'd spoken to Stiletto. Besides, this was her best contribution to the group. If she couldn't be useful, why even be involved?

It was still daylight when they parked at a lot outside the vampires' nightclub. There was no sign of the lines that would snake out the front door. Those would materialize with the dusk. No one answered when she rapped at the front door, so they made the long trek around the building looking for a back entrance.

The loading dock had a container truck pulled up to it. People moved back and forth from it, unloading boxes on dollies. One of them stopped to glare at the two of them as they walked up.

"We're closed," the dark-haired human man said. "Come back at sunset." With his build he could have been one of the bouncers Cassidy had walked past on her previous visits. He gave no indication that he recognized either of them.

Cassidy pulled the pendant Stiletto had given to her and held it up, the red gem managing to wink, even in the shaded back alley. "We've been invited."

"Ah." He tucked the dolly against the nearest wall. "If you'll come with me, I'll show you where you can wait until the Lord can see you."

Cassidy smiled thinly. "Of course." She was no happier to be entering the vampires' den now than she'd been any other time. The creatures gave her the creeps. Despite her confident words to Snow and the Alphas, she was fully aware that they could be walking into a terrible situation, which was why she'd told Snow to stay behind. Her girlfriend had given her a look that plainly said, "You're not the Alpha of me," and had followed along anyway. As they made their way through the warren of back halls that made up the nonpublic areas of Faint, the lone wolf's scent betrayed little concern. It stayed a mellow lavender.

She did her best to remain as Zen as Snow. If she was half as successful, it would be a good front.

"Stay here," the bouncer said after leading them to a small, lushly appointed room. He disappeared as soon as they sat down side by side on a crushed velvet fainting couch. The decor was fussy and overworked. Someone had taken a lot of inspiration from Victorian aesthetics.

"This is nice," Cassidy said, her voice laden with heavy irony.

Snow snorted. "If you like that sort of thing." She took in the oriental rug, the rosette-patterned wallpaper, the elaborately detailed lamp on a nearly as elaborately carved small sideboard. "I was around for the tail end of this fashion. Didn't see much of it in the circles I ran in."

"You were born in the Victorian era?"

"Technically, the very end of it. Mama's pack wasn't so rich as to put together a whole room like this, but we had bits and pieces." She pointed at the lamp. "I could swear I've seen that exact one before."

"You're a hundred and twenty years old."

"Somewhere in there." Snow lifted one shoulder. "I stopped counting a long time ago."

"I see." Cassidy licked her lips. She'd heard about age-gap romances, but a hundred years was a lot. How long was she going to live? She hadn't given it much thought. Lately, existing through the next day had seemed hard enough, let alone thinking in decades-long terms. That was a long time to keep her head on a swivel.

Snow bumped her with her shoulder. "You okay?"

Cassidy dredged up a smile from somewhere. "Just coming to terms with some things."

"You're looking a little wild around the eyes."

"Weird that." Cassidy gave a hollow laugh that sounded in no way genuine, even to her. "It never really occurred to me how long I might live."

"Does it matter? Wolven don't tend to care too much about age. All of the people you've been running with would be pushing elderly or dead if they were human."

"I'm going to lose a lot of people. Humans, I mean."

"Ah." Snow slid her arm around Cassidy's shoulders and pressed a kiss to her cheek. "All made wolven have to deal with those thoughts sooner or later. There's joy with the pack, if that's any comfort."

"A little." Cassidy snuggled down into Snow's embrace. "There's comfort with you too."

"That's sweet." The voice was familiar and unwelcome in such a personal moment.

Cassidy stood. "Stiletto." She extended the pendant toward the vampire, trying not to show any surprise that she seemed to have materialized out of a shadowed corner of the small room.

The vampire waved the pendant away as she moved too gracefully over to a cushioned wooden chair. She alit and tilted her head at Cassidy, her hands stroking over the carved dragons' heads that made up the chair's arms. "To what do I owe the pleasure of your visit? Have you found your pack?"

"We have. Or at least my Beta. We weren't able to scout the location thoroughly, but there's a very good chance the rest of my— our packs are there."

"That is excellent news. Any word yet on who's behind their disappearance?"

Cassidy shook her head. "We'll look into it while we get our wolves out, I'm sure. Which is where you come in."

Stiletto arched an eyebrow. Cassidy hadn't remembered her having this much poise when she was alive. Granted, her opinion of then-Hunter Stiletto hadn't been great. For one thing, Cassidy had still been angry with Mary Alice for having kept secret her own association with the Hunters. For another, Stiletto had made it clear that she thought Cassidy belonged in government hands. For what purpose, Cassidy wasn't quite sure. At least now she could be sure that Stiletto wasn't about to sell her out to her former employers.

"Where they're being held has high walls, cameras, guards. The whole deal." Cassidy took a deep breath. "I'm hoping you have a vampire who can help with the computer side of things. Our group has a lot of skills, but I'm the closest to a techie we've got, and that's very sad."

"You need a hacker." Stiletto sat back in the chair, her brow pulled down in a thoughtful frown. "I don't have many vampires with that particular skill set, likely for similar reasons to yours. There is one among my attendants who has the skills. I'll see if they have any interest in helping you."

"Attendants?"

"A human. More than employee, less than one of us. They prove useful during the hours of the day when our kind can't venture outdoors." Stiletto smiled thinly. "All our attendants are here by choice. We don't hold anyone against their will."

Cassidy dragged down her questioning eyebrow. Would they even know if they were being forced?

Stiletto was on her feet. Without even a blur as she stood up, one moment she was seated in the chair, the next she was standing next to it. "I'll check with my attendant." Her head snapped around to stare Cassidy in the eyes. "Any word from my predecessor?"

Her eyes were deep pools that enticed Cassidy to plunge into their depths. Red light flickered at the bottom, luring her in to explore. A sharp pain in her side cleared her head long enough to look away from the vampire.

"I haven't heard from her," Cassidy ground out through gritted teeth. Her wolf was enraged, demanding that they exact some sort of retribution on the one who had just tried to…To what, exactly? Hypnotize them? Enthrall, maybe. What had happened?

"If you say so." Stiletto stepped into her line of sight, but Cassidy refused to look directly at her face again.

"I do say so." It was even true. She'd been speaking with her mom about once a week, but had never so much as heard Carla's voice in the background. Sophia Nolan hadn't let slip where they were, if she even knew, and Cassidy hadn't asked. The less she knew about her mom's whereabouts, the safer she was. When she had her pack back, she'd do something about her mom and Mary, but until then, she couldn't lie to the Vampire Lord of Chicago about what she didn't know.

"Very well." Stiletto opened the door, letting a desperately needed draft of fresh air into the room. "You may follow me, or feel free to stay here, or even partake of what Faint has to offer while I search out my attendant. The club is about to open and you're free to indulge yourself in whatever way you like." Stiletto's smile promised dark pleasures.

Cassidy bit the inside of her lip to keep from responding. "We're coming with you." She reached out for Snow's hand.

"Of course." Stiletto's smile widened. "Why take a moment of respite when you can keep pushing." The smile melted away. "You look tired."

"Tired doesn't get my wolves back." Cassidy stood. "Are you going to help or not?"

CHAPTER SEVENTEEN

The way was unfamiliar. Stiletto led them away from the sitting room, deeper into the bowels of the building.

Cassidy practically radiated irritation. Stiletto had been pushing her buttons. Snow squeezed the hand that still held hers, trying to remind the Alpha that they were here for a reason, which didn't involve allowing vampires to pick fights with them. Her girlfriend sneaked a look over her shoulder, and Snow smiled reassuringly. Cassidy squeezed back once, and the animosity she was displaying receded somewhat.

They were led through back areas, indistinguishable from the others Snow had been in. She'd seen more of Faint in the past month than she had in the decades she'd been visiting Carla. The halls twisted and turned, taking them to the top of a staircase remarkable for its mundanity. Until now, even the back areas had held some mystique, but this was simply a set of concrete stairs bound by unadorned metal railings.

The descent was a quick one, and they emerged into a plain hall with low ceilings. Doors marched along each side of a hall that wasn't nearly long enough by half to run the entire length of the nightclub.

Snow glanced at the doors, listening for movement behind them. The area was awash with the smell of humans, and the rows of doors reminded her of a dormitory. Was this where the vampires' human "attendants" lived?

Stiletto stopped in front of the third door on the left and rapped on it. "Delfina," she called out.

An immediate rustle met her voice, and moments later a deadbolt was being thrown. The door opened, revealing a small human woman and a dark interior behind her.

A young Latina woman drifted into the light from the hall, tucking chin-length straight black hair behind her ears. Her skin was nearly as tan as Dale's. Snow assumed this woman didn't see as much sun as the Kenosha Alpha did. Small earrings glittered in each earlobe, and little silver, gold, and copper hoops marched around the rim of her left ear. What makeup she had on was tastefully done and applied so skillfully it almost appeared as if she wasn't wearing any. Her fingers were devoid of decoration and her nails were short. The royal blue pantsuit she wore would have been out of place in the club where most of the patrons seemed to prefer clothing that was tight or strewn with strategically placed holes, or both.

"Yes, Lord?" Her voice was low and questioning as she looked into Stiletto's eyes.

"These two"—Stiletto indicated Snow and Cassidy with a languorous wave—"have need of someone who's good with computers. Are you willing to hear what they have to ask?"

The hacker's eyes sharpened at the question, and her face lost some of the worshipfulness it had taken on when she'd met Stiletto's gaze. "And you approve?"

"If you do." Stiletto leaned forward in a conspiratorial manner. "It's for a heist."

"More of a prison break," Cassidy said. She looked behind them toward the stairs. "Can we talk inside?"

Stiletto raised an eyebrow at Delfina, who nodded and stepped back. The Vampire Lord walked in as if she owned the place.

Cassidy hesitated in front of the open door. She dropped Snow's hand and stepped through the threshold into a reasonably sized apartment, one that would rent for a fair amount of money anywhere else in the neighborhood. There were no windows, but it boasted many more amenities. A bathroom was visible off a spacious living room that was dominated by a large television mounted to the wall. Beneath the TV was a cabinet with all sorts of electronic equipment. Snow wasn't up on all the latest entertainment gadgets, but she recognized an original Nintendo game system among a number of other newer and sleeker devices. A small stack of boxes rose from behind a scuffed leather couch. They'd been labeled in black marker. Most had been opened but had been closed back up. A few were still sealed with pristine packing tape.

"I'm Delfina." The woman leaned against the living room wall. She reached a hand out toward Cassidy. "So, you need someone who's good with computers."

"Uh…" Cassidy took Delfina's hand and shook it. "Yes. That's right. This is Snow. You can call me Five Moons." She glanced toward Stiletto as if expecting her to take the lead, but the vampire stared back without expression.

"What are your qualifications?" Snow asked when Cassidy seemed a little at a loss.

"Yes," Cassidy said. "Qualifications."

"I'll need to know more about the job." Delfina placed one hand on her hip and studied them. "So is it a heist or a prison break?"

"Prison break. We have some…family who've been gathered up, and we want them back."

Delfina smiled, her teeth gleaming white in the dim interior. "Right to it then. I can respect that."

"They're being held in a decommissioned prison that's had some upgrades." Cassidy spread her hands. "We don't know how many, and we don't want to get close enough to check. If we spook them and they run, who knows if we can track our people down again."

"I'm good with stealth," Delfina said. She examined her fingernails. "How's your OPSEC?"

Cassidy shook her head. "I don't follow."

"Not good." Delfina looked back at Stiletto. "They're amateurs."

Stiletto shrugged. "Not amateurs, exactly. I'm sure if you need any of them to tear apart a small army, they could do that for you. They did exactly that downtown a few weeks back."

"That was you?" Delfina's look back at Cassidy was surprised. "Maybe we can work together."

"And we take your word for it?" Snow said.

The hacker opened her mouth, a frown settling over her brows.

"Delfina works for us," Stiletto said, crossing the room to stand next to the human. "You could take my word for it." Her tone was innocuous, enough so that Snow was certain that doubting her would definitely be taken as an insult.

Delfina's smile was brittle.

"Snow's right," Cassidy said. "I appreciate you lining someone up for us, but I need some reassurance that she's got what it takes to get the work done."

"An audition." Delfina curled her upper lip. "It's been a long time since anyone asked for one of those."

"More of a demonstration." Stiletto gently laid a hand on the small of Delfina's back.

The smaller woman shuddered delicately. "I could be convinced," she said, a little out of breath.

Stiletto smiled and turned back to Cassidy. "Not all pressure needs to be unpleasant." She cocked her head at the Alpha. "I imagine you've had trouble accessing your funds. If Delfina can provide them to you, would that be enough reassurance for your purposes?"

Cassidy nodded.

"Very well then." Stiletto looped Delfina's hand through the crook of her arm. "This way."

Arm in arm, the human and vampire crossed through a dining area with more cardboard moving boxes than furniture and slid open a door into a smaller room which had the look of a converted bedroom. If Snow had thought the living room had had more than its fair share of equipment, this room put it to shame. It was difficult to parse out the jumble of equipment and screens. There were two desks and at least six monitors on various mounts. That didn't count the couple of laptops that graced the tops of the desks. More equipment was piled on every horizontal surface. She could only hazard a guess at the purpose of the various devices.

The hacker settled herself into a sleek desk chair and looked back at them before flicking a switch. The rig came to life, lights blinking into existence, bathing her face in stark brilliance and shadow. The planes of her face had already been sharp, but the contrasting lighting honed those edges to razors. A flicker of dark delight passed over her face, and she wiggled her fingers, then turned to face the screens.

"Bank?" Delfina asked.

"Uh, Bank of America, Alliant, and First Chicago." Cassidy stepped up to stand awkwardly at Delfina's elbow.

The hacker gestured at a chair half-buried under a stack of square plastic boxes. "A long-timer, a credit union, and a megacorp. Good, I like a challenge."

"What makes them a challenge?" Cassidy gathered the boxes in her arms and sat down. She looked around for a moment before deciding to hold onto the items. There weren't many places to deposit them that wouldn't require moving other stuff.

Oddly, as packed as the room was with various things Snow had no context for, it was devoid of the packing boxes they'd seen everywhere else in the apartment.

"Big advantage to hacking from here is the firewalls are second to none," Delfina said as she started typing away at her keyboard. "The Masters might not be up on the latest tech"—she threw a glance over her shoulder at Stiletto—"but they don't skimp on anything."

Stiletto moved forward until she stood at the back of Delfina's chair. "No matter what the others think, we live in a world of technology. Nothing is going to change that."

"Is that why you overthrew Carla?" Cassidy asked without looking away from the monitors.

CHAPTER EIGHTEEN

Delfina's heart rate soared at the question, but Cassidy was only paying the tiniest bit of attention to her. What she was doing on the screens was interesting, but Cassidy could only follow it so far. She might have been facing the monitors, but her attention was focused almost completely on the vampire behind her. The one who stood between her and Snow.

For all the good it did her. Stiletto might as well have been a wooden statue for all the emotion she betrayed.

"We had some differences of opinion," was all she said. "I didn't know you had an interest."

"Your predecessor showed up on my doorstep in the middle of the night. It's difficult not to have some passing curiosity regarding the circumstances." She tried to keep her voice as dry as the vampire's but suspected that was impossible.

"If you're so concerned, perhaps you'd like to experience vampire politics firsthand."

Cassidy tried to catch a glimpse of Stiletto's reflection in the monitors, but there was nothing there. Was the former Hunter offering what Cassidy thought she was? Was it even possible to make a wolven into a vampire? Maybe Snow would know.

Delfina kept typing and clicking with the mouse. "This will go faster if you have account numbers," she said, breaking the tense silence.

"I have some notes on my phone." Cassidy pulled the device out of her pocket as the hacker swung around in her chair to stare at her in disbelief.

"Have you had that thing running the entire time you've been on the run?"

"I put it on airplane mode when I'm not actively using it." Cassidy might not have been skilled in OPSEC, or whatever Delfina called it, but she knew a few things. She'd watched network television growing up. Her mom loved shows like *Law & Order* and various crime-scene procedurals.

"So you're slightly less detectable for a portion of the time." Delfina shook her head. "We'll handle that once your money is squared away." She turned back to the screen. "The numbers?"

Trying to pretend her face wasn't flaming red at the rebuke, Cassidy read off the numbers. Delfina nodded, not even writing them down.

"Do you need that again?" Cassidy asked once she was done with her recitation.

"Nope." Delfina tapped a fingertip to the side of her forehead. "Got them all here. Besides, you won't need them much longer." She continued to type and move windows around her various screens.

Cassidy tried to keep up with what she was doing, but Delfina flicked back and forth between open windows and tabs with such speed that it was impossible. She knew enough about computers to get by in college. The most techie work she'd done had been some HTML editing and figuring out some Visual Basic for work in Excel. Delfina was light years ahead of her in skills and in comprehension. After a few minutes, Cassidy gave up trying to parse out what she was doing.

She had to look around to get a bead on what Snow and Stiletto were up to. Her girlfriend was leaning against the wall next to a decent-sized closet. Stiletto was nowhere to be seen. She inhaled, trying to sniff the vamp out before remembering that they had no discernible scent. There had to be some way of tracking them. Cassidy snorted a little bit at her own hubris. Because none of the wolven who'd come before her had ever thought of that.

Snow raised one eyebrow in silent question and Cassidy shrugged in return. She was getting punchy, and it wasn't difficult to figure out why. Yes, coming to get someone who could run the technical side of things on this prison break was important, but while she hung out in a nightclub basement, Luther was being held in an actual prison. If she was lucky, the rest of her pack and the packs of the Alphas who'd thrown in with her were also there. If she wasn't...Well, she'd have wasted time on potentially no more than one of her wolven. She would be glad to have Luther back, but she was certain Hammer wouldn't be thrilled about spending his time on one of her wolves. Bone and Marrow would either think it was hilarious, or they'd put their muscle behind Hammer. With all three Alphas arrayed against her, she could be kicked out of their uneasy alliance, and that was the best possible outcome. The worst would be death, for herself and possibly for Snow.

A gentle touch on the small of her back made her start in place. Snow's aroma washed over her and Cassidy relaxed.

"Are you okay?" Snow murmured. "You're getting really tense and you smell like you're a hair from biting someone."

"I'm fine," Cassidy lied. Snow would pick up the untruth, but if the hacker and the vampire were listening in, they might believe her. Not that she'd been especially good at dissembling before she was inducted against her will into the ranks of the wolven. Her mom had always known when she was fibbing, and so had Mary.

Mary. Another loose end she would have to track down. Same with her mom.

"If you say so." Snow wrapped an arm around her shoulder in a loose hug.

Cassidy allowed herself to melt into it for a moment before standing up straight. Her mom. Tonight was when she was supposed to call. She hauled her phone out of her pocket and held it up. Her mom would be calling soon.

"I have to take a call," Cassidy said.

"You really shouldn't," Delfina responded before Snow could say anything. She didn't bother turning around in her chair. "Every time you do makes it more likely the Feds will track you down."

"Don't you have amazing firewalls here?" Cassidy asked. "If I'm not safe from Fed intrusion on Faint's property, am I safe anywhere?"

"Probably not," Delfina said. "I mean we do, but you're not safe anywhere. Not really. Welcome to the reality of living in a digital world."

"Well, I'm just going to have to risk it."

"Head to the roof then." Delfina gestured behind her toward the door. "Take the stairwell all the way up."

"Thanks." Cassidy caught Snow's eye and gestured with her head in Delfina's direction. She raised her eyebrows in mute plea. Someone needed to stay behind and make sure this audition went as well as it could.

Snow chewed on her lower lip for a second, then nodded slowly. Hesitation dripped from her in a leaden cloud.

"Thank you," Cassidy mouthed. She vowed not to take too long. Her calls with Sophia were a vital lifeline for her, but it wasn't like they had a whole lot to say to each other at the moment.

She made her way out of the hacker's playroom and through the living room.

"Do you need something?" Stiletto's quiet question stopped Cassidy in her tracks.

She held up her phone. "I need to make a call."

"Is the reception no good down here?"

Cassidy flashed her best attempt at an easy grin. "It felt rude to be talking in Delfina's ear while she was working. I don't mind going to the roof."

"I should come with you." Stiletto stood from the couch, then in the next breath was standing next to her.

Cassidy didn't jump back, but it was a near thing. "I'll be fine on my own." She made no effort to hide the frost in her voice.

"We've had a dearth of your kind to feed from," Stiletto said. The dark red motes in the depths of her pupils intensified. "I can't guarantee your safety if I'm not there."

"And you can't guarantee Snow's safety if you're with me on the roof." Cassidy pulled herself to her full height and allowed the strength of her personality to creep into the space between them. "If anything happens to Snow, I'll make whatever went down between you and Carla look like a Sunday stroll in the park." She opened herself to the wolf, pulling on her strength, knowing full well that her eyes were shining their mismatched crimson and blue. Her teeth came to dangerous points, and she didn't stop her muzzle from lengthening, even though the changes brought with them a terrible bone-deep ache.

"Is that a threat, cub?" Stiletto asked, her voice silky and soft.

"It's a promise." What was the term for a baby vampire? Cassidy didn't know off the top of her head, so she dredged a term out of the paranormal romances she'd read once upon a time. "Fledgling."

Stiletto stared at her. The small point of red in her pupils had consumed their entirety, and her iris was being swallowed even as it expanded to take over the corneas. Her eyeteeth had dropped and were on full display when she grinned.

"If you won't accept my protection, then you'll have no reason to come whimpering to me if someone makes a snack of you."

Cassidy cocked her head. She could have looked away from Stiletto's gaze. Part of her knew it would have felt like tearing her own skin off, but she could have. Staring the Vampire Lord in the eyes and allowing her wolf to stand between her and the vampire's attempts at domination felt much more insulting. The wolf wouldn't let her back down, but she didn't really want to. She could handle herself against a vampire or two. Maybe not if they were Stiletto's caliber, but she was pretty sure that the vampire would have divested herself of any competition when she consolidated her power over Carla's court.

"I can handle myself. If one of yours tries to take me, I can't guarantee their safety."

"If they attack you, they're fair game." Stiletto closed her eyes and inhaled. She might have been getting herself back under control, but the action reminded Cassidy too much of the way wolven inhaled the scent of those around them. The vampire turned on her heel. "I'll keep an eye on your wolf."

Cassidy took a step. The first one was the hardest. Her limbs were stiff from holding herself against Stiletto's compulsion. "Eyes only," Cassidy growled. "I'd hate to have to make an example of you if you touch her."

The soft laugh she got in response wasn't encouraging. She slowed as she reached the door, caught between wanting to protect her girlfriend, but needing to know her mom was all right. With the hold Carla had over her mom, and the help Stiletto offered in the rescue of Cassidy's wolves, she was caught between two vampires. Why were all of her choices bad ones?

A quick call. That's what Cassidy needed, then she'd be back to keep an eye on the situation. She swallowed hard and shoved open the door to the hall.

CHAPTER NINETEEN

When the door opened behind her, Snow sneaked a look over at it. She'd taken up a position where she had a better view of what the hacker was getting up to, but she wasn't sure what Cassidy thought she would be able to accomplish. While she wasn't a complete neophyte to technology the way some wolven were, Cassidy's comfort with it far outstripped her own.

Stiletto stepped into the small room and nodded to her. Snow focused on her chin and nodded back. It was good policy to avoid looking a vampire in the eyes. They could do things to make their prey more malleable, and a lot of it seemed to stem from eye contact. She was practiced in avoiding the gazes of others, and it was second nature. Carla had never been successful in rolling her, but the former Vampire Lord of Chicago had relied on sex to try to get her hooks in. Since Snow had no desire for the more carnal side of life, Carla hadn't been able to mold Snow to her will the way she had so many others.

"She does good work," Stiletto said quietly. She moved nearly soundlessly, and Snow had no doubt that to a human, her movements would have been impossible to hear. As it was, Snow was barely able to pick up on the soft shush of cloth against cloth. The only time Stiletto breathed was to talk. Undead or not, the larynx still required the movement of air across it to work.

"I'll take your word for it." Snow crossed her arms. "This isn't my area of expertise."

"No, you gather information in more…traditional ways."

"That's right. People will say a lot to someone they don't feel threatened by."

Stiletto tilted her head to one side as if to say she couldn't completely agree with the statement. "Being under threat loosens a lot of tongues."

"But can you believe what they're saying?"

"You can."

"It gets difficult to parse out truth from terror, after a while."

"Hmm." Stiletto tapped her bottom lip with one finger. "You may have something there. In training, they taught us that torture couldn't yield reliable results, but out in the field…"

"In the field?" Snow carefully didn't look over at the vampire.

"I served a number of tours overseas where I learned that training only gets you so far. You learn a lot on assignment."

"The real world."

"Indeed. There's so much more to it than most people will ever experience." Stiletto smiled, the light from the monitors bathing her dark skin in cool highlights, rendering the shadows dark voids. "I'm glad I didn't stay stuck in that box."

"Does Malice have the same training you do?"

Stiletto shot her a look and grinned. She knew Snow was fishing, but the wicked glint in her eyes said she didn't mind being caught. "She does. We were very close at one time. Went through training together. You might say we were as close as sisters."

Snow raised her eyebrows in surprise that she didn't dare vocalize. It was a good thing that Cassidy wasn't there to hear that. Though the Alpha had confessed that she and Malice had had a falling out, Snow knew she was deeply concerned about her sister's fate. To find out that someone else claimed to have been as close as she and Malice once were would sting.

"What do you want, Stiletto?" Snow looked back at Delfina's screens but kept all her other senses trained on the vampire. She wasn't sure how well vampires could read the wolven. Years of exposure to their kind had taught her that their senses were keen, definitely sharper than those of humans, and that they perceived some things the wolven could not. They didn't have the same advantage the wolven did when it came to sense of smell, and she was reasonably certain that her kind were better at sifting truth from lie, at least in most situations. Torture was a different matter, and she had been telling the truth when she said it was difficult to parse out anything other than fear.

The vampire was after something. There was no reason to talk to her otherwise. Snow hadn't come to trade information. Honestly, she wasn't sure if she would, not without a major need. Carla had been a known quantity, but Stiletto was a mystery. She wasn't sure if she had the energy to deal with the enigma this new Vampire Lord represented.

Stiletto's smile was audible in her voice. "Not one to beat around the bush. I like that. Carla spent too much time worrying about lubricating the wheels she intended to turn. That's not my style." The vampire paused as if to invite comment, but when Snow said nothing, she continued, "Where is my predecessor?"

Snow pursed her lips. The question wasn't surprising. That the vampire had come right out and asked it was. "I don't know. The last I saw her, she was at the hotel with Cassidy's—" She bit off the end of the sentence before she could divulge that Sophia Nolan had not only been at the hotel, she'd also been in Carla's company.

"Cassidy's…"

Of course the vampire hadn't missed that. Snow waved a hand dismissively. "You know, Cassidy's wolves." The lie slid easily off her tongue. While she made it a policy not to lie to her own kind, the practice didn't extend to nonwolven.

"I see."

"How did you know about that?" Snow asked. It was time to get Stiletto's mind on something other than wondering what she'd almost said. "She seemed convinced that she'd made it to North Side's den without a tail."

"No one moves in this city without my people knowing about it." Stiletto sounded almost bored. "Surely that's no surprise."

"Were they your people already?"

"For longer than Carla would believe."

"I see." Snow chewed on her lower lip. "Did you know she was heading to North Side?"

"I didn't see that coming. It made sense when I considered that she hadn't landed at any of her safe houses. Do you want to know who told me?" The question was delivered in an arch tone that could have come from Carla's throat.

"Only if that information comes without any strings attached."

"I could be convinced to let it go for a light feed."

Snow pretended to consider the offer. The situation felt tense. She was feeling her way along an unfamiliar cliff edge. Decades of dealing with Carla had made her aware of where and how she could get away with sidestepping that vampire's will. She had no such feel for Stiletto. The new Vampire Lord might have come up under Carla's watchful eye, but she'd already demonstrated herself to be cast from a far different mold.

"No, I'll keep all my fluids to myself," Snow finally said. "Not that the offer isn't tempting."

"Pity." Stiletto sighed. "Let your Alpha know the offer extends to her."

"Not my Alpha." The denial was automatic. "But I'll let her know."

* * *

Once in the stairwell, Cassidy trotted up the steps two at a time. The door at the top of the stairs was propped open, and the scent of crisp outdoor air drifted into her nostrils. She paused and listened, hoping there was no one else up there. For the first time in a long time, the universe was prepared to throw her a bone. There was no sound of movement on the other side of the door. Cassidy pushed it open and slipped out onto the roof.

The chill spring air whipped past her. Chicago was living up to its nickname. There were a couple of spots that seemed like they'd offer decent shelter. She picked the one furthest from the door but stayed turned to watch it. If anyone else came up on the roof, she wanted to know. She could feel a far-off bass beat vibrating through her feet. Every time a door would open downstairs, dance music would swell until the beat was more than a rhythmic pulse coming up through her shoes.

Cassidy keyed the number for her mom's phone. She kept it out of the contacts and erased it from the phone's memory after each use. Given Delfina's dismissive response to her attempts at keeping her location hidden, she suspected it wasn't enough. But without knowing what else to do, she would keep doing her best. She would have to cross her fingers and hope. If they were lucky, Delfina would pan out and could help them close that particular gap in their defenses.

The phone rang once, then connected right away.

"Cassie-bean?"

Cassidy closed her eyes from the relief of hearing Sophia's voice. "It's me, Mom." Her eyes popped back open when she remembered that she didn't want to be observed while on the roof. "How are you?"

"Still keeping on." Her mom let out a long breath. "And you?"

"Better than last time." Cassidy gripped the phone. "We have a couple of leads, so that's something." If anyone was listening, that would have to be vague enough.

"I'm glad to hear it. You said you had some leads last time, too."

"We'll just keep running them down until we find our people. Are you being treated well?"

"I can't complain, except I get lonely during the day."

"I can see that."

"Have you heard anything from Mary?" Her mom's voice broke a little on her other daughter's name.

"Nothing more." Cassidy's response was gentle. "Sorry." She hadn't told her mom about losing Ruri's star. Hadn't even been sure where to start that explanation. As far as Sophia knew, Mary was as missing as she had been a couple of weeks ago.

"*She* says she has contacts in Chicago and will reach out to them soon." There was no need to ask who "she" was. By mutual understanding, they'd both stopped using Carla's name.

"Maybe that'll help." But probably not. That statement also went unsaid. There was so much Cassidy wanted to say during their weekly chats, but it was so hard. Either she was trying to keep away from the other Alphas and their keen ears, or she was on a roof trying to make sure vampires didn't get close enough to report back to Stiletto that Cassidy had a line, however tenuous, back to Carla. How long had it been since she and her mom had just chatted? It had been months. The last real conversation she could remember had been at the restaurant Sophia had taken her and Mary to. How long ago had that been? Was it really all the way back to early October?

"Maybe so."

"Any word on when you'll head home?"

"Not yet." Sophia laughed softly and not completely sarcastically. "I'm kept in the dark on places and timing. Which is ironic, since I'm the one who's up during the day."

Cassidy closed her eyes and leaned against the half wall that was her windbreak. "I'll come and get you as soon as I'm done here."

"You'll do no such thing. As soon as you're done there, you'll go find your sister and you'll bring her home." Up until now, Sophia's voice had been soft, unsure of itself. Now, it cracked at her through the phone, urging her to action.

She didn't know where to start. Deep down, she knew Mary was incredibly capable. Wherever she was, if she was still alive, she was taking care of herself, hopefully with Ruri by her side. Her mom didn't have that knowledge.

"Sure, Mom." There was no point in arguing. That could happen after she retrieved her wolves.

"Good." If Sophia had picked up any dissembling in her voice, she was choosing not to acknowledge it.

"So, same time next week?"

"The time works." Her mom's voice warmed as she smiled. Cassidy could almost picture it, warm and soft. "I'll be glad when we can have a nice long talk again."

"A conference call. With Mary."

"With Mary." Sophia sighed, the weary sound cascading down the line and tearing another little rent into Cassidy's soul. "I love you, sweet pea."

"I love you too, Mom."

"It's not long enough."

"It has to be for tonight. I'll call."

"I know." The line went dead. She stared at the front of her phone for long enough that it went to sleep, leaving her staring at a dark mirror of her own face. One day, this would all be over. It would have to be, right?

Her reflection had no answers.

CHAPTER TWENTY

Snow watched the back of Delfina's head. Stiletto was as still as a statue next to her. If she was breathing, Snow couldn't tell. She would have to get a whole lot closer, and she wasn't about to do that. The hacker was still muttering to herself as she typed, but she seemed to have dropped into a rhythm of sorts. The clacking at the keyboard had increased in its intensity, and more windows were flying past on the screen.

Snow still wasn't sure precisely what she was supposed to be keeping her eye on. If Cassidy requested a summary, she could let her know that Delfina was an excellent typist and knew her way around a mouse. She would occasionally catch something she knew up on the screen for a moment, but then Delfina would close whatever email account she was snooping in and would move on to something heavy in text that was too far away for even Snow's keen eyes to make out.

Cassidy hadn't been gone for very long when the door to Delfina's apartment opened. Snow perked up when she recognized her girlfriend's footfalls over the carpet. Cassidy's scent reached her nose, warm and vital, and she inhaled deeply. It had been unnerving to sit next to Stiletto but smell only Delfina. She would never get used to that odd vampire trait.

When Cassidy placed a hand on Snow's shoulder, she covered it with her own.

"How are we doing, time-wise?" Cassidy asked.

"I've transferred the contents of your credit union account," Delfina said, without taking her eyes from the screen. The pace of her typing flagged for a moment, then started back up. "Low-hanging fruit first. The banks are going to be tougher nuts to crack, but I have a decent chunk of funds hanging out in a crypto wallet for you."

"We're on the blockchain?" Cassidy sounded disgusted. "I don't want to be associated with that."

"Relax, I'm not minting you a portfolio of NFTs. I'm just routing your money through a few wallets. When it comes out the other side, it'll be nice and clean. This is a way faster way to launder it than sinking it in laundromats or a Wisconsin daycare."

"Wisconsin daycare?" Snow didn't recognize the reference.

"There used to be all sorts of scams related to daycares, especially in poorer areas." Delfina waved her hand. "I didn't think you'd want to go through the rigmarole of applying for a license, so we're going crypto instead."

"Mm." Cassidy was not at all impressed.

Delfina stopped typing and swiveled around in her chair. "Have you seen enough?"

"Not until I have a bank statement," Cassidy said.

"I can get you that, but it's going to take some time yet." Delfina looked over at Stiletto. "It'll take longer with an audience."

The vampire smiled, her lips tight. "We have an empty apartment, if you'd like to stay until Delfina is ready."

Snow stiffened, and Cassidy squeezed her shoulder reassuringly.

"No offense, but you keep talking about the wolven shortage at Faint. Of course I trust you, but the other vampires…" Cassidy shrugged. "And you're so new to your position."

Silence descended on the room. Delfina's face went blank, but Snow could smell her wariness. It wasn't full-blown fear, but she was concerned. There was no such indication from Stiletto. She already held herself with the preternatural stillness many vampires developed, and her face might as well have been a mask.

"You could stay in my room," the hacker said. She turned back to her keyboard.

Snow looked over at Cassidy, raising one eyebrow. She could use the sleep. Doing so under a vampire nightclub wasn't ideal, but it would be better than finding somewhere safe in the van.

As if she could read Snow's mind, Cassidy nodded thoughtfully. "That'll work," she said. Her jaw clenched as she tried to stifle a yawn.

"Down the hall, across from the bathroom," Delfina said. She pointed vaguely toward the door to her office. "Now get out so I can work."

Snow stifled a snort of amusement but couldn't quite hold it back at Cassidy's automatic bristling from being told what to do. She snagged her girlfriend's arm. Cassidy was willing to be pulled from the room.

The apartment wasn't so large that the hacker's vague instructions were difficult to follow. The bedroom was a decent size, especially compared to Snow's most regular sleeping quarters. She'd loved sleeping in the VW bus, but even she had to admit that it hadn't exactly been roomy.

The furnishings were of good quality, but nothing fancy. One wall held a number of boxes labeled "clothes-bedroom." Through the partially open closet door, Snow could make out only a few items on hangers. How long since Delfina moved in down here? The place smelled like her, but the rooms were all at different levels of moved in to.

Cassidy sat on the edge of the bed and stared down at the floor.

"Tired?" Snow perched next to her.

"Yeah." Cassidy kicked off one of her shoes, then the other.

"Me too." Snow bent down and undid her laces. By the time she'd stripped down to her T-shirt, Cassidy was already under the covers. She tried not to grimace as she slid between the sheets. Delfina's scent covered them. The sheets were clean enough, but they'd been slept in. She didn't like being buried in a stranger's stench.

Snow stretched out and tried to get comfortable. The attempt to relax on her right side didn't work out, so she switched to her left. That was no better. She flopped onto her back.

"Problems?" Cassidy's grin was audible in the question. She reached out and pulled Snow to her, molding their bodies together.

When she wrapped her arm around Snow's waist and snugged her in tightly, Snow couldn't keep from sighing. Cassidy was there. They would keep each other safe. Some of the day's tension started to leach from her body.

"I'm good. This is good." Her words were muzzy, even to herself. The stress of the past few weeks drained from her. It was temporary, she knew that, but for the moment, it was the best she had, and she wasn't going to squander the opportunity. She let her body melt back against Cassidy.

Her girlfriend was also relaxing, and she snuggled her chin into the crook of Snow's shoulder. But even as Cassidy drowsed off, she didn't let go.

CHAPTER TWENTY-ONE

The rap on the door to the hacker's room was all it took to wake them.

"What's going on?" Cassidy called.

"Your money's all yours again." It was Delfina. "Come say hello to your cash."

"Give us a minute."

There was no answer except the shuffle of footsteps away from the door.

It took only a few seconds to get her clothing back on. Snow was a little slower, and Cassidy tried not to fret. The moment of truth was coming up. Either they had a hacker, or they'd be starting the search over again and at a big disadvantage.

Delfina's computer lair was much as they'd left it, save for the addition of multiple cans of various energy drinks that now occupied one corner of her desk. It didn't seem she had a favorite brand. Only now did Cassidy notice the mini fridge under the desk. It shared a color and style with the equipment in the room.

"You're back." The caffeinated beverages had done little to keep bags from forming under Delfina's eyes, but her knee jiggled with an excess of energy.

"We are." Cassidy stepped to one side, giving Snow a protected corner to slot into, one that she could bar with her body if things went bad.

Snow sidled in next to her, then did that peculiar trick where she melted off everyone's radar. Even Cassidy, who had become attuned to her girlfriend's presence, could easily forget about her if she wasn't paying close attention.

"Good." Delfina stretched, then turned back to the screens that were still the room's only source of illumination. She clicked around with her mouse and keyboard, then maximized a window to take up a bank of four monitors. Even across the room, Cassidy could see that this was a bank account's balance page. At the bottom was a significant balance, but it wasn't quite right.

"That's not all of it."

"Of course not." Delfina clicked again and cycled through two more screens, one showing an account at a different bank and another showing a page at an investment site. "Figured I could invest the money you were setting aside for taxes, insurance, and utilities."

"Um." Cassidy peered at the screen with its charts and graphs. It was a good idea. As much as it pained her to admit it, they weren't going to need that cash to be liquid for a while, and it made sense that it should be somewhere that could make them some money. Hopefully they wouldn't have to do without it for too long. "Go ahead and pick some starter stocks. I'll come back when I have time and round out the portfolio."

"We got a stockbroker here," Delfina said as she swiveled back to face the monitors. "La di dah."

"Gotta get some use out of that education." It was something she should have thought to look into before this, frankly. The pack hadn't done much investing, but Cassidy knew she could do something with the money to grow it. If they didn't spend it getting everyone back, that was.

"I take it this means you're happy with Delfina's demonstration of her skills." Stiletto's smooth voice interrupted her nascent plans for diversifying the North Side Pack's portfolio.

"I'm convinced she has what it takes to shift money around under the noses of a bunch of banks. I can only assume her skills extend to other areas." Not that she had any choice. Delfina might turn out to be a thin straw to grasp. Hopefully she didn't break when the Alphas put her to use.

"Excellent." Stiletto's lips stretched into her thin smile, the one that radiated far more menace than humor. "We can discuss payment."

"Payment?" Cassidy turned on her heel to glare at the vampire. "You said I could come to you for support."

"I did. However, without knowing what kind of aid you might need, I wasn't in a position to put a price on it. Now I am."

Snow stepped in close and slid her arm around Cassidy's waist. As much as she wanted to lean into the support, Cassidy couldn't bring herself to do so, not in front of the vamp. Her wolf bristled at Stiletto's mercenary turn, but she wasn't hostile. Yet. There was no point in reacting until they knew what they were dealing with.

"What's on the table, then?"

Even as Cassidy inhaled her next breath, Stiletto was standing next to her. Air from the vampire's sudden movement washed across her face and was followed by the touch of cool fingers a moment later.

"We've had a dearth of *wolven* blood these past few weeks." Stiletto caressed her cheek, then trailed her fingertips down over the swell of Cassidy's jaw to land lightly on the pulse in her neck.

Cassidy licked her lips. While Stiletto lacked the lush promise that Carla had oozed, there was no denying her charisma. Dark-brown eyes flashed deep red, drawing Cassidy into their depths with far more subtlety than her predecessor had chosen to wield. She found herself wanting to impress this vampire, to please her in such a way that her reward would be…

Her center clenched, and her face heated in equal parts lust and embarrassment. Snow would be able to smell her excitement. That thought alone should have quashed her rapidly rising ardor, but instead it added an edge to the thrill that wasn't at all unpleasant.

"You seem interested," Stiletto whispered into her ear. She let one fingertip ride on the galloping pulse point.

If it would please you… Cassidy wrenched her mind away from the thought. That wasn't her.

"How about a favor?" Her voice was rough, and she leaned into it. Let Stiletto believe she was offended at the thought.

"You can do me a favor." Amusement tinged the vampire's tone. "A little bit of your blood. Your kind restores it so quickly it won't slow you down for more than a few minutes. Half an hour at most."

"Huh." That was true. What was the big deal? Her body would make more blood. Besides, they really needed Delfina's skills. Any chance they had of getting their packmates back rested with her. "I'm not just going to give you carte blanche on my bodily fluids. How much do you want?"

Stiletto's lips curved in a smile so sharp it was nearly feral. "*I don't want your blood.*" She slipped her arm around Cassidy's waist, supplanting Snow's embrace.

The lone wolf tightened her grip for a moment, then released it when Cassidy shook her head.

"Are you sure about this?" Snow's question was a murmur meant only for Cassidy's ears, but the vampire's grin widened when she heard it.

"We need a hacker." There would be no other deals forthcoming. Cassidy stared at Stiletto's mouth, noting the long white fangs against plump dark lips. "If you don't want my blood, then why are we talking?"

"You won't be feeding me. You'll be feeding a brace of those who have demonstrated their loyalty."

"A brace?"

Stiletto held up her hand, all fingers extended.

"Five of them?" Cassidy's lust dissipated as if it had never been, leaving behind clammy shaking hands and a feeling in the pit of her stomach that was all too familiar. Her wolf snarled and snapped within her. They were cornered, helpless. For a moment, five distorted wolven faces looked down at her.

Stiletto tilted her head and considered Cassidy, her eyes seeing too much for the wolf's comfort. "I promised them blood from the source." The vampire leaned in and breathed the words into Cassidy's ears. "I can't go back on that. I can instruct them to feed on you one at a time." The whispers weren't an attempt to be sexy; there was no fanning of the flames of her ardor. The vampire's tone was on the sympathetic side of dispassion.

Cassidy clenched her jaw. Her wolf subsided enough that she could think. "I can do three."

Stiletto considered the offer for a moment. "Four, or we have no deal."

"Cassidy?" Snow's anxiety scoured the inside of her nose with spiky blue barbs.

"I'm okay." She looked back at her girlfriend and summoned a smile from somewhere. "Really, I promise." Cassidy took a deep breath. "Four it is."

CHAPTER TWENTY-TWO

Despite her brave words, Cassidy didn't feel very okay as she was escorted through silent halls. The wolf paced under her skin, ready to break through at any sign of danger. Or more danger. It felt like they were in plenty of peril already.

They left the employee—no, attendant—apartments and mounted the stairs past the main floor of the club. The second floor was as expensively appointed as the first, but more muted. The excess on display below gave way to understated elegance that somehow screamed more of money than all of the sumptuous gilding the first floor had to offer.

"One at a time," Stiletto said as they made their way down a hall lined with plush gray carpet that sucked the sound out of each footstep, even to Cassidy's sensitive ears. A line of vampires stared at her. Deep within their pupils was the same mote of deep crimson that lurked within Stiletto's. How had they known to gather here? Had Stiletto been so certain that Cassidy would acquiesce?

"Through here." The vampire opened a door wrapped in quilted leather to reveal an understated waiting room. "They'll come in singly, feed, and leave. Those are their instructions. If you want more, you'll have to ask for it."

"The blood meal will be more than enough." Cassidy took a deep breath, then stepped into the room.

"If you say so," Stiletto said as she passed. The smirk was clear in her voice, and Cassidy refused to meet her gaze, not wanting to see it plastered on the vamp's face. "The first one will be in momentarily. Make yourself comfortable."

There were plenty of places to sit. Did she choose the tall wingback chair swathed in dark red velvet or the daybed heaped with tasseled pillows? There was even an upholstered window seat, but a quick peek past the heavy curtains showed nothing but wall.

The chair was the way to go. No one would be cozying up to her there. This was a business transaction, nothing more. Cassidy didn't want to encourage any idea that it might be more than that.

She lowered herself to the seat, her heartbeat a hollow thud in her ears. With Cassidy seated and no longer moving, the wolf's pacing increased to near frenzy. She swirled around inside of Cassidy, who had to bite down on the inside of her lip to maintain control. Would a vamp want to take blood from her if she was in wolf form? Surely, they wouldn't appreciate a mouthful of fur to go along with their blood meal.

She couldn't stop the strangled snicker that bubbled up in her throat. It dried up when the door opened and in stepped a white man so tall, he stooped a bit as he stepped through the threshold. He was a couple of inches shy of actually touching it, so perhaps the move was one born out of habit, from a time when the height of doorframes wasn't dictated by building code.

The wolf snarled, as if to say now was not the time to be concerned with local ordinances.

"Alpha." The vampire's voice was deep and too sonorous for his slender frame. He touched a hand delicately to his chest and bowed slightly in her direction. "You honor me."

"Do I?" The question was little more than a croak, but the vampire quirked a brow in understanding.

"You do." In a blur nearly too quick to follow, he was standing to one side of the chair. "We are to show you every deference." He grinned slightly, his lips parting just enough to see lengthened eye teeth. "Of course, I would regardless. Unlike some of my...compatriots." An accent Cassidy couldn't place shaded his words.

"I appreciate it?" This was not how she'd expected things to go.

"Shall we start?" He leaned over her, his eyes pooling into the deep red depths she'd come to understand meant a vampire was ready to feed.

"Yeah." Cassidy lifted one hand, hoping he'd take the hint.

The vampire trailed one hand down Cassidy's arm. Even through the fabric of her shirt, his cool touch raised a wave of gooseflesh in its wake. The shiver spread up her arm and down the right side of her body, raising even more of the small, tingly bumps along her side and back, all the way down her thigh. He grasped her arm, cradling it above and below the elbow, and slowly raised it to his mouth, keeping his gaze locked with hers.

All Cassidy could see were his eyes, even as he opened his lips, licking them in deliberate anticipation. He caught her continued stare and winked once, then drove the fangs into her arm.

"Oh god." Cassidy grasped at the arm of the chair as sensation curled and crested within her. The twin points of agony were so close together they nearly felt like one. The vampire's throat worked, pulling her blood forth from the small punctures, each suck sending a small spike of pain through her that was answered by a throb between her legs. She didn't want to like this. She screwed her eyes shut to close out the sight of the man suckling at her arm, small rivulets of blood welling up around where his teeth pierced her skin and dripping down to stain the fabric of the chair's arm.

Each pull inched her a little higher toward ecstasy, but before she could attain that peak, the vampire was raising his head.

"Exquisite," he whispered, then bent to lick away the stray drops that had escaped him. He waited a moment, as the small wounds were already starting to heal, then ran his tongue over the punctures. Cassidy's ardor had begun to diminish, but it came roaring back. "Is there anything I can do for you?" His tone dripped with the knowledge of the heat that suffused her body. His own face had grown ruddy, his lips fuller and redder.

The wolf wasn't averse to what he was offering. They had a need, one that gripped them both. In her mind, it would be a simple coupling, then they'd be done. Cassidy wasn't so certain that the vamps would let them go once they got their claws in her. She didn't know if she'd want them to.

"I'm good." She pulled her arm from his grasp, and he made no attempt to keep it.

"Pity," was all he said, before he was standing by the door, without having crossed the room. "Maybe some other time."

There won't be another time, Cassidy vowed in her head, but she said nothing aloud. How was she going to endure three more feedings without begging one of them to fuck her?

The vampire let himself out, closing the door softly behind him.

Cassidy breathed deeply, doing her best to slow her tripping heart rate. The wolf was still watchful, but less frantic than she'd been. Now that they'd experienced their first feed, the wolf wondered what their previous fuss had been about. She wasn't thrilled about how exposed they'd been during the act but reckoned they could pull themselves together quickly if necessary.

When the door opened again, Cassidy had to swallow the whimper that rose in her throat. An Asian woman with an asymmetrical bob of black hair floated into the room.

"Cassidy." She smiled down at the floor, then looked up, catching Cassidy's eyes with a glance that promised so much she had to grab both arms of the chair to keep from getting up to meet her.

She kept it together through that feed and turned down the vampire's offer after she lifted her mouth from the soft flesh directly above Cassidy's left collarbone. The vampire trailed her finger along the back of Cassidy's neck and twined it quickly in her hair before letting go and seeing herself out.

The third vampire was a white woman with intense gaze and presence to rival one of the Alphas. She insinuated nothing, but her frank offer to fuck Cassidy until she screamed was as tempting as the previous more delicate propositions. Part of her wanted the woman to stand over her and do what she wished to her, but the wolf was having none of it. She went away empty-handed, leaving Cassidy panting and desperately trying to regain her composure.

By the time the fourth vampire—a Black man whose beard and build reminded her uncomfortably of Hammer—left, Cassidy counted it as a personal victory that she hadn't taken any of them up on the offer for something more than her blood. The last one had seemed particularly disappointed. His eyes had flashed to a brighter red for a moment, and she'd wavered on the edge of accepting him before remembering that anything more than her agreement with Stiletto could be dangerous. Her pack didn't need someone at its head who was addicted to what the vampires could offer. And if her mind was so addled for want of a vampire's touch, would she even be able to wrest them free of their kidnappers?

"Suit yourself," he'd said, then the door was closing behind him.

The deep breathing exercises weren't doing much to calm her down. The heat between her legs was nearly unbearable. She slid a hand down the front of her pants, fingers tangling in wet curls before closing them over her mound. She hadn't even touched her clit, but the simple proximity wrenched a guttural moan from her throat.

The door opened again, and Cassidy closed her eyes. She couldn't take one more. There wasn't supposed to be another. Hot tears leaked out from under her eyelids and scalded twin trails down her face. It wasn't fair. How was she supposed to withstand this?

* * *

Snow watched the door from across the hall, where she'd posted up on the other side of a half-column. The fourth vampire barely looked her way as she did everything she could to shrink her sense of self down into her own body. No one had said she couldn't come along and lurk while Cassidy was paying Stiletto's price.

Pulled along in the vampire's wake was the smell of Cassidy's arousal. There was no smell of sex accompanying it. Snow shook her head. Her girlfriend had to be in agony right now. That had been the fourth and supposedly final vampire. She didn't see any more queuing up for their turn, but she forced herself to wait a few more seconds to be certain.

Stiletto was even newer to being head of her people than Cassidy was. While Snow knew less about the hierarchy of vampires than she did about the wolven, she was still impressed by what she saw. All four vampires had been old and powerful. By her mental reckoning, sunrise was already upon them, though likely not by much. This deep in the building, there was little chance the light would penetrate, but younger vampires would be compelled to seek dark places deep in the earth and to sleep while the sun was out. She didn't know how much longer they could resist the urge, but none of Stiletto's chosen were among that number. Wolven blood, and that of an Alpha, would bind them that much more tightly to her, and she'd gain a reputation among her people for being generous with those who stood at her back without stabbing it. Snow hadn't thought Cassidy would ever agree to allowing her blood to be taken, and yet Stiletto had maneuvered her into a position where she was forced to agree to giving blood to not one, but four vampires. It was impressive—and a little frightening. She would have to keep an eye on this new Vampire Lord. Preferably from a distance.

No one else showed up, not even Stiletto, who would presumably tell Cassidy that her duty had been fulfilled. Snow crossed the hall and pulled open the door to the room where Cassidy waited.

Her arousal was nearly strong enough to taste, and on its heels came a spike of something too close to despair for Snow's comfort.

"Cassidy?" She hurried to her girlfriend, kneeling in front of the tall chair and taking note of the unbuttoned pants and the hand shoved down their front.

The Alpha opened weeping eyes, relief slackening her face when their gazes met. "What are you doing here?" she whispered.

Snow's throat ached with sympathy at the strain in her girlfriend's voice. "I came to check on you. How are you holding together?"

Cassidy's laugh was hollow. "I don't think I can walk."

"Did they take that much blood?" Fury wasn't an emotion she was accustomed to, but that didn't stop the rage from welling up inside her chest. Her jaw ached as her wolf tried to ascend.

"Not that." Cassidy looked down at her, dismay in her eyes. "If I don't come soon, I'm going to…" She heaved a long sigh, then inhaled deeply through her nostrils. "That didn't help as much as I thought it would." Her eyes brightened from brown and muddy hazel to bright red and blue around the edges.

Snow hesitated before placing a hand on Cassidy's thigh. "I can help you with that, if you want."

Cassidy's eyes flared to full brilliance before she clamped them shut. "I can't ask that of you." She tried to move her leg out of Snow's gentle grasp.

"You're not asking me. I'm offering."

"You don't want to do this."

"I don't want to see you in such discomfort. You're in pain." Snow placed her other hand on the opposite leg and squeezed gently. "You need this. Let me do this for you."

More tears leaked out from under Cassidy's eyelids, but she allowed her legs to fall open in mute surrender.

"Good." Snow stood up enough to lightly kiss Cassidy's lips.

Her girlfriend's mouth opened under hers, and Snow assumed an initiative she rarely took. She delved into Cassidy's mouth, teasing the tip of her girlfriend's tongue with her own, deepening their embrace in a way she knew Cassidy would like.

This was all about Cassidy and what would satisfy her. Snow would get nothing from it. Nor did she expect to. This was an act of mercy for someone she cared about very much.

She ran her hand down the front of Cassidy's stomach, over tense muscles. The Alpha removed her hand from her pants, allowing Snow access. She skimmed past the already open button at Cassidy's waistband, then slowly lowered the zipper. The scent of Cassidy's arousal was already heavy in the air, but it spiked as Snow took her time gaining access to the contents of Cassidy's pants.

Her girlfriend panted, even as Snow slowly inserted her hand down past the waistband, sliding lower until she felt the curls that guarded Cassidy's mound. The act wasn't a difficult one; she'd performed it on herself more often than she cared to acknowledge. Doing it to someone else was fairly novel, but with Cassidy's reactions to guide her, Snow knew she could bring her Alpha to completion.

The tangled hairs were slick with Cassidy's fluids, and Snow's fingers skated through them, parting her folds and gaining full access to Cassidy's sex. She trailed the tip of one finger around the swollen prominence of Cassidy's clit, drawing forth another moan that shaded into a relieved sob. Encouraged by her girlfriend's response, she repeated the motion once, twice, a third time, then froze as Cassidy grabbed her wrist and thrust herself against Snow's hand.

"There," Cassidy panted. "Right there. Oh god, keep doing that. Don't stop."

Snow redoubled her efforts, sliding her fingers back and forth along either side of Cassidy's clit as her girlfriend threw her head back against the chair. Her head thrashed left and right as she whimpered, nearly in time with Snow's strokes. Cassidy's thighs clamped down around Snow's hand, holding it in place as Cassidy stared sightlessly upward, then screamed her release at the ceiling a moment later.

The smell of sex filled Snow's nostrils, and she tried not to wrinkle her nose. When she moved to pull her hand back, Cassidy opened her eyes to look at her.

"I'm not quite done. Is that all right?"

The quiet question nearly undid Snow. Even in the midst of Cassidy's ferocious need, she still had the wherewithal to consider Snow's boundaries. Snow nodded.

"Thank you. Just keep doing what you've been doing." Cassidy lifted her hips and slid her pants down past her knees.

Snow kept her eyes locked on Cassidy's. Her girlfriend shuddered when she opened her thighs and the room's comparatively cool air hit her steaming sex.

"Go on," Cassidy whispered. "Do that thing again."

Snow grazed the tip of Cassidy's clit with her finger, causing the Alpha to bite down on her lower lip. Her eyes rolled back into her head for a moment. She panted, and the smell of her lust, which had subsided a bit, ratcheted up again, filling Snow's nostrils, overwhelming everything else.

She brought her other finger into play, straddling Cassidy's clit in the way that had been so effective a minute ago.

"Right there," Cassidy grunted. "I just need…" She brought her hand up and spread the folds of her vulva with two fingers, sliding them up and down her slit to coat them liberally with her own juices, then pushed them inside her vagina. She gasped aloud at the penetration, then withdrew her fingers and plunged them deep inside again.

Snow watched, entranced at the way the fingers disappeared up inside her, at the tension that was building within her. She matched Cassidy's movements, running her fingers up and down beside her clit in the same rhythm with which Cassidy penetrated herself. With her free hand, Cassidy grasped the back of Snow's arm. Not the one that was currently engaged; she wasn't so far gone as to impede half of what was bringing her so much pleasure.

"Yes…" Cassidy whined. "Oh god, yes. Like that. Oh god, Snow. You don't…You feel so good. You're—"

Snow never found out what she was, as Cassidy's barely coherent sexual ramblings devolved into complete gibberish. She kept up her part of the strange dance in which they were engaged, fascinated at the play of sensation and emotion across Cassidy's face and body. She was doing that. It went on for longer than she would have believed, knowing how much sexual frustration Cassidy had built up.

When the final release came, her Alpha's entire body stiffened and trembled as she let loose a scream that was more wolf than human. The roar echoed in Snow's ears and around the room, as Cassidy sat upright, her back arched and unseeing eyes staring into nothing. Then, like a marionette whose strings had been cut in one slice, her body collapsed, leaning forward against Snow, who had to scramble to keep her from pitching forward.

"Are you okay?" She pushed back damp tendrils of hair from her girlfriend's forehead.

"Hmm?" Cassidy blinked up at her.

"Are you all right? That seemed…intense."

"Uh, yeah. I think so. I may have grayed out a little at the end there." She smiled and stretched languorously, seemingly unbothered by the fact that her pants were down around her ankles. "That was amazing."

"I'm glad it worked for you." And she was, though part of her tensed, waiting for the request to do that regularly.

Cassidy laid her head on Snow's shoulder. "I know that was hard for you, and I really appreciate it."

"I couldn't leave you in that state."

"I'll have to make sure it doesn't get to that point again. I don't want you to have to feel like you need to step in like that."

"I was happy to do it. To help you."

"And I love you for that." The words were slightly slurred. Cassidy relaxed against her, suddenly boneless as she drifted off into a postcoital nap.

"Oh, Cassidy." Snow maneuvered her girlfriend back into the chair. How she wished that the L word had come up in a different context. What did Cassidy mean by that? Did she love that Snow would spring to her aid when she was in need, or did she love how sex with her had felt? The first she could work with. The second would lead only to her own heartbreak.

CHAPTER TWENTY-THREE

The back of the van was so stuffed with equipment that Delfina was wedged into a gap space between the front seats and the piles of boxes. Cassidy had asked if she preferred to sit in the passenger seat. After all, she or Snow in wolf form could make themselves comfortable in places that weren't great for humans. The hacker had brushed her off and was currently slumbering, her face propped against a monitor box. Her many energy drinks had worn off about an hour outside of Chicago.

The rest of their drive across Illinois and into Iowa had been uneventful. Snow drove, and she'd been quiet since they'd left Faint, hacker in tow. She had been helpful, if reserved, as they accompanied Delfina from seedy electronics store to pawnshop to big box electronics store to get what little she couldn't get at the previous locations. The hacker had been chattering a mile a minute, full of interesting facts about why it was best to get things at mom-and-pop stores, which needed much more community support than soulless corporate chains. Cassidy didn't disagree, but it had been difficult to get a word in edgewise as Delfina continued to ride the high of her caffeine overdose.

It had been late morning by the time they'd gotten on the road, and now that they were back in Iowa and nearly to the prison, it was midafternoon. They needed to swing by and pick up Hammer before heading to the accommodations Delfina had set up for them. Cassidy looked back at the stacks of boxes and couldn't imagine how or where the South Shore Alpha would be able to squeeze in.

Snow took them up the road to the prison, then past it. Cassidy reached over and placed a hand on her leg. She was rewarded with a quick smile and a squeeze of the hand before Snow had to let go to maneuver the van onto the overgrown track they'd found a couple of days previous. She put the car in park near where they'd parked the last time.

"Now what?" she asked. Delfina didn't twitch, either when the car stopped or at Snow's words.

"We wait, I guess." Cassidy opened the passenger side window and stuck her head out. She inhaled deeply of the clean Iowa air. It was a far cry from the polluted and sometimes putrid air of the Windy City. It was a good thing it was so windy there. If the stench lingered all the time, she didn't know that any wolven could have lived with it long term.

"Anything?" Snow asked.

"He's been through a couple of times." She nodded toward the base of a large tree. "He's claimed that." She wrinkled her nose at the strong smell of Hammer's urine and had to quash the urge to relieve herself over it. The two of them weren't on the best of terms at the moment and getting into an actual pissing match wouldn't help that.

"Yeah, I'm getting that now," Snow said. She scrubbed her nose with the back of her hand. "Might as well get comfortable." She squished herself down into her seat and closed her eyes.

Cassidy couldn't blame her for wanting a bit of shuteye. Her own attention was drawn back toward the tall walls of the supposedly decommissioned prison. If they were just going to sit around, surely it wouldn't hurt anything for her to take on furform, then get a little closer and see if she could pick up on any more of her pack.

"Don't do it," Snow murmured, not opening her eyes.

"Do what?"

The innocent voice wasn't convincing enough to keep Snow from cracking her eyelids and giving her a sidelong look. "If I know you, you're about to decide that you should go check things out."

"Would that be so bad?"

"Only if you get caught." Snow's eyes slid shut again. "I'm sure you can guarantee that won't happen." The irony was so thick in her voice that Cassidy could have poured it over waffles.

"I won't get caught."

Delfina snorted from behind the passenger's seat.

"Okay, fine. I guess I'm overruled." Did she really want to be told what to do by a human? Especially one who was beholden to vampires, at that. Her wolf rumbled, not satisfied that they should acquiesce so easily, but not really wanting to expend the energy it would take to put someone in their place.

"Fortunately, we won't have to rely on you keeping your nature in check much longer." Snow lifted her nose and inhaled. "Hammer is coming."

"His name is Hammer?" Delfina pushed herself up so she could see past the backs of the front seats. "Where is he?"

Her question was answered when Hammer pushed his massive shaggy head in through the passenger side window.

Cassidy grimaced as his scent invaded her space. "Hi, Hammer." She gestured to Delfina, peering out between the seats, her mouth partially agape. "She's our new hacker."

Delfina reached a hand across the back of the seat. It might have been an attempt at a handshake, or it could have been an invitation to smell her.

Hammer expelled the air from his lungs in a loud whuff that probably sounded like a greeting to the human. Cassidy knew it as the kind of sound a grown wolf might use to dismiss a cub, a warning that further pestering would result in physical chastisement.

"Pleased to meet you." Delfina shifted to include Snow in her next statement. "I've set up a base of operations for us. It's a county over. I've memorized the directions. Before we get anywhere near where we'll be staying, I need your phones."

Silence reigned inside the van.

"I don't have one," Snow finally said.

Hammer grunted.

Cassidy tried not to grind her teeth. "Mine's been on airplane mode since we crossed the Iowa border. Surely that's good enough."

Delfina turned to face her, sticking out her hand in mute insistence.

"You don't understand—" She bit off the rest of the protest. How much did she want to tell the vampires' lackey that she was in contact with her mom?

"Everyone always has a good reason why they get to be the exception," Delfina said. "All it takes is one slip and we're up to our necks in Feds, military, the mob, white supremacist domestic terrorist cells, you name it."

Cassidy sent a desperate look over at her girlfriend. Snow's eyebrows creased in a sympathetic frown, but she shook her head as if to say she couldn't back Cassidy up on this one.

"You brought me on for what I know." Delfina reached her hand closer. "Let me do what I'm good at."

A deep rumble started in Hammer's throat. Hackles that Cassidy didn't have in skinform tried to raise along her back and shoulders, but she shoved the phone toward the hacker with poor grace.

"Good." The phone disappeared into a pocket. "It was smart of you to put it in airplane mode."

It felt too much like a mollifying pat, so Cassidy kept her mouth shut. Hammer panted happily in the window, no doubt enjoying the taste of her aggravation.

"Hope you don't mind getting cozy, big guy." Delfina directed the last to the South Shore Alpha. "It's a little tight back here."

"He can probably squish in up front," Cassidy said. She wasn't going to enjoy being in such close proximity with him, not feuding as they were, but he was still important to the success of their endeavor.

Hammer grunted again, then dropped to the ground. The sounds of his shift were familiar, and moments later he was standing next to the truck, naked as the day he'd been born. He showed no sign of being affected by the cold.

"I'll get in back," Snow said. She was crawling over the driver's seat before Cassidy could object.

Cassidy climbed over behind the wheel before Hammer could climb in. At least she could be the one driving.

Delfina shoved some of the boxes around, opening up enough space for the lone wolf, who settled in, making herself much smaller than Cassidy would have given any human-shaped person credit for a few months previous.

Hammer had pulled open the door and was settling himself in the passenger seat. He stared straight out the front windshield.

"It's about time you got back," he said. He slicked one hand down the opposite arm to remove some of the fluids that remained, then flicked it out the open window. "Our people are definitely being held in that place."

CHAPTER TWENTY-FOUR

Hammer's words jolted Cassidy, demanding that she act. She turned to look in the direction of the prison. Her wolf needed to move, but she held onto the steering wheel, refusing to give in to the wolf's demands.

"Did you see them? Was it everyone? Who's holding them?"

Hammer held up his hands. "Didn't see. Heard. I recognized the voices of some of my own, but the call was taken up by many. There were dozens." He stroked his chin, ebony fingers disappearing into the dense black beard. "The howling didn't last long, and it didn't happen again."

"When did they do it?" Snow asked.

"Maybe a couple of hours after you all left."

"The timing is interesting." The muscles in Cassidy's thighs flexed. She wished she could get out of the van and stretch her legs. The wolf needed to pace as much as she did. Instead, she started up the van and set it in reverse. "What does it mean?"

"I don't know." Hammer shook his head. "But the place was buzzing like a hornet's nest for a while after. Lots of humans were moving around inside, some outside. They had guns."

"So there's a big guard contingent." Cassidy shifted her gaze in the rearview mirror to lock eyes with Snow. "I'm glad we didn't go for the frontal assault. I wish we could find out exactly what we're up against."

"Isn't that where I come in?" Delfina hung over the back of the seat, making no attempt to disguise her frank perusal of Hammer's naked form. She waved a hand toward Cassidy. "Take a left at the bottom of the hill."

Cassidy nodded and took the turn carefully.

"I suppose it is," Hammer said to the hacker's question. "So long as you know your stuff. And are trustworthy." He leaned forward, subtly sniffing the air as she responded.

"Hey, you all are the experts on werewolves. I've got the tech covered, and I'm damn good at what I do." Delfina relaxed a bit back into her little nook, but not so far down that she couldn't see out the windshield.

"Wolven." Cassidy firmed her grip on the steering wheel.

"Hmm?" Delfina raised an eyebrow in question.

"Could you not?" Cassidy lifted a hand to block the hacker's very forthright stare. If not for the assault of Hammer's scent, it probably wouldn't have seemed so aggressive, but now she was on edge. The last thing they needed was the wolf forcing her way to the surface and disemboweling their tech expert, especially not while Cassidy was driving.

"Not what?"

"The eye contact. It's a little…aggressive." She allowed enough of the wolf to bleed through that she knew her eyes would be glowing, and her teeth lengthened. Cassidy displayed the sharp fangs.

"Oh." Delfina dropped her eyes.

"Thanks." The sibilants were blunted by her teeth, but it helped drive the message home, so Cassidy made no attempt to hide the change to her speech. "We call ourselves wolven. Werewolf is considered impolite among our kind. It would be like calling a vampire a fangbanger to their face."

"Ah." Delfina nodded gravely. "Thank you for the clarification."

"Speaking of fangbangers…" Hammer's nasty grin telegraphed that the insult was deliberate. "How do we know you won't put your masters' needs before our own?"

"My masters' needs are your own," Delfina said. "I've been given an assignment by them, and you're it."

"No little extra secret bits of the job? No setting us up for failure?" Hammer made no attempt to hide that he was smelling for any signs of dishonesty. He watched the hacker closely. Snow was also leaning toward Delfina.

"The Lord wants you to succeed as much as you want to," the hacker said. She met Hammer's stare for a few heartbeats, then looked away. The air tasted of truth. "I am not your enemy. I will do everything in my power to help you get your family back."

"Huh." Hammer leaned back, contemplating her for a long while before looking back out the front windshield.

Silence descended inside the van.

"No sign of the twins," Hammer said after the quiet had gone from uncomfortable to unbearable. "I can fill you in on what I saw while you were gone."

"You'll have to repeat it all for Marrow and Bone," Snow said. She tossed him a small throw blanket. From the wrinkles, it had been wedged somewhere.

Hammer dropped the throw over his lap. "I have no problem with that. I'll hold off on my ideas for getting into that place until they get back with their getaway driver." He glanced Cassidy's way, meeting her gaze and holding it. "How long do we give them before we get started ourselves?"

"We need to do some recon, so I guess until we've gotten a good look at the place and pulled our plan together. If they're not back by then, we'll have to move on." Cassidy chewed on her lower lip. "The longer we take, the more chance there is that they'll move our wolves."

"Or start eliminating them."

Cassidy glared at the scenery out the windshield. "Do you have any evidence of that?" She groped for the points of light that made up her inner starscape. At first feel, it seemed complete, with the glaring exception of Ruri's star. She reached out to them, one after another, and cradled them to her so she could get a good handle on who was there and who might be missing. They were all there but one.

"Nothing like that." Hammer's mouth twisted into a dissatisfied grimace. "But we still don't know why they want them. Clearly, they've gone to some effort not to kill too many off. From my pack, only Briella is gone."

"And Marquis," Snow reminded him quietly.

"And Marquis. Even that predated their sweep. We'd be foolish to assume that whatever premise they're operating under will last forever. Recommissioning a prison is no small thing. I doubt even the military can keep up a penitentiary for wolven secret forever."

"I'm missing Jimmy," Cassidy said. Snow reached over the seat and grasped her shoulder. "I don't know when he dropped off." She smacked the steering wheel with the palm of her hand. "I wish I could get a sense of how they're doing, not just if they're alive or not."

"It's better than wondering," Hammer said.

"Maybe." She blinked rapidly to keep the tears from obscuring her vision so much that she had to pull over. "I agree with you. The situation could change more quickly than we know. Hopefully Delfina can figure out how to monitor their communication pretty quickly."

"Until then…" Hammer glowered. "I hate waiting, but not knowing is worse."

"So, what did you see?" Cassidy asked. She scrubbed away the tear tracks on her cheeks.

"They're bussing people in. Some are guards, probably military, but I don't know for sure. They're also bringing in staff. That's a much smaller group."

"What's the camera situation?"

"They have plenty along the front and sides of the building, but since no one's done any yard maintenance outside the walls, I've been able to get pretty close without being seen. There are plenty of blind spots." Hammer sighed. "I've mostly kept away, just in case."

"And their schedule?"

"Three standard shifts for the guards. The staff are only around for two."

"But it's consistent."

"I don't have much data, but from what I've seen, it's lining up."

"That's something." Snow reached over and wrapped her hand around the back of Cassidy's neck. "Schedules can be exploited. It'll allow us to plan."

"Once Marrow and Bone are back, we can get down to it," Hammer said.

"We could start now," Cassidy offered. "What about recon?"

Hammer put his feet up on the dashboard. "Anything we come up with now will be speculation. Let's sleep on it, then get something concrete enough to actually work with."

The answer made sense, but Cassidy burned to do something, anything to forward their cause, to keep more of her wolven from dropping off her radar.

"We do this right, or not at all." Hammer crossed his arms over his chest. "No one is going to jeopardize anyone's wolves because they can't be patient."

"Yes, fine." Cassidy set her jaw, trying not to glare over at the other Alpha. "It's been a long day. I need to sleep on it. Maybe tomorrow... When the twins show up."

Hammer nodded. "Tomorrow."

* * *

Snow stood behind the van, the doors open while Delfina and Cassidy mounted the steps to the McMansion that was apparently their base for however long it took to launch their rescue operation.

"There's a lockbox on the handle," Cassidy announced.

"I have the code for that," Delfina said. Even from across the yard, her scent was faintly tinged with anxiety.

Snow wondered if she should clue the hacker in on exactly how much the wolven could pick up from her on scent alone. She was accustomed to being the odd one out of any group of her kind, and here was someone who was even stranger than she. Delfina would be at a serious disadvantage. But she belonged to the vampires, no matter her assurances that she wouldn't betray them. Maybe if they'd been dealing with Carla instead of Stiletto, they could have figured something out where the human would be on more even footing, but at the moment, it would be to their combined advantage if she wasn't too comfortable. Not that they wanted her floundering. There was a thin line to tread here: one where the hacker could be effective, but if she had some other instructions that could hurt Cassidy or Snow, or even the other Alphas, they'd be able to see it coming.

"So tell me about our hacker," Hammer said. He'd found an exceedingly wrinkled pair of sweatpants somewhere and was watching Delfina from across the yard.

Snow chewed at her lower lip. "She seems to know her stuff. She was able to retrieve North Side Pack's finances from the various banks that were holding them without tipping anyone off."

Hammer stroked his beard. "That's handy. I should talk to her. I haven't wanted to touch South Shore's money for similar reasons."

"Guess so." The less she said about Delfina, the better. Snow was prepared to be aggressively noncommittal about her.

On the front porch, Delfina entered the code into the lockbox, then retrieved the key. She let herself through the front door.

Cassidy looked back at Snow, giving her a quick nod before stepping in after the hacker. It seemed her girlfriend wanted to clear the house before she came in. That was fine with Snow, except the part where it left her mostly alone with her thoughts. Hammer didn't seem interested in further discussion, which just left Cassidy and her declaration of love after…

Snow's mind veered away from contemplating the act too closely. She was glad that it had made Cassidy feel good and had brought her the satisfaction she needed, but having love coupled with the act was troubling. The best way to move past it was by talking about it. She knew that, but she wanted to enjoy Cassidy's company a little longer without introducing that difficult conversation into it. Who knew how the Alpha would react?

Fortunately, she wasn't left alone with her worries for long. After only a handful of minutes, Cassidy trotted down the steps to the front porch and joined them at the back of the van.

"Delfina wants everything in the living and dining rooms," she announced.

Snow grabbed an armful of boxes and headed into the house. She inhaled deeply as she crossed the threshold. The home had a peculiarly sterile scent to it, one interrupted only by the scents of Delfina and Cassidy.

"That goes in the corner there." Delfina pointed into the living room toward the windows. "Small box can go on the dining room table."

Snow dropped off her load where she was bade and turned, nearly colliding with Hammer, who was right behind her. Between the three of them, it didn't take long to empty the van. The hacker started unboxing and setting up equipment as soon as it showed up. She was so engrossed in her work that she didn't notice the three wolven standing around staring at her until Cassidy cleared her throat.

"What?" Delfina didn't look up from the cords she was plugging into the back of a chunk of machinery.

"How can we help?" Hammer asked.

"Give me some time to get things set up."

"How long will that be?" Snow sidled up to Cassidy's side and insinuated her arm around her girlfriend's waist.

"At least a few hours." Delfina glanced around, her eyes distracted. "Once the hardware is set up, I'll get everything running. Install software, drivers, make sure everything's calibrated and working together. Get the firewall set up, run down my script library…" The volume of her voice diminished until she was muttering a series of steps to herself. "Don't expect it to be ready to go until tomorrow morning." She turned away from them and got back to her setup.

CHAPTER TWENTY-FIVE

Snow and Cassidy sat in the van. They'd parked it as close as they could to the spot they'd been in only a couple of days previous. Snow had rolled down the windows, and the cross breeze was nice, but it was also dragging Cassidy's irritated scent across her nostrils. They'd been sitting and waiting on Bone and Marrow for thirty minutes of the allotted hour, and Cassidy had been stewing ever since they'd gotten there.

"We'll be done soon," Snow murmured. She patted Cassidy on the thigh.

"I'm not very good at sitting around and doing nothing." Cassidy folded her arms across her chest.

"Do you want to talk about anything?"

"Like what?"

"I don't know." Snow chewed on her lower lip. They could talk about Cassidy's ill-timed use of the L word. Or they could talk about anything else. "How's your mom?"

"She's fine." Cassidy curled her lip. Frustration and pent-up energy roiled around her in a swirl that directly contradicted her words.

"Are you sure?"

"No?" Cassidy exhaled a long breath. "I'm not sure. She doesn't seem to be in a worse situation than the past couple of weeks, but I don't know…She feels like one more ticking time bomb I have to deal with. Everything is taking too long. I just want to get to the part where I can bite the problem and make it go away, you know?"

"I can see that." Snow smiled at her girlfriend with sympathy.

"I'm not letting it get to me, I promise." Cassidy took Snow's hand and interlaced their fingers. "You're the only one I can let out my frustration with. Is that okay? I'm not dumping my feelings on you, am I?"

"You're not dumping on me. At least not in a way that would be inappropriate for people who are dating."

"Well, good." Cassidy grinned. "I hope I don't have to tell you to let me know if it gets to the dumping-on-you stage."

"You'll be the first to know."

Cassidy nodded, and her scent eased into something a little more companionable than pouty. They sat in easy silence for a few minutes before Cassidy spoke up again.

"So, weird question."

Snow waited for Cassidy to ask, but her girlfriend had gone silent. "Are you asking something, or making random statements?"

The pointed question startled a laugh out of Cassidy. "Just trying to figure out the best way to ask it."

"Then shoot from the hip. We've been through enough that you shouldn't have to second guess asking me much."

"I'll remind you of that the next time I accidentally insult you."

"I expect nothing less." Snow squeezed Cassidy's hand. "So what's eating at you?"

"Aside from my wolf?" Cassidy took a deep breath. "So you know how Alphas have special names?"

"Yes. Pretty sure I introduced you to the concept."

"Well, it occurred to me when you said that, that Snow probably isn't your given name. I was just wondering how you could end up with an Alpha name when you keep telling me how submissive you are?"

"It's not an Alpha name." Snow let her voice trail off as she debated how much to tell her girlfriend. Or even how to tell her. "I don't really think of myself as submissive, you know."

"I didn't know. I always think of it as the opposite of dominant."

"I suppose you could make that argument linguistically, but it doesn't feel right for me."

"Fair enough. So how do you label yourself? And what does that have to do with your name?"

"I think of myself as non-dominant, I suppose. Submissive implies that I allow myself to be placed on the bottom rung of the ladder by which wolven rank themselves. I don't really bother with the ladder, if that makes sense. It's a lot easier now than when I was a cub. There wasn't really anyone else like me in my mama's pack. When I was a wee cub, it didn't matter, but it became more obvious as I got older."

"How so?"

"It took me a long time to shift. Longer even than it does now. A lot of the younger cubs took a while, but they got better and faster at it. I did too, but not nearly as much as them. So they'd push me around. You know, like kids do."

Cassidy's scent was warm with compassion. "I don't know why it's so encouraging to hear that kids are dicks, no matter the species."

"Well, wolven cubs have a lot in common with humans. Plus they start measuring themselves against each other really young. I endured a lot, and mostly dealt with it by holding myself apart. At a certain point, they became more interested in jockeying for power than picking on the weird kid. There was a period of a few years that actually weren't terrible for me. Then puberty happened."

"Ah."

"Indeed." Snow realized she was clutching Cassidy's hand pretty hard and tried to let go, but Cassidy firmed her grip. It was just for a fraction of a second, but long enough to get across that her girlfriend didn't mind having the blood flow to her fingertips restricted.

"If it's too painful, you don't have to tell me."

"It was a very long time ago. It shouldn't have this much power over me still."

"But it does."

"Yeah." There was no big secret as to why it did. Snow didn't need a therapist to know that same pattern had repeated itself many times over the decades.

"Well, you don't have to tell me if you don't want to."

"I don't mind." Either the story would give Cassidy more context for the ways Snow was damaged, or it would drive her away before she could really break Snow's heart. It was a win-win, right? She shook out her hands. "Okay. They called me Snow after everyone started getting interested in each other's bodies and exploring them. It was a joke."

"A cruel one. They were calling you frigid."

"Yep." Snow laughed, but there was no humor in the sound despite her best attempt. "Best way to defang a joke is to take it on. Pretend it isn't hurting until it really doesn't anymore."

"Did it work?" Cassidy's voice was so gentle that Snow couldn't stop the sob that escaped her.

"Clearly." She tried to laugh again, but it came out more as a wet burble escaping her throat than an actual expression of humor. "Well, a lot of the time. Besides, it's a little funny. I ended up with a name similar to the ones bestowed upon the top echelon of a pack. Me, whose presence barely extends beyond my own nose."

"If you don't like it, I can call you your real name."

"No." Snow shook her head hard for emphasis. "I am Snow now. No one's called me by my real name in a hundred years. Even Dean called me Snow. The only one who still used it was Mama and she's been gone for a century. I wouldn't recognize it if you tried to hang it off me."

"Snow it is then." Cassidy leaned over to nudge her with her shoulder. "I love it, and it suits you."

"Oh, well. I have to keep it now."

"Mm-hm." Cassidy shot her a highly amused look. "Glad to help."

A strange shimmer in the rearview mirror interrupted Snow before she could tell her girlfriend how much of a smart-ass she was.

"What the hell?" She turned around in her seat, peering into the cargo area. It was much cleaner than it had been for weeks, which gave her an unobstructed view of the shimmering curtain that had opened across the back doors.

The curtain parted, and a dapper man with the palest skin she'd ever seen ducked his head as he stepped into the back of the van. His outfit was immaculate and seemed more suitable to a night out on the town than crouching in the back of a stolen van. Tapered dark-blue pants ended in shiny gray loafers. One hand was shoved deep into the pocket of something that looked as if a cardigan and a blazer had had a baby, inheriting the worst traits of each of its parents. The cut wasn't helped by the large gray-and-blue houndstooth pattern. The other hand held a hard-sided brown leather briefcase, of a style Snow hadn't seen in years. The leather shone, in as immaculate shape as the rest of his outfit, except the hair. He'd spent a lot of time on it, that much was clear by the calculated tousle he'd managed to cultivate. The style was at odds with the streaks of silver at his temples.

"Move it." The voice was familiar. Bone or Marrow pushed past him, followed by her sister.

The second sister glanced around and looked Snow in the eye as the shimmering pattern that still crawled around the edge of the doorway winked out of existence. She waved vigorously from her bent position. That was almost certainly Bone.

"Snow!" She pointed at the fancy lad. "We have our wheelman!"

Snow cocked her head. The man balanced awkwardly between a squat and a crouch didn't have the look of someone hardened enough to have been bestowed a criminal title. If it had been anyone else, she might have been inclined to offer some benefit of the doubt, but Marrow and Bone were well known for their bizarre senses of humor. Surely if she waited, they'd produce some grizzled crook from somewhere and laugh and laugh about how they'd gotten her good.

What had been up with the curtain? She stared at the trio, trying to wrap her brain around what had just happened.

"Snow, you tilt that head of yours any further and you'll tip over on it." Now that was definitely Marrow. There was no mistaking the sharpness that Bone still lost whenever they talked.

"He's the real deal," Bone said.

The wheelman looked around, taking in the area. He shifted into another pose, this one possibly meant to look dignified.

Snow blinked, then looked over at Cassidy. Her mouth wasn't hanging open, but her scent was gobsmacked.

"Are we just going to hang around in the woods?" the man asked. "I thought you had an important job for me. One that couldn't possibly wait."

His scent was human—or at least mostly. There was a strange tang to it, one that wasn't completely covered by what was likely an expensive cologne. She'd encountered a similar oddity to a human's scent trace a couple of other times. One was out in Navajo Nation, a medicine man who had been well-known to the packs out there. The wolven had accepted him, which was unusual, as they'd steered clear of most of the other humans in the area.

"Cool your jets, Byron," Marrow said. "We have a job and you still owe us for pulling your fat out of the fire."

"Hammer's waiting for us at the house," Cassidy said.

"Then let's get going." Marrow sat, her legs folded under her and gestured at Byron to take a seat. "We don't have all day."

CHAPTER TWENTY-SIX

"Introductions are out of the way," Cassidy said. She leaned forward, her hands braced against the table. The whole crew was there, or at least Snow supposed that was what they were now. Four Alphas, one vampire-entangled human hacker, one magical wheelman, and her. Hammer had been standoffish with Byron, and the Gary Alphas were giving Delfina some impressive side eye, but no one looked as if they were going to resort to immediate violence. The scents around the table were guarded, but not aggressive.

Hammer stood, moving into Cassidy's space, reminding her of her place. Cassidy refused to be intimidated, maintaining her stance before grudgingly moving away from the head of the table as if it had been her idea. The twins shifted where they sat, but Delfina and the wheelman sat up straight in their respective seats.

"Delfina, how much do you know about our target?" Hammer asked.

Cassidy nodded as if the question had come from her. Snow made a mental note to talk to her about her working relationship with the South Shore Alpha. The sooner they had it out, the better. Hell, if they needed to fuck to get some of their mutual antipathy out of their systems, she would support that, but they couldn't continue in this vein.

"Very little beyond that it's a decommissioned prison in the area." Delfina stood and crossed over to the dining room, pulling up her chair in front of a veritable bank of monitors. "And the address is?" She opened up a mapping website and waited, her fingers poised over the keyboard.

"Silent Heights Penitentiary." Cassidy moved to stand directly behind the hacker's chair, cutting Hammer off before he could do the same. Instead, he posted up right at the North Side Alpha's shoulder.

On one of the living room couches, Bone elbowed Marrow and pointed at the two Alphas jockeying for space. Marrow snickered, the sound growing into outright hilarity when the wheelman looked over at her, one eyebrow raised in delicate question.

"We'll tell you later," Marrow mouthed.

"Silent Heights," Delfina said as she typed the words into the search box. Moments later, they were looking at an aerial shot of the old prison's grounds.

Cassidy pointed at a smaller building within the walls. "I bet that's where Luther is. It's the only structure close enough that I would have felt him."

"I wonder if the others are being held in the main building," Hammer said. "There are people who come and go out the main gates. Not many, but enough to keep part of a prison going."

"So, we know where they are." Bone crossed into the dining room to lounge on one side of the window. "We need a better idea of what's going on inside."

"You said they have cameras on the walls?" Delfina asked.

Hammer and Cassidy nodded at the same time.

"Let me see if I can track a feed from here. It's a long shot, but better to check now than take the risk of going onsite."

"Fair enough." Hammer's words were easy, but his scent already carried hints of frustration. Cassidy's wasn't far behind.

The group watched in silence as Delfina's fingers performed a staccato dance across the keyboard and mouse. She would type for a few seconds, then click around in an unfamiliar interface. A few moments later, a screen heavy with white text on a black background would pop up. Delfina would stare at it while muttering to herself, then would type some more. Then another screen would be brought up. Ten minutes ticked past, then twenty. They passed thirty before Cassidy and Hammer exchanged an equally annoyed glance.

"Any luck?" Hammer asked.

"Not so far," Delfina said. "I just want to try a couple more things."

They had no choice but to wait as Delfina continued to type and click, the sounds getting sharper as each tactic was apparently rebuffed. Finally, she pushed herself away from the table and its piled equipment. She swiveled around to face the gathered wolven and Byron.

"I can't get in. I need to be there to establish a connection. I'll install a back door. From there we should be able to peek in on what they're doing."

Cassidy clapped her hands together. "Guess we're going for a drive."

The gathered Alphas stood and headed for the front door. Byron rolled his eyes, then looked over at Delfina, who cleared her throat.

"Is everyone going?"

Snow nodded from her dark corner. She was glad the hacker had said something. Speaking up in front of the entire group wasn't her style, but the folly of a van full of Alphas pulling up outside the prison where how many dozens of wolven were being held couldn't be overstated.

Delfina scoffed at the surprised expressions that were turned on her from every direction. "You can't all be in charge." She waved a hand. "Pick someone. I don't care who."

"We have the experience." Marrow pushed past Bone. "We've pulled operations against the Feds before. We should be in charge."

"A couple of jokers who keep their pack together because no one can stand up against two Alphas?" Hammer sneered. "You'll excuse me if I don't take your word about your experience."

"What is it?" Cassidy said on the heels of Hammer's dismissal.

"What?" Bone asked.

"What's your experience?" She cocked her head, her posture somewhere between curious and aggressive.

"We bombed a number of power plants in the seventies and eighties," Bone said. "The Feds called us ecoterrorists before we became…" She held her hands up behind her head to evoke wolf ears.

"We were recruited because of our work with ELF." Marrow stood tall. "We started with Earth First, then moved on when we got tired of tree-spiking." She grinned. "We struck some harsh blows. Shut down a coal power plant. It had to be replaced. So yeah, we've got some background working with groups on shady shit."

Bone raised her eyebrows. "You could check our bona fides, but the people who could vouch for us are either dead or in prison."

"Or him." Marrow jerked a thumb over her shoulder at Byron.

Snow regarded him. The human looked to be in his thirties. There was no way he'd been running around blowing up polluters when

Marrow and Bone claimed to have been active. Still, there were no traces of lies in their scent, and there was that strange inhuman note the lingered around Byron.

Hammer shook his head. "I can't follow these two." The words were directed at Cassidy, as if he believed she might back him up.

Cassidy looked back and forth between Hammer and the twins. "Look, I don't know who should be running this," she said slowly. "I don't think it should be me. I'm happy to be support on this one."

Marrow strode toward Hammer, only stopping once she was well within his personal space. "Sounds like we need to settle this the traditional way."

"Sounds like." Hammer's lips peeled back from his teeth in a mockery of a grin. "Which one of you wants to go up against me?"

"What do you think?" Marrow asked without breaking their stare. "You want to take him apart, or do you mind if I do it?"

"You do it," Bone said. "I don't have a horse in this race."

"Good." Marrow continued to look into Hammer's eyes.

"Fine." He shoved the Gary Alpha away from him, then gripped the bottom hem of his shirt. "We have a challenge. You and me."

"Me and you." Marrow kicked off her shoes.

It didn't take long for the Alphas to undress. Muscles and skin rippled as they removed their clothing. By the time they were naked, each had flowed from skinform to betweenform.

"The backyard," Bone said.

"You stay out of this," Hammer growled, his words distorted by the muzzle that jutted from his face.

"She doesn't need any help." Bone pushed her sister in front of her, pausing to wipe some of the fluid that clung to Marrow's fur on her pant leg.

Snow waited for everyone to clear the room after the Gary Alphas and Hammer. Cassidy went with them, but not before glancing her way. Delfina and Byron followed along with the group. Once the house was empty, Snow found a spot to sit by the front door. She didn't watch challenges if she could avoid it, and she always made sure she had a clear escape route when one happened.

CHAPTER TWENTY-SEVEN

The challenge fight between Marrow and Hammer was short and brutal. To Cassidy's surprise, Marrow came out victorious, but not unscathed. It took a few hours before she could move her right arm, and the rent along her ribcage was likely to scar. Hammer hadn't fared any better. Cassidy would have put her money on him, especially after he'd demolished her by the stream the previous week. She'd believed he was the biggest threat among their little group, but Marrow didn't seem to feel fear.

In the face of her onslaught, Hammer had been hard-pressed to keep her from opening up a major artery. In his desire to protect himself, he'd lost the fight.

The hacker and the wheelman had watched from the deck and had gone back inside the house when it was clear Marrow had won. Snow hadn't come out, which hadn't worried Cassidy. Her girlfriend's star had shone steadily from the direction of the house for the entire fight.

When they all reconvened in front of Delfina's bank of monitors, Hammer raised no objections when Marrow started issuing orders.

"You two"—Marrow pointed at Hammer and Cassidy—"you stay here with me. Bone will accompany Snow, Delfina, and Byron to the prison."

"What?" Cassidy stared at the Gary Alpha in disbelief. Her wolf sprang to alertness. Neither of them wanted to leave Snow unprotected.

Hammer grabbed her by the upper arm and squeezed in warning.

"You'll go along with this?" She transferred her incredulous glare to him.

"She won the challenge. Like it or not, she is Alpha."

"The hell she is. She is *an* Alpha, not *my* Alpha."

"You can still challenge, Five Moons." Marrow sounded as if the prospect of facing off against Cassidy was the dullest event imaginable.

For a moment she was tempted, but then Snow sidled into her field of view and shook her head.

"Your Snow will be fine," Bone said. "If we get caught, she has the best chance of making it out of there. No one stealths like her."

"If you say so." The words were meant for her girlfriend, but Bone nodded. "The hacker I understand, but why Byron?"

"You'll see." Marrow nodded at Delfina. "I assume you have a way of communicating with us that won't get us picked up by the heat."

The hacker nodded. "Burners." She pointed at a duffel bag of brick-like cell phones. "We'll bring a SIM card and swap it out once we call."

"Good." Marrow stared at the group. "Get going. The sooner we get the lay of the land, the sooner we can really get down to planning."

Cassidy was left to watch forlornly as the other group piled into the van and drove off.

Marrow turned to her and Hammer. "Good. Now you two can get over your crap."

"What?" Cassidy looked sidelong at the South Shore Alpha, then returned her attention to Marrow. "We're fine."

"You're not. And I won't have whatever is going on between you getting in the way of the rest of the team." She dropped her hands to her hips and glared at them. "I don't care if you talk it out, fight it out, or fuck it out. Just get over it." Marrow turned on her heel and stalked out of the room.

"The hell?" Cassidy couldn't believe her ears.

"She's not wrong," Hammer said.

"Isn't she? We've been managing all right since our…scrap."

"Scrap?" He grinned. "Is that what you call getting your ass handed to you?"

Cassidy bristled. Her wolf didn't like the challenge to their prowess. "You didn't exactly shine against Marrow."

"I'll have my time again." He watched her closely. "Unlike you."

"What's your problem with me, anyway? What did I do to you?"

"You called me away from my people when they needed me most."

"And I paid for that as harshly as you did." Cassidy cocked her head. "You can't think I did it on purpose."

"If I thought that, I would have put you down a long time ago." Hammer walked toward her.

Cassidy stepped back and shifted to keep her shoulder toward him.

He smiled grimly and kept walking, circling around her. "You're too young in your position. Too inexperienced."

"Well, yeah."

Hammer blinked at her agreement. "You don't know what you're doing."

"Also true."

He stopped in his tracks. "Then what are you doing as Alpha?"

"The best I can." Cassidy exploded toward him, planting her hands on his shoulders and shoving him back with everything she had. "Same as you."

Hammer staggered back a couple of steps, then planted on his back foot for a second before launching himself at her.

She tried to sidestep his outstretched arms but was unable to completely evade his grasp. He wrapped an arm around her waist and brought her to the ground, then gripped massive hands together and raised them over his head. Cassidy had enough time to throw herself to one side. The hardwood floor dented where she'd been the moment before. The boards buckled into the subfloor with a splintering snap. He grunted as the impact shivered through his arms. Cassidy took advantage of his momentary distraction to strike the side of his head with her elbow. The grunt turned into a guttural howl, then he was throwing himself at her.

Their fight was messy and inelegant. It was also free of lupine interference. When Cassidy's wolf didn't rise to Hammer's challenge, Cassidy abandoned everything she'd learned about fighting as a wolven and relied on the roughhousing she'd picked up scrapping with neighborhood kids until puberty had made fighting with the boys a losing battle. Unlike in her tween years, her punches were effective. Her wolf might be curiously apathetic about this fight, but Cassidy didn't lose the strength she'd gained from her transformation.

She rained down punch after punch on Hammer's stomach, chest, and arms. He worked to bat them away and returned them with interest, rocking her back on her heels. Again, the wolf's gifts kept her from going down. His eyes were bright and his teeth bared, but he wasn't shifting either. There was no challenge here, no fight for dominance of their little pack. Marrow had claimed that. This was a chance to settle some scores.

They brawled for long enough that Cassidy's arms were starting to ache. Sweat drenched her face and back, slicking her shirt to her skin. She panted as she took another swing at Hammer, this one at his face.

He closed his hand around her fist and dragged her forward until his face was in hers. "Feel better?"

Cassidy turned her head. "About what?" she grumbled.

"About losing to me." He let go of her hand, pushing it down.

Her fingers throbbed where they'd been crushed together in his grip. "I could take you."

Hammer barked a laugh. "I know. You have. You will again. And so will I." He turned away from her. "Learn to lose, kid. It's a much better skill to have under your belt than winning all the time."

Cassidy snorted. "Losing means dying."

"If an outsider wants to take your pack, yes." Hammer shook his head. "I'm not an outsider. I don't want your pack. Killing you gets me nothing."

"Then why did you fight me the other day?"

He shrugged. "To put you in your place. To blow off some steam. It wasn't supposed to start some big rivalry between us. I forget how new you are."

"I can't help being my age."

"It's so damn frustrating. You just don't get a bunch of stuff. Do you know how hard it is to treat you as Alpha and cub?"

"Do you know how hard it is to be that?" She didn't appreciate the comparison to being a baby, but couldn't deny the accuracy of the description either.

"You do things that are incredibly...rude. And then you have ideas that could actually work." Hammer clenched his fists. "It's like I'm in the middle of whiplash between wondering how you're going to insult us next but having to pay attention because in the middle of the affront is something that might pan out."

"I don't want to be in charge," Cassidy said. She speared her fingers through her hair. "I don't even know what I wanted in the pack. But when I was thrust into it, there was no one else who was remotely close to me in dominance. My wolves didn't have anyone else. What was I supposed to do? What do I do now? I can't abandon them, go running away just because things have gotten difficult. I'm just doing my best to get my people back. I can figure things out once more urgent matters have been sorted."

"And then you say things like that." Hammer crossed his arms. "It would be a lot easier if I could just hate you, Five Moons."

The words had been grudging, but the tone sounded like approval. Warmth filled her ribcage, and Cassidy grinned. "Why would I want to make things easy for you?"

"No reason you should start now," Hammer grumbled. "No sense in switching horses midstream."

"Exactly." Cassidy bumped him with her shoulder. "You could call me Cassidy, if you wanted."

"Cassidy." He seemed to be tasting the word. "If you must, you can call me Robert." He held up a hand. "Only Robert. Never Rob, or Bob, and certainly not Robby or Bobby."

"Robert." Cassidy nodded. "It suits you."

"In a way Cassidy doesn't suit you."

"What does that mean?"

"I don't think I've ever met a wolven named Cassidy. The name smacks of a bubbly irreverence. It's very human."

"My dad loved the Grateful Dead. Sorry I don't live up to your expectations."

"I'm not. You continue to surprise me, Cassidy Five Moons. Sometimes even in good ways."

"And you, Robert Hammer." Cassidy looked up at the South Shore Alpha. "Are we done with our pissing match?"

"For now." He stuck his hand out toward her. "Until we are whole with our packs again, I am proud to consider you packmate."

"Likewise." Cassidy reached her hand out and allowed it to be engulfed in his.

The grip of his handshake was powerful but controlled. He could have crushed her fingers if he'd wanted, but then so could she. Cassidy was conscious of their restraint as they engaged in a very human gesture of partnership.

"So, no fucking then," Marrow said as she poked her head around the edge of the doorway.

"Sorry to disappoint," Cassidy said. "You should have put on some music before you left."

"Really set the mood." Hammer raised one eyebrow. "An ultimatum isn't especially sexy."

"You're just not hanging around with the right partners, then." Marrow came the rest of the way into the room. "I know both of you well enough by now. Don't tell me you aren't working on some ideas for solving our little problem." She crossed past them and plopped herself down on the living room couch. "Now that you're capable of looking past your own noses, why don't you lay some of those ideas on me?"

CHAPTER TWENTY-EIGHT

Snow and Bone hunkered down behind some bare bushes that had been planted at the edge of the parking lot across the road from the prison. The hill fell away at a steep slope, which didn't give them a lot of room, but they were well hidden from multiple angles. Snow approved of Bone's choice for concealment.

From her cross-legged position on the ground, Delfina unslung her backpack, then gestured impatiently toward Snow for the large plastic case, which she handed over. The hacker had insisted on carrying it on their trek up the hill from where they parked but had reluctantly relinquished it after ramming it into a tree for the fourth time. Snow wanted to see what Delfina was up to, but the larger part of her knew that making sure no one was coming up on them was more important. She caught Bone watching her out of the corner of her eye and turned to catch her ex's gaze. Bone pointed at her eyes with two fingers, then gestured in a circle around them.

"Already on it," Snow breathed. She took quick stock of the area, then backed away from their little group. There was a better vantage for watching to one side, one that would allow her to keep Bone and the others in view while also getting a decent view of the doors of the prison. She eased herself over to the new point and settled without even a crinkle from the dead leaves and branches that littered the ground under the trees.

She heard the high-pitched whine of electronic equipment being powered on and Delfina muttering to herself again. The hacker liked to talk herself through things, it seemed. It was just as well that she wasn't expecting deep tech-related conversation with anyone else.

"Anything?" Bone asked. Snow had to strain to hear her, which was good. If her words had been clear, then they would have carried enough that a human with exceptional hearing might have picked them out by the road.

"The signals are weird," Delfina said. "I can't get a good read on them. What I'm getting most is interference. I'm gonna fine-tune my calibrations." There was silence as the hacker fiddled with her equipment.

Snow watched with interest as someone exited one of the guard towers atop the wall. The figure was holding some kind of rifle loosely, but at the ready. They wandered down the top of the wall, keeping more of their attention on the space inside the walls than out. Snow was certain she could have leaped out of her hiding place and done jumping jacks without attracting their attention. The figure continued to the next guard post and back, each time giving only the most casual perusal of the grounds outside the prison. After a few minutes of this, they disappeared back into the tower from which they'd first emerged.

"Still nothing," Delfina announced a short while later. "Well, not nothing, but none of what I'm getting is useful." She sighed and closed the lid on the black plastic case. "That's all right, I have a backup." She pulled the backpack over and removed a much smaller box. She opened the top and pulled two objects out, then fiddled with them for a bit.

"Is that a drone?" Bone asked.

"Mm-hm." The hacker kept tinkering a moment longer.

"Can you deploy it that direction and come around from the bluff side?" Bone asked. "Don't want anyone to catch sight of it that could lead back to us."

The grunt she got in return was indignant. "Of course," the hacker said. "It's not my first day on the job. Besides, what do you know about drones, Weather Underground?"

Bone snickered quietly. "Weather Underground? Is that the best you can do? Now that was a group that got things done." She clapped a hand down on Delfina's shoulder, then tightened her grip. "You do you, but if you blow us, I will end you." The last was delivered with as much good cheer as the first had been. Snow was reminded that while Marrow might be the sharper of the two, Bone's edge was still plenty keen.

Delfina stiffened but didn't say anything. The cool spring breeze blew a spike of much colder fear past Snow's nostrils. From the way Bone's smile widened, she hadn't missed it either.

The somewhat chastened hacker launched the drone, watching it for a moment before transferring her attention back to the monitor and joysticks in her hands. Byron and Bone crowded in around her. The high-pitched whir of the drone's tiny rotors faded quickly. It was so small that Snow couldn't track it for long. She'd had no idea they made drones that small until Delfina had picked one up during their shopping trip. Had that really only been yesterday?

Byron continued to watch over Delfina's shoulder. "Can you get a good look at the doors and windows on the outside of the building?"

"You collecting architectural details?" Delfina fiddled with the controls, then sat straight up. "Shit!"

"What happened to the feed?" Bone asked.

"It just cut out." Delfina adjusted something, then leaned closer to the screen. "Damn thing didn't even make it over the walls." She poked her head up to take a quick look over the concealing hedge before Bone could grab the scruff of her neck and yank her back down. She pulled free of the Gary Alpha's grip and peered back at the screen. "I need the drone back. The log cuts off. I don't have any data on why it died."

"Not to mention if someone finds it…" Bone looked over at Snow, then sidled away from the humans toward her. "Can you get it?" Bone asked, pitching her voice low enough that no one beyond them would be able to hear it. She placed her hand around the back of Snow's neck and pulled her in close. She was one of a handful of people with which Snow could tolerate such closeness, but she pulled away anyway.

"You're asking me to endanger myself for a piece of equipment."

"An important piece. One that could expose us if it's discovered." Bone's explanation warmed into cajoling. "You're the one who's most likely to pull this off without being caught. We can't send those two in." They both turned to look at the humans who were watching the small monitor in Delfina's hands. "I can try. I might even be successful. Your chances are much higher. No one skulks like you do."

Snow sighed. "Flattery will get you nowhere…"

"But…" Bone seized on the unsaid word, a small smile playing around the corner of her mouth.

"But you're right."

"I love it when you say that."

"Only because you hear it so rarely."

"And I cherish every one." Bone wrapped her up in a one-armed hug, letting Snow go before the embrace could start to feel like a wordless request for something further.

"I'm not shifting here," Snow said. "It's too open. Let's find ourselves some decent cover."

"Fair enough." Snow followed Bone back over to the humans.

"We're moving out," the Gary Alpha announced before heading back down the hill, toward a dense clump of evergreens. Bone drew the humans off to one side and started quizzing them on the contents of the video Delfina had gotten from her drone. Snow was grateful for the distraction as she made her slow way through her change. Once she'd assumed the silver form of the other half of her soul, she made her way up and nipped a fold of cloth on Bone's arm.

"Oh good, you're ready to go." Bone angled the small screen Delfina had been using to observe the drone's video feed. "It looks like the drone cut out about ten feet from the wall. It shouldn't be too far from there." The images were difficult to follow. The wolf's brain didn't want to believe that they were depictions of something that had happened elsewhere and at a different time.

"I was trying to fly over the west wall," Delfina said.

"That's the closest one to where we are. Where the sun sets."

Bone's clarification was welcome. Concepts like cardinal directions became fuzzy when she was in furform. Wolves didn't think that way. Ten feet was also difficult, but a little easier to envision. Snow made her way around to the black case on the ground next to the hacker. She pawed at it, trying to get it open.

"Pop that lid, would you?" Bone said.

After Delfina opened the top, Snow stuck her nose inside. The smells of plastic and electronics were difficult to tease apart. Both were alien to the wolf. Snow sneezed, trying to clear her nostrils before trying again. She closed her eyes and inhaled deeply. It would help to remember some of the plastic scent; the drone had been sitting in it, after all. It would hold onto some of that, but being a thing of metal and its own plastics, those scents would come through most strongly. She sniffed until she thought she might be able to recognize the scent when she ran across it.

"Good luck," Byron said as she turned to make her way toward Silent Heights.

Bone shook her head. "She doesn't need it."

Snow wished she shared her ex's confidence in her abilities. Still, Bone was right about one thing. She was the one with the best chance at recovering the drone. Beyond that, she was the one the group could afford to lose. Bone hadn't said so, hadn't even alluded to it, but Snow knew where she stood. She always knew what her relative rank and worth were.

She lowered her torso toward the ground and began purposefully slinking toward the prison walls.

CHAPTER TWENTY-NINE

More cover by the tall stone walls of the prison would have been nice, Snow decided. The cameras from their previous visit were still very much in evidence. She surveyed the entire western edge of the wall and noted two of them. She tried to wrap her mind around the concept of field of view. It helped if she envisioned the cameras as crows who would set up an alarm call if they saw the wolf skulking toward their nests. Crows weren't much of a threat on their own. One or two were an annoyance, but if more came down, even the strongest wolf could be in for a lot of pain. And Snow was not the strongest wolf. That was all right. She was the sneakiest wolf. There might not be a whole lot of cover, but she'd done more with less in the past.

Now if only she knew where the drone had ended up.

The sweep of the cameras was methodical, and after a few minutes of observation to determine their pattern, Snow snaked her way around and under the saplings and shrubs that had been allowed to grow up in the years since the prison was closed. She dived into a clump of dead grasses and waited for the nearest camera to look the other way.

As she panted, air moving over her tongue, she tasted a bit of plastic in the air. The unnatural whiff was familiar; she'd held it in her nostrils a few minutes before. Snow swept her own gaze across the ground, looking for a tiny piece of matte black plastic. All she saw were shockingly green bits of new grass growth poking out through the brown of dead leaves.

The cameras continued their mindless swivel, still seemingly unaware of her presence. Snow left off her attempt to see the downed drone. She needed to penetrate further into the coverage of the other camera. Not too far down the wall, a couple of scrubby shrubs had been allowed to establish themselves. She would have to time things perfectly to get under the bushes before the camera's lens swept back over her. As soon as the camera's swivel cleared the grass, Snow launched herself toward them.

She slid under their dubious cover, her belly pressed to the ground. Every rock and stick under the shrub was jabbing through her fur into soft skin, but she paid little attention to the sudden discomfort. Her attention was taken up by the camera that was swiveling her way yet again. It kept moving, not stopping to focus on her hidey hole. She let out a long breath, then started tallying up her options for her next place to hunker down. As she inhaled, the scent of plastic and electronics tickled her nose again. This time it was much stronger. The damn drone was nearby.

Snow turned her head slowly, trying to trace the scent back to its origin. It took a few passes to narrow it down to the wall directly to her left. She'd been expecting the drone to be further into the field. Delfina had said she'd been about ten feet short of the wall before the signal had cut out. On the other hand, if it had been moving forward, there could have been enough momentum to keep the drone moving instead of falling straight out of the sky.

When Snow finally picked it out, the little device was sitting about two stretched-out wolf-lengths up the wall. It teetered on the very edge of a piece of stone that jutted out a little further than those around it. She glared at it, then back at the swiveling camera. Could she get to the wall, climb it, grab the drone, and be back under the bush before the camera's sweep brought her back in range? She looked back toward the edge of the forest where Bone and the humans were waiting. There was no sign of them, which was good, but she could have used the comfort of seeing someone who was on her side.

What if she shifted to skinform, then knocked the drone down with a rock? No, that would leave her stranded naked in the middle of a field. She could probably make it back to furform, but the transformation would be lengthy. And if the camera caught her midshift, she would be a sitting duck.

She hooked one claw around a pebble and popped it out of the ground. An experimental swipe confirmed that the wolf wouldn't be able to throw anything with the accuracy she'd need. The only way to get the drone was to hope she could time her move to the exact point in the camera's sweep where it wouldn't be able to see her and be back down and under the bush before it panned back.

The camera had completed three more passes before Snow felt like she'd pinned down the timing well enough to risk it. She inched around under the shrubs until she was pointed at the wall, taking her time so nothing would look untoward to whoever might be monitoring the camera's feed. She had to assume it was being watched at all times. Her tail could be a problem, and the last thing she needed was for it to flop out from under the shrub's branches and give her away, so she tucked it in hard to her side. Under might have been better, but she was going to need it for balance when she went up the wall. She bunched up her hindquarters and held, waiting for the right moment to release.

Her heart thundered in her ears and vibrated her ribcage as the camera hit its outermost swivel. She would have to wait another second, maybe two before she could—There!

Snow launched herself across the mostly dead grass toward the wall. If she could time it right, she could run up it. Hopefully she could get decent purchase that way. She'd seen humans doing this. They called it parkour. If a human could do it, then so could she. At least, that was what she told herself as she galloped across the space between the wall and her bushes. The first few steps up the wall worked as she'd hoped. She was higher than she'd have been able to manage through jumping alone.

The drone was just above her, all she had to do was reach out and tap it off the ledge with her snout. At the first tap, the drone skittered back a fraction of an inch. She was so close, and yet the camera would be making its way back soon if it wasn't already. Snow hooked her front claws around a stony outcropping and pulled herself up, giving her enough room to sweep the ledge, knocking the drone free. She let go, following the drone down and hoping it didn't get hung up somewhere else.

She glanced over her shoulder as she dropped and caught a glimpse of the camera. She couldn't quite see the lens, but it was close. There was no way she'd be able to grab the drone and get back to the bush. Even if she left it, she'd be hard pressed to make it back to cover in time.

As she hit the ground, her legs were already moving to get her back to safety.

"Hold still!" Byron's voice sounded in her ear.

She froze, wondering how he'd gotten up to her without tipping off the cameras, or worse, without her noticing. A hazy gray bubble enveloped her, and she went even more still. How had this exceedingly localized fogbank come to be?

"Keep still," Byron said again. He was nowhere in sight, and she wasn't picking up the slightest whiff of his scent. The only thing she could smell was the drone, which was sitting right past the end of her nose.

Snow stared at the gray shroud that enveloped her, then realized it was textured. This wasn't fog, it was an image of stones stacked atop each other. If the camera was seeing what she was, she was completely camouflaged.

"And go," Byron said.

Snow didn't wait. She scooped the drone off the ground in her jaws and dashed for the safety of her shrubs. She made it with plenty of time. Her muscles shook from the tension she'd been keeping them under, but it wasn't time to relax, not yet. Now she had to get out.

She waited, timing things to get back to the blind spot, then darted from cover. The way back was quicker than the way there had been. She'd already timed it out and was able to flow through the invisible obstacle course without much effort. The last dash to the woods was as fast as she'd ever moved. She wasn't sure where the others had ended up, and she didn't really care. All she wanted was to be somewhere free of cameras.

She plunged deep into the trees before she felt comfortable stopping. Even then, she put a big oak between her and the prison. She allowed the drone to roll free from her jaws, then pressed herself to the ground, panting heavily. Every muscle in her body vibrated.

As she lay there, she picked up the sounds of feet crunching through dead leaves. The smells of her companions reached her nose before she saw them.

Bone crouched down by her head. "I knew you could do it."

Delfina snatched the drone up from the ground and studied it closely. "It's a bit damp."

"It's not like she has pockets," Byron said.

"I didn't know you could do that illusion thing," Bone said. "Is that new?"

Byron lifted a shoulder. "It didn't come up before."

"Illusions?" Delfina didn't look up from her drone.

"Sometimes." Byron didn't sound like he wanted to elaborate.

Snow could sympathize. She pushed herself to her feet and headed back toward the van. She needed some time away from this damn prison. Cassidy's arms sounded like the right place to be.

CHAPTER THIRTY

With the intel Hammer had gathered while everyone had been away, they were able to generate a decent number of ideas, all of which hinged on what Delfina could discover at the prison, but Cassidy was pleased with their progress. There were two stacks of paper on the table: one for discarded ideas and one for potential plans. The papers with the best ideas were spread out across the table top.

Bouncing ideas off Marrow and Hammer had felt good. Cassidy enjoyed feeling like part of a team, and now that she could let go of some of the crap that had grown up between her and Hammer, he was actually pretty fun to be around. He had a way of seeing to the heart of the matter. His mind was agile enough to poke holes in even the most likely sounding scenarios. Cassidy was paying more attention to his body language and scent and less to her own reactions to his words and had come to realize that he wasn't trying to be an asshole when he shot down half her ideas.

Marrow stood at the head of the table, rearranging the scraps of paper with their best plans. "I like what I'm seeing here," she said. "There's a bunch of different ways we can go. What Cassidy's hacker finds will tell us which direction is best."

Cassidy looked over at Hammer. "Are you really going to be comfortable infiltrating that place?"

"No problem. I've already identified a likely candidate to switch with. They've hired custodial staff, and there's one with my build and coloration." He ran one hand over his chin. "I'll have to lose this. My face hasn't been naked since the sixties."

Cassidy squinted at him. "So your big disguise is to lose the beard? Don't you think you'll need something else."

Hammer shrugged. "I've seen how humans treat each other based on skin color. I'll be one more Black man in a menial job."

"So that's our first step," Marrow said. "We can do that one without having to wait for the hacker to get back with her intel."

"Getting eyes on the inside will be a huge help," Cassidy said.

"And if I can see where our people are being held…" Hammer leaned against the table, turning his head as he perused their various schemes.

"And see who's left. Do you think Hazel's people are in there also?" Marrow's voice was uncharacteristically soft.

"Could be." Hammer's face turned thoughtful. "I've met a few of them and should know them by smell."

"Do we break them out too?" Marrow asked. She gazed out the front window as if the trees surrounding the house were the most interesting things she'd ever seen.

"Of course we do." Cassidy sat up straight in her chair. How could Marrow ask such a thing?

"And if they're being held by pack?" Marrow's eyes met hers and held them. "And if we have to make a choice?"

"No." Cassidy drove her finger down on the table. "We need to agree that everyone gets out. We get our people out in the order we come upon them. No preference for our own packs. Otherwise, what's to keep us from getting in there and scattering?"

Hammer expelled a snort of air through his nostrils. "Five Moons has the right of it."

"Just making sure we're all on the same page." Marrow looked away from Cassidy.

"There's one other thing we need from in there," Cassidy said. "Getting our wolves out is one part of the problem." She held up a hand when Hammer clenched his fists. "The bigger part. But we'd be foolish not to take the opportunity to get some information on who's behind this. I don't want to get our wolves back only to have them taken again."

"That makes some sense," Hammer said. "We'll have to rely on our hacker to do so. How much do you trust her?"

How much did Cassidy trust her? Not any further than she could throw the vampires' vassal, which admittedly was much further than she could have when still human. "She's an unknown quantity," Cassidy finally admitted. "Let's just say I have every confidence she'll do the job we ask her to. I don't really know what she might do above and beyond that."

"But you're keeping an eye on her." Hammer's response wasn't a question. It shaded into the space between statement of fact and being an order.

Cassidy nodded as she reminded herself that they were good now. She didn't have to assume his statements were meant in the least charitable interpretation. And she *was* keeping an eye on Delfina.

"Where are the others? Shouldn't they be back by now?" The sun had traveled high enough in the sky that even Cassidy could tell it had been at least a couple of hours since Snow had left with Bone and the humans.

Marrow closed her eyes for a few seconds. "Bone says they're on their way back. They hit a snag."

"Is everyone all right?"

Marrow cracked one eye open. "You mean is your mate all right?"

"Not my mate, but sure." The term, when applied to Snow, might make her want to grin widely, but that wasn't a discussion she and the lone wolf had had yet. Besides, she was pretty sure that "mate" had a specific connotation among the wolven, and she wasn't sure they fell into it.

"Sounds like she's in one piece."

Cassidy tried not to feel too relieved, knowing it would come out in her scent to the other two Alphas.

"Why don't we break until they get back?" Hammer suggested. "Seems to me like we can't move until we hear what they've found out anyway."

"That works for me." She and Hammer turned to look at Marrow, who flipped a hand at them.

"Go, get some fresh air. It's time for recess."

Recess. All three wolven trooped out to the back deck, but that was where any resemblance to grade school ended. There was no tetherball or four-square. Thankfully, there were no screaming human children running around either.

"How far out is Bone?" Hammer asked. He leaned on the edge of the railing, gazing into the dense pine trees that surrounded the house.

"Maybe thirty minutes," Marrow said.

"Then there's time." He stepped out of his sweatpants, then pulled his shirt off over his head. His form started to blur even before the shirt was completely off.

Cassidy wasn't far behind him. Through the snaps and grinds of her bones and muscles reforming, Marrow dryly said: "Guess I'll hold down the fort while you two run off and play."

Hammer looked up at her, his tongue lolling out of his mouth as if to say, "You wanted to be in charge, so have fun with that."

Cassidy's laugh came out as a short bark.

Marrow rolled her eyes but didn't seem too put out by their responses. She headed back inside.

The wolf was ascendant now, but Cassidy stressed that they didn't have long. The concept wasn't one the wolf really wanted to acknowledge, but when Cassidy reminded her that Snow would be back soon, the wolf perked up. They had a short time to pass, and it was far easier for both of them to do so in furform.

They followed the twisting bright orange rope that was Hammer's scent through the tangle of the trees.

* * *

By the time Bone guided the van up the twisting drive to the corporate retreat house, Snow was ready to be out of the vehicle. She'd opted to remain in furform, not wanting to expend the energy that shifting multiple times demanded. That had meant she'd been relegated to the back of the van with Delfina. Bone drove and Byron chatted quietly with her throughout the drive. If Snow had really cared, she could have listened in on what they had to say, but Delfina took up most of her attention. The hacker was tinkering with the drone and control pad, presumably reviewing logs and trying to determine why or how it had failed. Whatever she was finding wasn't to her liking, and she was getting more and more worked up.

There was an undercurrent of fear to her scent. The top layers were indignant frustration and bewilderment. Finally, Snow crawled over to her and nosed the digital equipment out of the way. She lay her head in Delfina's lap. Humans liked to cuddle with furry things. It was an instinct the wolven shared. Snow wasn't sure about the hacker yet, but she did know that if Delfina tried to attack her, she would come out a distant second in that contest.

Delfina hesitantly placed a hand on Snow's neck and, when she didn't react, gave it a gentle scritch. Snow leaned into the contact, and the smell of Delfina's anxiety eroded to the thinnest thread. Snow didn't have a whole lot of use on this mission, but this was one way she could help, and she was glad to do it.

Still, when the van slowed to a stop, she was on her feet and at the back door. The hacker would be fine. She wanted Cassidy.

As if her desires had summoned her, Cassidy bounded up to the back of the van. The late morning sun glittered off the crazy patchwork quilt that was her pelt. The brightness muted the odd eyes, though they still sparkled with excitement.

Snow jumped down from the back of the van and went straight to her, rubbing her head along the side of Cassidy's neck to bury her nose in her girlfriend's magnificent ruff. This was home. She inhaled deeply, pulling Cassidy's aroma inside of her, allowing it to coat her nostrils, before expelling it slowly.

Cassidy waited a moment, then cavorted halfway up the front steps of the house, pausing to look back at her expectantly. Bone and the humans were already heading inside the house. Snow followed along behind Cassidy, who let her through the door first, then took one last look out over the front yard before joining her.

"We'll need everyone in skinform," Marrow called out from the living room. "Time to start pulling things together."

Cassidy nodded her shaggy head and took off up the stairs to the second floor, Snow tight on her tail. The North Side Alpha took the first turn in the bathtub, shifting to skinform with an ease Snow couldn't help but envy. She was glad for her girlfriend's presence in front of the tub when it was her turn to shudder her way through her own transformation. Having someone to watch her back made all the difference. At the very tail end of her reversion to skinform, Cassidy disappeared. She was back in seconds.

"Someone left your clothes outside the bathroom door," her girlfriend said. "There's a Gatorade too." She placed the clothing and drink on the edge of the sink, then passed over a towel.

Snow rubbed herself down with vigorous strokes, then pulled on her clothes. The drink was more than welcome after a shift, and she chugged it down greedily as they descended the stairs to the living-dining area.

"'Bout time." Marrow looked away from them as they entered the living room and over to the rest of the group.

Snow tried not to let the comment get to her. She knew it was aimed her way, but Marrow's statement was vague enough that she doubted anyone else picked up on it.

Bone smacked her sister on the arm but was ignored for her efforts. Cassidy placed her hand on the small of Snow's back and stood straight behind her.

"So what's the deal?" Hammer asked. If he noticed the tension, he chose to ignore it.

"It's not good." Delfina looked over at the drone in its case. "Something killed my drone. We aren't going to be able to see what's going on inside without actually getting onto the grounds."

CHAPTER THIRTY-ONE

"Get on the grounds?" Cassidy pushed away from the doorframe. She locked eyes with Marrow. All of their plans had hinged upon having a good look at the layout of the place before going in.

"Infiltration will be harder without a good layout," Hammer said.

"What do you think?" Marrow ignored Cassidy's gaze as if it was nothing. She looked over at Byron.

"I need to see one of the windows inside whatever..." He turned to Delfina. "Is it a field?"

The hacker spread her hands. "Do you know what a Faraday cage is?"

Byron nodded.

"It seems to be similar, except it's running without the actual physical cage. I have no idea how they set it up. Theoretically, the idea is possible, but we should be decades away from realizing that kind of tech."

"Fair enough." Byron tapped his lower lip thoughtfully. "If there's a gap in this field, do you think you'll be able to run a signal through it?"

"Maybe. I don't know how big the gap would have to be."

"Maybe about the size of a tower window."

"That could do it. How would you do that?"

Byron grinned and fished a string of glowing crystals out from under his shirt. "Magic." He turned to Marrow. "Let's see what we can scare up online. I need the best schematic of the building that we can find and photos, preferably from the outside and inside."

"Magic?" Delfina turned to face her bank of monitors. "We're actually going to magic our way into a prison. Now I've heard everything."

Cassidy gave Snow's shoulder a squeeze, then moved past her. "I can help," she said. "I'm an excellent Googler. If you're looking for pics, I can help track those down."

Wordlessly, Delfina reached under the table and produced a decidedly unimpressive-looking laptop. Cassidy had seen more elegant looking bricks. The hacker powered it on and unlocked the login screen.

"Knock yourself out," she said.

The living room was tense as Cassidy and Delfina bent themselves over their respective keyboards. Cassidy went straight to Google, looking up Silent Heights Penitentiary. Sure enough, there was a "Friends of the Penitentiary" page. She clicked through to the website and learned that they'd given tours for a long time before canceling them abruptly a couple of months previous. That was interesting. Even more so was the note stating that there was no firm date for when tours might resume. She clicked away from the main page, looking for photo galleries. Soon she was paging through image after image on the group's Instagram account. That led her to hashtags related to the prison.

Delfina muttered something about building codes and started trying to log into Clayton County's website.

"What do you think, Byron?" Cassidy asked. She swiveled the laptop around so he could see a set of photos that an urban spelunking group out of Dubuque had taken during a trip through the old prison. Judging by the dates on the photos, they were a little less than ten years old.

He leaned in to peer at the images, then reached past her, flicking through the online gallery. "This could work." Byron stopped on a fairly innocuous photo of a window. It was one of the artsier pictures in the group, likely chosen for its dramatic lighting as the subject matter was fairly mundane. "Can we get a view of the other side?"

"Garbage," Delfina grumbled from next to them. "The state of these plans is deplorable."

"Maybe try the state historical society," Snow said to her. "They should have more money than a rural county."

"I can try…" Delfina bent back over the keyboard.

Cassidy zoomed in on her photo, trying to determine if there was anything about the view out the window that might tell them where it was from. She wasn't going to be as cantankerous as the hacker, at least not out loud, but she wasn't impressed with the photo descriptions on this site. There were no GPS coordinates embedded in the files, which could have made things so much easier. Unfortunately, the view out the window was dark and indistinct. She copied the image and downloaded it to the desktop.

"You have Photoshop on this thing?" she asked.

Delfina shook her head. "I got GIMP."

"I don't know that one." She knew image editors in general, however. Mary had given her a hard time about her Fashion major, first for signing up for it, then for dropping it. It was difficult not to feel vaguely triumphant that something she'd learned in university finally had a direct application to her postcollege life. Her mood soured when she realized she couldn't call her sister up to gloat; she couldn't even leave her a voice mail.

It was slower going than Photoshop would have been, but Cassidy was able to import the image and start working on contrast and sharpness. Slowly, a triangular shape started to appear from the dark mass of pixels.

"Is that the peak of one of the towers?" Byron asked.

"Could be." Cassidy opened the tab with Google maps and zoomed in on the prison in satellite view. "What do you think?" She pointed at the facade of what seemed to be the original prison building.

"The angle isn't quite right." Byron chewed on his lower lip while glaring at the screen. "I bet it's on that side, though. Can we get more views of the outside?"

"Your wish…" Cassidy went back to combing through photographs.

"Got it!" Delfina crowed. She double-clicked on a file, and black-and-white copies of blueprints opened up across two of her monitors. They'd had been scanned from originals that hadn't been well cared for, but the lines were mostly legible.

"It's a lot smaller than the satellite view shows," Hammer said.

"Looks like they've added on to it over the years," Bone said. She pointed at the yard. "It's missing those buildings in the middle."

"Also half the main complex." Marrow leaned back in her chair. "Still, it's a good start. I don't think the walls have changed too much."

"Prison's something like a hundred years old," Delfina said. "Plans from back then aren't going to be super complete."

"More like a hundred and fifty," Cassidy said.

"There, you see?" Delfina pointed at the plans on the screen. "This is nothing short of a major miracle. You should all be really impressed."

"You did an excellent job, dear." Marrow grinned at Delfina's scowl. "Still, it could be useful. Make sure you hold onto that. Now, can you find us anything more recent, say with ductwork or plumbing lines?"

"Some people have seen too many heist movies," Delfina grumbled. She turned back to her keyboard.

Cassidy and Byron went back to comparing images to each other and the murky, pixelated blobs she had salvaged with her Photoshop clone.

"That's the one," Byron finally said. He pointed at a window high up on the main building. A metal catwalk had been built to connect it to the stone wall's original ramparts. "Check that angle. It gets the very top of that guard tower. It's pretty close to the right size, too." He peered through the living room, then turned back and tapped on the lower right-hand corner of the image on the screen. "Where is it? Bring up the aerial map again, would you?"

Bemused at the wheelman's building excitement, Cassidy obliged him. She zoomed in on the main building, keeping an eye out for that metal catwalk. Sure enough, it was in the satellite image.

"That's it." Byron nodded, his eyes gleaming. "Zoom out."

Cassidy tapped to back the image further out.

"Slower." He patted her on the shoulder. "Zoom back in, then out again, but slowly."

"Do you want to drive?"

Byron shook his head. "Just do it. Please."

The last was tacked on as if he'd been admonished about his manners often as a child. Still, he wasn't being rude, merely excitable. He also didn't set off the same dominance instincts the wolven did. After a moment, Cassidy complied with his request.

"Perfect." Byron's eyes were glued to the screen. "Back in one more time. Slow on the way in too."

If she'd been with her friends from college, Cassidy would definitely have made a dirty joke at that last line. Over by the dining room table, Bone smothered a snicker.

"Got it." Byron stood up straight and pointed at Delfina. "Grab your drone." He stalked into the dining room, then threw open one of the smaller windows.

"Here we go," Bone said as she walked past Cassidy. She looked over at Snow, who was still standing in the corner where Cassidy had left her. "You're going to want to see this."

"See what?" Cassidy pushed away from the table.

"The front end of what you saw in the van," Marrow said.

Byron pulled the necklace of crystals from under his shirt. It was less a piece of jewelry and more a series of bulky, hard-cornered rocks that glowed, even in the light of the sun streaming through the windows. He undid the clasp on the silver chain and removed two sizable crystals, then returned the rest of them beneath his shirt. After placing the crystals on the windowsill, he licked his finger and began tracing designs along its bottom edge, then up one side of the casing. He paused once and pointed vaguely in the direction of the group who was watching his antics with emotions that ranged from giddy to completely confused.

"Water," Byron said. When no one responded, he snapped his fingers, then pointed toward them again. "Come on."

Bone and Marrow jabbed each other with their elbows. Marrow must have come out second best in their contest. She rolled her eyes, then headed off toward the kitchen. As water splashed into a cup, Byron continued to trace invisible symbols over the sash. He'd started down the other side when Marrow stomped up to him and shoved the glass in his direction.

"Mm." He took three large gulps, then handed the cup back to her. "Thanks."

Marrow stood close by, watching as he completed his symbols. He grabbed the crystals and stepped back.

"Here it comes," Bone said.

The wheelman muttered words in a language Cassidy didn't recognize. He repeated the same strange phrase, his voice raising with each cycle. He threw his head back and shouted those same unintelligible words at the ceiling one last time. The crystal in each hand flared an incandescent white so bright that Cassidy had to put her hand up in front of her eyes. They shone with a harsh glare for one breath, then another. Then in the moment between her third breath and the next, the light died.

Cassidy lowered her hand and stared, blinking away the after image.

"What just happen—" The rest of the question died in her throat. The living room window no longer showed the tree-lined front yard of the house where corporate warriors went to figure out how to live with themselves in their line of work. It opened onto an open area lined with rough yellow stone walls.

CHAPTER THIRTY-TWO

"How did you do that?" Delfina rushed up to the edge of the window and peered at it. She poked the frame where it had abutted glass only a moment earlier.

"Magic." Byron grinned. He stuffed the two crystals into his pocket. They were dark and dull, lacking even a hint of their former glow.

Snow sized up the dandy. Magic would certainly explain why he smelled not quite human. She had her thoughts on how humans ended up with the ability to do magic, but as usual, had no way to prove any of it. The skill was exceedingly rare, so much so that she hadn't recognized the traces when she'd smelled them on him.

"Can you fly your drone through there?" Byron pointed behind the hacker.

"I sure can." Delfina flipped open the case with the drone.

Snow stiffened as the scent of plastic reminded her of being stranded out in the open with those cameras swiveling her way. A warm hand caressed the small of her back.

"You all right?" Cassidy asked, her voice soft.

The contact reminded her that she was well and truly out of that situation. Hopefully, she would never have to endure it again. "I'm good." She snagged Cassidy's hand and squeezed it. "Now that you're here" was left unsaid. It wasn't a sentiment she wanted to air in front of the Gary Alphas.

Snow raised her voice. "So you can talk in my head and make illusions and portals in thin air. Any other talents you've got up that sleeve?"

Byron grinned and mimed tearing the sleeves of his cardigan off his shoulders. "Those are the showstoppers, I'm afraid. Telepathy only works when I can see the other person. Illusions don't take much energy unless I have to hold onto them for a long time. Portals are a whole hell of a lot of effort."

Hammer stroked his chin thoughtfully. "Why don't we just portal inside the prison, grab our people, and portal out?"

Bone shrugged. "It would be doable on a small scale. We've used him like that before."

"But it takes a lot out of him," Marrow said. "It's easy to pop open a portal and drop a firebomb through, then close it up."

"Moving as many people as we need to…" Bone eyed the wheelman. "What do you think?"

"First of all, I need a physical portal," Byron said. "Something to anchor it, like a door or window frame. Second, I need to be familiar with the place where the portal is anchored and where it's coming out. I can get around some of that with pictures and seeing the environment, like we did online just now, but it gets way, way harder. And then holding it open…" He shook his head. "I'd love to be your silver bullet—"

"I see what you did there," Marrow said.

Byron's face creased with a quick grin. "—but it's not that simple."

"We can make this work," Delfina said. She dragged an overstuffed armchair over to the window and took a seat in it. The high-pitched whine of the drone's engines filled the room, then suddenly diminished as it flew across the sill.

"Byron's talents don't change much about our plans," Marrow said. "We still have the same basic tasks. We have to complete our recon, infiltrate the prison, and identify where our wolves are being held."

"After that it's break them out of whatever holding pens or cells they're in," Hammer said. "We'd be fools not to assume they're locked up."

"Then get them out," Bone said. "And us with them."

"And open enough space between us and whoever's in that place that they can't pick us all right back up again," Cassidy finished.

"Parameters haven't changed, people." Marrow turned and pointed back into the dining room. "Let's leave the hacker to her toys." She swept out of the room.

Byron lingered a moment. "Anyone looking toward the window will see you looking out," he said. "Try to make sure you're keeping out of sight."

Cassidy laid a hand on his arm. "Why don't you stay with her and keep an eye out? I don't think she'll be able to watch the monitor and the guardhouse."

Byron shot a look over at Bone, who nodded. "I can do that, I guess," he said.

"Good." Cassidy definitely didn't bristle when the human got someone else's permission over hers. It certainly didn't bother her that the someone wasn't even the wolven who had won herself the opportunity to head this little venture.

She joined the Alphas and worked with them to spin up more plans and poke holes in them as the humans performed their digital recon. Snow tried to slip out of the room, but Cassidy was able to cajole her into joining the rest of the team at the table. She didn't say much, but her insights skewered more than one plot.

They continued that way into the afternoon and evening, with breaks for lunch and dinner. The Alphas and Snow took to the outside to find their dinners, while Delfina and Byron drove into town. After dinner, Delfina had much more to report. The detail she was able to add around the physical makeup of the area was invaluable, but she still hadn't been able to hack into the wireless network being used in the prison. Her signal through the portal simply wasn't consistent enough. After throwing a mouse across the room and dashing it to pieces on the far wall, Delfina finally admitted she wasn't going to be able to infiltrate the network.

"Guess it's up to me to get the lay of the inside," Hammer said. He scrubbed at his beard as if saying goodbye to it.

"We've pieced together what we can from that ancient blueprint and the photos Cassidy found," Marrow said. "It's not enough."

"And it wouldn't tell us exactly where our wolves are being held anyway." Bone stood and stretched her arms until they popped in their sockets. She sighed with relief.

As if that had been a signal, everyone shifted in place or stood up, working muscles grown stiff through inactivity. It had been hours since dinner.

"We've got a start," Marrow said. "Let's implement the first pieces, then regroup in a couple of days." She stood and draped an arm around her twin's shoulders, leaning against her sister. "You know your tasks."

"Yep." Cassidy popped up out of her chair, trying to stifle her own groan of relief as her butt finally rebounded from the shape it had been forced into. The chairs hadn't been uncomfortable at first, but she had close to twelve hours sitting on her ass today. How did humans with office jobs manage?

Her stomach swirled with a slightly sickening combination of anxiety and too much time planning with not enough doing. She had assignments, and her wolf wanted them done as much as she did. The wolf also wanted them to be rested and energetic for the coming tasks. It was as close as Cassidy had ever known her to admit that the future existed and should be prepared for.

"You ready to head up?" Cassidy asked Snow, who nodded.

The lone wolf had been quiet the past couple of days since they'd left Faint. Cassidy smiled at her and received a quick grin in return. Maybe she was just overwhelmed with all these people in one place. Snow seemed to prefer not to have to deal with large groups.

They went through what had become their regular evening routine. Cassidy pulled off her shirt and pants and was crouching down to assume furform when Snow reached out a hand.

"How about skinform tonight?" She slid between the sheets, as naked as Cassidy. They didn't have pajamas. They barely had a full change of clothing.

"I can do skinform." Cassidy grinned. "Skin on skin is as nice as fur on fur, in its own way."

"I'm glad you think so." Snow pulled back the sheet and blanket on the other side of the bed.

Cassidy took the invitation and pulled the bedclothes up over her shoulder. It was cool between the sheets. "Is it all right if I cuddle up to you?" Asking still felt right in skinform.

"Of course." Snow turned away from her, allowing Cassidy to take up position behind her as the big spoon. She relaxed back into her girlfriend's arms. "Can you get the light?"

"Of course." Cassidy reached past her and tugged on the bedside light's pull chain, plunging the room into darkness. She snuggled in, sharing Snow's sigh.

Tension bled out of the lone wolf's limbs and Cassidy found herself unwinding with her. She tucked her chin on top of Snow's shoulder and allowed herself to start drifting toward sleep, but it eluded her. For a few minutes she lay there and thought that maybe she was nervous about their first concrete steps toward rescuing their wolves. Cassidy was no stranger to anxiety-induced insomnia. In school, she'd come up with a series of steps toward complete relaxation that she used when she was keyed up about exams. She ran over the broad outline of what was coming up, but without getting mired in the details. When that didn't work, she allowed herself to identify what she was worrying about, then how she would handle those hypothetical situations if they came up. That still wasn't doing the trick, and Cassidy was forced to envision herself skiing down a long slope. It was her version of counting sheep and had been her go-to for getting to sleep for years, but even that wasn't helping.

Snow shifted, snugging the blankets higher around her shoulder. "Are you awake?" she asked.

"I am." Cassidy ran one hand over the small of Snow's back in what she hoped was soothing circles. "Can't sleep?"

"No." Snow moved again, this time sticking a foot out from under the covers.

"Am I making you too hot?" Cassidy tried to scoot away, but Snow grabbed her arm and held it tight around her.

"It's not that." She paused. "We need to talk about the vampires."

"Oh." Cassidy realized she was squeezing Snow's ribcage and loosened her grip. "I didn't know that was going to happen. That I was going to get that worked up, I mean. I'm really sorry you had to do that for me."

"Cassidy." Snow wormed her way around in Cassidy's embrace until they were face-to-face. She cupped Cassidy's jaw between her hands. "I don't regret doing that for you. It was clear you were in a state that didn't feel good, and I'm glad I was able to bring you the relief you needed."

"Oh. Well, good…" Cassidy allowed her voice to trail off. If that wasn't what Snow was mad about, then what was it?

"Do you remember what you said?"

"I said a lot, I think." Cassidy's cheeks burned as she remembered how out of control she'd been. Even when her heat had been at its most intense, she'd never needed to come that badly. She had some vague recollections of begging Snow to keep doing what she'd been doing as they'd chased the orgasm that would finally allow her to come down from the peak the vampires had stranded her upon. "I don't think it made a lot of sense. You probably shouldn't read too much into it."

"Ah." Rather than reassuring her girlfriend, Cassidy's words pulled a spike of blue anguish from her.

"Was that not—" Cassidy tried to gather Snow to her again, but the lone wolf pulled away. "I thought that's what you wanted…"

"What I wanted to hear?" Snow hiccupped a strange laugh that was more sob than mirth. "Turns out I have no idea what I wanted to hear."

"I don't understand."

"That's quite clear." Snow sniffled. "That's what I get for beating around the bush. So you really don't remember what you said, at the end, when it was all said and done?"

"I really don't," Cassidy confessed. "I was exhausted, and I think I actually dozed off for a few seconds."

"You said, and I quote 'And I love you for that.'"

"I did?"

Snow nodded. "Right after I said that I was happy to step in to help out with your…" She gesticulated with one hand as if searching for the words. "…libido problem."

"Oh. That doesn't sound great in context, does it?"

"Not really."

Cassidy chose her next words carefully. "Are you mad about me using the L word, or about the context?"

"Well, before you said that you didn't remember so I shouldn't pay attention to it, I thought it was both. But hearing you say that…" The stench of sadness rolled off Snow again.

"I see. I'm going to talk through this. Let me know if I get too far off base…" Cassidy mulled over Snow's revelations. "So you've been sad that I said I loved you in a way that made it sound like I only loved you because you could get me off. Is that right?"

Snow tucked her head down so it was lying on Cassidy's chest. She nodded.

"And you thought that you were mad about the fact that I said I loved you in that moment."

"Mm hm." Snow's voice was small in the dark.

Cassidy found herself wishing she could see her girlfriend's face. Smell was all well and good for getting a bead on what she was feeling, but being able to look her in the eyes felt like it would have more weight. But Snow had waited until the lights were out before broaching the topic.

"But it turns out it's just the context, and you're not mad that I said I loved you, except then I accidentally took it back. Do I have all of that right?"

"It sounds silly when you say it out loud."

"I don't mean it to." Cassidy stroked her fingers through the abundant curls of Snow's hair. "Not at all. I'm just nailing down the facts of our conversation so I can respond to them in a way that makes sense and that neither of us can misunderstand."

"If you say so."

"I do say so. Did I miss anything?"

"No, I think that's a decent summary." Snow's voice was grumpy.

"All right. Here's what I'm thinking. Nothing has changed."

"What?" Snow's body stiffened under Cassidy's hands.

"No, it's true. Look, I'm not going to ask you for sex. That ball is firmly in your court. You served it into mine that one time, and I lobbed it back. If a situation comes up where you want to send it back my way, I'm happy to receive it, but that's as far as it goes." Cassidy concentrated hard on the truth of her words. She meant them, and she wanted to make sure she smelled like she meant it. She had no idea if she could intensify the scent of whatever emotion she was feeling, but it didn't hurt to try.

"Okay." Snow's aroma shaded from complete anxiety to anxiety mixed with relief. It made for an interesting swirl of lavender that Cassidy hadn't seen often.

"As for the second part…" She hesitated. Was now the right time? It was so soon, and they were about to engage in something incredibly difficult. Their lives and the lives of many, many others hung in the balance.

"The second part?" Snow asked when the pause had dragged on too long.

"Well, there's no way I could love you just because you gave me an orgasm."

"Um…" Snow's scent edged away from relief into confusion and was shading into the alarming shade of virulent red that Cassidy associated with anger.

"Because I loved you before that, you dork," Cassidy hastened to add.

The laugh came out half snort, half wheeze. "You're the dork."

"No, you are." Cassidy gathered Snow in close and tucked her head in the crook between her neck and shoulder. She blew a light raspberry on her girlfriend's skin, delighting in how she squealed and giggled. They fit together so nicely, in skin and furform. There would always be room in her arms for Snow.

CHAPTER THIRTY-THREE

The next week passed in a flurry of tasks and preparation. Every day there was something else to do. Snow contributed as she could but felt constantly overshadowed by the Alphas. She found herself spending more and more time with the humans. Delfina always needed another set of eyes on some set of data, or maps, or blueprints. Snow had looked at so many versions of prisons that she started to dream about them, but not as buildings. No, her dreams were filled with lines on pages that somehow still managed to trap her within them.

Cassidy spent as much time as she was able to with her, but it was never enough, not when Snow knew what awaited them at the end of their preparations. Hammer was gone most days, on his infiltration of the prison. He came back late each night smelling of cleaning products and rage. The prison employee he'd switched places with was a janitor, one who didn't spend much time in the areas where the wolven were held. He was able to get close enough to the captured wolven to smell them twice, and the information he was able to bring back was instrumental in firming up their plans.

Alarmingly, both times he'd gotten within sniffing distance of the wolven, he'd come out unable to access his wolf half. He'd been stuck in skinform for hours after the end of his shift. The Alphas had exchanged angry and fearful glances when they'd heard that, but it had become simply one more item to factor into the never-ending puzzle that was this prison break. Not being able to shift would be a hindrance, to be sure, but even in skinform, they were still faster and stronger than humans. A quick experiment the twins had been only too happy to carry out had revealed that Hammer still healed at the same rate.

The plan grew in complexity as the days wore on. No one was happy about that. Marrow and Bone even sniped at each other over it. Whatever had kept Hammer from transforming meant the frontal assault idea went thoroughly out the window. Its only virtue had been simplicity, and Snow wasn't sad to see it go, but she suspected some of the Alphas had been holding out hope that the solution might actually be that uncomplicated.

And so the twins disappeared, sometimes with Byron to fulfill his wheelman duties and sometimes on their own. It seemed that beyond being able to weave illusions and craft portals, Byron was also an accomplished car thief, and Bone and Marrow were putting his talents to good use. Slowly, the driveway to the house was filling up with all manner of vehicles: a random assortment of vans and passenger cars, as well as some delivery trucks and a couple of semis. Delfina had to take a call to reassure the owners of the property that nothing untoward was happening. She lied with the smooth confidence of someone who knew that more existed in life than what the human on the other end of the line knew. In that moment, Snow could see the tiny hacker as a vampire. The certainty that Delfina was being groomed to become one of Stiletto's kind was impossible to exorcize from her brain. The thoughts were unhelpful. Delfina could have been half vampire, and it wouldn't have mattered as long as she continued to aid them in the ways only she could.

Each day flew past quicker than the next, until Snow, the Alphas, and the humans were sitting around the dining room table one evening a week later, waiting for Hammer to get back from his shift.

He swept through the doors, the scent of his agitation preceding him. It was so strong Snow didn't understand how the humans couldn't smell it.

"I got to that building," he said, without any kind of preamble save his distressed state. He pointed at Cassidy. "The one in the middle of the yard. Where Luther is probably being held."

The Alphas sat forward, almost as one, their attention riveted to Hammer. Snow leaned back in her chair, trying to spare herself some secondhand apprehension.

"It's not good." He reached up to tug at a beard that was no longer there. When there was nothing to grip, he ran both hands over his recently shaved scalp in agitation. "There's definitely some medical shit going on in there."

"Medical shit?" Bone's voice was low and dangerous. "What type of medical shit?"

Hammer gestured down at his barrel chest. "Do I look like a doctor? But I know medical fuckery when I see it. That's not even the worst part."

"How can that not be the worst part?" Cassidy asked.

"That's where the cubs are being held."

The Alphas were on their feet, statements of outrage and concern overlapping in a deafening cacophony.

"The cubs?"

"Who does that to younglings?"

"We can't wait. We have to go now." Bone leaned forward and pounded her fist on the tabletop. A muffled crack pierced the angry turmoil of the Alphas' voices.

The humans had scooted back from the table, and Snow had to tear her attention away from the emotional scrum to focus on their surroundings.

"Marrow, we have to move now," Hammer said. "We can't afford to wait any longer."

"We don't have everything in place yet." Marrow shook her head. "If we push this too much, it'll all fall apart. The semis need to be placed."

"So we do it tonight," Bone said.

"Look, I want to get this moving as much as the rest of you." The words were true. Marrow was resolute in her scent and her body language. Her eyes shone the same brilliant amber as her sister's. "But everything needs to be just so. We need to be just so. The better rested we are, the more on top of our game we are, the better the chances that this will come together without any problems."

"So we're leaving our cubs in the hands of assholes who experiment on them just so we can get a good night's sleep?" Hammer's voice was high with incredulity.

Marrow put her hands on her hips. "Are you initiating a challenge?"

Snow caught Delfina's eye and glanced over at Byron, then deliberately looked at the stairs to the second floor. The hacker gave her a tight grin before taking the wheelman firmly by the arm and hustling him out of the room.

Hammer hesitated as the humans took themselves out of harm's way. He wanted to challenge Marrow; they could all smell it.

"If any of you want to try for the top spot, that's fine by me." Marrow swept her eyes across all of them. "I can take any one of you. I'm the best person to head this little caper, and you know it. So maybe start thinking with what's in here"—she tapped her forehead—"and not what's in here." Marrow thumped the left side of her chest. "If you want to see your wolves alive, you'll listen to what I'm saying. If you want to squabble about it, I'll beat your asses, and then we'll still do things my way."

Hammer scrubbed his hands over the fuzz on his scalp. He wanted to take her on, but something was holding him back. "One more day," he finally ground out. "No more."

"That's all I ask. One day to get everything set as well as it can be." A small smile flashed across Marrow's face as she tried to be gracious in victory. "Besides, we still need to pick up the explosives."

"We could have done that in the morning and been good to go at lunch," Bone said quietly, without looking in her sister's direction.

"Laundry drop off is first thing." Marrow shook her head. "It's literally the first task. We can't open with an anomaly. That's asking for trouble. You know this."

Bone didn't reply, but she did turn to meet her twin's eyes. She nodded, but unhappiness oozed from her pores.

"One day then," Cassidy said. "I've got my own preparations to see to." She stood. "If we're not doing any challenges, I'm going upstairs."

None of the Alphas said anything, though Hammer nodded. Snow ghosted away from her chair at the end of the table. None of the others even twitched. She was pretty sure they'd forgotten all about her.

Cassidy hadn't. She was waiting for Snow just outside the doorway from the dining room into the hall. When Snow reached for her hand, Cassidy reached back, just as she always did.

"Time to talk to your mom?" Snow asked.

Cassidy nodded.

* * *

She stared at the brick-like phone in her hands. This would be her last call to her mom before they started this insane plan that could work—no, that had to work—to get their people back. What was Cassidy supposed to say to her? "So long, hopefully I don't get killed, leaving you alone without any daughters?"

It had possibility but lacked a certain panache. It was a good thing Sophia Nolan had no better idea where her daughter was than Cassidy knew where her mom was. She couldn't rat Carla out to Stiletto, and Sophia couldn't show up on the doorstep of a supposedly shuttered prison asking after her daughter.

"Do you want some space?" Snow asked, her voice hushed.

"From you?" Cassidy tried to grin at her girlfriend but knew it was coming out pained. "Never." She patted Snow on the leg.

"Okay." Snow caught her hand and threaded her fingers together with Cassidy's. "I'm right here."

"I know." Her smile warmed to genuine appreciation. She took a deep breath and typed in a quick text message to her mom's number warning her of the incoming call from a number that wasn't in her phone. Not that she really needed to bother. Her mom picked up every call that came through, even the ones her phone company helpfully labeled as Scam Likely. Cassidy gave her text a minute to sink in, then dialed her mom's phone.

The first ring was cut off halfway through by Sophia's breathless, "Hello?"

"It's me, Mom. I said I was calling."

"Just in case. You can never tell with these unlisted phone numbers."

"Of course." They'd had this discussion before, and Cassidy wasn't willing to push it this time. "How are things in your neck of the world?"

"Good, I think." Her mom's voice took on a hollow quality as she cupped her hand over her mouth and the phone. "Carla's sending me home soon."

Cassidy sat up straight on the bed. "Really?"

"That's what she said," Sophia said in the same hushed tones. "I'm trying not to act too excited about it. I don't want to hurt her feelings."

"She's a centuries-old vampire, Mom. I don't think you can hurt her feelings, even if you tried."

Sophia tsked. "First of all, you should never assume someone else's emotional state, Cassidy Anne. Second, she's been different. Fragile. I don't think you'd be doing so well after your whole world was turned upside down overnight."

Cassidy kept her mouth shut, turning her mom's trick of silence as a weapon back on her.

"Oh." Sophia sighed. "I know it's been hard for you, sweet pea. I guess what I'm saying is that she was in charge in Chicago for decades and then was stabbed in the back by someone she'd taken in."

Snow closed her hand around Cassidy's ankle, giving it a warm squeeze as Cassidy struggled not to unload on her mom.

"Is that what she told you?" Cassidy kept her voice light and conversational.

"Not in so many words, but I picked it up. I'm good at reading between the lines."

Not as good as Carla was at heavily implying. "I see."

"Anyway, I'm going to have her send me back to Chicago, not New York. I have to check in with Mr. Gunn."

"Mr. Gunn?"

"The private detective I hired to find your sister, remember?" She'd stopped trying to be discreet, and Cassidy was treated to the full force of her disapproval.

"Sorry, Mom. It's been a hectic month." And it had been. Cassidy didn't think she'd truly appreciated exactly how much had happened before saying the words. "But this too shall pass, right?"

Sophia laughed. "Don't quote your dad at me."

"You should really go back home. Chicago is way too dangerous. I can't believe you want to go there after everything that's happened."

"I can't not go back. Your sister is out there somewhere. If you're too busy to bring her home, then it's up to me."

"Mom." The line of conversation was so well worn that Cassidy could see where the argument was going to end and exactly which steps would take them there. Time to stop soft-pedaling the conversation. "Either you get killed going after her, or you get her killed. Is that what you want?"

"If you would help, we'd have twice the chance of finding Mary."

"With two of us, there's twice the chance that we'll all die." Cassidy took a deep breath, keeping her voice stern, but not slipping into commanding. If that happened, her mom would go against her wishes to spite her. "I'll handle it as soon as I'm done. We're close to wrapping things up here."

"Are you?" Sophia's voice lightened considerably. "That's the first time I've heard you say anything positive since you left town."

"Left town" was a terrible euphemism for what had happened that night nearly a month ago. It did nothing to capture the grief and pressure Cassidy had been grappling with since. Without Snow, she wasn't sure how she would have gotten through it. There would probably have been an ill-advised challenge to either Hammer or one of the twins that she likely wouldn't have survived.

"The next couple of days are going to be…tense. If you don't hear from me at our regular check-in next week, then…"

"Is it that bad?"

"Maybe. I don't want to leave you hanging, but I also don't want you to worry."

"I don't think that combination is possible, dear."

"I know." Cassidy sighed. "Promise me you'll head home after you leave Carla."

"I don't know…"

That was more concession than she'd gotten so far. "I'll visit you at your apartment. We'll talk over plans for finding Mary." Up to this point, Cassidy had refused to talk about what came next. Part of her was worried that laying future plans would only lead to them being disrupted; the other part had been too wrapped up in the current mess in front of her.

"Good." Sophia's voice was steadier than it had been for a while. "I'll make up the guest bedroom. Don't make me get the covers changed for nothing."

"I won't." Cassidy grinned. Her shoulders relaxed and she nodded. "I love you, Mom."

"And I love you, Cassie-bean. I *will* talk to you next week."

"Yes, Mommy." Cassidy smiled as she disconnected the call. It was just like Sophia to believe that she could make the universe conform through sheer force of will.

She stared at the phone for a moment. Snow leaned her head on Cassidy's shoulder, wrapping one arm loosely around her waist. That was one problem handled. If only the next one could be solved with a little bit of give-and-take.

CHAPTER THIRTY-FOUR

That last day was a blur of preparation and high levels of anxiety. It got to the point where Snow was finding it difficult to be around anyone who wasn't Cassidy. Fortunately, Bone and Marrow cleared out with Byron. They took the two semis with them. Hammer had left early to show up for what was probably his last shift as a custodian for the prison. It was a good thing too. The rage he radiated was deep enough that even the humans were picking up on it.

Cassidy was left back at the house with Snow and Delfina. They worked in the back of the box truck they'd spent the better part of the week converting. The two wolven were there to be extensions of Delfina's will. This was her show. The back of the truck needed enough room for the equipment she would use to hack into the prison's systems, but it also had to look like the inside wasn't so much shallower than the outside. Byron had said he could help with that, but the less work he had to do to mask reality, the less power it would take him.

At the beginning of the previous week, he'd given them each a crystal to keep on their person at all times, with special instructions to the wolven to make sure they held onto it while shifting. Every morning he checked the crystals, and if they glowed brightly enough, he would hand them another. For some reason, and to the wheelman's delight, Snow's crystals filled up the most quickly.

Byron was close-lipped about what exactly the crystals did for him but given his performance with the portal in the living room window, Snow had to assume that they functioned as some sort of battery for his magic.

The sun was closing in on the horizon when Delfina declared herself pleased enough with their efforts. The small closet they'd constructed hummed with machinery to the point where Snow and Cassidy didn't enjoy being too close to it. The high-pitched whine was manageable when the door was closed, but it was still audible to their sensitive wolven ears. Snow didn't want to think about what it would be like to be shoved in that room while in furform.

They trooped into the house and changed out of clothes grown sweaty with the exertion of playing carpenter for a day. The day's clothing was tossed in the corner instead of being laid aside to be reworn. If they truly were pushing forward with the plan the next day, then nothing would be left behind at this house. If it was important or expensive enough to hold onto, it would be tossed through a small portal to be retrieved later. Anything not being worn or carried into the prison would be destroyed.

Cassidy and Snow shared a quick shower. Snow knew Cassidy enjoyed the feeling of her hands, so she soaped her girlfriend down, avoiding any areas that could result in unnecessary arousal. Then she turned her back and allowed Cassidy to do the same for her.

By the time they were out and toweled off, the Gary Alphas and Byron were back. The wheelman was preparing a meal for him and Delfina, under the assumption that the wolven would go get their food from the land. He was correct. If this was going to be their last night before who knew what was going to happen, Snow itched to be back in furform. Spending time as her wolf self would help calm the thoughts that twisted in her head. The constant what-ifs and doomsday scenarios weren't helpful, but knowing that didn't stop her from thinking it.

Marrow stood next to the table, leafing through the lists, drawings, and plans they'd generated over the past week. Every now and again, she'd pass a piece of paper to Bone, who would review it, nod, then hand it back.

"We all good?" she asked absently when Snow and Cassidy entered the room.

"To Delfina's satisfaction," Cassidy said. "Byron should take a look to make sure it'll work for him, but if we're moving tomorrow, I don't know that there's much we can do about it."

"What about your errands?" Snow asked.

Marrow looked up, a little surprised that Snow was asking directly. She hadn't been speaking up much, except when something in the plan seemed unnecessarily dangerous.

"They went well. Everything is in place."

The front door swung shut behind Hammer. His agitation wasn't at the same fever pitch as it had been the day before, but he was still on edge.

He stalked into the dining room, standing closer to Marrow than strictly necessary. "We move tomorrow." It wasn't a question.

Marrow moved away from him to the head of the table. She braced her arms against the top, peering at the papers that were strewn about. "That's everything on the list." She looked up and made eye contact with her sister.

Bone nodded. "It all checks out."

She turned her attention to the South Shore Alpha. "And you marked the path inside the prison?"

Hammer nodded.

"Then we're good to go."

"Tomorrow," Hammer reiterated.

"Tomorrow." Marrow's tone matched his. Her eyes raked the assembled crew, daring any of them to contradict her. She skipped over Snow, then looked back and caught her gaze, holding it for the same amount of time she'd afforded to the Alphas. She raised her voice and looked over at the humans. "Tell us you're with us or leave."

Delfina's eyebrows shot up under her bangs at the blunt request, but Byron stepped forward.

"Of course I'm with you," he said. He grinned impishly. "Why would I miss out on all the fun we have planned?" He pulled the string of crystals out from around his neck. Each glowed brightly. "Besides, I haven't been this full up since the last job we pulled."

Marrow and Bone stalked to either side of him. Their faces distorted, muzzles protruding and sprouting fur while the rest of them remained human. Behind him, Delfina's scent soured with disgust and a soupçon of fear. The twins inhaled deeply as they thoroughly invaded his space.

"He speaks truly," Bone growled.

As one, they turned to Delfina.

"Are you with us?" Marrow rumbled.

"I'm not backing out now," Delfina said. The fear in her scent increased, but there was no trace of duplicity. "I have a job to do, and I'll do my best."

The Gary Alphas squeezed in around her. Byron moved into the dining room to keep from being shoved out of the way. They took their time inspecting the hacker, and though they never touched her, at times only a whisker separated their noses from her skin.

"No lies," Marrow said. It was both a report on what they smelled and an instruction to the hacker and, by extension, the rest of them. Not that there could be any question about the motivations of the wolven, but the humans were wild cards. The twins seemed to have decided that Delfina represented the greatest weakness in the crew's cohesiveness. Snow couldn't blame them. They had a track record with Byron, but Delfina was an unknown. Her loyalties were divided. As long as their mission was also in the interest of the vampires, they were in the clear. But what if that changed?

Marrow shook her head, allowing her muzzle to pull back into her face, though Bone kept hers protruding. She panted, looking ridiculous with her tongue lolling from a half-human, half-wolf visage. Bone's eyes twinkled when they met Snow's.

"I suggest you two get a good night's sleep," Marrow said to the humans. "We'll be up at five to get things coordinated and on the road. The laundry truck does its pickup/drop-off by eight at the latest."

Delfina nodded and headed back into the kitchen where her dinner was waiting. Byron clapped his hands together and surveyed the wolven.

"Keep your crystals on you as much as possible tonight," he said. "I assume you're going out for your nightly run. Beyond that, if you could make sure you go through a lot of doorways that would be really helpful."

"Doorways," Cassidy said, in a flat tone that indicated she had no idea what the wheelman was going on about.

"Doorways. As many as possible. Also going in and out from inside to outside would be even more effective. It would really help a lot. I'll get those crystals back from you in the morning." With that, he gave them a curious half-bow and headed to the kitchen as well.

Snow stared after him. The human was prone to pranks and tricks, which explained how he got along with the Gary Alphas so well. She wouldn't put it past him to give them the instructions merely for the entertainment factor.

"He's joking, right?" Cassidy asked.

"Maybe," Marrow said. "But let's act as if the request was made in good faith."

"Sure," Hammer grumbled. "Like when he told me he'd seen deer out back so he could watch me shift in midair when I threw myself off the back deck."

"You could have given the air a teeny-tiny sniff first," Bone said, her words a little garbled by her muzzle.

"I'm going for a run," Cassidy announced. "You coming?" she asked Snow.

"Of course," Snow said. A joint hunt was exactly what her jangling nerves needed. The stakes had ratcheted up as soon as Marrow and Hammer had agreed that their operation would kick off in the morning. If Snow had any hope of sleeping well overnight, she would have to thoroughly tire herself out.

She followed Cassidy onto the back deck and fished a softly glowing chunk of crystal out of her pocket before stripping down to her bare skin. When this was all done, she was going to have to congratulate the hacker on her choice of hideouts. There were no neighbors to see them, and they had access to a small state park. The park was getting over-hunted, but the river that ran through was stuffed full of trout. There was plenty of food to eat, and if they had to look a little harder than the first night, it would only go further toward Snow's goal of tiring herself out.

By the time she finished shifting to furform, Cassidy was the only one still waiting. The other Alphas had disappeared into the woods bounding the small property.

Cassidy panted a lupine smile, then turned and trotted down the deck's stairs. Snow followed on her tail. One more hunt, one more bit of normal before they gambled everything. Only the next day would tell them how well their luck would hold.

CHAPTER THIRTY-FIVE

The white gate guard with the name tag that read Witzig was taking a long time with her ID. Snow tried to look more bored than nervous, but she was grateful the human couldn't smell her nervousness. Delfina had assured her the fake IDs she'd procured for all of them would be indistinguishable from the real thing. They'd certainly looked convincing enough, but now that it was in this woman's hand, while she checked back and forth between the small picture and Snow's face, doubts were shoving their way into her mind.

"I gotta run this," the guard said. She turned away to key numbers into a small handheld device, shielding it from the spray of rain that blew in under the overhang on the guard shack. "Where's Castor?" she asked.

Snow shrugged. "Out sick, I guess. Better him than me. I can't afford the day off."

"Your bosses don't give you PTO?"

"Not when you've only been on payroll a coupla months."

"Ah." Witzig looked at her screen a little longer. "You're clear." She handed the ID back. "Randy," she called into the small guardhouse. "Get your ass out here! It's inspection time."

Snow waited as a tall male guard as pale as his partner came out of the hut carrying two poles, a bored expression on his face. He handed one off to the other guard, then popped up the hood on his jacket. They angled the poles so the mirrors at the end reflected the truck's undercarriage and walked toward the back at a reasonable clip. On a less crappy day, they might have taken longer. But neither seemed thrilled at having to brave the elements. There was nothing to find. Snow banged twice on the panel between the cab and the cargo area, then jumped out of the truck and followed along behind the guards, her own face protected from the rain by her stolen uniform cap. When they got to the back, she pulled open the door. Hammer and Cassidy blinked at the sudden light. Hammer gave a small wave.

Even though Snow knew the two bags of laundry on the far side of the Alphas were the twins disguised by one of Byron's illusions, she saw nothing to indicate that it was anything other than reality. The male guard looked in and grunted once. He took the female guard's pole and disappeared back around the guard shack.

Witzig accompanied Snow back to the cab.

"Where's the loading dock?" Snow asked. "It's my first time doing this run."

"Sure." The guard stepped back and pointed through the tunnel that ran through the layers of chain-link fence in front of the stone walls. "Take a left when you get through. You'll want to back it, though. There isn't space to turn the truck around in there." She grinned, her sober demeanor changing suddenly. "One of your coworkers figured that out the hard way."

"Roger that." Snow throttled the urge to give the guard even a lazy salute. It was difficult. Everything about her screamed military. Prison guards didn't usually wear camo, for one. The M249 that swung on a strap from her neck seemed like overkill for a regular prison, but if you were tasked with stopping the escape of wolven, it was probably much more effective than whatever was standard issue. Not that Snow knew much about prisons, having managed to avoid them all of her very long life. She did know that most such institutions had a policy of not allowing firearms on the persons of the guards in the cell blocks with the prisoners, but those patrolling the walls and the gates were probably exempt.

She backed the truck down a long corridor bound by the innermost layer of chain-link fence on one side and the wall of one of the older buildings on the property. It wasn't the oldest one; they'd confirmed that on the original blueprints. It was a good thing that Byron had gone over the operation of the truck with her, and she'd had a week to practice. Even so, she had to take her time, but she managed to get to the loading dock without trouble. The constant rain wasn't much of an obstacle. At least the storms promised by that morning's weather forecast had yet to show up. If everything went to plan, even those wouldn't impede them.

Once at her destination, she jumped down and walked around to the back. Another guard opened the rollup door that accessed the prison proper. Hammer was already extending the ramp to the loading dock. Cassidy stood behind him, a laundry cart at the ready.

"Big load today," Snow said to the guard. "You the one to sign off on the manifest?"

"Is it?" The Latino man had more five o'clock shadow than Snow had expected from someone this early in the morning. Still, it was only 7:30. He could have been about ready to come off the night shift. He took the proffered clipboard and peered at it. "I really wish y'all would go digital."

"Small town Iowa." Snow rolled her eyes. "What else do you expect?"

"That's for sure." The guard pulled a pen out of one of the many pockets of his fatigues. He signed the papers with a messy flourish, then stashed the pen away. He moved to one side of the door and watched while Cassidy and Hammer rolled their carts past him.

"I'm into the video feed," Delfina said in Snow's ear. "See about ducking back inside the truck. I want some clean footage."

It got her away from the drips at the edge of the loading dock roof. Snow backed into the truck and busied herself further down the cramped aisles. She tried to avoid Byron's illusion, but it was so convincing that she only knew where it was when a portion of her body disappeared into it. They couldn't do anything about that guard until Delfina finished her technical wizardry. One minute passed, then another crawled by, accompanied by the hypnotic drum of rain on the truck's roof. Snow tried to sound busy, pushing things around and thumping big objects into the side.

Finally, Delfina's voice sounded again in her ear. "Loop is in place. Call him in."

Snow dropped a short stepladder onto the ground in the narrow aisle. She cried out in pain.

"You all right in there?" the guard called out to her.

Bone and Marrow moved stealthily through the illusory back of the truck and took up spots on either side of the door.

"Nope." Snow affected a hiss of pain. "Oo, that hurts. Can you give me a hand?"

"Hold on," he said. His footsteps echoed through the loading dock. "What—"

He hadn't even come around the corner when Marrow reached around to grab him by the collar. She swung his body inside, right at her sister who received the guard's flailing strikes without flinching. Bone wrapped her arms around his neck, holding him in a grip he couldn't break out of, no matter how much he battered at her with his arms. Bone took the abuse, her face set in a grim mask as she tightened the hold. It took too long before the guard's struggles tapered off completely. Bone kept her chokehold going a little longer before easing him to the ground.

Marrow gave her sister a quizzical look, then grasped the unconscious guard around the jaw. She gave a savage twist that was accompanied by two vicious snaps. The guard's final breath was a strangled cough.

"Too soft." Marrow shook her head. She was already going through his pockets. "Here we go," she said, holding aloft a few sets of heavy-duty zip tie handcuffs. "Some for you." She passed half a handful to her sister. "The rest for me." She stashed the ties in the uniform coveralls the entire crew was wearing. She would have to shuck the laundry disguise at some point, but until then, it would explain their presence.

Bone grabbed the dead guard's radio and disappeared into the illusion to drop it off with Byron and Delfina so they could monitor any chatter and relay it across the comms to the wolven.

"You know what to do?" Marrow asked Snow.

She nodded. Her choice would have been to be in the prison with Cassidy, but if that wasn't the case, better to be out here with the humans. Someone needed to keep an eye on Delfina.

Marrow clapped her hand on Snow's shoulder. "You'll be great."

Bone emerged from the back of the truck. "We're on."

Delfina's voice insinuated itself into Snow's head via the tiny earpiece, identical to those the others wore. "Loading dock is clear. Proceed with the next phase."

Bone and Marrow each grabbed a cart and pushed them through the doors into the prison.

"Here we go," Snow said. "Whee."

* * *

Inside, Hammer led them to the laundry room. The way was direct, but long. This back corridor was mostly featureless, the institutional gray paint flaking off and baring large patches of old paint and even the original plaster in places. Occasionally, they'd pass through a T-junction that split off deeper into the hulking edifice. They cleared an abandoned checkpoint, its gate half off the hinges and leaning drunkenly against the wall.

The laundry room looked as if it had once been a place where clothes were actually cleaned. A large, empty space took up two-thirds of the room. The footprints of machinery were visible beneath layers of dust. Someone had gone to the trouble of sweeping away a couple of decades of detritus around the tall shelves that took up the smaller portion of the space, but that seemed to have been the only effort toward cleaning. On the far side of the room was a steel door with a bar across it.

Hammer caught Cassidy studying it. "That leads out to one of the unused cell-blocks," he said, his voice hushed.

"Got it." She looked around. "Does anyone come down here?"

He shook his head. "Not much. Dirty linens are dropped off here, and the clean ones picked up, but the blocks where our people are being kept are on the other side of the prison."

"Ah." Cassidy tried to bring up a mental image of the prison's layout and pinpoint exactly where they were. She had no idea how successful she was. Her spatial reasoning wasn't the best. Marrow had drilled the prison's layout into all of them, but she'd had a particularly hard time of it.

"Where's your map?" Hammer asked.

Cassidy pulled out the creased piece of paper and unfolded it.

He pointed out the lower left-hand corner. "We're here."

"Makes sense."

To his credit, he didn't look at her as if she was the biggest flaw in the intricate rescue plan they'd formulated. Cassidy started pulling actual bundles of laundry out of her cart. It had been fully stocked when they'd stolen it from the company that contracted with the prison. They'd had the house's washer and dryer running for three straight days to get everything cleaned.

Hammer started unloading his cart as well. If anyone stopped by or checked the lone security camera, they would see the two of them working diligently.

"Video loop in the loading bay is set," Delfina said through Cassidy's earpiece. "I'm taking care of yours. Continue with what you're doing until I say otherwise."

"Understood." A glance over at Hammer confirmed that he'd received the same set of instructions. Together, they kept moving packages of linens out of the carts and onto the shelves. When that was done, they started loading bags of soiled linens back into their carts. The dirty bedclothes smelled strongly of wolven. Cassidy's eyes moistened whenever she caught a whiff of one of the wolves from her pack. There was Beth, mixed in with hints of Blair and Carlos. Blair's scent sent her eyes from moist to full-on tears. She hadn't smelled her wolven for months. Blair's disappearance felt like the start of this whole affair, but she was here. It was all Cassidy could do not to clutch the linens to her face and inhale, coating the insides of her nostrils with the scent of her missing packmates.

"Clear out of the laundry room for a few minutes," Delfina said a moment or two later. "I need footage of the empty room. Finish loading up the carts and take them with you, though. It'll be good to include that footage in the loop."

"But what's my motivation?" Cassidy said. Hammer looked over at her but didn't crack even the tiniest smile. "Because she's directing us like we're actors…" Her voice trailed off when Hammer shook his head and pushed his cart through the door.

Cassidy and her cart followed him out.

Hammer put his hand up to his ear. "How long do you need us gone?"

"Not long," Delfina replied. "Give me two minutes."

"Can do." He looked over at Cassidy. "Ready to kick this off?"

CHAPTER THIRTY-SIX

"Are you for real?" Cassidy asked. She glanced around the hall as if they might get caught speaking out of class. "I've been waiting for this moment for weeks."

"Are you prepared to kill the humans here if that's what it takes to get our people out?" Hammer's face was deadly serious. It was typically somber, but at this point it was downright funereal.

"I've already taken out more humans than I can count." Cassidy tried not to think about how easy it had been to snuff out all those lives in the woods. They'd been so fragile.

"That was in the heat of the fight. Will you be able to do it when your blood isn't already up?"

"Hammer. Robert." Cassidy lifted her chin and looked the South Shore Alpha directly in the eyes. "I'm prepared to do whatever it takes to get my wolves and yours out of here."

"Excellent." A tiny sliver of a smile escaped his dour facade. "We may actually survive this thing, then."

"The twins are on their way." Delfina's update came right on the heels of Hammer's encouragement. "I've taken over and looped footage for all the cameras in your area. Working on the ones between you and your targets."

Cassidy pressed her finger against her earpiece. "Roger." She looked back over at Hammer. "Time to get changed, then." Her wolf twitched within her. She'd been quiet so far, but now that things were ready to get rolling, she was becoming more active. Cassidy allowed her to ascend a little further. It would be good to have the wolf's reflexes at the fore.

Hammer shoved his cart back inside the room and rooted around at the bottom. He pulled out a familiar set of navy blue coveralls. These had been his work uniform for the past week. He tossed a similar set over to Cassidy. They stripped down to their underwear and pulled the coveralls up.

A few moments after they'd donned their custodian disguises, Bone and Marrow entered the room. Cassidy pulled out the fatigues Hammer had purloined days earlier. She crossed her fingers that they fit the twins better than her coveralls fit her. She'd had to roll up the pant legs and cuffs and hope no one would look at her too closely.

The Gary Alphas grunted almost identical thanks. They were as focused as Hammer, but on them it was a lot stranger. All signs of the joke-making, prank-pulling Alphas were gone. Their movements were eerily similar as they changed into their uniforms.

"Almost forgot," Hammer said. He dug around in the bottom of his cart and came up holding a couple of batons. "None of the guards go anywhere without these." He pressed a button on the handle of one, which produced a rapid clicking sound and a strobe light effect at the tip.

"Stun batons." Marrow's lips were pressed together in a tight line, but she held out a hand for one.

"That'll slow one of us way down," Bone said. She reached out for the other.

"It'll drop a human in their tracks," Cassidy said.

"That it will." Hammer's grin had a vicious edge to it. "I've got one in my cart."

"If there's nothing else…" Marrow looked around at the other wolven. When no one said anything, she pressed a finger to her earpiece. "Delfina, we're moving out."

* * *

"They're on the move," Delfina said in Snow's ear. "Pickup/drop-off is estimated to take thirty minutes. We've eaten into more than half that window."

"Good to know." Snow loitered in the back of the truck. If any more guards came out to check on them, she would be the one to neutralize them. She waited a few more minutes, then retracted the ramp and closed up the back of the truck. She climbed into the cab and pretended to turn on the engine. She hadn't heard from Delfina that there were eyes on the driver's seat of her truck, but it felt better to move forward as if there were.

After miming a couple of turns of the key, Snow climbed out of the cab and popped open the truck's hood. She and Byron had discussed at length how many spark plugs they should disable. He was of the opinion that they should err on the conservative side. He wanted just enough of the leads removed to keep the car from moving. Snow wanted a statement. She poked around under the hood, ignoring the rain that ran down the back of her neck, and deftly removed three of them. After poking around a little longer for show, Snow closed the hood and hopped back up into the truck.

It took a few tries, but when the engine finally turned over, it sounded like a rock tumbler. A series of rattles and knocks issued from beneath the hood. Snow put the truck in gear and tried to ease it forward. The pace of the rattles picked up, the truck rolled forward a foot and a half, then refused to move. She pressed her foot to the ground, revving the engine until it sounded as if Hell itself had come to pay a visit, but they weren't going anywhere. She affected a concerned look, cut the power, then got back out of the truck.

After a few minutes pretending to troubleshoot the engine, Snow realized that no one was going to come over to check. Her back hunched against the dismal weather, she started on the long trek toward the guardhouse at the front gate. Her feet splashed through puddles along the crumbling asphalt drive. The female gate guard saw her coming and left the booth to meet her.

"You can't be wandering the grounds, ma'am."

"I know that." Snow let some exasperation creep into her voice. "I wouldn't have to wander all the way out to you if my truck was running. The dang hunk of junk isn't working worth a damn. No matter how much I crank her, she only goes a little ways before she stops."

"Sounds like my last girlfriend." The gate guard grinned and slung the rifle around her back, then hitched up her belt. "Let's see what's going on." She pressed the button on her radio. "Randy, I'm going to go check on the laundry truck. It's busted or something."

"Roger." Randy's reply was filled with static and only barely intelligible.

"So how you like working for Suds 'n' Duds?" the guard asked as they trudged back toward the loading dock.

Snow mentally rolled her eyes. Trust her to end up with someone who wanted to chat. From what she smelled off the guard, the woman was interested in her. Snow affected an indifferent shrug. "It's a living, I guess. Didn't exactly grow up hoping to be the driver of a laundry pickup service one day."

"Oh no?" Witzig shot her a look out of the corner of her eye. "What did you want to be?"

"Never really thought about it."

"Oh, come on. Every little kid dreams of being something."

"When I was younger I thought about getting into genetics research." That much was true. If she could have found some way to research why wolven existed, Snow would happily have dropped everything to pursue that.

"Damn, that's a lofty goal."

Snow shrugged. "Well, life gets in the way. Had some family troubles, and then there was never the money or the time to actually work on making my dream happen." She nodded toward the guard. "What about you? You always wanna be a prison guard?"

Witzig chuckled. "Not exactly. This is definitely not where I saw myself. It's all right though. It's temporary. One more bump on the road to bigger and better things, you know?"

"I hear that."

"Now speaking of roads, let's see if we can get you back on yours." Witzig approached the truck with its raised hood. She hoisted herself up onto the bumper to peer inside, then reached out and started testing connections.

Snow kept back a little ways. The plan hadn't accounted for someone who actually knew enough about cars to diagnose her sabotage to be stationed at the front gate. Her wolf whined within her skull. The tips of her fingers itched a bit as she contemplated what she would do if the guard was able to figure out what was wrong. Eliminating her would be bad. Randy at the gate would realize something was up when she didn't return. Snow supposed she could radio to the gate that something had come up and at least slow him from checking too quickly. That was likely to be a very short-term fix. What if he got suspicious that it wasn't Witzig's voice? Snow's powers of impression were terrible. Still, the radios were of indifferent quality. She might be able to pull it off.

"Do you want me to crank it?" Snow asked.

"Not yet." Witzig leaned way over to investigate something at the back of the engine. "Your filters are in terrible shape." She poked her head out to look at Snow. "Yeah, turn it over. I want to see what it sounds like."

Snow climbed into the front seat, still debating over what to do with this guard who was entirely too clever for her own good. After checking to make sure Witzig couldn't see her through the open hood, Snow pressed on her earpiece.

"Gate guard fancies herself an expert on cars," Snow murmured as she turned the key. "What do you advise?"

"That's inconvenient," Delfina said. "Let me run the numbers on some options."

That wasn't the answer she wanted. Snow cranked on the ignition again when the truck didn't start the first time. Could Byron portal the guard away? She wouldn't be able to run to get anyone, at least not for a while. Snow daydreamed about the kind of environs in which they could strand the guard in. Somewhere even crappier than this. Could Byron get her to the Arctic Circle? She was jolted from her reverie when the engine caught and sputtered its way to dubious life.

"That sounds real bad," Witzig shouted as Snow joined her in front of the truck again. "You've got a couple of problems that I could see. The isostatic flow through your carburetor is probably compromised. That's what's making the worst of the racket. Also, your distributor cap is loose. Looks like it's missing the gasket. Probably got old and crumbled away."

Snow blinked at the guard. Granted, she hadn't spent much time working on newer engines, but she'd had to do a lot of her own work on her bus. What she hadn't done herself, she'd assisted with. Most of what was coming out of Witzig's mouth was gobbledygook.

"So it's stuck?" Snow asked slowly.

"Yep. You're not going anywhere without a tow." She reached up and removed the brace holding up the hood, then let it drop. "I can hang out with you while you wait."

"Oh!" The pieces fell into place for Snow. The guard didn't know anything about cars. She must have figured she could impress Snow by pretending. This was an elaborate pass. She wondered if it had worked before.

"You'll need to come back to the booth to call out," Witzig said. "Cells don't work in this place." She gestured vaguely at the stone wall behind them. "Too much interference."

"I do need to call this in," Snow agreed. "Just let me lock up the back."

"Sure."

Snow walked around back and reactivated her earpiece. "False alarm. I'm headed to the front to call this in."

"Acknowledged," Delfina replied. "How you feeling?"

"So far, so good." The words were a lie, her pulse was pounding in her ears, her pits were sweatier than they'd been in years, and her wolf wouldn't stop pacing, but Snow could fake it for a little longer. She shook the doors to make sure they were latched, then headed around the truck, smiling when she saw Witzig. "Let's go give my boss the bad news." A clap of thunder met her pronouncement, and a heavy curtain of rain obscured their view of the guard shack.

Witzig sighed. "What a shitty day."

"And then some," Snow agreed.

CHAPTER THIRTY-SEVEN

"The truck's cover is set," Delfina reported through Cassidy's earpiece. By the way the other wolven looked around, she was speaking to them also. "Everything is proceeding according to plan."

"Doesn't that feel like she's jinxing it?" Bone muttered to Marrow.

"This is us," Hammer announced as they drew abreast of an elevator with scarred and dinged up doors. He stopped and looked over at the twins. "Best of luck."

"Break a leg or whatever," Cassidy said.

"I thought that was only good luck in the theatah," Marrow said. She drew out the "aaah" at the end in what was supposed to be comedic proportions, but the gray, peeling walls pulled the air out of the room. It seemed like this place had been constructed to assassinate joy. The dull peals of thunder that penetrated the wall did nothing to help the mood.

Cassidy shrugged. "It's acting. Figured it would work."

"We'll make it work," Bone said.

"Yeah, work it, girl," Marrow said. She gyrated her hips but stopped almost immediately. There couldn't have been a less amusing set of motions to make.

"Take care of yourselves and our people," Hammer said. "That's all that matters. We're counting on you."

"And we'll do what we can to lessen the heat on you," Cassidy assured them.

"I know, I know," Marrow groused. "That's the whole point of the plan."

"Then let's get started with it." Bone walked a few steps down the dingy corridor before looking back at her sister, who followed a moment later.

"Going up?" Hammer asked as he leaned over to press the elevator call button.

"Do we have a choice?"

The South Shore Alpha made a show of looking over the single button. "Nope."

"Then up it is." Cassidy stared at the door. There were no numbers to tell them what floor the elevator might be on, and it was taking forever. "Does this thing even work?"

"Most of the time." Hammer took a casual glance down the hall. "I've only had to carry my cart up the stairs once. It's old as hell. Definitely wasn't part of the original construction."

"Well, that's peachy. We better not sit out this whole thing because we get stuck in a rickety-ass jumped-up dumbwaiter." Saying the words "prison break" out loud felt like inviting trouble down on their heads. For some reason, complaining helped take the edge off.

"We can always bust out through the service hatch and crawl to the next floor."

"Carrying our carts?"

The two Alphas shared a glance and burst out laughing. Cassidy regretted the outburst almost immediately. Their guffaws were swallowed by the walls around them, and a leaden silence descended around them as soon as they snapped their mouths shut. Silent Heights Penitentiary really did hate happiness.

Before too much longer, the elevator chugged its way down the shaft. Cassidy was pretty certain the machinery wasn't supposed to sound like that. Even the "ding" when the elevator doors opened sounded sickly. Her wolf didn't want to get into the metal box. The walls of the prison already pressed in on her. The elevator's scarred and beaten interior was too small. For a moment, she flashed back to being stuck inside the bespoke prison Mary had constructed. The one she'd kept them in when they'd first been turned. She could feel the closeness of the impenetrable walls.

"Are you coming, Five Moons? Cassidy?" Hammer's voice broke through the spiral of claustrophobia that threatened to overwhelm her.

"Uh, yes." Cassidy licked her lips. "I sure am." The wolf resisted every step she took toward the elevator, but somehow she pushed herself over the threshold, even remembering to take the other janitor's cart along with her.

"You smell of terror," Hammer said as the elevator door ground closed.

"Bad memories."

"Of elevators?" His voice was nearly casual, devoid of the judgment she expected.

"I spent a lot of the month between when I was bitten and I shifted for the first time closed up in a metal container." She looked around at the walls. At least the peeling fake wood paneling was nothing like Mary's box. "It was about this size."

"Very bad memories." Hammer's own scent was shading toward anger again. "Who would do this to you?"

"Mary didn't know what else to do."

"Your sister?"

Cassidy nodded. "It's not like she could approach one of you for help. I can imagine how well the packs would have reacted to such a request." It felt strange to defend Mary for choices that Cassidy was still angry with her about.

"Maybe so." Hammer stared into space as the elevator continued to work its way slowly upward. "I suppose we'll never know now."

"That we won't." Cassidy kept her eyes on the door. As soon as it started to open, she was already pushing her cart toward it.

Hammer exited behind her without further comment. He took the lead, pushing his cart through the halls with a studied nonchalance. He'd coached her on how to move once inside the prison. No one would look at them twice if they took their time. Rushing around was guaranteed to draw the attention of the guards. Apparently, they preferred the employees complacent. Her wolf bridled at the slow pace.

"Should I still be feeling my wolf?" Cassidy asked, careful to keep her voice down now that they were heading toward a wing of the prison they knew was occupied.

"I only lost contact with mine in the cell blocks and the medical building. Unless something's changed, you should have full access to the wolf until we end up in those areas."

"Good." This area of the hall was being swept on a regular basis, unlike areas downstairs. Cassidy wished she could pull out her map to check it but forced herself to rely on Hammer's guidance instead. He was the closest thing they had to an expert on the prison.

"Through there." The door on the indicated side of the hall was wide. Hammer pulled the huge ring of keys off his belt and searched through it until he found the right one. The lock opened with only a bit of jiggling, then they were passing through into an area that wouldn't have been out of place in an older office building. The large room was divided by cubicles, which were still mostly empty at this hour of the morning.

Hammer reached down and snagged a small wastebasket from next to a nearby desk. He nodded for Cassidy to take the other side of the room. With a reluctance she hoped the other Alpha didn't pick up on, Cassidy started down the cube farm aisle. The first few cubes were empty, and Cassidy started to relax a little bit—until she rounded the corner of the next cubicle. It was occupied by a human in the same fatigues she'd seen on the guard at the loading dock. She hesitated for a moment, then reached in for the garbage can. The man's shoulders didn't even tense. For a moment, Cassidy wondered what he would do if she flicked the back of one of his ears. Clearly, Marrow, Bone, and Byron were rubbing off on her. She emptied the small can into the larger one on her cart and kept on. There was no more relaxing, no sense that maybe this wouldn't be so bad. If they had any hiccups in here, that man would die.

She completed her slow circuit of the office, meeting up with Hammer in front of a large enclosed office. The door was shut and the room was dark, the blinds on the windows hanging half open.

Hammer tried to turn the door handle, but it was locked. He jiggled it a couple of times, but it didn't budge.

"What are you doing?" The man from the cubicle stood at the end of the row. He was taller than he'd appeared, sitting down. He held himself straight, with a military bearing that went well with the fatigues he wore. "The inner office is off-limits to custodians. You should know that."

Cassidy scratched her head. "I don't know anything about all that. We were just told to give it a deep clean." She hoisted the small vacuum cleaner out of her cart. "Came prepared and everything."

"Who told you?" The man approached slowly, his hand drifting toward the pistol at his waist.

"It was—" Cassidy turned to look at Hammer.

"Parsons," he finished smoothly. "Duty board was clear. It said to clean the inner office."

"Parsons." The guard moved his hand away from his sidearm. "This should be easy to clear up. I'll give him a call." He turned to head back to his cubicle.

Cassidy and Hammer shared a glance before erupting into motion. While Hammer sprinted back the way he'd come, Cassidy hefted the vacuum and threw it at the back of the guard's head. Even as she let it go, she was already moving toward him at a full run.

The guard had half a second to turn before the small appliance collided with the side of his face. A couple of shouts of alarm issued from the other side of the open office, one of which was cut off by a wet thunk. The wolf surged through Cassidy, lending her strength and speed. Most of all, the claws and teeth were the most welcome.

Cassidy restrained herself from opening the guard's throat at the last second. They were supposed to leave as little trace as possible. Once they moved onto another area, they didn't need a bloodbath behind them to alert anyone any sooner than they had to. She molded her hands into fists and came up under the guard's chin. He tried to block the blow, but she was too quick.

His head snapped back with an audible crack, and he wobbled back two steps but didn't go down. Across the office, another scuffle was occurring. Cassidy spared it no thought. Hammer was there, and he would take care of what needed to be done. She stepped to the side, allowing the injured guard to shift to keep her from getting behind him.

Cassidy stepped in, grabbing his shoulders and bringing him toward her. His forehead met hers. Stars spangled behind Cassidy's eyes for a second, and she lost her grip on the man. He collapsed as if someone had severed his brainstem. The center of his forehead sported a massive welt. Cassidy stooped in close to him. Shallow breaths wheezed through his open mouth. Good.

She stood, peering over the cubicles in Hammer's direction. A moment later, his head popped up like a meerkat's on the savanna. Cassidy raised one eyebrow in question. Hammer nodded and gestured toward the door. After a quick thumbs-up, Cassidy gave the room a quick circuit. In addition to Hammer's aroma, she was able to identify three other recent scents. They corresponded to each of the unconscious personnel in the room. She picked up each one and deposited them by the door to the inner office.

"Hope you had some good footage of the area before things went a little sideways," Cassidy said into her earpiece.

"Feed was replaced before you entered the room," Delfina assured her. "There's no indication anyone else knows you're in there. Second group is undetected as well."

"Good."

By the time she'd collected all the guards and confirmed that the room was empty aside from them, Hammer had located a keycard. He waited until she approached with the last body, before waving it in front of a small gray reader. The security device looked much newer than anything else in the office. He gestured for her to precede him in, then turned to grab the other two unconscious guards.

Cassidy deposited her target, then went for her cart. It had been shoved to one side in her rush to get to the man who was going to call them in. She pushed aside the large trash bag and fished out a length of rope, which she brought back into the office.

Hammer was prowling through the space, opening filing cabinets and rifling through them. As Cassidy knelt to truss up the first guard, she noticed that there didn't seem to be much in the way of paper in the cabinets. There wasn't much to the room at all. The furnishings were Spartan, with only a couple of desks and as many office chairs. A wooden chair sat in the corner, but from the layer of dust and the damage to the varnish, it hadn't seen use since the prison was decommissioned.

The South Shore Alpha slammed shut the cabinet drawer, then came to help tie up the remaining humans.

"Empty?" Cassidy asked.

Hammer grunted in irritated assent.

"I guess that leaves the laptop." She indicated the small black computer that sat in the center of the nearest desk.

"That's all you." Hammer lifted his hands as if to say "not it."

Cassidy grinned but crossed the room to sit in the office chair. "This one's for you," she said into her earpiece. "Time for you to earn those big hacker bucks."

"I can't do anything if you don't open it," Delfina groused.

Cassidy pulled open the lid and powered on the computer.

"Move the camera up," Delfina said. "I can't see much from where I am."

Cassidy unclipped the small camera from the button of the snap over one of her breast pockets and affixed it to her lapel.

"Better?" she murmured as the screen flickered to life. To no one's surprise, they were confronted by a login screen.

"Much," Delfina said. "Okay, plug the unit into a USB port."

Cassidy complied, having to turn the unit over when she inevitably tried to insert it the wrong way first.

"Good. Now hold down power and hit the restart button on the screen."

"Got it." Feeling a little bit like a puppet, Cassidy followed the hacker's instructions. Hammer prowled behind her, closing the blinds on the windows.

They continued, Delfina murmuring instructions through the earpiece and Cassidy doing her best to follow them quickly. The hacker had stressed how important it was to get the timing right. They had a couple of false starts and had to start over from the beginning each time.

"How much longer will this take?" Hammer grumbled. "We have other work to do."

Cassidy ignored him. This time she hit the right combination of keystrokes and right-clicked at the proper time, and a command line box appeared.

"Let's go!" Delfina chortled. "We're nearly in." She rattled off a line of code that Cassidy faithfully typed in. "Now hit Enter."

Holding her breath, Cassidy tapped the Enter key and watched as the computer thought about it for a second. Her heart dropped when the screen went black, but a moment later, she was looking at the soothing blue of a generic Windows background.

"Let's back this puppy up," Delfina said. "Do I have to walk you through copying files?"

"I think I got it," Cassidy said drily. She replaced the unit with a slender black hard drive. She watched, impatient, as the files moved over one at a time. Hammer still paced in front of the windows.

When the last file had moved, Cassidy reached for the drive.

"Hold on," Delfina said. "Let's check for hidden files." Once again, she puppeteered Cassidy through the steps, complaining about the inferior quality of the Wi-Fi signal the entire way.

The hacker exposed a hidden partition on the drive with many more digital documents. Cassidy cringed at the thought of how much longer it was going to take.

"Hey, if they went to this much trouble to hide it, there has to be something good on it." Delfina sounded positively gleeful. "I can't wait to get my hands on that. Make sure you hold onto that drive."

"Yes, ma'am." As the final file hit the hard drive, Cassidy snatched it from the computer. She slid the drive onto a key ring, then threaded that through a stout chain around her neck. The chain was big enough that it wouldn't choke her if she had to take to furform.

"See you in a few," Delfina said.

"Let's get out of here," Cassidy said to Hammer.

"Finally." Hammer jerked the door to the office open.

CHAPTER THIRTY-EIGHT

Cassidy scanned the hall outside the office in either direction. She inhaled deeply, tasting the air for any trace of human that wasn't a few hours old.

"I've found something," Delfina announced through their earpieces.

"So?" Hammer said. "We're about to head to the next target."

"This is worth the detour," the hacker said. "There's a system that's dispersing something into the cell blocks and med wing. How much do you want to bet it's whatever is suppressing your ability to change."

The South Shore Alpha looked back at Cassidy. His jaw was set, but he raised an eyebrow as if asking her opinion.

Cassidy pressed a finger to her earpiece. "How certain are you that it's the wolfsbane?"

"Or whatever they're using. Why else would it only go to those areas?"

"Being able to shift would be a huge help," Cassidy said to the other Alpha. "Our wolves would be able to fight back way better if there's a snag in the plan."

"Deviating from the plan makes snags," he said. "But you're right." He touched his earpiece. "How much of a detour?"

"It's in the control room," Delfina said.

"That's the opposite direction from the med wing. Why can't you just hack it?"

"They have some heavy-duty firewalls. I need a hard point to gain access."

Hammer blinked. "And you expect us to do that. I'm no tech geek, but that sounds way harder than copying files."

A new voice came over their earpieces. "Don't forget you have me," Byron said. "I've got the juice for a small portal."

Cassidy met Hammer's gaze. "We have to do it. This could be huge."

He closed his eyes but contacted Delfina again. "We're on it, but it better not take long."

Hammer turned, heading down the hall. Again, Cassidy was forced to follow along in his wake. Even with the weight of the cart, he was moving at what was a jog for him but would have been a quick clip for most humans. She thought about asking him to slow down, but the truth was that she and the wolf needed to be moving with some speed, even if they were going the wrong way.

The way to this new target wasn't the straight shot they'd had to the office. When they came around the final corner to see a reinforced door emblazoned with the word "Control," Cassidy grunted with relief. Only then did Hammer slow. Windows on both sides of the room that bordered the hall gave it a curious fishbowl exterior, if fishbowls were made with wire sandwiched into the glass.

As they got within ten feet of the control room, Cassidy realized her wolf was gone. She stumbled. The only other time she'd felt this had been when Hammer had dosed her with wolfsbane at his den. She'd hated it then, and it was so much worse now that they were in the stronghold of their enemies.

"Not great, is it?" Hammer asked.

Cassidy shook her head, wondering how she would fight without the wolf to guide her.

Hammer approached the door and rapped on it. There were more people crammed into the room than had been in the office. They appeared to be at various duty stations, keeping an eye on multiple monitors at each. One of the guards looked over at the door and gestured for Hammer to keep moving.

The South Shore Alpha picked up his mop and showed it to the guard through the window, then pointed at the floor in the control room. Another guard looked over. Both men were in the same camouflage fatigues they'd seen on the guards in the office. The second man stood up and walked toward them, then leaned against the wall next to the door.

The small intercom crackled to life with a spittle of static. "We don't need a cleaning," the guard said, his words garbled, but recognizable.

Hammer waved his mop again.

The guard gestured to the intercom on their side.

The Alpha made a face, but pressed the button and leaned in to talk to it. He spoke smoothly but dropped syllables.

"Say again," the guard said.

Hammer grimaced and repeated his statement, dropping different syllables this time.

The guard snarled in frustration and pushed the door open a crack. Cassidy reached forward and grabbed him by the collar, elbowing the door from his grasp and pulling him out into the hall. As soon as he'd cleared the doorframe, Hammer rushed inside. The heavy door was already swinging closed. Without giving up her grip on the front of the guard's jacket, Cassidy pivoted to keep it from closing. She went down to one knee, launching the guard back into the room and into the nearest desk. The massive metal furniture had been state of the art in the 1960s. It might no longer be cutting edge, but it was solid. The guard impacted it, then slid down the side, blood smearing in his wake.

Across the room, Hammer had taken on two more guards. One waved a stun baton in what was probably supposed to be a threatening manner. In a movement that was almost too quick to follow, Hammer slid his hand beneath the man's guard and batted the baton to the side with contemptuous ease. He reached over and grabbed a female guard by the throat while the first one tried to drop him with a kidney punch.

A door to Cassidy's right opened, and a slender Asian man with close-cropped brown hair stepped into the room. His fatigues were black instead of the camo they'd seen on the other guards.

"Shashka, there's another one."

The man in black fatigues looked over and grinned when he saw Cassidy. She stepped over the body of the man she'd thrown into the desk. Long before most humans would have bothered, this Shashka had his hands up and was adopting a defensive posture. It didn't stop him from advancing, but clearly, he wasn't taking chances.

A loud cry was cut off with lethal finality. It wasn't Hammer's voice, so Cassidy didn't bother looking over. He could handle a couple of measly humans, and so could she. She curled her fingers automatically, expecting claws to spring forth from the tips. The skin didn't itch, nor was there even the slightest bit of an ache. Excitement still rose within her, a desire to pit her strength against her opponent's to see who would come out on top. She grinned with teeth too blunt to do decent damage.

The man in black slid to the side, dodging her first swing with galling ease.

"What's the matter?" he asked, his voice deep and resonant. "Missing something?" He closed on her, punching her twice in the short ribs. Each blow felt like someone was driving a spike into her torso.

Cassidy brought an arm down to sweep his fists away as she swiveled back to put her shoulder between them. Whoever this Shashka was, he was fast. Nearly as quick on his feet as she was, and with way more experience. That much was evident when he circled to keep Cassidy from landing a clean hit on him. A couple of her punches made contact, but they were glancing blows at best. He didn't seem to notice any but the hardest strikes, and even those pulled only the barest wince out of him.

"I've taken out countless of you animals," Shashka hissed. "Every one of them had more fight in them than you do." He spat at the ground in front of her.

It was an obvious ploy to get her to rush in. Even without her wolf, she could see that. Cassidy simply kept circling and weaving, not slowing long enough for him to get a good bead on her. The man in black stayed with her, his movements smooth and confident. She'd seen someone move like this before.

Mary. He's a Hunter. Her foot came down on its side, her ankle folding. Cassidy tried to keep rolling with the stumble. She went down.

Shashka saw his opening and struck. He swooped in, swarming over her, hands chopping and striking. Cassidy curled in on herself, raising her arms to cover her head, keeping the most vulnerable parts of her body protected. She caught at the wiry arm as it came sliding around her neck but couldn't stop the onslaught. The man in black slid behind her. He locked his legs around her waist and braced one hand against the back of her head, locking his arm in place against her windpipe.

She grabbed at his arms, but without the claws she was used to fighting with, her struggles had little effect. As her lungs began to labor for air, she tightened her focus. She had one task to accomplish. She dug her fingers into the Hunter's arm and tried to tuck her chin. His grip was too strong, so she abandoned that tactic and rolled. The

Hunter might have taken on wolven in the past, but he'd forgotten that they were nearly as strong in skinform as they were in furform. He tightened his grip as he moved with her. That was fine. Cassidy already couldn't breathe, so making it so she could not breathe even more didn't put her any further behind.

She dragged herself to her feet, fighting against his weight the entire way. Oddly, moving slowly didn't make her as out of breath as quick motions did. Now was the time to be deliberate. She only had so much air left; her pulse throbbed, a twin timpani in her neck and ears. The Hunter hung off her back, trying to slow her down with his weight, but that wasn't really the problem. They were too far from the wall for her to throw herself at it, so Cassidy reached out for the nearest desk.

Her vision was deteriorating into a strange tunnel, and it was getting difficult to gauge distances. Cassidy twisted and rammed her back into the edge of the desk. The sturdy ancient furniture held, and Shashka let out an explosive grunt in her ear. His grip loosened enough that she could drag in half a breath of air. It wasn't nearly enough, but the edges of her vision cleared, and she had enough energy left to try the maneuver again.

With all of her mass behind her, Cassidy threw herself at the desk. If she could have cut him in half on the metal edge of the desk's top, she would have.

This time he let out a strangled howl, and his grip slipped again, enough for Cassidy to hook the fingers from each hand around the insides of his elbows and yank them apart. This time she was able to suck in a whole lungful of oxygen. She dropped her chin and sank her teeth into the Hunter's wrist. Tendons and skin crunched under the strength of her bite. Hot blood soaked her mouth, a sensation she'd never experienced in skinform, but in that moment, she didn't care.

A blow struck her across the back of her shoulders, but she didn't relinquish her grip. It was slow going with blunt human teeth, which she hoped hurt so much more. There were arteries in the wrist that would slow him down. All she had to do was find one.

"Let go of me, you bitch!" Shashka pounded at her with his free arm, raining blow after blow down on her back and shoulders. He was close, but his angle wasn't great, so Cassidy shrugged most of the strikes off.

She continued to gnaw at his wrist, burrowing into the flesh, seeking the gout of blood that would tell her that he would soon be no one else's problem ever again. Her mouth filled with iron, cloying and bitter. She snorted in ragged breaths through her nose and kept to her grim task with such focus that it took her a few seconds to realize that his assaults had ceased and that she was holding him up by the arm.

Cassidy whirled, desperate to make certain there wasn't another attack, but there was no new threat, only Hammer. The Hunter's head lolled on his neck at an unnatural angle. She dropped the arm and wiped her mouth on the back of her hand.

"Are you able to continue?" Hammer asked.

"Of course." Cassidy rolled her shoulders. They were sore. Her ankle throbbed where it had folded, but she could put weight on it. If she'd had her wolf, the shift to furform would have dispelled many of the aches and pains, but that was going to have to wait. If Hammer's experiences had been any indication, it would be some time before her wolf could emerge again.

"He walked right past the panic button." Hammer shook his head in disbelief. "Arrogant bastard."

"Hunter." Cassidy swallowed before continuing, "He was a Hunter. Moved the same way as my sister."

"A Hunter. That is not an option I had entertained."

Cassidy pressed her finger against her earpiece. "Delfina, give everyone the heads-up that we have Hunters in the prison."

"Hunters?" Delfina asked. "Is that the guy who got the drop on you?"

"It is."

"What makes you think there's more than one?"

"Two desks in the office. Both free of dust. This one was in charge here. My guess is they're running the whole operation."

"If there's another one out there, we need to get moving," Hammer said. "Once they realize they've been infiltrated, who knows how this will go."

Cassidy met Hammer's eyes and nodded. "Delfina, whatever you want to do here needs to happen now," she said. "We have to move."

"One second." The hacker's voice was distracted.

A shimmer filled the door the Hunter had come through. Byron stood silhouetted against a dark background lit only by monitors and the LEDs on Delfina's equipment. He reached toward them, a boxy device in his hand.

"Plug this into one of the computers," he said. "Then you can keep moving."

Cassidy snatched the device from him, then looked around for somewhere to plug it in. The portal closed, revealing a cramped office.

That seemed like a good option. She rushed to the desk. A much newer monitor than she'd seen anywhere else in this place rose proudly out of a sea of paper. She shoved away stacks of papers and open binders with schematics and drawings, looking for the CPU that had to be here somewhere. If they'd had the time, the manuals might have been helpful, but they were long past the window for research.

There was no CPU on the top of the desk, but her slapdash cleaning session revealed wires that threaded through a hole bored through the wooden top. She followed them down to where a tower had been shoved under the desk. There were plenty of open USB ports on the front, and she jammed the device's connector into one of the ports. For once, it went in on the first try.

Cassidy rejoined Hammer in front of one of the banks of old monitors. The quality was terrible, but good enough to make out what looked like humans packed into cells. She placed a hand on his shoulder and moved in so her chest was touching his back. There on the monitor was Naomi, and that over there sure looked like Jamieson.

"No sign of the twins," Hammer said, his voice rough.

"That's good, right?" Surely that meant Delfina was cloaking their movements. It definitely didn't mean they'd been stopped or captured.

"Sure it is." From his scent, the South Shore Alpha wasn't sure what to make of the lack either.

"Delfina would tell us if they'd been compromised." She tightened her hand on his shoulder. "There are contingencies, remember?"

"I know." He cracked a brief grin. "I even helped come up with some of them."

"Good. Then let's get moving." She pressed a hand to her ear. "Do you have everything you need from us?"

"I do," Delfina replied. "If I can crack this, I'll be able to turn off the suppressant. Hell, I could even open all the doors in this place."

"Silver linings." Cassidy turned to her partner. "Let's go get those cubs."

CHAPTER THIRTY-NINE

Cassidy and Hammer had to move quickly. They'd spent as much time as they dared cleaning up blood and had stuffed the bodies of the guards into the small office, then locked it using a key from Shashka's pockets. The dead Hunter had been deposited in Hammer's trash can and covered by bags, obscuring the body. They didn't have the time necessary to cover their tracks completely; all they could do was make it not completely obvious from outside that the control room had been breached. The top of her coveralls had been drenched with Shashka's blood. After a moment of thought, she'd unbuttoned them and tied them around her waist. Hammer had fetched her the undershirt of one of the dead guards. Fortunately, it was dark enough to conceal the blood, though the scent of bitter iron lingered.

They pounded through the halls, hoping Delfina could cover their tracks, not that there was anyone alive in the control room to see them. The office was still dark when they passed, which was a relief. For as much as had happened, it was still relatively early, at least as far as the workday was concerned. Hammer was adamant that there was only one way into the medical wing. Instead of waiting for another elevator, they dragged their carts down a flight of stairs.

They'd hit the landing halfway down when Delfina whispered the words they'd been waiting to hear.

"Marrow and Bone are in position. Byron has dropped off the explosives."

Hammer stopped on the landing and raised his hand to his ear. "We just need to get through the checkpoint, then you can blow it to hell."

"I'm watching your feed," Delfina said. "Once you're through, the twins have the go-ahead."

"Roger that." Hammer glanced over at Cassidy, excitement in his eyes.

She nodded and hefted her cart, taking it to the bottom of the stairs.

Hammer unlocked the bottom door with yet another key from his massive ring. They rolled on down the hall toward the sturdy metal gate that stretched across its length. The architecture changed, the walls going from ancient to merely old. The paint wasn't in as bad condition as it had been in the original building, but it was still chipped in places, revealing odd stains beneath. The pervasive smells of mold, dust, and dampness had some new additions. A sweet miasma lingered atop of the smells of age. Sharp chemical notes peeked through in colors Cassidy hadn't seen before. The bright pink and chartreuse traces among the scent haze were interesting and alarming.

Her own anticipation peaked when Luther's star popped into focus in her starscape as they approached an enclosed counter protected by scarred plexiglass. It dominated half the hall. Cassidy bit her lower lip to keep from breaking into a wide grin that felt inappropriate for this place.

A metal gate bisected the checkpoint. Behind the counter, a bored guard leaned back in a chair, rocking it onto its hind legs. The white woman's light hair was pulled back in a low bun that rested below her camouflage cap. Her eyes lit up when she saw them approaching. Her stun baton lay across her lap.

"Bit early to get started in there." She got to her feet and leaned on the counter.

"Parsons is short-staffed," Hammer said. "Told us to get the wing out of the way first."

"Fair enough." The guard gestured further into the wing with her baton. "They're all zombies in there anyway. Shouldn't be any trouble." She gestured for them to come up to the window. "Badges."

"Oh, come on, Girard, you know who I am by now." Despite his protestations, Hammer unclipped the laminated ID badge from his belt and pressed it against the glass.

Cassidy fumbled with hers.

Girard shrugged while scrutinizing his credentials. "The boss is around today, you know. Gotta mind our Ps and Qs." She turned to Cassidy. "Let's get this over with."

Hammer's badge had been working for him all week. This was the first time hers was getting any scrutiny.

The guard squinted at it. "You don't look like a Brenda," she said.

"It was my grandma's name," Cassidy replied.

"Poor granny." Girard reached under the counter.

Cassidy pulled the badge away from the window and tensed. Hammer's scent ratcheted from mild anxiety to on the edge of attack. The plexi was thick, but between the two of them, Cassidy was reasonably certain they could get through it. Whether it would be before or after the guard pressed a panic button would remain to be seen.

A loud thunk was followed by the squeal of metal on metal as the gate cranked ponderously back into the guard station, clearing the way for Hammer and Cassidy.

"Have fun mopping up drool," Girard called after them.

A spike of brilliant scarlet rage ripped through Hammer's scent, but nothing about his demeanor changed. The guard on the other side of the gate didn't look up from a battered paperback as they wheeled their carts past him.

Rumbles of thunder, made distant by the layers of walls, accompanied them as the station receded behind them. The hall continued for another thirty or so feet before ending at a pair of heavy metal doors. All the doors were metal here. Cassidy was getting heartily tired of being closed in by stone and steel. She could only imagine what it was like for her wolves and poor Hammer, having to put himself through this day after day. She owed him a case of beer after all of this. Maybe a truck full of beer. If he even drank it. So far all she'd seen him consume were tea and water.

They'd nearly made it to the heavy doors when a muffled thud shook the walls. A puff of dust sifted down from the ceiling above.

"The twins are moving," Hammer said.

"That they are. We need to also."

* * *

Snow rested her feet on top of the dashboard. Witzig had been summoned back to the guardhouse by her surly partner, which was just as well. Snow wasn't one to consign somebody to death simply for not picking up on her extreme lack of interest, but the woman had been truly oblivious.

Rain sleeted down the windshield. It might have obscured her from any cameras, but just in case...The lounge was calculated, not something she felt at all. The imaginary tow truck "Dispatch" had told her was coming was definitely not on the way. The previous week, Delfina had located the hard lines for the phone on the outside of the prison and had inserted her own redirect before they'd even acquired the laundry truck. When the gate guards had called out to Suds 'n' Duds to let them know what was going on, Byron had been at the other end of the line. He'd smoothly taken the information and promised to get someone out that way quickly.

That had been twenty minutes ago. If things were going as planned, Hammer and Cassidy should have been in the medical wing. Unless there had been a lot of resistance, the cubs should already have been rounded up. Bone and Marrow should have been leading the first group of wolven from the cells to the portion of the wall they'd identified as being vulnerable to explosives in a way that would allow them to obliterate a section, without bringing the entire thing down on their heads. It overlooked an area on the bluffs that gave them direct access down to the water. The Mississippi carved out a wide channel at the base of the bluffs, but parts of it acted more like a river delta. What they needed was a water landing. Wolven could survive a lot of damage, but a fall of a few hundred feet into the ground would still kill most of them. If they got lucky and hit mud instead of solid earth, they would be hopelessly mired and easy pickings for their kidnappers. Or they might be consigned to a slow and agonizing death from the elements and starvation.

Her thoughts sure were taking a dark turn. Snow wasn't usually this pessimistic. Maybe it was that they'd lasted twenty minutes without having to consider any of their contingencies, which was about fifteen minutes longer than she'd anticipated. Waiting for the first thing to go wrong was maddening.

"Heads-up," Delfina said through the earpiece.

A moment later the fitful quiet between peals of thunder was shattered by a loud explosion, followed shortly by the patter of small pieces of debris hitting the top of the truck and the ground. The guards at the gate were visibly distressed. One of them came out of the hut, shielding their face from the pounding rain to stare past the prison's original building. If that had indeed been Marrow and Bone blowing a hole through the exterior wall, the guard would be seeing a column of smoke. If the wolven were insanely lucky, the curtains of dense rain would conceal it, buying them a little more time.

Byron pulled open the panel they'd installed behind the seats. "We need to move."

"Yep." Snow scrambled over the seats and into the closet they'd built for him and Delfina.

The hacker didn't look up from the screens. "They're going over. You need to get to the trucks."

Snow nodded and followed Byron through the door into the back of the laundry truck. Once she closed it, the only light source was from the crystals hanging out of his shirt. A third of them were dark.

"Remember what I taught you and you'll be fine," Byron said as he slid two crystals off their silver chain and held them in either hand.

Glowing runes sprang to life around the interior of the truck's double doors. The doors flickered in and out of existence, the familiar shimmering curtain springing to life, then winking out before reforming.

"Portal's unstable." A crease of concentration furrowed Byron's brow. "That's weird." The final statement was an absent mutter as the wheelman bent all his focus to the task.

The flickering worsened, even as Byron bent his attention to it. He scrawled over glyphs, changing some, neatening up others, but the curtain continued to wink erratically in and out of existence. Finally, the shimmer vanished and the runes went dark as did the crystals he grasped.

"What happened?"

Byron shook his head. "The runes are perfect. As good as any portal I've ever made, and I've been doing this for a few decades. My best guess is someone moved the trailer trucks we stashed."

"Who would do that?" Her skin prickled, the fur on the back of her neck rising at the major gap that had been suddenly introduced in their plans.

"They're stolen and hidden on public land." Byron shrugged. "It could have been anyone."

The door to Delfina's hidey hole crashed open. "Get in here," the hacker snapped from the doorway, then disappeared back to her seat.

Snow eased open the back doors and glanced through the crack. No one waited. She closed it quietly, then scrambled to join Byron in the hacker's technology closet.

"What's the situation?" Delfina asked.

"Portal failed." Byron bit the words off in obvious irritation. "The trucks must have been moved."

"Then we have a problem. Marrow already went over with more than twenty wolven." Delfina scowled at her monitors. "Bone is pinned down with the larger half. We have nowhere to go."

"Why not here?" Snow asked.

Delfina flicked her a glance, the scorn in her gaze was almost tactile. "How are we going to fit sixty wolven in the back of this truck?"

"We don't." Snow shook Byron's arm. "Make the portal through the laundry truck to somewhere else."

He blinked at her. "Where to?"

"Does it matter? Anywhere. Just not here."

"That could work."

"We still need to get your people back through a prison crawling with guards who definitely know they're there," Delfina said.

"So the gloves are off." Snow grinned. She knew her eyes were glowing and her teeth were starting to come to points. "We're at our best when there are no limits."

"If you say so." Delfina's fingers danced over her keyboards, then she swiveled the mouthpiece of her headset down. "Bring your cargo back to the laundry truck," she said over the crew's open channel.

"Then I need to get in there and clear the path from our end," Snow said.

"If you're going to do what I think you are"—Byron pressed a crystal into her hand—"this is going to take more power."

Snow moved to the center of the truck and stripped off her clothing, kicking it to one side with only the barest thought about folding it. She wouldn't be wearing that again, even if she survived. She knew her own strength. Against one human, she would do just fine. Against a group...It would take fewer to overwhelm her than it would any of the Alphas. But if she could buy Cassidy and the others some time, it was worth it.

She dropped to a crouch, holding the crystal in her left hand, and called her wolf to her. The slow push of fur through her tender skin was torture. Her change was always slow, but this was a crawl compared to its usual clip. Experience had taught her that the slower the change, the more charge she infused into the crystals.

By the time she stood on all fours, fluids dripping off the tips of her fur, her sides were heaving as if she'd completed a particularly arduous hunt. The crystal rolled away from her front paw, shining brightly enough to throw her shadow across the far wall.

Byron bent down to scoop it up. "Thanks for the extra juice," he said before crossing to the back door.

He threw it open. It bumped into something, then swung back toward him.

"What the hell?" Byron shoved the door as hard as he could.

"The fuck?" Snow recognized Witzig's voice a moment before the door swung all the way open, revealing the guard at the back, her mouth agape.

Snow didn't hesitate. She hurtled forward to collide with the guard and send her stumbling back until she hit the loading dock's back wall. She kept moving, snapping and growling. Witzig was fast, and she slapped Snow's muzzle away a few times before she was able to get a good mouthful of the guard's arm. After that, it didn't take long to dismantle her. Before long, Witzig lay slumped against the wall, a pool of blood spreading from her. Snow stepped back, avoiding dipping her paws in the gore.

"I was going to ask if you'd be all right," Byron said. "Looks like you'll be fine."

Snow panted, trying to radiate confidence she didn't really feel. Fake it till you make it, wasn't that the saying? She would fake it until everyone was out, or she was dead.

CHAPTER FORTY

An alarm spun up, its shrill claxon grating on Cassidy's ears. It cut off a moment later, then spun up again.

"Damn alarms," Delfina grated through the earpiece. The shrill sound died abruptly. "Marrow went over the edge after half of the first group. Trucks were discovered. That escape route is burned."

She and Hammer exchanged a glance. "Any implications for our extraction?" Cassidy asked.

"None yet. Your plan is still to bring the kids to the laundry truck." Delfina sighed as the alarm went off again. "I'll update if things change. For now, keep to the plan. Got my hands full in here." With that, she disconnected their line.

"Keep on keeping on?" Hammer asked. He had his hand pressed against his side, keeping pressure on a bullet wound that was still leaking blood, even as it continued to heal. He wouldn't have to hold it closed for much longer.

"That's the plan." Cassidy wondered how much further off-course things had gotten. Sure, they'd tried to work out all the contingencies they could, but the trucks that were supposed to move the wolven had seemed safe across the river in Illinois. Their backup plans had been for things that could go wrong on the inside. The trucks weren't even in the same state. How had they been found?

Her own wounds ached, but they'd been superficial and had long since closed. They'd passed the checkpoint, but as soon as the explosives had gone off, the guard on their side had demanded they come back. When they'd kept moving, he'd pulled his sidearm, as had the guard on the other side of the gate.

It had been a short but bloody battle, one aided by Delfina unlocking all the doors in the prison. There had been no time to hide the bodies. Apparently, someone had found them, and they kept trying to sound the alarm. Their carts had been riddled with bullets, and they'd left them behind, but not before filling their pockets with enough of Delfina's gadgets to stock a Best Buy.

"How long did it take before that suppressor gas wore off?" Cassidy asked.

"About two hours," Hammer said.

"So not until we get out of here."

"Seems so." He flexed the fingers on his free hand. "I miss my claws."

"Me too." Most of all, she missed the counsel of her wolf. But they were still alive, so she couldn't be doing too terribly.

The medical wing was eerily empty. Hammer hadn't been allowed all the way into it, but he'd been close enough to hear the voices of their children. The way forward was slowed as they checked every room. It wouldn't do to leave a cub behind because they'd taken refuge in a closet. So far, the rooms off the main hall had been dusty and smelling of must, with the occasional moldering piece of furniture. There were plenty of rooms along this hall. They were too comfortable to have been cells. Cassidy thought perhaps they'd been treatment rooms once upon a time. Fortunately, she and Hammer were nearly at the end of the corridor. Another set of imposing double metal doors blocked their way. Those looked newer. Someone had cared enough to replace the handles and probably also the locking mechanism. The badge reader next to the door was definitely a recent addition.

Hammer removed his hand from his side and glanced down at it. The trickle of blood had stopped. He grunted with satisfaction and produced the Hunter's keycard from one of his pockets. The reader flashed green. He pushed on one of the doors. It didn't budge.

Cassidy grabbed a handle and pulled back, ready to give Hammer a hard time about not knowing which way the door swung, but it didn't move either. All the doors they'd encountered so far had been unlocked.

Hammer reclaimed the handle and shook it. The door rattled in its housing. "It's been barred," he said. "Maybe barricaded."

"Someone doesn't want us in there." Cassidy shook her head. "I hate to be a disappointment, but…" She pressed her shoulder to the door, planting her feet and shoving, churning her legs as if she was going to walk right through the solid metal. The door creaked and groaned, but barely moved. All that work, and maybe a fraction of an inch to show for it? Cassidy stopped pushing.

"Hold on." Hammer disappeared into one of the nearby rooms. There were some clatters and clangs, followed by the squeal of metal on metal. He came out carrying two rails from an examination bed. They were so rusted it was impossible to tell the original paint color. He tossed one to Cassidy, then posted up at the wall next to the doors. "Let's make a new one." He reared back and hit the wall with all of his impressive strength. The bar crashed into the cinder blocks, sending a spray of paint and concrete chips out in all directions.

Cassidy slotted herself in opposite Hammer as he continued to take big swings at the surface. She tried to time her hits between his, and he slowed his blows a fraction so she could take hers. The surface quickly went from pockmarked to divoted. As they both trained all of their strength on to it, the wall deteriorated further. It wasn't a quiet process, but they'd gone past the point of stealth. The faster they moved, the better. Luther's star blazed in her internal starscape. He was angry, filled with a towering rage that matched hers in intensity. Now was a good time to unleash that aggression. She wasn't worried about that well running dry; she would have plenty left when they finally came across those behind their pain. The Hunter, Shashka, was one of those, but the rest had all been flunkies. There had been no satisfaction in taking them out, beyond knowing that she and Hammer were still alive and one step closer to fulfilling their mission.

They made short work of the wall. After the first hole had been broken through, they used the long pieces of steel as levers to pop out cinder blocks. It couldn't have taken more than a few minutes, but each one felt like a lifetime. When the hole was large enough for Cassidy to poke her head through, she did so. The hall on the other side of the door was empty.

"We're clear." Cassidy fell to widening the hole so it would be big enough to fit through.

She crawled through first, then turned to lend Hammer a hand. It was a tight squeeze, but he managed, even if he did leave some skin behind on broken chunks of masonry.

Before them was a stack of furniture and debris. Whoever had shored up the doors had known what they were doing. It would take some doing before anyone would be able to get it or out that way.

Cassidy took a long look around, then lifted her nose to sniff at the air. The hallway continued on from the door and also split to the left and the right. She could smell humans and wolven most strongly down the main drag, but there were whiffs of wolven down the side passages as well. The top level of smells were human, and each held the stink of fear, except for one that stood out. That one had a silvery sheen of excitement to it. Someone was anticipating their arrival.

"Sides go up to the second level," Hammer murmured. "Offices and the like up there. Prisoners were kept downstairs. The gallery could also be used to suppress prisoners in the common area."

"Luther is through there." She pointed ahead and to the left. His star beckoned to her.

"Go get your Beta. I'll sweep the second floor and eliminate any trouble I find."

"What if I need you?"

"I'll be around." He grinned. "But I'd be surprised if there's anything you can't handle." Hammer held out his hand to her, his elbow bent and wrist crooked.

Cassidy hesitated, then went in, trying to imitate his stance.

He gripped her hand hard and pulled her in for a rough hug. "Alpha."

Cassidy smiled into his shoulder. "Alpha. Take care of yourself. You owe me a rematch."

Hammer shook his head and released her. "Why fight again when we already know you'll lose." He turned on his heel and trotted down the right-hand hallway.

She didn't like being alone, but Luther wasn't far. Besides, Hammer had confidence in her. She wasn't about to disappoint him or herself. All she had to do was be smart and ruthless. Hadn't she managed this far? Cassidy slunk down the hall. That this was probably a trap was very clear with the barricaded door and lack of guard presence. Someone was practically laying down a trail of roses and candles toward the main entrance.

Their intel on this part of the complex was hazy. It wasn't part of the original building, so they didn't have even sketchy blueprints. There were some photos that had been taken by the urban spelunkers group, but it seemed that this part had been off-limits to tours even before the prison had been reopened. Hammer had sketched in as much as he'd seen, but this far in they were truly blind.

Cassidy pressed a finger to her earpiece. "Anything on the cameras?"

"Those went down a little bit ago," Delfina replied. "There was a flurry of activity, then someone went through obscuring the lens on each one. I'm blind."

"It was worth a try." Cassidy kept moving slowly and soundlessly. At least the cameras couldn't be used to watch her, but any doubt that someone wasn't waiting for them was now gone.

The hall wasn't long, and at the end was yet another set of heavy double doors. Cassidy pulled gently on the handle, and it gave. She opened it enough that she could peer through to the next room. It opened into what might once have been a cafeteria. Rusted and broken tables and benches were shoved against walls painted with sprays of blood. Deep scratches and gouges marred the stained floor. She'd seen those patterns before. They were from wolven in fur or betweenform. But how was that possible? Hammer had said this area employed the same suppression of their wolf halves as the cell blocks did.

The ceiling rose two stories above, and the second floor looked down into the room. A railing ran the circumference of the gallery. Guards in camouflage fatigues glared down from behind the heavy metal rails. Each face was hard and betrayed no qualms about pointing rifles on the group that was gathered at the center of the room.

The smallest bodies were at the front, feet shuffling and heads lowered. Not one of the cubs dared look up. Behind them were older cubs not quite on the cusp of adulthood. Their arms wrapped around the shoulders of the smallest. At the back of the gathered cubs were five adults. Luther's nose lifted and his jaw flexed when he picked up her scent. He was ready to attack, rifles or no rifles. If it had been just him, Cassidy had no doubt that he would already be moving.

A tall, sexless figure whose pale skin contrasted with the black fatigues that Shashka had also worn stepped forward. Their short blond hair was covered by a black cap. They raised their chin to display a cocky grin and spread their hands as if to ask "What do you think?"

This had to be the other Hunter. Cassidy had suspected there was another one around. Apparently, it had been too much to ask for today to have been a vacation day.

"No need to be shy," the Hunter said, her voice surprisingly high and light. "We all know you're out there. We've been waiting." She turned her head, laying the back of her hand against her cheek, miming a conspiratorial whisper. "I was beginning to worry you'd miss the fun."

CHAPTER FORTY-ONE

Snow quickly licked spatters of blood from her paws a few feet away from the bodies of a couple of guards. She didn't concern herself with the blood that painted the walls behind them. As long as it wasn't on her feet, she couldn't lead anyone to her. She looked around, taking in the intersection of corridors. Between those and the high windows lining one side of the main hall, she knew where she was. The way behind her had been cleared of as many humans as she could handle on her own. It had taken all of her talents of stealth to ambush these last two. One had gotten off a few shots of a pistol, all of them going wide. The guards had had long enough to arm themselves. That wasn't unforeseen, but Snow wished they'd had more time. Hell, it would have been really nice if the entire plan had gone off without a hitch.

She moved slowly, taking care not to allow even the faintest click of nail on concrete to give her away. She wasn't sure how much closer she really wanted to get to the cell blocks. The suppression agent had been disabled, but did it still linger? They didn't know if whatever suppressed the ability of wolven to shift would force her into skinform or merely lock her in furform. It wasn't as if they'd had the opportunity to check, and she really didn't want to become unceremoniously human in the middle of a prison. Skinform was one thing. Naked skinform when being hunted by gun-toting guards was quite another.

There was a corner up ahead, past a checkpoint that stood open and abandoned. Where had those guards gone? Were they the ones she'd eliminated a minute ago? The skin between her shoulder blades itched. She couldn't ask Delfina. Even if the earpiece had fit inside wolven ears, she had no way of activating it, much less asking her questions. She missed her eye in the sky.

Despite not knowing what lay in store for her, Snow made her deliberate way forward. No one awaited her at the checkpoint, but the stench of human sweat was recent. The scent trail stretched out ahead of her. The guards had taken off in the same direction she was headed.

She peeked her head around the corner and found them, crouched in doorways on either side of the hall. That was unfortunate for her. How did she take them out without getting taken down herself? It would have been so much more convenient if they'd hunkered down together. She had to do something, though. This was the best way out of the cell blocks, which was likely why the guards had posted up here. Could she rely on her sneakiness to get close enough to attack? Maybe. But then how did she get across the hall without getting riddled with bullets? She'd managed to avoid getting shot this far, and she preferred to keep it that way.

Still, it had to be done. They would do a lot of damage against wolven trapped in skinform.

Her mind made up, Snow slunk forward. She'd been moving quietly before, but now she was less than a whisper, not even a stray thought grazing the mind of someone focused on something else. She hugged her presence in close, not letting a wisp of herself press out ahead of her. There was no breeze inside these stifling walls, and she'd never been gladder. Snow skulked down the hall, passing ten feet without notice, then twenty. She picked up speed, still being careful to move softly until she was within lunging distance. She was headed down the left side of the corridor, for no particular reason except that it had been closer.

"Look out!" the guard across the hall yelled.

Snow launched herself at the nearest guard who half-turned at the warning. She led with her teeth, closing them around the human woman's arm as she flung it up to try stopping Snow. The bones in her forearm snapped and Snow's mouth filled with blood as she closed her jaws with savage precision. She let her bodyweight bowl the screaming guard over into the dark room. It only took an instant to let go of the guard's arm and bite down on her shoulder where it met her neck. Snow shook her head back and forth, shredding through skin and muscle with ease.

The guard wasn't moving when she was dropped from Snow's jaws. A pool of ichor spread from her still form, and Snow ducked all the way behind the wall.

The other guard opened fire. Snow pressed herself to the ground as slugs punched holes in the plaster and lath walls. White powder and shards of wood rained down on top of her. The guard yelled a hoarse scream more of terror than anger as he continued to blindly pump bullet after bullet in her direction. When he stopped shooting, Snow pushed herself up from the ground.

The sound of metal on concrete was the only confirmation she needed. Snow darted from the room and across the hall as the guard panted, trying to reload his weapon.

He looked up as she crossed the threshold. His eyes widened, taking in her blood-soaked face and chest. Each footfall hit the ground with a saturated slap. The guard scrambled backward, abandoning the rifle he wouldn't be able to get loaded and leveled at her before she could get to him. The combat knife he pulled out of a boot sheath was a surprise. His first swipe opened a slice along the side of her muzzle. Only the twist of her head at the last minute kept him from taking out her eye. It might grow back, it might not, but now was not the time to put her wolven regeneration to the test.

Throwing herself to the side put her off her trajectory and she dashed past the human, who whirled with her, blade brandished between them. She pelted full force at the wall, leaping and twisting to run along it for two paces, then pushed off, coming toward him again. He'd gained his feet but was still too slow to be a real threat. Snow faked toward his left hand, and when he moved to intercept her, she dipped under his arm and casually ripped a chunk out of the back of his right leg, severing his hamstring in the process. The guard grunted in shock and went down to one knee. It took less than a second to reach back and bite through the artery on the inside of his upper arm when he tried to brace himself.

She danced away, not wanting to be painted with arterial spray, not that her coat was anywhere near pristine anymore. The guard stared at her stupidly as the vitality pumped out of his body with the final beats of his racing heart. He slid to one side, his terrified eyes never leaving hers. Snow watched him, counting the breaths, not daring to turn her back on him.

His last breath left him in a slow wheeze.

Her head jerked up as a strange noise hit her ears. She cocked her head, trying to make sense of it, then bounded from the room when she recognized it as the slapping of many feet against the prison's deteriorating linoleum floors. Down the hall came a mob of people. The scent that came from them was all wolven, though none were in furform. No one wore shoes. Bright hospital gowns flapped about their bodies, though not many made any effort to keep them closed. One figure stood out, dressed in the same fatigues as the guards. Snow knew that profile, she knew that scent.

"Snow!" Bone cried. She pounded up to her, leaving the other wolven in her wake.

She couldn't speak, but Snow stuck her nose in Bone's hand and gave it a quick lick.

Bone squatted and grabbed the ruffs of her cheeks. "Take them back. There are more coming. We—I'm staggering the groups. Less chance that everyone will get picked up." She looked around, catching sight of the guard's legs through the doorway. "There are more guards."

Snow pushed her head against Bone's shoulder, then looked up as the remaining wolven caught up to them. A few she recognized, but most were unknown to her. Naomi stood at the back, keeping an eye on the group's tail. The wolven waited, bodies tense, but without the posturing that so often accompanied first meetings. Snow headbutted Bone again, then turned tail, trotting along, knowing the wolven would follow her.

She guided them swiftly, but silently, through the halls. The irony of so many of her kind being guided by her was palpable. That every single one of them was more dominant than she only made the situation that much more absurd, but they all obeyed her. Every look was treated as if it came from an Alpha. Was this what it felt like to be at the top of a pack? She had a better understanding of why some wolven sought out higher positions. There was a strange headiness to having others fall in line with only a glance.

They were flying around a corner when she caught the smell of gun oil and sweat from up ahead. Snow tried to stop, her toenails scrabbling against the linoleum tile. Her nails caught for a moment, then slipped on another slick length. The wolven sprinted after her, a mere length of two wolves behind.

The first volley of bullets mostly missed Snow as she slid to one side. Fire streaked over her shoulder and along one flank. One slug thudded into her side, sending her reeling back.

Blood exploded among the ranks of the wolven who were rounding the corner. One woman, someone Snow vaguely remembered from her time with the Gary pack went down from a bullet to the jaw.

"Scatter!" Snow recognized Naomi's voice. The wolven scrambled to follow her order. Those who had already rounded the corner kept running, coming after Snow as she closed with the guards who crouched between a makeshift barricade that consisted of a table on its side and a couple of elderly chairs.

Snow hoped they would stay out of the line of fire. She darted from side to side, trying to ensure that any shot the guards lined up would be a difficult one. She wasn't in the habit of making herself an easy target. More bodies hit the ground behind her as she reached the barricade and vaulted over it.

Wordless shouts from the humans accompanied her arrival. One tried to turn to keep her in his sights, but she bulled her way under his arms and bit down as hard as she could. Her teeth hung up on some sort of body armor. She didn't stop moving but chewed to try to get through the toughened material. The guard hollered, beating at her with his arms. After making no headway with the armor, Snow shook her head hard. When her teeth slid free of the fibers, she angled herself, throwing the guard back over the barrier.

"Oh god," another guard said, frozen in horror as the wolven took their combined rage out on him. She raised her rifle to fire into the group, but Snow collided with her, bowling her over onto her side.

All it took was the snap of her jaws over the guard's neck, an old-fashioned throat ripping, before Snow was on to the next. This one had gotten their weapon up and had opened fire again. A wolven vaulting over the barricade lunged and grabbed the rifle's barrel, shoving it up toward the ceiling. Another set of hands reached out and grabbed the human. They were dragged into the mob, leaving Snow with only one to take down.

When the final guard realized he was on his own, he backed away from her as she advanced, growling. The fur on her ruff lifted as she sent her presence out from her body, pushing in on the human. Her lips peeled back from her teeth. The guard had seemed so brave a minute ago when he'd been crouched behind cover and firing at her and her people. He edged another step back, but Snow closed the distance between them.

She opened her mouth, allowing saliva mixed with blood to drip from her jaws as she anticipated snapping his bones with her teeth. The guard couldn't take it any longer. The air stank of blood and terror. He threw the rifle down and turned to run. In two bounds, Snow was on him. Her paws to the back of his shoulders sent him tumbling. He tried to pull a knife from his belt as he went down, but Snow grabbed his forearm between her teeth and shook her head, casually splintering the limb. Then, because she'd been raised never to toy with those less fortunate, she lunged forward and took his throat out as well.

The wolven were clustered around the two guards they'd eliminated. Naomi spoke quietly but firmly, directing them to strip the bodies and pass the pieces of clothing out. The more fragile of the wolven ended up with the boots, others ended up with the weapons. One of them sighted down the barrel of a rifle and nodded. It should have looked ridiculous with his hospital gown, but with the blood spatter he looked grimly practical.

Three wolven were down. One got back up after a moment and was helped forward, leaning on the shoulders of the two on either side of her. The other two didn't move. Without talking it over, two of the nearest uninjured wolven picked up their bodies. There was still the chance they might recover. If they didn't, at least they would be out of this place.

There was one more ugly little skirmish as they made their way through the halls. The guards were getting better at setting up around blind corners and opening up on them from cover. Two more wolven went down and had to be carried. Snow picked up another bullet wound and a stab to the haunch that had her limping. When the doors to the outside finally came into view, she wanted to howl in triumph. Her head drooping from weariness, she shouldered the door open.

Byron stood in the back of the laundry truck. He motioned her over, his hands easy to see as each grasped a bright crystal.

Snow accompanied her wolven into the truck.

"Through there." Byron pointed at the near door. It should have led to Delfina's little tech closet, but through the doorway were the cool dark greens of an evergreen forest.

"Through where?" one of the wolven asked.

"Is that safe?" Naomi shifted, her scent sharp with suspicion. She hoisted the burden of a body in her arms.

They didn't have time for this. Snow pushed herself through the group, dodging legs, nosing them out of the way when they didn't move for her. She trotted into the back of the truck and through the doorway without pausing. The smell of loam and rich earth made her want to drop to the ground and roll in it, but that would have to wait. Snow turned and looked back through the portal. On this side, it was anchored by a stone arch in the middle of a clearing. The wolven on the other side hesitated, then Naomi stepped into the back of the truck. As if they'd been waiting for someone to break their indecision, the group surged forward.

"What do we do now?" one of them asked after they'd all cleared the portal.

Snow looked back at the gathered group. They huddled together, with no regard for pack.

"We figure it out." The voice was Naomi's. Cassidy's interim Beta stepped out of the group. She'd been shoved into the position after Luther's disappearance but had moved ably into the role. Apparently she was still doing her best by the pack. Naomi gently placed the body she'd been carrying atop a bed of bright green moss under one of the massive trees. "There will be more."

Snow nodded. There would be more. She would do everything she could to see to that.

She stepped back through to the truck.

CHAPTER FORTY-TWO

Cassidy grimaced. So much for stealth. Not that she'd seen any way she could have sneaked into the large room. Aside from the second floor gallery, there seemed to be only a single entry, at least on the first floor.

"All that for little old me?" Cassidy called out. "You shouldn't have."

"We sure did," the Hunter replied. "You should come on in. We didn't make all these preparations for nothing."

"I'm good out here."

"Fine. I'll have to start killing the babies." She sounded as cheerful about killing the cubs as she did about pretending that this was all one big party.

Cassidy shivered. The Hunter would have been less frightening if she's started screaming threats. She pushed the door open.

"Hands," the Hunter called.

Cassidy wiggled them as she stepped forward. "I have two of them."

"Where I can see them."

"Ah." Cassidy raised her hands to shoulder level. "You should have been more specific." She stopped just inside the doors, taking a look up at the guards. There were five of them, and they were disciplined enough that none of them had turned their weapon or eyes on her. Instead, they kept their rifles leveled at the kids and their chaperones.

"Are you behind all of this?" the Hunter asked.

"Me?" Cassidy raised her eyebrows in surprise and shook her head. "I can't take credit, I'm afraid. Just along for the ride."

"That's too bad." The Hunter grinned, a nasty smile that slashed across her face for a moment then was gone. "I'd like to congratulate the one who put this together. It's screwed up quite a bit of planning."

"Mm. So sorry." Cassidy took another step, and the guards tightened up. She stopped.

"So what's the game plan here? Where do you think you'll go with all of these werewolves?"

Cassidy shrugged. "Home. That's all. Nothing more nefarious than getting our families back."

"Your home is gone." The Hunter tilted her head "You're North Side, right? That hotel of yours went up like dried kindling."

"Your idea?"

"It sure was." The smile was back, but this with a dark edge that promised pain. "You got a problem with that?"

"Of course I do." Cassidy stepped forward again. If she could get close enough to the Hunter, maybe she could surprise her and give Hammer a chance to move in on the guards above. It was risky. It wouldn't take much for them to start putting holes in the cubs. She had no idea if the younglings were as resilient as adult wolven were. "You can't really be surprised that we showed up."

"It would have been better for you if you hadn't." The Hunter looked past her and motioned someone forward.

A firm hand dropped onto Cassidy's right shoulder while the barrel of a gun was shoved into her back. Two more guards were directly behind her. She hadn't smelled them until they were right on top of her. The room was rank with various unpleasant stenches, and their body odor had mixed right in.

"I guess it's that you got the drop on us this time," the Hunter continued. "After all, you were so woefully ignorant of what was going while we were picking you off one by one. I should really thank you for getting all those Alphas together in one place. It made swooping in on your packs so much easier."

"Yeah, well." Cassidy grimaced, playing up the guilt she felt at the outcome of that idea. She still didn't feel great about it, but the reality was that she wasn't the one who'd kidnapped packs from across the Chicago area. This asshole and the rest of her assholes were. "Happy to help."

"Appreciated." The Hunter studied her. "Step forward." She pointed to a spot directly in front of her. "I want to see you in the light."

The barrel in her ribs ground in tightly, forcing her to step up. Still, Cassidy took her time moving across the room. Why did it have to be so large? And so devoid of cover. If Hammer was going to do something to help her out of this jam, he would be better off doing it sooner than later. This Hunter moved so much like Mary it was unreal. She missed her sister. Mary would have been a huge help with this whole operation. Out of habit, she reached out toward Ruri's star. It was still gone. One next to it winked out also.

"Beth?" Cassidy stumbled to a stop just out of the Hunter's reach.

The guard used the hand on her shoulder to propel her forward until she was practically nose to nose with the Hunter.

"Thank you, Agosto."

"Blight." The guard relinquished his grip and stepped back. The one with the gun in her ribs didn't move.

The Hunter, Blight, looked down at Cassidy. "You're so familiar." She grabbed Cassidy's chin and lifted her head up, turning it one way, then the other. "Have we crossed paths before?"

"You wouldn't be here if we had."

A nearly genuine smile flitted across Blight's face at the statement. "Ditto." She continued to examine Cassidy's face. "It's the eyes and the hair," she announced and let go of Cassidy's chin. She held up a hand, blocking her view of the top of Cassidy's head. "Darken the hair, change the eyes, and you're the spitting image of Malice. I didn't know she had a sister. I can see why she kept you from us. It's a shame about…"

"Shame about what?"

Blight's answer was cut off by the report of a gun firing overhead. One of the guards was yanked back from the railing and his weapon turned on the guard across the way. Everyone froze for a moment, then everything broke loose at once. The adult wolven threw themselves forward, shoving cubs down, trying to interpose their bodies in front of the weapons of the guards above. Those humans ducked as whoever was firing sprayed rounds above their heads.

That has to be Hammer, Cassidy thought as she swept the rifle barrel away from her back and stepped out of Blight's reach. She grabbed at each guard and yanked them forward. One was too surprised to stop her, the other broke her grip on his jacket. The first went stumbling into Blight as she lunged toward Cassidy, a short samurai sword in each hand. The hapless guard was skewered through the torso and dropped. Blight had to step back to free up her sword, giving Cassidy time to get behind the other guard.

Above, the guards were trading fire with someone Cassidy couldn't see. Luther and the others were shoving the cubs under the dubious cover of the tables and benches against the walls. A few of the adults sported spots of bright crimson, but none of the cubs seemed to have been hit.

Blight cuffed the other guard out of the way, but he didn't go down. Instead, he rubbed his ear and turned toward Cassidy. Realizing her error, Cassidy threw herself at him before he could lift his rifle more than a few inches. She grabbed the barrel and twisted, trying to yank it from his hands, but he hung on with grim determination. Aware that Blight was shifting to the side to try to flank her, Cassidy pivoted, keeping the struggling guard between her and the Hunter as best she could.

"Let fucking go," the guard hissed. He was much larger than she was, nearly as tall as Hammer if not nearly as dark. He gritted his teeth as he tried to regain control over his weapon, but Cassidy wouldn't be dislodged.

She threw herself into another pivot, hauling the guard around. Her grip slipped off the barrel, and he grunted in triumph as he yanked the stock out of her hand. This hand-to-hand combat thing was a pain. She needed her teeth and claws. More than that she needed her wolf. Since she had none of those things, Cassidy launched herself at the guard, wrapping her arms around his waist in a desperate tackle and hoping her unexpected strength would help bear him to the floor.

To her shock, the gambit worked. As the guard's back made contact with the ground, she was already rolling to one side, just as Blight's sword flashed past her face. The Hunter was quick, maybe even a match for Cassidy in skinform, which is why it was a shock when Blight made no attempt to slow the swing of her blade before it made contact with her ally. The sword was razor sharp and bit deeply into his shoulder, just missing the body armor that might have absorbed some of the damage.

"No witnesses," the Hunter whispered as he dropped.

Cassidy backpedaled as fast as she could, dodging slash after slash. If she'd only had one blade to worry about, she thought perhaps she wouldn't be working so hard, but Blight's hands worked in concert, each strike coming closer than the one before. She couldn't duck under the Hunter's guard; she couldn't maneuver to the side. Her only tactic was to back straight up, and she knew she wouldn't be able to continue that for long.

The gunfire up top was subsiding, the time between the loud cracks growing longer. Either Hammer was winning, or he was getting slaughtered. Cassidy couldn't risk a look to find out.

"Alpha," Luther cried out. "Behind you!"

Cassidy's back foot hit something that moved a bit. She swept her foot behind her, trying to dislodge whatever piece of trash she'd kicked.

"You good, Luther?" Cassidy called back.

Blight surged forward in a complicated series of cuts and stabs. Cassidy dodged and weaved, slapping one slice away a hair before it could sink into her upper arm. She wasn't fast enough to stop all of them. Instead she concentrated on letting through only those that wouldn't disable her. Blood stained her skin from half a dozen minor slash wounds, but many were already knitting back together.

"Better than I was, Alpha," Luther responded.

Whoever was up above shot down, hitting one of the fallen guards with a spray of bullets. Hammer seemed to have gotten the upper hand. All Cassidy had to do was survive long enough for someone to save her ass.

She finally hit the wall, hard enough to expel a startled huff from deep in her lungs. The Hunter paused, grinning widely. She knew Cassidy had nowhere to go.

Luther's voice rang out behind her. "You're on your own, Blight."

"Not for the first time, wolf." The Hunter spun at Cassidy, who tried to lunge away, but she didn't have far to go. Agony spangled through her whole body as a sword pierced her shoulder. Blight grinned and pushed in on her, pressing the length of her body against Cassidy's. She grunted softly, driving the blade through Cassidy, pinning her to the wall.

Cassidy locked eyes with the Hunter and didn't look away. She refused to give this maniac the satisfaction of seeing her flinch. Whatever the Hunter was looking for in her cruelty would not be found in Cassidy's suffering. And suffering it was. The blade felt like a hot poker. Every heartbeat sent more pain radiating from the point of injury as her wound tried to close and was reopened by the razor-sharp blade.

Blight stepped to the side, extending her other sword so it rested on the tender skin of Cassidy's neck. "Back it on up there, Luther," she said. "Unless you want to see how well your Alpha regrows her own head."

CHAPTER FORTY-THREE

"I like my head where it is, thanks anyway," Cassidy said. The handle of the sword quivered slightly in time with her pounding heart. "So, you use me as a hostage and actually make it out of here, what then? Do you really think we'll let you live after what you've done to us?"

"You'll have to find me."

"I'll just ask Mary where you all like to hang out."

"Mary?" Blight chuckled. "Oh, you mean Malice. Good luck with that. She's not coming to save you. She's dead, little sister. You're on your own."

On your own. Blight's words echoed in Cassidy's brain. She looked out, catching Luther's eye. He stood about fifteen feet away, a wolven flanking him on either side. From the set of his jaw, she knew that if she told him to come in, he would.

"I'm not alone," Cassidy said quietly. "I haven't been alone in months." She raised her voice. "Sorry about this, Hammer."

"If you move a muscle…" Blight drew the blade lightly across Cassidy's throat. It was so sharp that even that lightest pressure cut through her skin and sent a trickle of blood down her neck.

Cassidy smiled and closed her eyes. She didn't need to move to reach out to the points of light that surrounded her. Luther blazed the brightest, but there were others, cloaked as if viewed through cloud cover at night. She'd done this once before, but that had been mostly instinct with the wolf to help her along. This time, she reached out deliberately, imagining she was cupping the closest light in her hands. She drew it closer, into her orbit, until it blazed as brightly as Luther did.

She reached out again, this time grabbing a handful of stars. She gathered them in more quickly, with greater confidence. There was a feeling of resistance for some of them, but she plucked them free of whatever was holding them back and welcomed them among the starscape around her. There were still more stars that she could reach, and she did, until all the muted points of light she could see burned with the same steady light as Luther's.

When she opened her eyes, every wolven in the room was staring at her. Even the cubs under the tables and benches watched her, some with eyes that glowed in brilliant shades in the shadows. Luther's eyes shone, as did those of the wolven on either side. She felt the stirring of her own wolf within her, the groggy shifting of one who'd slept for too long and couldn't rouse. There was no time for rest. They had work to do, and those who needed their protection were right there in the room.

The wolf twitched, and Cassidy couldn't stop her head from jerking slightly in response.

"What are you up to?" Blight hissed.

"About five foot four," Cassidy gasped. "Why do you ask?" She grabbed her wolf by the scruff of her neck and shook her, willing her to wakefulness. They were the Alpha of the North Side Pack. They would not be stopped, not by this so-called Hunter, not by anyone else.

The wolf turned over within her and stretched, raking her claws down the underside of Cassidy's belly. The itch of fur blooming through her skin raced over the outside of her stomach. Cassidy clenched her teeth to keep from giving it away. She turned away from her wolf and to the shining stars around her. In her mind's eye, she pulled at the stars, dragging them ever closer. She shook them, in the rough but affectionate way she might grab one of them in furform, closing her jaws around their shoulder and giving them a friendly rattling of their bones. She willed them to awaken, to change as she was changing. It was slow and agonizing, but once they were in forms more suited to the fight, they would make this Hunter eat her words. Hell, they would make her eat her tongue.

Cassidy stared Blight in the eyes. The Hunter recoiled from what she saw in them, and as she did, Cassidy howled in triumph. Her skin split, sending fluids sluicing down her limbs to drip to the floor with individual splats that turned into a torrent. Her muzzle lengthened, her legs shifted and snapped.

The Hunter leaned in, aiming to slice Cassidy's head off, but her arm was already up. She skewered the muscles of Blight's bicep with her claws, digging in and twisting, aiming to wreak as much damage as she could. Blight's blood mixed with the liquid coming off Cassidy.

"Surprise," Cassidy growled, then stepped forward, the sword still embedded in her shoulder. She unfolded herself to her full betweenform height. In skinform, the Hunter had been taller than her, but no longer. They were eye to eye now.

Blight stepped back, abandoning her second sword and switching the remaining blade to her left hand.

Cassidy struck, swiping out with her arm, aiming to knock the sword away, but Blight whirled into the movement and was able to salvage the blade. She kept turning, trying to dart out of Cassidy's reach, but she wasn't letting up. The Hunter was too dangerous to be allowed to regain her composure. Cassidy lowered her shoulder and lunged into her, trying to get under the Hunter's center of gravity and lift her off her feet, but even on defense, Blight was too fast. She was difficult to wrap up, never breaking in the direction Cassidy expected.

The wolf watched her, studying the Hunter's movements, even as Cassidy tried to shut her down. She stepped in, sharing the load, seeming to whisper to Cassidy, "Strike here, strike now."

Cassidy shifted with Blight, then feinted to the right, away from the Hunter's sword arm. The Hunter twitched, already reacting to block the blow she thought was coming, but Cassidy reversed and was coming in over the blade.

Blight's sword bit deep into her forearm, slicing through skin and muscle until it hit bone. Cassidy and the wolf howled, this time in pain, but they moved into the slice, hard enough for the sword to lodge in their radius. Or ulna. Cassidy couldn't remember, and the wolf didn't care. United in their desire to take down their enemy, they grabbed Blight's neck with their other hand. A quick tightening of the fist around Blight's larynx was all it took. They dug their claws in behind the small organ, then tore it out in a fountain of gore.

Blight grabbed at her neck with one hand, her mouth bobbing open and closed, like a fish on a line gasping for air as it was lifted from the water. She struggled to remove the sword from Cassidy's arm, but her strength was draining rapidly as Cassidy and the wolf stared down at her impassively. The hilt slipped from Blight's hand as she toppled to the ground where she breathed once, twice more, then her chest stopped rising. If they listened for it, they might hear the last beat of her heart, but they didn't need it.

Cassidy and the wolf turned to the center of the room. Hammer stood not far from her in betweenform. The rifle grasped in his hands looked puny in comparison. A wolven in russet fur stood at his side, leaning against his flank. Behind him was Luther in furform and the remaining adult wolven. Only now coming out from their hidey-holes were the cubs. Some were in furform, but others had retained skinform. Cassidy suspected those who still looked human hadn't been turned yet. Snow had mentioned something about turning Dean, who'd been stuck in skinform until he was considered an adult by the pack. Only then had he been given his wolf.

"We're gonna have to talk about this, Cassidy," Hammer said.

She relaxed a bit at the use of her given name. If Hammer had been irretrievably angry with her, he would have called her Five Moons. Still, from his scent, he was not at all pleased.

"You'll get them back when we're all safe," Cassidy said. She closed her eyes and took stock of those who gathered around her. With a start, she realized that more of the North Shore Pack wolves shone among her array of stars. Beyond them were still more veiled points of light. She thought it might be the rest of the wolven in the complex.

They were coming with her also. Everyone stood a better chance if they were whole. It was easier this time, whether because she had practice now or because the stars of the new pack she'd formed pulsed around her. She didn't know and didn't have time to care. With a quick yank and twist, the stars of every wolven in the prison complex came to her. She breathed in, feeling the power of her people.

"For fuck's sake." Hammer stepped up to her and closed his free hand over the sword in her shoulder. "Get the objects out of your body before you start healing." He ripped the blade free, not seeming to notice when she grunted in pain. The sword embedded in her arm took more to get free. He was reduced to wiggling it as she moaned with each jerk. Being able to heal from nearly any wound didn't make them any more fun to endure.

The sword clattered to the ground and Cassidy took refuge among her stars again. A warm body settled itself against the back of her legs. Luther's star intertwined with hers, throwing his support in. With the exception of Hammer's star, which now orbited with the rest of them, the remaining nearby stars clustered in around her. A warm white light filled her bones, sending them to buzzing. She had to do something with the energy. Some of it she bled off into the unauthorized holes in her body, the rest she sent out to the others. That shake to wake the wolves of those in the room had worked, but this one was on a grander scale. Their lights surged in intensity, and Cassidy and her wolf grinned, tongue hanging out of their mouth.

When they opened their eyes, Hammer was over by the door. "I'll be right back," he growled. "Found something upstairs that might help."

Cassidy nodded. "We'll wait, but be quick. Something tells me they aren't going to let up on us just because we took out their Hunters."

Hammer nodded and slipped out the double doors.

At her side, Luther braced himself on all four legs, then started to shake violently, willing himself into betweenform. "It's been too long," he panted.

"I've missed you too." Cassidy threw her arms around his shoulders and buried her muzzle in the crook of his neck.

"That's not it," Luther said, his voice rougher than it would normally have been, even in betweenform. "I mean it is, but not just it. That's the first time in weeks that I've been able to shift at my own direction. They've been up to some serious shit here, Alpha. Worse than you know."

"I saw the blood spatter on the walls in the main room," Cassidy said. "Have they been staging fights?"

Luther nodded. "They have ways to keep us from shifting."

"We know that one. There was a suppression system in place in the prison."

"Did you know about the part where they've figured out how to make us shift whenever they want?"

CHAPTER FORTY-FOUR

Snow abandoned her usual stealth, opting instead for speed as she rushed to make her way back to Bone. Usually, she could do both, but fatigue was making her fumble-footed. Besides, there were so many pools of blood, and so many feet had already been through them, that she didn't feel she really needed to worry about avoiding them. Her fastidious nature was going to have to sit this one out. There was too much to be done to worry about niceties.

She skirted the makeshift barricade where they'd lost the first wolven of the group. A quick sniff at the air let her know that there were no humans nearby, but some had moved through since she'd shepherded her group to the safety of the laundry truck. She was halfway to the next hallway when she stumbled, tripping over her paws and going sprawling forward.

Cassidy was next to her. The feeling was so strong that Snow looked over her shoulder before scrambling back to her feet. Of course her girlfriend wasn't there, but it sure felt like it. If she closed her eyes, which she wasn't going to do with armed humans roaming the halls, she knew it would have felt like her Alpha was at her side. It didn't matter, she tried to tell herself. She had to meet up with Bone. Cassidy's presence, her acceptance meant everything to Snow, but this feeling, like a phantom limb but for a relationship was strange. Good strange, but odd nonetheless.

She trotted forward a few steps before realizing that the wounds she'd picked up while guarding the wolven were nearly half-healed. They'd been closing, but the process was slowed, probably from all the energy she'd expended today. She glanced down at her foreleg, and the wound she'd received when a bullet had winged her was gone. All that remained was a bald patch of pink skin. There was a small clatter of metal on hard ground as the slug that had been shot into her side was pushed out of her skin. Her gait improved immeasurably now that every step didn't jar the bullet.

Did Cassidy do this? She had no way of knowing, but it was awfully coincidental to be happening right after she'd felt Cassidy's presence so strongly. Did her girlfriend need her? Had she been trying to reach out for help? No, that didn't explain the sudden acceleration of Snow's healing. The cause didn't really matter, but Snow found that she liked the feeling that Cassidy was always nearby. She could feel her tail lifting higher, and she was moving with confidence, instead of only purpose.

The determination came in handy when she rounded the next corner and found herself face-to-face with a lone human guard. The woman half-lifted her pistol, but Snow looked her straight in the eyes and growled. She'd taken out more humans that she could count today, and she wasn't averse to taking out one more. This one could save herself, if she was willing to turn tail and run.

Snow did her best to communicate how badly a confrontation would go for the woman. She held the human's gaze, but hunkered low, not to protect herself, but gathering to spring instead. She crab-walked to the side, giving the woman space to run, but making it clear that Snow was moving past her, one way or another. Her growl intensified, and when the human didn't move quickly enough to suit her, Snow emitted one sharp, loud bark. The sound galvanized the guard, and she scooted past Snow, then turned and sprinted down the hall away from her. For a moment, Snow was tempted to give chase. Her instincts wavered between getting to the rest of her pack and making sure this guard wasn't a threat. From the fear in her scent, the human would continue running as long as she was able, but who knew if her resolve would stiffen if she met up with more of her kind.

But Snow couldn't kill the world. She could only save her little corner of it. Swiveling her ears to keep anyone from coming up behind her, she continued down the hall. The deeper she pressed into the prison without meeting up with Bone and her charges, the more worried she became. She slowed her headlong dash to a trot and kept her nose moving, hoping to catch any scent that would give her an indication about what went wrong.

She was nearly to the cell block when the scent of gunpowder seared her nostrils. As she reviewed the layout of this area of the prison in her mind's eye, she kept swiveling her head, scanning with all of her senses. There were distant shouts, then the distinctive crack of a firing gun. If she'd had her earpiece, she would have asked for details from Delfina, but that wasn't going to work now. She was on her own, except for the persistent sense that Cassidy stalked at her side. It was enough reassurance to keep her pushing forward, looking for the steps up to the higher levels.

The gates at the bottom of the stairs hung open, whether from Delfina's interference or because the guards were in too much hurry to close them after passing through. Snow flowed up the concrete steps three at a time, stretching her long body out to mount them as quickly as she could.

The sounds of gunfire and the smells of guards got stronger. This was the right direction. She kept climbing to the top level. The cell block had three tiers, and if she was an evil human guard bent on suppressing the movement of wolven below, that's where she would have gone.

Her instincts proved right. An array of guards lined this side of the cell block. At one time, the chain-link fence that ran the length of the heavy iron railing had been intact, but it appeared the guards had cut holes in it so they could lean out and fire straight down. They didn't need to worry about maintaining their cover from those who couldn't shoot back. The guard directly opposite the top of the stairs stuck his head out over the railing and raised his rifle just as Snow crested the last step.

She didn't hesitate, crossing the walkway and clamping her jaws around the waistband of the man's pants. She used her momentum to lift him up and forward, dumping him through the hole in the fence and sending him plummeting two stories to land on the concrete floor. He cried out when he hit the ground, then again as something snaked out from under the overhang and pulled him back, despite the hail of bullets that rained down as soon as the wolf exposed itself.

It wouldn't take long for someone to wonder how the guard had fallen, and Snow threw herself at the next, hoping she could catch them in the same position. The guard looked up as she closed and pushed away from the railing, training the gun at Snow. She immediately dropped into the evasive pattern she'd found reasonably effective, juking from one side to another, trying to be as unpredictable in her changes of direction as possible. The tactic mostly worked, save for the one bullet that creased the outside of her right shoulder, leaving a sizzle of pain in its wake. Snow chomped into the guard's hand, using her teeth to savage flesh and tendon. When the guard let go of the gun, Snow went after the other hand, this time clamping her jaws around the woman's wrist and shaking her head. Either she would hit a vein or the forearm would be unusable, Snow didn't really care which. Her only goal was speed.

The guard dropped to the ground, cradling her injured limbs to her chest, and Snow kept on past her. There were three more guards on this side, and they knew she was coming. Her ability to dodge incoming bullets was hampered by her attempts to keep the nearest guard between her and the other two. More bullets flew past her, and multiple streaks of fire bloomed to life on her skin, but Snow kept coming.

The guard tracked with her on her final approach, whipping the rifle around. Snow threw herself to the ground as he squeezed off another volley of rounds. When she bit down hard on his calf, he swore in the high-pitched voice of someone in the midst of unexpected agony. She let go, but only for long enough to lunge at his groin, biting through the soft flesh on the inside of his thigh. She kept up the pressure on her jaws as she pulled away, removing a lump of muscle as well as a large portion of his femoral artery. The guard toppled, the dark skin of his face slackening even as he crumpled to the ground.

A howl went up from below, overlapping wolven voices reverberating through the long hall. Dozens of wolven added their voices to the call until it filled the space. Each new voice gave her a new spark of confidence, a tiny shot of adrenaline. The longer they howled, the faster she moved. Bullets flew at her, but she was motion incarnate. Never stopping, never slowing, even as she changed direction with every other step. She flowed low then leaped, sidestepping in a ballet of fur, teeth, and claws that ripped the throat out of the first of the two remaining guards as she leaped past him.

Cassidy ran with her. No, this was someone else. Two someones, then three. Wolves raced down the walkway on either side of her, and more were coming up the stairs at the other end of the hall, still howling. The final guard threw down his rifle, but when the wolves didn't stop, he tried to climb through the hole that had been cut into the fence. He wasn't fast enough. Wolven teeth hooked onto the backs of his pants, hauling him back inside.

Snow stopped, letting the wolven pass her on either side. The last guard disappeared under an avalanche of fur. His cries were cut short almost immediately, but the wolves took their time. When the mass of fur dispersed, many were licking crimson off their jaws with long red tongues. They looked to her. Snow looked away.

On the other side of the walkway, more wolven were making short work of the guards who'd posted up there. A humanoid figure stalked among them, and it took Snow only a moment to recognize Bone in betweenform. As the last guard was swarmed under, Bone moved to the fence, and hooked her fingers through it. She glared across the void between the top tiers of the cell block, searching the gathered wolves on the other side. When her gaze caught Snow's, her mouth gaped in a lupine grin.

"Where's that girlfriend of yours?" Bone called out. "I'm going to kill her."

CHAPTER FORTY-FIVE

Cassidy and the adults waited impatiently by the doors. Aside from Luther, the others were the most dominant remnants of the South Shore, Gary, Aurora, and Joliet Packs. Luther explained that they'd been separated and told to keep a lid on the kids. Their absence from the rest of their packs not only weakened those but allowed their captors to force their cooperation in the various experiments that were being performed.

Cassidy wasn't sure which was worse, the experiments that tried to cure the wolven of their wolf side or the ones that forced the wolf to surface.

"Why would they do that?" Cassidy demanded. "After everything they did to try to 'cure' us?"

"Because if they can't cure us, they can use us," Amos, from the Gary Pack said. "When the wolf comes out after being cooped up for so long, it's beyond feral." He glanced back at the common room with its blood-stained walls.

"Can you imagine?" a small, but fierce-eyed female wolven said. In betweenform, her fur was a brilliant russet. None of the other wolven except the adults had chosen to shift out of furform. "Suppress the wolf for a while, then reverse the change and drop the wolf in the middle of your enemies."

"Oh, I can imagine," Cassidy said grimly. "Watch the cubs. I'm going to find Hammer." She sprinted up the stairs and followed her nose straight to the South Shore Alpha.

"Five Moons." He didn't look up as he gathered glass vials into a hard plastic case.

"We're burning this place to the ground," Cassidy said. Her voice shook with rage.

"That's an excellent idea." He shot a look over his shoulder at her. "I want to know what was done to our wolves." He lifted a vial up to the light. "But I'm on board with razing the rest of it."

"Good. I'll keep an eye on things downstairs. Holler when you're ready to light it up."

Hammer grunted and turned back to rifling through the refrigerator. The medical equipment was top of the line and clearly not original to the prison.

Cassidy made her way back down the stairs. "Hammer's collecting some things, then he's going to burn it all down."

"Good." Luther's voice was fervent, and his eyes gleamed.

Long minutes passed, and only the sounds of movement from the second floor kept Cassidy from going back up to check on the South Shore Alpha. To keep her mind off the time, she spoke softly with the cubs who were still in skinform. They answered timidly, their eyes darting, as if expecting the worst to come around the nearest corner. Cassidy couldn't blame them. She felt much the same way, though she went to pains to project assurance.

"Ready up here," Hammer called down from the top of the stairs.

"I'll move everyone out and hold the door open for you," Cassidy said. She turned to Luther and gestured him forward. "Get them out," she hissed.

He looked at her, eyes wide, then opened the doors out of the medical wing. Seeing no sign of humans on the other side, he moved through, gesturing for the cubs to follow. They did so without comment or complaint, the adult wolven following in their wake.

"Do it!" she shouted up to Hammer.

"Fire in the hole!" Hammer replied. A second later, the sound of metal hitting concrete reverberated down the concrete stairs, followed by the sound of footsteps dashing downward. On the heels of Hammer's footfalls was a rushing sound, like a massive intake of breath. Air rushed past her as it was pulled up the stairs, fuel for the conflagration that already crackled and spit.

Cassidy waited, holding open the door to the hall. As soon as he was past, she let it close. The flames smelled too much like they had when the hotel had gone up.

"That'll slow down any research they've got going on," Hammer said as they sprinted to catch up to the rest of the group.

It wouldn't. Cassidy had no illusions that the so-called researchers of the lab hadn't taken things home with them. The prison might be locked down digitally, but all it took was a flash drive. Burning it down had been about catharsis, but more than that it was a promise. This wasn't going to stand, not if Cassidy had anything to say about it.

Hammer trotted to the head of their small pack, then motioned the wolven to follow him. He pretended not to notice when everyone looked to Cassidy for confirmation, but his assumed indifference couldn't hide the spurt of anger in his scent. This was going to take some undoing. Pulling the wolven to her had seemed like a good idea. It still was, but Hammer didn't forgive easily.

* * *

Bone had changed her mind about splitting the remaining wolven into smaller groups. The gaggle of wolves that followed her down the hall was easily twice the size of the first one. Working their way through the prison with everyone but the Gary Alpha in furform was a completely different proposition than it had been with the group in skinform. The few guards who tried to stand against them were easily dispatched. Sure, some wolven sported new bullet wounds, but everyone was moving quickly enough and no one had gone down who didn't make it back up.

With Bone in betweenform opening doors that would be impassable without thumbs, they made good time, but there were noises coming from outside that were making Snow nervous. Interspersed with the persistent rumbles of thunder was the familiar rhythmic thump of helicopter rotors. She caught Bone's eye as they ran. The Alpha nodded grimly.

By the time they reached the loading dock doors, the sounds of the helicopters were loud and numerous. The roar of engines and blades filled the air.

Snow hunkered down, bunching up her hindquarters so she could dash out as soon as Bone handled this last door. When Bone threw it open, Snow launched herself over the threshold along with the first rank of wolven. They ran out onto the concrete dock.

The laundry truck was gone. Snow dug her claws into the hard surface, skittering to a halt as she took in the scene. Past the loading dock, half a dozen helicopters had landed or were in the process of doing so. Dozens of black-fatigued soldiers were debarking and streaming toward the prison's main doors. The stink of charred flesh filled her nostrils, but she couldn't see what was causing the smell.

"Where are they?" Bone asked, her voice sharp, if low. She crouched by the doors, as if doing so would hide her from any of the soldiers who would see her, see them all, if they only bothered to look their way.

As Snow stared, trying to figure out how this could have gone so wrong without her knowing, a strange sight caught her attention. A human arm was waving in midair, right at the edge of the dock. A moment later, Byron's head joined it.

"Come on," he said, motioning vigorously at them. "Before someone sees."

The recovered wolven exchanged glances but stayed frozen in the doorway.

"It's all right," Bone said. "He's with us."

Snow was already slinking toward the wheelman. With her example and Bone's encouragement, the other wolven followed.

At some point, Snow broke the plane of Byron's spell. A human corpse in body armor lay smoking at the very edge of the loading dock. The truck had half a dozen holes in the side. The door to Delfina's pocket lair was open but it wasn't as brightly lit as it had been.

"Delfina took some damage," Byron said.

Snow whined. Did that mean the hacker was injured or that some of her equipment was out? Or both?

Byron held up a glowing crystal, his scent both frightened and resigned. "This is my last one." He gestured around them with his other hand. "It's powering this. When it's drained, we'll be sitting ducks." He snickered, his eyes a little wild. "Little lost pups."

Bone shouldered her way into the truck. It was filling up quickly as wolves crammed themselves into every available spot. Most wolven enjoyed being in proximity with each other, but not like this.

"How many do you need to get us out of here?" the Gary Alpha asked.

"The portal takes a couple of crystals if I want to keep it going for more than a handful of seconds."

"So we're stuck here." Bone flexed her shoulders, moving her head around and popping a few vertebrae. "Looks like we get to see how many of them we can take down with us."

Snow whined and nosed at Byron's pocket where she could see the outline of more crystals.

"We're not completely sunk," Byron said. "If we can get some of these recharged before I lose all the juice I have in this one and the illusion goes down…" He sighed. "It's a long shot."

"I'll take a long shot over one in the head." Bone held out her hand. "Let me see what I can do."

Wordlessly, Byron fished a dead crystal out of his pocket and handed it to the Alpha. She held it between her hands and stared at it. What followed was the slowest change Snow had ever witnessed.

Bone gritted her teeth through the shift from betweenform into her human form in a process that took minutes. The process should have been nearly instantaneous for her. That she could draw it out was a testament to her strength. When she was finished, she shuddered naked in the back of the truck, fluids coating her skin. The crystal had started to glow. She looked over at Snow. "Your girlfriend isn't making this easy."

That made no sense. What did Cassidy have to do with Bone taking a long time to shift? Snow cocked her head.

"Never mind," Bone said. She took a deep breath and began the process of reverting to furform. Her wolf came much more easily, but when she stood as a full wolf in front of the group, stacked into the truck in whatever way they could fit, the crystal was only a little brighter.

Snow lifted her nose, a new scent coming to it. She'd assumed that the smell of iron had been coming from the dead guard outside the back of the truck, but the door was closed, and the smell was only intensifying. She nosed her way through the gathered wolven. Plenty of them smelled of blood, but this was different. It was human.

She shoved her way through the crammed-in wolves to the door at the back. She nosed it open and enough to eel her way inside.

Delfina's tech room smelled strongly of burnt circuits and blood. The hacker sat with one hand pressed against a hole in her side, not looking up when Snow joined her. She planted her paws on the edge of the desk and levered herself up to sniff at the human's face then her side.

"I'll live," the hacker gritted out through clenched teeth. "Time's running out for the rest of your crew, though." She clicked through camera views, showing the group with Hammer at the head and Cassidy taking up the rear.

Snow's heart lifted when she recognized Luther's form in the middle. He had a cub in skinform on each hip. They would be those like her brother, who hadn't been born with the wolf's gift within them. Those who could already shift padded along beside the adults, little balls of fluff who should have been out chasing each other, not skulking their way through prison halls.

Delfina clicked over to another view, this one showing black-clad soldiers pouring into the prison. They'd secured the empty cell blocks and were now fanning out across the complex. There were so many that at least some of them had to be on an intercept course.

"Five Moons and Hammer lost their earpieces when they shifted," Delfina said. "I can't warn them about what's coming."

The hacker couldn't warn them, but Snow could. She nosed at a paper copy of the prison layout, one that had started with the blueprints they'd found online. The hacker didn't look down, so Snow barked once. This time Delfina looked her way, and Snow pushed the paper over toward her. She looked at the screen with the soldiers and pawed at the map. Where were they?

"Ah." Delfina glanced at the monitor, then started scribbling on the plan. "They're here, heading this way. Safest route is going to be back through here. The back way through the laundry room is their best bet."

Snow snatched the paper and whirled to leave. Delfina yelled something after her, but she didn't stop. Cassidy needed to see this. She barked again, a clear announcement that she was coming through that was only a little muffled by the rescue plan in her mouth. The wolves crammed into the back of the truck somehow made enough room for her to pass at a full lope.

Bone saw what she was doing and paused in betweenform with the crystal clutched in one hand. She opened the door into the prison. "Be careful," she said.

Snow didn't slow. There was no time for caution, only to get to Cassidy and bring her and the cubs out.

CHAPTER FORTY-SIX

There wasn't a peep among the cubs as they were hustled through the empty halls, the adults trying to split the difference between speed and quiet. The scent of smoke followed them as the medical building burned merrily at their backs. Once inside the original prison building, even the thick walls couldn't keep out the sounds of helicopters. Cassidy and the adults traded worried looks. They knew what those sounds meant, and the growing anxiety among them was starting to trickle down to the youngsters.

Some of the older cubs in skinform carried the younger ones on their backs. They looked constantly to the adult wolven who'd been in the medical wing with them for reassurance. Those in furform stuck as closely to Cassidy at the back of the pack as they could. Getting around with them underfoot was complicated, and Cassidy had solved that problem somewhat by scooping up the two smallest, carrying one under each arm as if they were footballs. They sank their little claws into the fur that covered her arms in betweenform, giving themselves more purchase, and allowing her to move more freely.

She had to rely on Hammer at the front. He was back in his role as navigator, only now every step seemed a thousand times more fraught than it had on the way in. They had their cargo, but losing it now would be an even bigger blow than never having gotten to them in the first place. Frankly, Cassidy was all turned around. There was a cluster of wolven to the south and those with her. The other group had stopped moving. Maybe they were at the truck?

The hallway was too long and had too many rooms along it. Each was an ideal location for an ambush, a fact that Cassidy couldn't shake from her mind. She had to push the thought down and trust that those at the front of the group had cleared them. Her checking each one would only slow them down even more. The adults kept having to wait for her strange little entourage. Even if there were guards hidden in the rooms, Cassidy's arms were full of wolf cubs. She wasn't exactly in a good state for a scrap.

She checked on the other group again, reaching to see if she could get a good feel for them. Her wolf counseled her to stay present and pay attention to their current situation, but knowing there were helicopters out there made Cassidy's fur itch. The group was staying put, but the general feeling she got off them was one of uneasiness. Maybe that was feeding into her own anxiety.

There was one star that wasn't part of either group, one that shone so brightly that Cassidy didn't have to reach out to know who it was. Snow was on her own and heading their way. Why would she do that? Surely, she was much safer with the bigger group, not by herself. Snow didn't expose herself without a good reason, and if she was headed toward them, things couldn't be good.

"Hammer," Cassidy called out. "Snow is incoming."

"How could you possibly—" Hammer cut himself off when Luther laid a hand on his arm. "What do you make of it, Alpha?"

"I'm not sure, but I don't like it."

"Our options are to keep moving forward or hole up." He shook his head. "I'm all for moving."

"But not if we're heading into a trap." Cassidy stopped walking. "I really don't like this. Something is wrong. You know Snow. She's not coming here, alone, for her health."

"That's true." Hammer slowed but not completely. He turned his head enough to watch her out of the corner of his eye. "The office is coming up. It's more defensible than anywhere along this hall."

"I can live with that."

"So glad." Hammer strode off with more purpose in his step. His strides lengthened until he was nearly jogging.

"Come on," Cassidy said to the cubs. "Give a little run to catch up." She pushed herself faster and shifted one of the cubs so he was resting against her shoulder. "Grab on," she said to him. He grasped her shoulder as best he could with paws that weren't really made for such things. It was awkward, but she had one hand free.

The office was quiet when they approached. Hammer stood outside the door and ushered everyone inside. They wouldn't have to stay long. Snow was nearly to them.

Once inside, the wolven hunkered down below the level of the windows. The cubs were stashed at the back in cubicles. A quick admonishment to keep quiet was all it took. They looked up at Cassidy with eyes that were too knowing by half. They shouldn't have been wise to the necessity of keeping as still as they could. They should have been vibrating with energy.

Once the cubs were settled, Cassidy moved to the front. She tapped Luther on the shoulder and gestured to the back. He nodded and took Rocky with him. Cassidy moved forward until she was by the front windows, supplanting Hazel's wolf from her spot. Snow was nearby. Cassidy cracked the office door. When Hammer reached out to stop her, she shot him a glare that told him to step off. To her surprise, he actually did.

Snow darted past, low to the ground, then stopped and doubled back when she picked up Cassidy's scent. When she saw her girlfriend, she hurled herself at her, dropping a piece of paper in Cassidy's lap. She met Cassidy's eyes, then looked down at the paper, then back up.

Her ears were laid back to her head, and she kept looking behind her. Cassidy picked up the paper and tried to make sense of the lines that had been added onto it. Groups of X's outside the building had arrows leading to various areas inside. Some of them were awfully close to the path they were taking.

A large O had been drawn in the medical building, and that had a path that deviated quite a bit from the one they'd taken, the one they'd decided upon when planning.

"I think your hacker has devised a new exit strategy for us," Hammer said, his shaggy head hanging over her shoulder.

Snow gave a little growl-bark of assent. She stabbed her nose emphatically at the O's line on the schematic.

"We're going to have to backtrack quite a bit," Cassidy said. "Is this where the humans are now?"

Snow gave another assenting bark.

"So, they could have moved on." She drummed her fingers against the ground, then looked up at Hammer. "What's your read on this?"

"The hacker's been right so far. We both know helicopters mean reinforcements and possibly ones more battle-hardened than those who've been guarding our wolves here."

"Then we follow Delfina's map. Let's move out."

CHAPTER FORTY-SEVEN

Snow scouted ahead of the group. They'd been hustling for a while, trying to ignore the persistent thump of rotor blades outside. Even with them running as swiftly as they could, the soldiers in the prison were closing in fast. They could hear their boots on concrete and shouts between squads as they tried to intercept the wolven. The cubs were flagging, slowing them further, though the adults did what they could to move them along. She ran, knowing that delays would be deadly, but they were running out of options.

Snow slowed at an intersection and scoped it out, then barked once, indicating the hall was clear and they could keep going. The turn to the back way into the laundry room was up next. She threw herself toward it, running the fastest she'd ever managed and went skidding into the last junction. Again, it was empty, and she barked as she ran to the side the group needed to take.

Hammer made eye contact with her and nodded, then put his head down and found a burst of speed from somewhere. Luther pounded grimly at his heels, teeth gritted in a grim mask of determination. Snow had sometimes thought the wolven was inflexible, but that hardness wouldn't allow him to waver, not when he had three cubs on him. As they ran past her, Snow waited for everyone to go by, then slotted in at the rear. There was just the short hall to the laundry room's back door. She hunkered down around the corner and watched down the hall.

"It's barred," Hammer yelled. "We have to break it down."

There had been no indication that the door was blocked on the map. Snow fretted. How long would it take for five wolven to break down a door, even one that was barred? Yes, there were two Alphas in the group. With all the time in the world, that door would come down, but could they do it quickly enough to avoid the soldiers closing in on them?

A sullen boom echoed down the hall, followed by another and another as the wolven threw themselves at the metal door. It didn't take long before each body's impact on the door's surface was accompanied by the tortured squeal of metal under pressure. Snow risked a glance back. The door was bowed in significantly, and a gap had opened up between it and the frame, but it was only large enough for the smallest among them to pass through. Cassidy threw herself at it, shoulder first, and the door gave way another handful of inches.

She couldn't watch her girlfriend. Cassidy had things well in hand. One of the adult wolven in full furform slunk back to join her. She knew this one by sight; he'd been with the Aurora pack. Snow was pretty sure both Crag and his Beta had perished in the fight at the Alpha meeting ambush. He was strong, much stronger than Snow, but what else was new? She pulled back, allowing the Aurora wolf to watch, but stayed glued to his flank.

Already, the sound of booted feet drifted to her ears. The soldiers were trying to sneak up on them, but they weren't quiet enough to avoid their sharp wolven ears. The Aurora wolf growled, drowning out the creeping sound of rubber-soled steps. Snow jumped up and darted down the hall, threading her way through the youngsters who waited patiently, casting glances toward the progress being made against the door and the hallway opening.

Snow grabbed Cassidy's left hand in the signal they'd used those weeks ago in the forest. She hoped her girlfriend would remember what it meant when she bit down lightly on Cassidy's fur-covered hand.

"They're coming?" Cassidy asked.

Snow let out a soft whuff of agreement.

"It needs to come down now," Cassidy said. She grabbed Luther and Hammer and pointed at the door. "You're our two heaviest. I need you to give that thing everything you've got."

"Yes, Alpha," they chorused. Hammer's scowl of concentration deepened into irritation when he realized what he'd said. He and

Luther backed up a good ten feet from the door. They crouched, then on a signal only they could divine, launched themselves toward the stubborn door at full speed. At the last moment, they dropped their shoulders and collided with the metal surface with a concussive boom. The hinges squealed, high and shrill.

Snow's heart dropped as it seemed the door was going to hold on, but a second later, the bar on the other side finally gave way, dropping to the floor with a sharp clang. The door swung into the room, listing crazily. Only the lower hinge was still even partially intact.

As one, the cubs and remaining wolven flowed through the opening. The adults, led by Hammer, headed for the far door, followed closely by the skinform cubs. As they had the entire time, the furform cubs waited, clustering close to Cassidy for comfort. In that instant, Snow realized what Cassidy had done and why Hammer and Bone were so angry with her. She'd somehow forced the pack bond with all the wolven in the prison, including the other Alphas. Including Snow. Was that why she felt like Cassidy was always with her? It explained why the furform cubs were so clingy but those who couldn't shift yet were more willing to seek shelter with the others. At least for now, the former Alphas were leaving their quarrel with Cassidy until later.

They had bigger problems. The ripping snarl of the Aurora wolven chased them down the hall and through the doors. A human voice raised in pain, but on its heels was the report of a rifle, which was joined by more. The wolf yelped high and sharp once, then was silent.

Across the room, Hammer was already out the door with wolven racing after him. Luther was waving them through, but with the commotion at the end of the hall, he looked back.

Cassidy was halfway across the room, urging the slower cubs on. Once again, she'd gathered a number of them in her arms. Another wolven carried a couple as well. Cassidy also looked back, cringing as the pain of losing one of her wolves hit her. Snow was just through the door, nudging the slowest of the cubs with her nose. They were running as fast as they could, but short legs could only go so fast and they'd been going for so long. The little stumbles of earlier were now amplified into trips and tumbles. Each time one went down, Snow was there to grab them by the scruff and pull them upright. It felt a bit like she was playing a game of reverse-whack-a-mole, only with far too many stakes riding on the outcome.

"Luther, no!" Cassidy's shout came as Snow was righting another of the cubs. They'd made it halfway across the room.

The North Side Beta had shot past her and was righting the door, trying to push it closed in its frame. Bullets hit the other side with sharp impacts and whines as they ricocheted into dusty corners. The heavy metal that had impeded them so before was now shielding the cubs from being torn to shreds.

"Go!" Luther roared as he leaned against the door, blocking the entrance as thoroughly as he could. "Get them out of here."

Cassidy hesitated, and the cubs slowed, milling about her in confusion.

"You can't come back here." Luther braced his back against the warped metal and dug his heels into the ground. "I've got this."

"Luther…" Cassidy backed toward the opposite door. She couldn't go to him, not with the cubs heeling to her so tightly. She looked down then back at him. "Luther."

"I know." Luther smiled, as gentle an expression as Snow had ever seen on his face. "You'll do so well."

Tears flooded from Cassidy's eyes and were soaked up by the fur on her face. "Dammit, Luther." She backed through the door, not breaking eye contact with her Beta until she could no longer see him.

"Take care of her, Snow," Luther said. His voice was soft, even to her ears, and she was confident that no one else had heard it.

She risked a look back at him and dipped her head in assent. Then she was also through the doorway. All they had left was the long hall ahead of them, then they would be at the loading dock.

CHAPTER FORTY-EIGHT

Luther's name pounded into Cassidy's brain with every stride. Lu-ther. Lu-ther. She was aware of him, his star shining at her back as they drew further and further away. She'd slammed the door after Snow and the last of the cubs had come through it, and now they scurried down the hall. A gap had opened between the front half of their group and the back half. The two adult wolven in furform had dropped back and were assisting Snow in keeping the kids moving as quickly as was possible.

Behind them, the laundry room was suspiciously quiet. She couldn't help but wonder what the humans pursuing them were planning. Her wolf scraped her claws along the inside of her ribcage. They had one task, and it didn't involve space for mourning. That could happen later, when the time was right. Luther was gone. Best to treat him that way and not to waste energy they didn't have on someone who was already dead.

The advice was solid, if harsh. It felt like the wolf had opened up a hole in the bottom of her ribs, one that was draining cold liquid into her belly. That didn't matter. All that mattered was the next step, and the one after that.

Lu-ther. Lu-ther. Lu-ther.

A massive concussion behind them blasted hunks of masonry and twisted metal debris through the doorway. Cassidy whimpered as Luther's star winked out. She swallowed a howl and broke into a run. The cubs' stars were smaller lights compared to those of the adults. They twinkled more quickly, but more dully. She poured her energy into them, willing them to shine brighter.

Something must have worked. The cubs were running faster, their trips and falls disappearing. Even the most uncoordinated among them ran swift and true.

They didn't have much time. Whatever had taken Luther out could easily be trained on them next. There wasn't far to go, but the middle of Cassidy's back felt so open and unprotected. Looking back wouldn't help. It was an invitation to tripping herself and taking down half a dozen cubs. She forced herself to keep looking forward, hyperaware of the shine of Snow's star behind her. Her girlfriend would be the first one struck.

When they turned the final corner before the doors to the loading dock, Cassidy finally took that last look over her shoulder. Snow was the very last wolf. At the far end of the hall, figures in dark clothes were pouring through the doorway. Snow paused as the last of the cubs were able to round the corner, then ducked out of the way.

Gunfire rattled down the hall, chewing plaster and paint off the walls. Chips of concrete flew up where slugs hit the floor. A light above shattered, raining shards of glass down in their path.

Snow grunted as she was hit by one bullet, then another. She kept running, leaving a trail of blood behind her as she sought shelter in the hallway.

"Where the hell is the truck?" Hammer roared, his voice carrying through the open door to the outside.

The truck was gone? Had they left after Snow got the map from Delfina? What was the hacker playing at? Cassidy growled, and her wolf rose within her, threatening to break free. She pressed the wolf down. If the truck was gone, they would need people with thumbs. There was always the possibility of getting to the woods. All that stood between them and the trees was the chain-link fence. With the razor wire on top. How would the cubs fare against it?

She hesitated just inside the door, not wanting to expose herself and the cubs by going outside, but knowing that their pursuers weren't far behind. The helicopters were pulling away, having dropped their cargo of soldiers in the large open space at the front of the main building. Dozens of soldiers were running toward the prison, intent on getting in through the main doors. Curtains of driving rain obscured them somewhat. Maybe that was why no one had noticed them. Yet.

Snow shot past her, taking a direct line toward where the truck had been parked. Hammer and the other wolven watched her go by as they found what meager cover they could, trying to get their bearings. She flowed low to the ground, then disappeared into thin air. A second later, her head stuck back out, looking particularly strange divorced from the rest of her body. She gave a loud whuff while staring Cassidy in the eyes, then disappeared again.

The wheelman had some talent with illusions. Cassidy hoped this was one of his, otherwise everything had gone completely off the rails. They were already so far off the plan that it was barely recognizable.

"Come on then." Cassidy pushed away from the doorframe, trusting that the cubs would follow her.

Hammer and a good portion of the group had already breached the invisible barrier. Cassidy passed through and almost ran into the South Shore Alpha's back. She edged around him and saw why he'd stopped. It was a good thing that Byron's illusion extended a little way out from the truck, as the back was already packed full of wolven.

A brief howl rippled through the wolven crammed into the back when they saw Hammer and her. It was low, not so loud that it should attract attention over the still departing sounds of the helicopters.

"We can't all drive out in this," Cassidy said.

"We sure. As shit. Can't," Bone agreed from further into the truck. She stood naked, a bright crystal clutched in her hand. Her chest heaved as she struggled to breathe. As soon as her gulping breaths slowed under control, her face tightened into a mask of concentration. Fur slowly sprouted along her limbs and down her stomach. Fluid dripped slowly off her, landing with quiet splats in the puddle of effluvia at her feet. By the size of it, she'd been at this for a while.

"We need one more," Byron said. The crystal he held in his hand was growing dimmer and dimmer. "I need two to activate the portal." He pulled a spent rock from the cluster around his neck. "Snow, could you? You fill them the fastest."

The lone wolf heaved a sigh, but trotted up to Byron, taking the crystal in her mouth. She stepped out of the van, onto the very edge of the loading dock where she was still obscured by the wheelman's illusory blind. Adult wolven slunk out of the back, freeing up space for the cubs. Between the whimpers of those in furform and the sobs of those in skinform, some had seen their parents. In unspoken agreement, wolves without cubs made way for families to reunite.

"Stay close enough to touch the truck," Byron said. "You'll still be covered by the illusion."

Inside, wolves licked faces and shoved muzzles against necks and shoulders. Hammer stepped over the gap between the loading dock and the truck and swooped a little girl up in his arms. The fur around his eyes was suspiciously wet as he held her close. The last time Cassidy had seen her, she'd had her hair done up in bright pink barrettes. Those were conspicuously absent today.

"Poppy!" She sobbed into the dense fur of his shoulder.

Not all the cubs were in the truck. A handful of those in furform still clustered around her. Cassidy bit her lip as she realized they hadn't seen their parents. Either they'd gone over the edge with Marrow's group or they hadn't come out of the prison. Her own eyes were starting to prickle, but she pushed down her despair, hoping the little ones wouldn't pick up on it. She moved into the truck, helping over the younglings whose legs were too short to make crossing even that small gap a sure thing. She crouched down, making herself as small as possible and pulled the cubs in close.

They nuzzled in, their noses cold and wet. One fell asleep immediately, with another close to nodding off, eyes sliding closed as they stood on their feet.

At the edge of the platform, Snow's entire frame shook. She held the crystal in her mouth, powerful teeth wielded gently to keep from cracking the faceted rock. Even as her muscles quivered and twisted with such vigor that they were visible beneath her fur, the crystal was brightening, or so Cassidy thought. It could have been a trick of the light or wishful thinking. She knew how exposed they were, felt it in her bones. If Byron lost his illusion, or if someone thought to take a quick turn past the loading dock, they were sitting ducks. Worse than. Ducks could fly away. All they had was each other and a purposefully disabled vehicle. It had seemed like such a good idea when they'd planned it out. They hadn't counted on needing to take everyone through it.

Further into the truck, Bone growled as she powered through her change, pausing in betweenform for a few moments to regain her strength, then pushing herself into full furform. When she finished the transformation, the crystal under her paw glowed brightly enough to light up the back half of the truck.

By the edge of the loading dock, Snow's crystal was definitely brighter. She was halfway to betweenform, the line of fur rippling down her body like grass bending before a gentle breeze. The change was glacial, but the crystal was lighting up much more quickly than Bone's had. The Gary Alpha was already working her way back to betweenform.

"We're nearly there," Byron said. He looked up front, gauging Snow's progress, then leaned over and tapped on the door to Delfina's hidey-hole. "Time to pack it up."

The door opened, accompanied by the smell of fresh blood. Cassidy's stomach growled as the wolf took notice. When they realized it was coming from the hacker, the wolf subsided.

"Are you sure?" Delfina called through the door. "I'm going to set this thing on fire when we go, so you better be seconds away."

"Not quite," Byron said. "But start wrapping it up."

"Sure thing, Dad."

Cassidy could hear the eye roll. She tightened her grip on the cub in her lap and stayed as still as she could, watching her girlfriend. "I'm right here, Snow."

Her girlfriend's shape was human enough that the nod wasn't out of place. Her front legs looked more like arms now, even if they were still covered with fur. It was shorter, but the play of light and dark was still striking. Snow wrapped fuzzy fingers around the crystal, digging its edges into her palm as if that would help with the pain. Agony rolled off her in sharp red waves spiked through with blue. Cassidy found herself biting her lip in sympathy as her own limbs threatened to cramp from the tension. The cub in her lap lifted its head to lick the underside of Cassidy's chin until she cuddled it closer.

By now, Snow had clawed her way into betweenform. There was a point between skinform and furform where there was a certain amount of equilibrium, where the wolf and human sides of their personalities were at enough of a balancing point that you could get a bit of a rest in the process. At least, that was how Cassidy experienced it. Snow couldn't seem to find that sweet spot. She panted heavily, each breath a strained whistle. The stink of her pain filled Cassidy's nostrils. The cubs whined and pawed at their noses, sneezing in an attempt to clear it, but every time they did, the next inhalation brought Snow's suffering right back into their muzzles. Cassidy's heart pounded. It took everything she had not to go to her girlfriend.

Dark gray arms lifted the cub out of her embrace.

"Help her," Hammer said.

Cassidy sobbed with relief. "Stay with him," she ordered the cubs when they started climbing to their feet to follow her. She pointed at Hammer until they settled, then lunged for Snow. She gathered the lone wolf to her, holding her as tightly as she dared without adding to Snow's agony.

"I'm here," she whispered into quivering wolven ears. "I'll always be here."

CHAPTER FORTY-NINE

Snow had been lost in her own pain for what felt like an eternity. Logically, she knew it couldn't have been that long, but the longer she held herself in betweenform, the more her grasp on time and what was going on around her slipped. Between waves of torment, Snow would crack open an eye to check on the crystal's progress. It was difficult to focus on, the sharp planes blurring and doubling, but it was brightening and much more quickly than the ones she'd filled up for Byron at the house. Of course, she hadn't spent any time holding onto betweenform then. She wasn't strong enough to hold betweenform, and her control was starting to fray. Her pain would spike and the wolf would push herself to the fore, trying to take on whatever was hurting her. Her bones would start the shift back to furform, and Snow's mind would clear for long enough to wrest control back from the wolf and to force herself into that unnatural balance between her two pure forms. The wolf was rising within her once more, and she knew she didn't have the energy, the strength of will, to keep her at bay. If Snow lost her handle on betweenform, she didn't know if she'd be able to come back.

Warm arms closed around her, and a familiar scent filled her nostrils. Cassidy smelled of home and safety. She'd felt the Alpha at her side for a while now, but it was nothing compared to being held by her. Snow allowed her muscles to relax, collapsing into her Alpha's embrace. She didn't need to waste the energy on staying upright. Cassidy was here now.

She sneaked a peek at the crystal. It was so much brighter than it had been. Every moment she continued to hold onto betweenform with tooth and claw, its brilliance intensified. Cassidy's presence allowed her to bear the terrible pull between her two forms more easily, but it wasn't in any way an effortless task. It wasn't that the pain lessened, more that her capacity to withstand it increased. Snow concentrated on maintaining betweenform through one more breath and then the one after that. As long as she only had to hold it for as long as it took to drag in one more lungful, then expel it out slowly through her mouth, she could withstand the pain.

There was a tug at her hand. She became dimly aware that someone was saying something.

"—let go." Byron's voice was low and had a cajoling edge to it. "Come on, now, Snow. Let me have it."

Snow looked up at the wheelman and tried to relax her grip. Her hand was clenched in as tight a fist as she could make, and it wouldn't release, no matter how much she struggled to let go. She shrugged. There was more than one way to solve any problem. If her hand couldn't let go, then maybe she didn't need it anymore.

With a long exhalation, Snow ceded her body to the other half of her soul. Even as the wolf rolled into her, the transformation was slow. Her energy reserves were so low that she was having problems keeping her eyes open.

"I got you," Cassidy said.

The words were the last thing she heard as the wolf took over and Snow's consciousness retreated. The loading dock receded from her until it was no more than a pinpoint in the dark, and then even that was gone.

* * *

Snow's final change took tense seconds. Byron flitted above her, then reached in and grabbed the crystal as soon as her paw had changed enough that it could no longer maintain its hold.

He shoved the crystal that had been powering the illusion into his pocket. Any remaining brightness was too dim for even Cassidy's eyes to see.

"We're doing this," Byron yelled. "Everyone be ready to move through."

His call was echoed outside the truck as far-off voices were raised in alarm. They were too far off to make out the words, but the tone was unmistakable and getting closer.

Delfina shuffled around inside her lair for a few moments, then levered herself out the door, a hand clamped down over a wound in her abdomen. As she shut the door behind her, puffs of smoke escaped, and the light of the screens was replaced by ominous orange flickers. "We don't want to wait around too long," the hacker said.

"No kidding." Byron's retort was accompanied by the spang of bullets against the side of the truck. What color remained in his face drained completely as he clutched the crystals and started to mutter under his breath.

Cassidy stood, hoisting Snow's unconscious body into her arms. "Get closer to him," she ordered Hammer and the cubs. "Line up on the other side of the truck," she called out to the adult wolven outside. "Keep it between you and what's coming until you make it through."

She pushed forward through the crowd of wolven in the truck, moving them back with the force of her presence so Hammer and the cubs would have the room they needed.

More rounds ricocheted off the side of the truck. The too-familiar sound of a helicopter grew louder.

"Hurry it up, Byron," Hammer yelled.

Byron squeezed his eyes shut, lips moving more quickly, but still carefully forming each syllable.

Cassidy held Snow close, as the thump of rotors grew more distinct even over the patter of rain above.

"There!" Bone pointed at the deep green woods that snapped into existence in place of the door to the burning hidey-hole. On the other side, wolven stood, moving toward the door, holding out hands as they saw the youngsters frozen in front of it.

"Go on," Cassidy shouted. She lunged forward, bringing the youngsters in furform along with her.

Byron stood next to the portal, his arms at his sides and the already dimming crystals in his hands.

Cassidy lumbered through, trying to herd the cubs while holding Snow tight. The little group broke into a stumbling run, pushing the kids in skinform ahead of them. They stepped through, only to be pushed further into the glade by those behind them. The pit of Cassidy's stomach fell away, then abruptly returned as she made her way over the threshold. She cleared to one side, making way for those behind her, casting about for somewhere to put Snow. Delfina came in on the heels of the youngest cubs, and on her heels were the adult wolven.

How long would it take forty wolven to get through the portal? They were in furform, so not that long, hopefully.

Cassidy laid Snow at the base of a massive conifer, then returned to the portal. She stood, encouraging each wolf through, yanking to the side those who stopped just through the portal to clear the way for those behind. On the other side, Byron stood in that peculiar, rigid-legged stance. Cassidy could only see one of the crystals from where she stood, but it had lost more than half its brightness.

Still, the wolven came in a flood of fur. One ducked as a bullet pierced the side of the truck. The wolves kept coming, flowing lower to the ground. Byron didn't move, even though the hole had pierced through less than a foot from where he stood.

And then, the stream of wolven ended. Every one stood on the other side of that portal. Cassidy ducked back through, scanning the truck and through the back doors to make sure no one had been left behind. She checked her starscape, looking for twinkles that remained, but there were none. More bullets punched through the truck, leaving bright points of light that were starting to rival those in her starscape.

"We gotta go!" Cassidy tried to grab Byron, but he fought her off and shoved her toward the doorway to the evergreens.

Cassidy lunged toward the doorframe, her knees and elbows pumping, her tail out behind her. She pivoted even as she cleared the edge of the portal and grabbed Byron by the elbow, yanking him backward over the threshold with so much force that he collided with her. They collapsed backward in a tangle of limbs. A crystal was knocked from Byron's hand. The portal winked out soon as it left his grasp, leaving behind a stone doorway set into the ground in the middle of a forest glade.

Cassidy thrashed around, shoving Byron off of her. She looked up as two figures approached in betweenform. "We made it out," Cassidy said to Hammer and Bone. "I can't believe we made it out." Her heart lurched when she remembered. Luther's absence from the stars swirling around her cut deeply, as did Beth's and Jimmy's. There would be more absences to discover in the days to come, as those she wasn't able to claim, to save, were discovered.

Bone coughed into her hand as she loomed over Cassidy. Hammer was less subtle.

"It's time to give them back," he growled. "You took them, and it's time to let them go."

"Of course." Cassidy looked around for her girlfriend, spotting her under the tree. "Give me a second." She scrambled to her feet. "I was only borrowing them. I just needed…" She waved her hand back and forth in the air in a way that enlightened nobody, herself least of all.

Off to the side, Byron was helping Delfina sit on a large rock. He lifted the edge of her shirt and hissed in sympathy at what he saw there.

Around them, wolven were reuniting with mates, rediscovering their pack members, and drawing cubs near. A couple of cubs in furform and one in skinform lingered near a small fire that the first group of wolven through had built. Some of the excitement dwindled as the tension between the Alphas built and overwhelmed the lighter emotions on display.

The wolven, both in fur and skinform, shifted to regard the three Alphas in betweenform. Hammer and Bone followed her as she knelt next to Snow. Her girlfriend was breathing, but slowly. Cassidy smoothed the fur on top of her head. Snow's eyes drifted open.

"I'm waiting," Hammer said, his arms crossed, one finger tapping against the charcoal fur of his bicep.

"Give me a second," Cassidy said. She sat, crossing her legs and pillowing Snow's shaggy head in her lap. "I'm not too sure how I did it. Let me see how to undo it."

All eyes were on her, but she tried not to let that faze her. It was impossible not to labor under the weight of all their combined expectations.

"Just need to…" Cassidy glared up at Bone and Hammer. "You need to give me some space. Your whole deal is drowning out everything else."

Hammer glared at her, but Bone willingly gave her the space she requested. She drifted over to a clump of Gary Pack members. Or they would be pack members again soon. Those who'd come through with the first batch seemed a little confused about the fuss, but they watched as closely as those whose alliances had been forcefully taken.

"Okay." Cassidy squeezed her eyes shut.

She tried to push the stars away from her, in clumps at first, but they kept springing back as soon as she released them. Then she tried one at a time. Bone and Hammer's stars seemed like they were working, but even they would come drifting back into her orbit. Each failure made her dig deeper and try harder, pushing out with all her might.

The wolven were getting restless, those in skinform murmuring to each other while those in furform were in constant motion.

Finally, Cassidy had to stop pushing. The pads on her palms and soles were slick with sweat. She panted, her chest rising and falling too rapidly. Snow lifted her head and gave the underside of her jaw a quick lick.

If the wolven wouldn't be pushed away, maybe Cassidy could remove herself from the equation. She took a deep breath, then concentrated on pulling in on herself. She contracted her sense of self down to its most compact, not letting even the slightest tendril escape. The stars stilled in their orbits, drifting in place until Hammer's pulled free, followed by Bone's, then the rest. One by one, each wolf spun free of her orbit until all that was left was Snow's star. It blinked rapidly, distress emanating from it.

Cassidy didn't know what to do. If she tried to pull Snow back in, would the other wolves come back?

She leaned forward, burying her face in the thick ruff about her girlfriend's shoulders.

"I'll pull you back, if you want it," she said quietly. "I had to let everyone go. I didn't know how else to do it."

Snow licked her again, practically bathing Cassidy's face with her tongue.

She laughed; it seemed like a better option than sobbing with relief. "Noted." Cassidy looked up at the wolven, who still watched her. "You can all go back to your Alphas now. Thank you for letting me borrow you."

CHAPTER FIFTY

Six weeks later…

"Do you smell her?" Bone called down to Snow from the boughs of a tall pine tree, her words a little garbled by the long muzzle that stuck out of her betweenform face. Lone wolf no longer, Snow had asked to be brought in to the North Side Pack when Cassidy had reclaimed her pack members. Cassidy had been happy to oblige, if a little surprised. Cassidy's packmate was barely visible on the forest floor below, even in her silver wolf form.

A single bark drifted up in response. It had an irked edge to it, one that said clearly that the answer was the same as it had been the previous five times it had been asked.

On the other side of the trunk from Bone, Cassidy was also in betweenform. It was great for climbing trees, and Bone had been insistent that they have two sets of eyes looking out during the arrival of Marrow and the missing pack members. She wanted to be able to set eyes on her sister, but she also needed someone to watch the skies. They were all quite antsy about flying objects, namely helicopters. Not that Cassidy could blame any of them. If she never saw another helicopter again, she would die happy. Luckily, the Maine woods had very few of them.

They'd had other obstacles to navigate. There was a semilocal wolven pack who hadn't taken too kindly to the tattered remnants of five packs appearing, even on the edge of their territory. The remaining Alphas had met with them, and after some tense negotiations that resulted in a couple of new scars to add to Cassidy's growing collection, they'd come to an understanding. The refugees, as the locals had taken to calling their group, could stay until Marrow showed up with the rest of them. After that, their choices were to join the Bar Harbor Pack or decamp.

Byron's aunt had been happy to put them up, though she didn't like people in her house. They were welcome to stay on her grounds and in any of the outbuildings. Most of the wolven had kept to furform since escaping their captivity, which had been helpful. The North Side Pack's first hunt had been a sad one, but they'd gotten the chance to mourn Luther correctly. The Beta hadn't been the only hole in their ranks. Beth, Jimmy, and Zoya would also never run with them again. A handful of those who'd come on that last run were no longer members of the pack. During the Great Switch, as it had come to be known among the packs, some of the North Side's number had ended up in other packs. Of course, they'd gained from other packs, those who had formed close bonds with North Side Pack members during the Silent Heights ordeal and those whose packs had dissolved with the loss of both Alpha and Beta. And then there were the orphaned cubs. Two of them had chosen to remain with Cassidy's wolves.

It had been Cassidy's intent to grow the pack. She'd made that silent promise to her wolves those many weeks ago. The irony of it all stung deeply.

"How about now?" Bone called.

Despite the fact that Cassidy could see Snow below them, she didn't answer. Cassidy felt her, glowing brightly at the edge of her vision.

"Snow?" Bone craned her neck to glare down at the ground.

"Oh, she hears you," Cassidy said. "Pretty sure she's done with the questions every five minutes."

"Cassidy, if I had your talent for feeling your wolves"—Bone's grin told her that the double entendre was very much on purpose—"I wouldn't have to keep asking."

"So use your own talent, Noor. How far does Marrow think she is?"

"She's not answering either." Bone's voice was pure disgruntlement. "Maybe she got tired of me asking."

"Huh," Cassidy said. "I can't imagine."

"I'm sure you can't," Bone said in a tone that Cassidy had no problem seeing right through. If she could, it was because Bone wanted her to.

The Gary Alpha seemed to enjoy being caught out in ridiculous lies. The more outrageous the falsehood, the more entertained she was by the whole thing.

Cassidy and Bone had spent a lot of time together, and she'd come to genuinely enjoy the other Alpha's company, enough so that they now used each other's first names. She could see what had drawn Snow to her in the first place those decades before. For her part, Snow had gotten easier around Bone. She hadn't minded when Cassidy spent some time with Bone during her last heat. There were a couple of other wolven in the other packs that Cassidy had gotten to know physically too. So far, their arrangement was working out well. When Cassidy had an itch that Snow wouldn't scratch, she'd find someone to couple with, then return to her girlfriend. Snow genuinely didn't care about Cassidy seeking physical satisfaction with others, and their own relationship had grown even more solid as a result. She loved having someone to snuggle down with at the end of the night, and she knew Snow felt the same way. There was something incredibly gratifying about waking up curled up with her every morning.

Below the tree, Snow moved away from the trunk. It was difficult to tell, but Cassidy thought her nose might have been lifted.

"Did you get something?" Bone yelled.

Snow didn't answer.

"No sign of whirlybirds," Cassidy said. She'd picked up the slang from Bone and Snow. Cassidy used it because she felt like someone out of the 1950s, which entertained her to no end.

"I'm going down." Bone dug her claws into the branch below her and swung out of the tree without even a smirk at the unintended dirtiness of her turn of phrase.

"Guess I'll stay up here and keep an eye out," Cassidy said to no one in particular. "No going down for me, more's the pity." If no one else was going to make a joke about it, then she might as well.

It wasn't long before she took in the first whiff of wolven she didn't recognize. She'd gotten used to the myriad new aromas of the mixed wolven packs that she dealt with on a nearly daily basis, but this was a new one.

After leaping from one branch to another until she was close enough to land without risking injury, Bone let go and hit the ground with a thud that Cassidy felt through the trunk forty or so feet up. She loped off in the direction Snow had gone, using her sinewy betweenform arms to pull herself along.

Cassidy gave the sky one last careful look, but there was no sign of anything untoward in any direction. She thrust the claws of her left hand into the bark of the trunk and jumped off her branch, trusting the friction of her claws to slow her descent. Her feet hit another branch, and she shifted to one side and repeated the maneuver until she was a mere twenty feet up. She gathered her legs under herself and leaped clear of the tree, tucking and rolling when she hit the ground, then popped up. A healthy layer of moss and pine needles meant she didn't have anything to worry about on landing, as long as she didn't come down on a stump or rock. Spring had come and gone, and they were into the throes of early summer. This one could last forever, as far as Cassidy was concerned. The past winter had been far too traumatic to even think about the next one.

She picked up the silver thread of Snow's scent and traced it through the underbrush. Bone's golden scent meandered along a similar trajectory. Cassidy and her wolf enjoyed the lope through the woods. The forest was different than the ones they'd become used to in the Midwest. This felt older, more established. The character of the trees was different, and the understory was more open.

Cassidy caught up with the others in a small clearing. She sauntered into the open area just as Marrow in betweenform caught Bone up in a crushing hug. In furform, they were nearly indistinguishable, except that they felt different in Cassidy's starscape. There was an affinity with Bone that she lacked with Marrow. Whether that was from the nearly two months they'd spent together in Maine or that Marrow hadn't been caught up in the bond Cassidy had forced with the wolven at Silent Heights, she didn't know.

The scent of joy filled the clearing as the twins were finally able to be in each other's company for the first time in many weeks. They'd spoken regularly—even half a continent hadn't been enough to sever their telepathic bond—but Cassidy knew as well as anyone that communication was a poor substitute for contact. Snow sidled up next to her, her own scent tinged with the reddish pink of happiness for the Gary Alphas.

The rest of the wolven were in furform. Two sidled forward, coming up to greet Cassidy, who went down on her knees to gather them close. They'd been gone from her pack for far too long.

"Do you want me to reclaim you?" she asked, bracing for disappointment.

Carlos and Gene licked her face, bathing the muzzle in warmth breath and their scent. At their enthusiastic agreement, Cassidy opened up. She had more practice now and drew them carefully in, excluding the stars of the wolven nearby. There was some resistance; the stars weren't coming cleanly to her.

Marrow looked up from her embrace and made eye contact with Cassidy. She nodded once, then the tension around the stars was gone and they whirled back into Cassidy's orbit. Their joy at rejoining her fold couldn't be faked, and she found herself panting with happiness as they wound around her, rubbing their scent on her fur and picking up hers in turn.

Bone and Marrow picked their way across the clearing, each with an arm over the other's shoulder. It took a lot of coordination to maneuver like that, but they already moved as one.

"Head back to the cliff house?" Bone asked.

"Sounds good to me." Cassidy nodded. "Hammer knows you're coming."

"I'll try not to be too loud," Marrow said.

Bone snickered and bumped her sister with her shoulder.

"Byron is picking up the hacker and Dale," Cassidy continued, ignoring Marrow's comment. "Delfina's good to debrief us on what she pieced together from the files we snagged."

"So you did get those out," Marrow said.

"That I did. I'm ready to find out who's behind all this bullshit."

"And you waited for me." Marrow placed an insincere hand over her heart. "I'm touched."

"In the head, maybe." When Marrow curled her lip, Cassidy held up a hand. "No disrespect intended. I've gotten used to your sister."

"Ah." They tightened their grip on each other for a moment. "Well, she's definitely touched in the head, so I can see how you made that mistake."

"Very funny." Bone's embrace was threatening to turn into a headlock. Given the amount of time they'd roughhoused when the five of them had been living out of the stolen van, Cassidy decided she needed to move on before things derailed any further.

"We figured we were well out of their reach. They had no way of knowing where we ended up, and your group was on the move, so…" Cassidy shrugged. "It took Delfina a while to unencrypt things and pull the threads together. By the time she had a good understanding of what was going on, we knew it was only going to be a couple of weeks before you got here. So we waited."

"Not that we want to wait too much longer," Bone said. "Which is why we're heading to the debrief now."

"We'll get there faster in furform." Marrow looked back and forth between them.

"You're not in charge anymore," Cassidy said. "That mission is over. But since you're speaking sense…" She leaned forward until her hands touched the loamy ground and called her wolf fully to the fore.

CHAPTER FIFTY-ONE

It felt a little odd to be back in clothing. Snow had spent the majority of her time since they arrived at Byron's aunt's property in furform. After the events of the previous weeks, the immediacy of the wolf had been a lifesaver. She and Cassidy had passed the time simply being. That it had been together had been even better. For the odd sojourn she'd taken into skinform, she'd rarely bothered to go clothed, especially once the days had gotten warmer.

Still, Byron's great-aunt Gwyn disapproved of them being in her house in furform. She complained about it upsetting her cats, of which she had many. Her cats weren't as alarmed by the wolven presence as most usually were. Still, they belonged to a witch, so perhaps they'd had to deal with more strangeness than the average housecat. There was one for every room, it seemed, and the rambling Victorian mansion had many of those. A black-and-white, tuxedo-patterned cat had vacated a chair next to the dainty metal table that had been set up for the laptop in the aunt's attached greenhouse. The computer was flanked by two monitors that barely fit on top of the table, which hadn't been made to act as a staging area for a presentation such as this one.

The aunt was a strange one. It was no surprise that she smelled similar to Byron, both in a manner that suggested they were related and the extra bit of zest that confirmed she was also capable of performing magic. She hadn't batted an eye when they showed up and had wasted no time in setting the wolven to filling up crystals for her and her nephew. The back porch was ringed with shining rocks at various levels of dimness. Every time they shifted there, the crystals grew a little brighter.

Beyond that, Gwyn didn't care if the woods on her property were full of wolven, and she definitely didn't seem like the type to turn stool pigeon, so if her rules stated they should only come into the house in skinform, then who was Snow to disagree.

The Alphas and their Betas were arrayed in a semicircle in front of the screen. Byron slouched in a chair among them. No one had made any comment when Cassidy had announced that Snow was coming, even though Naomi was there as Cassidy's Beta now, permanently in the position for as long as she wanted it. Given that Snow was technically no longer a lone wolf, her presence could have been contested or led to each Alpha bringing one more along. They'd rolled with it, as if there had never been any question in their minds about Snow's presence.

The laptop's screen reflected the image of the waiting wolven back at them. Delfina wasn't on the call yet.

Byron glanced at his phone, one of the burners Delfina had provided them with those months before. "She's getting set up."

"I don't understand why you couldn't have just brought her here," Hammer groused. His bulk looked a little ridiculous in the tiny wrought-iron chair. It couldn't have been comfortable, but he lounged in it as if he intended to stay put for hours.

"Her employers were a little put out about the condition in which she was returned," Byron said.

"We did send her back with a hole in her side," Bone pointed out.

"A patched hole." Hammer indicated the door into the main house over his shoulder. "The witch was very helpful."

"Yes, Aunt Gwyn is awesome," Byron said. "It's a pity the bullet wound scarred." He looked down at his hands.

They all had scars. Even Marrow had shown up with one above her left shoulder blade. The awkward silence that grew out of his statement was interrupted by Delfina's face on the screen.

Snow recognized the background. Delfina was back in her apartment at Faint. The room was dim, but the edges of the equipment behind her were familiar.

Delfina squinted out at them. "Everyone made it back?" She looked over at Marrow. "And in one piece too. Congrats."

The greeting she received in return from the gathered Alphas was warm. Snow wondered if Delfina understood how rare that was. Wolven tended to be suspicious of nonwolven, Alphas most of all. Would they have been so warm if they'd known that Stiletto was probably somewhere off camera? Or maybe she wasn't. It was daytime, after all.

Delfina smiled at the warm welcome, but her face sobered quickly. "So do you want to chat, or should I get into things?"

"From the look on your face, I think jumping in would be good. Unless someone disagrees." Cassidy looked around the group, then leaned forward when no one spoke up.

"Right." Delfina exhaled. "I have notes and kind of a presentation. I'm going to share my screen."

"I'll pop you on the big monitors," Byron said. "The Alphas are a little...too busy to do it."

Cassidy drew herself up as if she was about to disagree, then slouched back into her chair. Snow had no doubt that the North Side Alpha could handle the technical aspects, but she was pleased to see Cassidy wasn't pushing it. The Alpha was finally starting to get a feel for when she needed to put herself out in front and when she could step back.

"Yeah, sure," Delfina said, sounding distracted. She clicked around on her side, and her face was replaced by a view of her screen. There was an email on it. "So, thing is, someone out there is gunning for you, and they're using the Hunter program as cover for it."

Every eye in the room except Byron's went to Cassidy.

"So the Hunters are in on it?" Hammer asked slowly, never looking away from the North Side Alpha.

"Not exactly." Delfina seemed oblivious to the sudden tension. "It looks like some Hunters are. Or former Hunters. From what I can tell, there's a group of rogues. They used to be Hunters but faked their own deaths, either at their own hand or the hands of what they call supranormals."

Cassidy looked at the others. "That's what they call us. Well, us and vampires and demons, and probably the fae too. It's how they lump everyone together."

"Don't know that I care to be lumped in with the vamps," Marrow said.

"Looks like they're on some crusade to rid the world of 'undesirable' elements." Delfina hooked her fingers into air quotes. "They picked on the wolven first, I think, because you all are easier to find and don't tend to have the political power the vamps do. No one seems to know what the deal is with demons. And the other shifters tend to be solitary." She caught Byron's eye through the screen. "Witches don't seem to be on their radar at all."

"So what's their big plan?" Bone asked. "Why go to all that trouble if all they want to do is kill us?"

Delfina smiled crookedly, then flipped from the email to a report. "Because they don't want to kill you. Or at least not without making you useful first. It looks like the prison was a big part of their effort to cure you. When that didn't work, they—"

"Tried to figure out how to control the change," Hammer said. "I've heard the stories from those in the medical wing."

"That's right. What you may not know is that they intended to set compromised wolven after the vampires. The plan there was to get them to wipe you out. Or to wipe each other out." Delfina flipped through a series of emails. "They're using code names here, but it looks like they had at least four rogue Hunters involved."

"Is Malice on the list?" Snow asked.

Delfina started a little, then made eye contact with her through the screen. "There's only a few mentions of Malice in the files we picked up. Seems like someone tried to feel her out for the op but quickly concluded she'd be a liability." Delfina looked away from them, at another screen. "Here it is. They say she's 'too soft.'"

The scent of dread filled the air as Cassidy shifted in her chair. "Do you know who the Hunter in New York City is? They have to have their own, right?"

"Let me see…" Delfina tapped away at her keyboard, then looked at one of her other screens. "The New York Hunter is someone called Mace. Looks like they weren't successful in recruiting them into their extracurricular activities either."

Cassidy sagged back into her chair, but not before directing a meaningful look Snow's way. Her mom had only gotten back to her New York apartment about a month ago. It sounded like she was out of the crosshairs for a little while longer. Snow was glad they weren't going to have to do something about her. Sophia Nolan was intense, especially when it came to her daughters. There had been no change on the Malice and Ruri front. The former North Side Beta was still missing, and presumably so was Malice. She and Cassidy had discussed what to do next but had been awaiting the debrief with Delfina before coming to a final decision.

"How about handlers?" she asked. "Do you have any information on them?"

"That's a little sketchier, but there's a list."

"And it has Malice's handler on it?"

Delfina nodded.

"Maybe we can do some of our own recruiting," Bone said. "The Hunters who haven't faked their own deaths could be a good place to start."

"There's at least one who's working both the legitimate side and this black op," Delfina said. "They're careful not to name them. They also don't name their contacts in the military, the CIA, and at least one sitting member of Congress."

"The military one would have to be highly placed to have access to as much firepower as they leveled against us," Hammer said.

"Same for the one in the CIA," Snow said. "I don't imagine just anyone gets read into the Hunter program."

"And someone or someones in Congress?" Dale shook her head. "Looks like I need to take my pack deep underground. You all are already moving far from your original dens. I think it's time we followed suit."

"Think twice if you're heading north of the border," Marrow said. "We ran into a pack who wanted to challenge us to a hockey game for the privilege of passing through."

"Really?" Dale blinked at the Gary Alpha. "I thought our area was pretty hockey mad, but that's insane."

Snow nodded. She'd heard stories about some of the northern packs. There was a reason she had spent most of her time out west and south.

"All right, then," Dale said. "So not heading north of the border, at least not without our skates." She looked back at Delfina on the screen. "Where are the remaining Hunters? Seems like it's a good idea to avoid them."

"For sure," Delfina said. "I'll email you the list."

Dale shifted uncomfortably in her chair.

Cassidy snickered. "You'd be better off mailing a packet. Byron, do you think your aunt would mind if we use her address?"

Byron shrugged. "Should be all right."

"Seriously?" Delfina asked. "You want me to mail this stuff?"

"We'll reimburse you postage, if that's the problem."

"No, the problem is that it's ridiculous in this day and age." Delfina shook her head. "I feel like I'm dealing with my grandparents. Does one of you at least have a laptop?"

"Used to," Cassidy said. "It went up in flames with the rest of my stuff at the hotel. I'll be getting a new one soon."

"I know your email. I'm going to send you some things. I was able to make decent headway on the correspondence, financials, and databases, but there are medical files that I don't have the background to break down."

Snow looked over at Cassidy and nodded. She'd audited a number of classes related to genetics throughout the decades. She wanted a look at those files.

Dale's Beta spoke up. "I was a doctor, once upon a time. I'd like to get my hands on those."

"Do you have email?" Delfina asked.

Jane shook her head. "I'll get it from Five Moons, if that's all right with her."

"Of course," Cassidy said.

"Good." Delfina sat up straight, the top of her head disappearing past the top of their monitor. "Now that you have the synopsis, let me run you through the details."

It took two more hours of parsing through screenshots and emails. Half the time Snow wasn't sure what she was looking at, but various Alphas would be nodding. She knew Cassidy had a background in finance, and she seemed to be following the money parts. Hammer seemed to have a good handle on the military aspect of things. Rocky, his new Beta, would lean over and whisper something in his ear, then Hammer would relay his question.

Coupled with what they'd found in the prison, not much of it was surprising, but it was all alarming.

Eventually, Delfina's presentation came to a close. The greenhouse was still warm, even though the sun was almost below the tops of the trees. Delfina signed off, and everyone stood immediately. There had been a lot of fidgeting among the wolven for the last half hour.

"Dale," Cassidy said. "You and Jane should stick around. We're going for a run, all the packs. It would be good to have you along."

"Agreed," Hammer said. He'd stiffened when Cassidy spoke up on everyone's behalf, but his scent was only half as annoyed as his body language had been.

"I think we can manage," Dale said. "The pack doesn't expect us back until late."

"Good." Cassidy leaned over and caught Snow's hand, drawing her up to stand next to her. "We should gather the packs. Where are we going tonight, Byron?"

"There's a place I've been to in upper Michigan. I was thinking there, unless someone thinks we'll be accosted by hockey-playing wolven?"

"In June?" Bone rolled her eyes. "Don't take us to an indoor rink, and I'm sure we'll be fine."

"Besides," Marrow said, "everyone knows Michigan isn't Canada."

Byron's eyes twinkled as the twins rose to his bait. The three of them wandered out of the greenhouse, bickering amongst themselves. The other wolven followed along.

Cassidy didn't accompany them. She kept her hand wrapped around Snow's and waited.

"We have some choices to make," she said when they were alone.

"That we do." Snow caressed Cassidy's cheek, then gave it a gentle peck. "Are you ready?"

CHAPTER FIFTY-TWO

The North Side Pack was the last one back through Byron's portal. The hunt had gone well, even with such a massive group of wolven. The wheelman had chosen wisely. The patch of forest he'd opened up to them had been untouched for quite a while. While it hadn't been large, the scrubby grasslands surrounding it had also been empty. If Cassidy had to guess, she would have said the area had been a farm a decade or so previous. There had been plenty of space in which to roam, the game had been plentiful, and the number of humans they'd run into had been zero.

As usual, she and Snow had worked in tandem. Snow had hunkered down, and Cassidy had flushed game toward her. The former lone wolf was so good at hiding that she was able to get the drop on their prey almost every time. Cassidy had enjoyed the hunt with her but had also relished the time spent with the pack. Running free with them wasn't something she would ever take lightly again. Each hunt felt precious, and she tried to fix each one in her mind once she returned to skinform. The wolf's amusement at her new practice felt more indulgent than judgmental. She knew how much they'd gone through to regain their wolves.

The wolf put their paw down on one of Byron's crystals, covering it with their shaggy mitt. She receded, allowing Cassidy to ascend, as the faceted stone swelled with brilliance. Around her, the others were doing the same.

"Naomi," Cassidy said, "could you gather the pack and hang out by the standing door?"

Her Beta nodded, her shirt halfway over her head. "No problem, Alpha. Should they all be in skinform too?"

"Whatever's comfortable." She looked across the clearing, to where Hammer stood, still in full furform. "I need to talk to the Alphas, then I'll be by to address the pack." Dale and Jane were to the side of the portal, each halfway dressed. She would have to go looking for Marrow and Bone.

"I'll be right back," Cassidy said to Snow, who was nearly through her transformation. She swung by where Dale and Jane stood, making eye contact with Hammer and motioning him over. She hoped he wouldn't take offense at the gesture, but he'd been prickly ever since the events at the prison.

"Five Moons," Dale said. "Thank you for the invitation to the hunt."

"Of course." Cassidy smiled. "We've been through so much together. It felt right to run with you while we had the chance."

Hammer was making his way across the clearing, his head cocked in question.

"We need to talk," Cassidy said. "Just the Alphas. It can be quick. Probably should be quick. Do you know where Bone and Marrow are?"

Hammer considered it for a moment, then whuffed once. He turned away and trundled into the nearby woods.

"I hope that means he's getting them," Cassidy said.

"If Hammer didn't want to pitch in, he wouldn't have," Dale said. "That wolf has always been comfortable doing his own thing."

"Because the rest of the Alphas are so good at taking a back seat."

"Oh no." Dale grinned. "I'm driver seat or no seat."

"That's what I thought." Cassidy laughed.

"How are you doing?" Dale watched her closely as she asked the question.

"I have my pack back."

"That's not an answer."

Cassidy sighed. "It's a mixed bag. I got the North Side wolves back and then some, and things with Snow are great. Like, really great. I love the time we get to spend together, and how well we work together. Only…"

"Only?"

"There's so much that needs to be done."

"Like what?" A voice cut through the darkness. It took a moment for Cassidy to pick up the figures in the shadows and to realize the question hadn't come from the Alpha she'd begun to consider a friend, but from her sister. Marrow quirked an eyebrow at her, Bone by her side. Hammer was discernible only by the orange embers of his eyes, but as they continued to move into the clearing, enough moonlight picked out the edge of his dark fur that she could see him.

"I know at least some of you are considering heading out with your packs soon. Finding new dens," Cassidy said, purposefully keeping her voice quiet. "But I still think there's strength in numbers."

"Numbers, is it?" Marrow asked.

Next to her, Hammer's form began to shift as he made the transformation out of furform.

"Yes, numbers." Cassidy gestured around her. "You've seen how it can be when we work together. We took down a prison."

"We lost wolven," Bone said, her voice soft.

Hammer pushed himself off his hands and knees and took his full height, not caring as usual that he was completely nude. "You heard the hacker," he said in his deep rumble. "There's some serious firepower aimed at us. Smaller targets are harder to hit."

"Bigger targets can hit back harder," Cassidy replied. "You can't deny that you like to hit back."

Hammer waved his hand back and forth as if to say "maybe yes, maybe no."

"I think it's interesting that you're the one who keeps pushing for us to be one big happy pack," Marrow said, her tone accusatory. "That would be awfully convenient for you, wouldn't it?"

"Not really," Cassidy said. "Snow and I are leaving."

Marrow's head snapped back at the response, her eyebrows shooting up her forehead in surprise. "Why would you do that?"

"Unfinished business. Things I have to do, but don't want to drag the packs into."

"That's not what I expected," Marrow said.

"Yeah, well. I don't want to be queen of the wolven. Sorry to take away your boogieman." Her smile was grim, but Cassidy didn't care. She was tired of tiptoeing around the subject. "I can take your wolven away from you. I'm not going to, but you only have my word for it. Maybe this will convince you that I'm not some power-hungry monster. I'm not MacTavish." She added the last part quietly.

"You might not be that bastard of a rogue," Hammer agreed, "but you can't blame us for being concerned. If we're all together and something happens, what's to stop you from stripping us of our wolven again? Even if it's done for the best possible reasons, it still…" He clapped a hand on her shoulder. "You frighten me, Cassidy." His voice was sincere; the silver in his scent was too.

"Yes, well." Cassidy covered Hammer's hand with hers. "I frighten me too, Robert. I'm not cut out for this Alpha business. Not right now."

"You did fine," Bone said.

"Got your wolven through a hell of a sticky patch," Dale added.

"Not all of them, and not well." Cassidy quirked a half-grin at them. "I didn't say I was out of the Alpha game forever, but I need to learn more about us. I can't do that if I'm trying to do my best by my pack."

"Not many Alphas know when to retire gracefully," Hammer said.

"Then I want everyone to hear all about the mountains and mountains of grace that Five Moons had."

The Alphas clustered forward, rubbing and sniffing in the ways of packmates about to part. Even Marrow got in there, wrapping Cassidy up in a hard hug and inhaling her scent deeply. It was a goodbye, but Cassidy was sure she would see these wolven again, provided she managed to survive long enough.

Once she was thoroughly coated with the scent of the other Alphas and had provided her own to each of them, Cassidy took her leave of the group. Bone glanced her way and smiled, before turning back to the Alphas, who were already deep in conversation. It hurt a little to be cut out so quickly, but Cassidy reminded herself that she was the one who'd initiated breaking those ties. As hard as it had been to say goodbye to the Alphas, her own pack was going to be so much harder.

As she walked back to the clearing, Snow separated herself from the shadowy side of a tree.

"You doing all right?"

Cassidy nodded. "We'll be back. Or we'll visit wherever they end up."

Snow took her hand and squeezed it once. "Leaving is hard, but I can tell you that coming back is one of the best feelings in the world."

"I'll have to take your word for it."

"Don't worry. I'll make sure to remind you I was right when the time comes."

"What would I do without you?" To make up for the dry tone, Cassidy leaned in for a kiss.

"You ready?" Snow asked when they parted.

Cassidy licked her lips, partly from nerves but also to savor Snow's unique flavor. "Doesn't matter. This needs to happen now."

"Just remember, when you let them go, make sure you still keep me close."

"Always." Cassidy took a deep breath and made her way back into the clearing with its lonely stone doorway.

The pack awaited her, Naomi at the front. The various groups were freely mixed together. There was no longer any difference between the original wolven who'd come to North Side under Dean and those who'd remained after MacTavish was excised. The new wolven, a few from each of the surviving packs and more from the disbanded Aurora and Joliet Packs swelled the ranks to numbers larger than even Dean had enjoyed, or so Snow had told her. Deeper in the crowd were the cubs, likely nodding off in the arms of one of their many foster aunts and uncles.

"What did you want to say to us, Alpha?" Naomi asked. Her eyes glowed a soft magenta.

Cassidy walked right up to her and pulled her into a hard hug, then stepped back. "I'm leaving." She reached back her hand for Snow's. "We both are."

Naomi straightened, her brow furrowed in confusion. "What do you mean? When will you be back?"

"I don't know," Cassidy said. "When I'll be back, I mean. There's a lot to be done, and we don't know exactly where to start." She put her hands on Naomi's shoulders. "I'm releasing the pack of their bond to me. I'm hoping you'll take on my mantle."

Murmurs rippled through the crowd and a wave of sorrow washed over Cassidy. The scents were accompanied by the combined feeling of sadness that emanated from the starscape of the wolven she hadn't yet relinquished.

"We're going to find Ruri and my sister," Cassidy said. "And then we'll make a decision about how to handle those who took you. They were only the tip of the claw, one that was supposed to hook out our guts and leave us too weak to defend ourselves." She stood straighter, making deliberate eye contact with every single of the wolves who called her Alpha. "They failed in their plan. The packs may be fewer in number than when we started, but we are so much stronger. Both in the bonds we've forged with the other packs here and the bonds we've forged between each other."

"A bond you're breaking," Naomi said quietly.

"A bond I'm setting aside for you to pick up. I know you'll do amazing things. Besides, the other Alphas need some time to forgive me for what I did to them during the breakout."

"You saved us."

"But not without damaging their trust in me. I'm going to miss you, Naomi. You made me a much less terrible Alpha than I would have been on my own."

Naomi grabbed her up in a rough hug, burying her nose in Cassidy's shoulder. "You would have gotten there on your own, eventually."

"Maybe." Cassidy returned the hug, glorying in the feel of her Beta against her. She closed her eyes and reached out to the stars in her orbit, touching each one and acknowledging them before letting them go. She'd finally figured out the trick of it. With each star that dimmed, she was a little weaker in spirit. The wolf whined within her as she stripped them of their bonds. She didn't like the feeling, but she was ready for the coming hunt.

When Cassidy let Naomi go, the only star that still blazed within her sphere was Snow's, and it burned with compassion. It was that empathy that finally did Cassidy in. Tears welled up in her eyes, and she cleared her throat around the large lump obstructing it.

She looked at the gathered wolven, hers no more. "I'll miss you all," she said hoarsely. "I wish I could have gotten to know more of you better. I wish we hadn't lost anyone."

"You'll always have a place here," Naomi said.

"We'll see how you feel about that after you settle into the top spot." Cassidy gave Naomi's arm a playful swat.

Gene's voice rang out of the crowd. "You're not getting away that easy." He pushed his way to the front and threw his arms around her.

It took much longer to perform the impromptu ritual of parting than it had with the Alphas. The cubs were beside themselves, and Cassidy and Snow had quiet words for each of them. By the time they finished their farewells, the moon had risen high overhead. Cassidy reluctantly drew back, away from the circle of wolven who watched her and Snow leave, eyes gleaming in the darkness. She walked backward, keeping them in sight as long as she could, before too many trees obscured them from her view.

"That was hard," Snow said, her steps nearly soundless on the loamy forest floor.

"Hardest thing I've ever done," Cassidy said. "And that's a high bar."

"It is." Snow tilted her head. "Was, maybe. Are you ready for what comes next?"

"It doesn't matter. We need to find Mary, or what happened to her. I'll call my mom tomorrow and let her know we're heading to Wisconsin." She tapped her lower lip "I need to get a laptop."

"Sounds like a plan." Snow stopped in front of the small outbuilding at the end of a long, somewhat overgrown road. "Mind if I drive?"

"Of course not." Cassidy passed the keys over to her girlfriend. The moonlight glinted off angled letters on a soft leather keychain.

Snow moved around to the open garage door and grabbed the edge of a tarp that covered a large boxy shape. She gave it a tug and it came free, revealing the curves and lines of a battered Volkswagen bus. "She's not much to look at right now," Snow said. "But the engine is tip-top. Rocky and I sunk a bunch of time into making sure all the mechanicals and electrical are humming. She'll get us where we need to go."

"Then what are we waiting for?" Cassidy climbed up into the front seat. "Let's go find my sister."

Bella Books, Inc.
Women. Books. Even Better Together.
P.O. Box 10543
Tallahassee, FL 32302
Phone: (800) 729-4992
www.BellaBooks.com

More Titles from Bella Books

Hunter's Revenge – Gerri Hill
978-1-64247-447-3 I 276 pgs I paperback: $18.95 I eBook: $9.99
Tori Hunter is back! Don't miss this final chapter in the acclaimed Tori Hunter series.

Integrity – E. J. Noyes
978-1-64247-465-7 I 28 pgs I paperback: $19.95 I eBook: $9.99
It was supposed to be an ordinary workday...

The Order – TJ O'Shea
978-1-64247-378-0 I 396 pgs I paperback: $19.95 I eBook: $9.99
For two women the battle between new love and old loyalty may prove more dangerous than the war they're trying to survive.

Under the Stars with You – Jaime Clevenger
978-1-64247-439-8 I 302 pgs I paperback: $19.95 I eBook: $9.99
Sometimes believing in love is the first step. And sometimes it's all about trusting the stars.

The Missing Piece – Kat Jackson
978-1-64247-445-9 I 250 pgs I paperback: $18.95 I eBook: $9.99
Renee's world collides with possibility and the past, setting off a tidal wave of changes she could have never predicted.

An Acquired Taste – Cheri Ritz
978-1-64247-462-6 I 206 pgs I paperback: $17.95 I eBook: $9.99
Can Elle and Ashley stand the heat in the *Celebrity Cook Off* kitchen?